Hunt for
the Enemy

Rob Sinclair

Clink
Street

Find out more about Rob and his books at
http://www.robsinclairauthor.com

Books by Rob Sinclair

The Enemy Series:
Dance with the Enemy
Rise of the Enemy
Hunt for the Enemy

For my wonderful wife.
Thank you for putting up with me, xxx

PART 1

Killer instincts

Chapter 1

July 2000
Marrakech, Morocco

It was summer. It was hot. No, not hot, scorching. The sun blazed down, heating the ground and everything around. Humid, sticky air seemed to seep through cracks in the road and from the walls of the sand-coloured buildings, rising upwards, choking everyone who breathed it. Carl Logan drove through the twisting city streets in a rusty old tin can of a car that clunked and jerked and whined every time he changed gear and every time the engine revved. He wore a pair of khaki linen trousers and a thin cotton shirt, but with the windows of the car fully wound down, the stifling air burst against his face and he was dripping wet. A thunderstorm had not long passed, leaving behind wispy grey clouds in the sky. Even though the fierce sun had done its best to burn away the remnants of the rain clouds, the humidity levels remained peaked.

And yet Logan was almost oblivious to the debilitating conditions. Because today was the day.

Three years of gruelling, agonising training had brought him to this point. The training had been more than tough; it had been life-changing, taking him to the brink physically on numerous occasions. He'd suffered terrible injuries, been hospitalised for weeks on end. It had been mentally draining too. From the intensive mock interrogations to the mind-bending psych evaluations, he'd felt like he was losing his mind. In many ways, he probably had. Numerous times during the training he'd questioned why he was going through it at all. Why he was committing his life to this cause that just three years before he'd not once considered.

But those thoughts were buried deep now.

Finally the training was over. It was time to show his true worth.

Logan had been in Marrakech for four weeks, but the full details of his first assignment for the Joint Intelligence Agency had only been relayed the previous evening by his boss back in England, Mackie. No details or explanation had been offered as to why the targets were on the JIA's radar and Logan hadn't asked. The targets were on the blacklist and that was all Logan needed to know. The JIA had hammered into him that his job wasn't to ask questions. It was to carry out orders.

Sitting next to Logan in the passenger seat of the car was John Webb, a fellow JIA agent. Webb was a number of years more senior than Logan and had been a close mentor over the previous twelve months as Logan assimilated himself into the life of a field agent. The first two years with the JIA had been non-stop training, not even a hint of a real assignment. For the last year, he had been shadowing others in the field, learning.

Now it was his time to shine.

Logan had admired Webb from the very first time they'd met. After a troubled upbringing, like Logan's, Webb had come into his own since joining the JIA ten years previously. He had an air of respect and dignity and yet he was tough and ruthless. The job of an agent was a loner's one – there wasn't the time or capacity for close friendships. And yet Logan had enjoyed the time he'd spent with Webb and he could tell the older agent had relished the opportunity to act as guide and tutor.

'Take this next left,' Webb said in his bass voice.

Logan took his foot off the accelerator and the car slowed. He was beginning to turn the wheel when a moped came sweeping up on his inside. Logan slammed on the brakes, narrowly avoiding a collision. Oblivious, the moped driver sped off into the distance. Logan clenched his hands on the steering wheel, attempting to return his focus to the task at hand.

'Everything okay there? You seem a bit distant,' said Webb.

It was the second time already on the short drive that Webb had questioned Logan's state of mind.

Logan shot him a look.

'I'm fine. I didn't see him. That's all.'

'Okay, okay, only asking.'

Logan put the car into first gear and eased around the corner, into a cramped side street. On one side it was lined with industrial bins and bags of rubbish from the various shops, cafes and restaurants that occupied the parallel street at the front of the buildings. On the other was a series of ramshackle buildings, anything from two to five storeys tall. Cars and mopeds were parked tightly up against the buildings here and there.

The alley was narrow and dank – and dark, which at least provided immediate relief from the ferocious sun. They drove for a couple of hundred yards, Logan keeping the pace slow, winding the car through the at times impossibly narrow gaps where other cars had parked a little too far from the side of the road.

'This is the place here,' Webb said, ducking down and looking up through the window at the building on the right-hand side. 'Pull up wherever you can.'

Logan drove just past the building and the nearest space, then put the car into reverse. He swung the vehicle back toward the wall, only stopping and re-aligning the steering when the rear of the car was a few inches from making contact. He misjudged it. As he turned the car in, there was a scraping noise: the bumper raking against the building.

'Easy there!' Webb shouted. 'Come on, man. Just keep it cool.'

'I am cool,' Logan said.

'Then straighten this thing up and let's get inside.'

Logan pulled the car forward a couple of feet, then eased it back into the space, this time missing the wall without any trouble. He and Webb opened their doors in unison. Webb squeezed his muscled frame through the six-inch gap that Logan had given him – it was the only way to park the car and still allow other vehicles to pass. They couldn't afford to block the street, which would cause unnecessary commotion.

Logan went around to the boot and opened it up. He picked up the larger of the two black aluminium cases that lay there. Webb took the smaller, lighter one. After shutting the boot, Logan followed Webb around to the door of the building. It was derelict, a set of apartments that was in the process of being sold on for refurbishment. Most of the other buildings either side were in a similar state of disrepair, including those that were still occupied. The worn door to the building had a simple lock. Logan stood watch, eyes darting up and down the street and over the surrounding buildings, as Webb expertly picked the lock. It took less than ten seconds. Webb pushed the door open, its warped wood creaking and straining.

'Come on, follow me,' Webb said, heading in.

The building was dusty and dark inside but the air felt cool and dry. Webb did a quick recce of the ground floor, looking for any signs of life. There were none. He headed for the bare wooden staircase and Logan followed, lugging the heavy case with him.

'You're sure you're ready for this?' Webb asked without turning.

'Yeah,' Logan responded.

'You know, it would be understandable if you were nervous. This isn't for everyone.'

'I'm not nervous.'

'I'm just saying, don't feel bad if you are. Training is one thing. But doing this for real? Not everyone can hack it.'

'Whatever you say.'

'But I know you can do it. I wouldn't have let Mackie pass this job to you otherwise.'

'Okay, I get it.'

'You ask me, I'd say you're a natural. Some people just don't have it. Others do. I'm sure you'll be fine.'

'I never said I wouldn't be.'

'Okay, okay. So let's just get this done.'

They passed the fifth and final floor, after which the staircase became narrower and steeper. At the top, they came to a stop at a gun-metal door. Webb pushed down the security bar and the door swung open to reveal the flat roof of the building.

Webb walked out and Logan followed, wincing as the blast of superheated air smacked him in the face. He followed Webb across the burning roof tiles to the far southerly corner. From there they had an unobstructed view toward the Kasbah district with its mix of old-world charm – the sumptuous colours of the rooftop gardens of luxury riads and the minarets from its many mosques poking proudly into the sky – together with the deep blue of the rooftop pools and gleaming glass of flash new hotels.

Webb kneeled down and opened up his case, then took out his spotter's scope. Logan came down beside him and placed his larger case next to Webb's. He undid the thick clasps and opened the lid to reveal the green and black AWSM sniper rifle, snug in the deep foam interior of the box.

Logan took out the rifle and attached the bipod, then quickly gave the rifle a once-over, making sure the mounted scope was securely in place. He opened a pouch on the case lid to reveal five shiny .338 Lapua Magnum cartridges and placed them one at a time into the rifle's detachable magazine. With all five cartridges neatly inside, Logan clipped the magazine onto the assembled rifle and set it down on the ground.

'Fifteen forty,' Webb said, looking at his watch. 'The target isn't scheduled to arrive back until sixteen hundred.'

'May as well set up the spotting position now,' Logan said. 'Get our sights ready.'

'Agreed,' said Webb. He lay flat on the ground and pushed his scope through a gap in the worn concrete wall that lined the rooftop.

But Logan didn't lie down next to Webb to align the sights on the rifle. There was still plenty of time for that. Instead, he stood up, leaving the assembled rifle on the floor, and fished in his pocket for the plastic cord that he'd stashed there just a few minutes before the two agents had left the safe house.

'The distance to the front entrance of the hotel is six hundred and seventy-three yards,' Webb said. 'The drop is forty-three feet.'

Logan knew the measurements already. He and Webb had been through every last detail numerous times. Webb's repetition was just part of the routine. Everything had to be perfect for the shot. They would only get a few seconds. But Logan was confident he would take the shot exactly as planned. The distance wasn't that difficult. The rifle could handle twice with ease. Logan himself had managed close to two thousand yards in training. Six hundred and seventy-three yards wouldn't be a problem.

'Wind speed is close to zero,' Webb said, looking at his hand-held anemometer. 'But I'll keep rechecking. And we should take readings from different spots on the rooftop over the next hour just to make sure. If we get another storm coming over, it could change significantly.'

'Okay,' Logan said, as much to himself as to Webb.

He took a deep breath.

And then he was ready.

Logan wrapped the cord tightly around both of his hands, leaving just two feet of flex in the middle. He was aware that his breathing and heart rate were speeding up, but he was sure it wasn't nerves. Just adrenaline and anticipation.

With Webb still preoccupied, Logan stepped over his colleague, one foot either side, then quickly dropped his weight to the ground, his knees pinning down Webb's arms. Webb immediately let go of the anemometer, squirming for just a second before Logan swept the flex under his colleague's neck. He used his left hand to wrap the cord around a full turn and then he pulled back and out, hard and fast.

Webb rasped, trying to shout out but unable to with the crushing pressure on his windpipe. He kicked and writhed and squirmed. But Logan had taken him by surprise. The experienced agent simply hadn't been ready and there was no way he was getting out.

Webb coiled and bucked but Logan held firm. He pulled on the cord, using every ounce of strength he could muster, his arms, his whole body tensing and straining. His face turned red, his knuckles white. Veins throbbed at the side of his head; his biceps bulged. But all the time he focused on just one thing: pulling as hard as he could.

Pained sounds escaped Webb's lips but they were quickly becoming weak, shallow. He clawed at the ligature cutting into his neck. Droplets of blood dripped onto the ground beneath him. It was wound so tightly there was nothing for him to grasp.

Soon, Webb began to scrape and rake at Logan, but he was too far gone already for it to make a difference.

When Logan felt the resistance from his associate wane, he only pulled harder. The cord dug into his hands, sending a shock of pain up through his arms. But he didn't let up – he just kept on tugging, harder and harder.

Webb's body went limp and it flopped down, melting into the rooftop. Even then, Logan held tight a few seconds longer, keeping Webb's lifeless head suspended in the air.

When Logan finally released the grip, unwinding the cord from around the neck, Webb's face thudded down against the hard floor with a sickening crack. And then he was completely still.

It was done.

Logan stood up, panting, sweat pouring down his brow. He unwound the cord from around his hands and a rush of blood coursed through them, making them throb and sting. He saw several lines of indented red flesh on his palms and the backs of his hands where the plastic had dug in and cut into his skin. Logan dropped the cord and put his hands to his knees for just a few seconds as he got his breathing back under control. His whole body ached from exertion.

When he was ready, he kneeled down next to Webb's body and rolled his former colleague onto his side, away from where he had been spotting.

After taking one last look at the man who had so readily mentored and guided him, Logan fished his phone out of his pocket and dialled Mackie. He picked up after just two rings.

'I'm in position,' Logan said.

'Good,' Mackie replied. 'And you're alone?'

'I am now.'

'Excellent. Then call me when it's done.'

Logan ended the call and put the phone back in his pocket.

He didn't know why the targets had been chosen and he hadn't asked. They were on the JIA's blacklist and that was all he needed to know.

That was his job now.

He picked up the rifle and looked through the scope, eyeing the hotel entrance, six hundred and seventy-three yards away.

And then he lay down and waited for his second target to arrive.

Chapter 2

Present day
Moscow, Russia

When Angela Grainger looked through the spyhole and saw the man standing on the other side of the door, her legs suddenly felt like jelly. Because the face she saw was one she had never expected to see again in her life.

And yet the feeling that washed over her was more than just surprise. There was also delight, relief, embarrassment, confusion and regret. Such an awkward combination.

She wondered for just a second whether she should open the door. Perhaps she should just pretend she wasn't there, go and lock herself in the bathroom and hope, pray, that he would go away.

But she couldn't do that. Regardless of the confusion that was sweeping through her, she had to know why he was there. And how he had found her.

More than that, even though seeing him on the other side of the door scared her, if she didn't open the door, chances were she might never set eyes on him again.

She reached out and turned the handle before she could talk herself out of it.

And there he was.

Carl Logan.

Despite her uncertainty, she felt a flutter in her heart as she looked into his deep-green eyes and couldn't help but smile – something she hadn't done in too long.

Their affair, more than a year ago, had been fleeting, but it had affected them both deeply. Yet their relationship had been doomed from the start. She'd lied to Logan. She'd betrayed him. Then she'd shot him.

After that, she'd gone on the run, leaving behind everything she knew – her job, her money, her life that she'd built tirelessly over many years – and with it her capacity to love.

And yet here he was.

Had he come for his revenge? Or to take her back to America to face justice?

No. She didn't think so.

Not that it made her feel any happier. Because with the door open, she saw the look in his eyes. The blood on his clothes. And the gun in his hand.

'It's not safe here,' he said. 'We have to go.'

More than anything, on hearing his voice, the feeling that washed over her was relief.

She didn't need to ask what he meant. She already had a good idea what was happening.

Carl Logan wasn't there to kill her, or to turn her in.

He was there to save her.

Chapter 3

There had been no gunfight, no ambush from the Russians, no planted bomb ready to tear down the apartment that Angela Grainger had been holed up in. No path of resistance at all.

Perhaps Lena's parting words as Logan had left her bleeding to death on the warehouse floor had been merely a red herring, one last attempt at deceit.

Or perhaps the final assault was still to come.

Either way, Logan and Grainger had escaped from the apartment in Khoroshyovo-Mnyovniki entirely unimpeded. But both knew their ordeal was anything but over. The CIA, the Russian FSB, even the JIA, to which Logan had been loyal for so many years, would be after them.

They had already fled some two hundred miles from Moscow, quickly escaping the city and heading south, passing through largely forested terrain. Their only plan thus far had been to travel as far and fast as they could – increase the distance between themselves and whoever was now following them. The further they went from the starting point, the wider the arc of where they could be. Although it wasn't like Logan to run from his problems, right now he wasn't sure what else he could do. His immediate priority had simply been to get Grainger to safety.

They were travelling in a clapped-out saloon car that had been parked in the frozen apartment grounds and had taken Logan only seconds to hot-wire. Luckily it'd had an almost full fuel tank and in the five hours since their departure from the apartment block, they hadn't yet needed to stop.

Logan had barely spoken to Grainger during the journey. There was an unease between them; neither was sure how to treat the other after what had happened in America, a whole year before, when Grainger had shot Logan and gone on the run. The longer the silence in the car dragged out, the harder it became for Logan to think of the right thing to say. So he did what he'd always done best: kept his mouth shut. He'd learned a long time ago that silence was better than bullshit.

Despite the awkwardness in the car, standing in the doorway of the apartment, looking at the woman he'd once held so close to him, had been a poignant moment. A brief one, though.

His words to her had been simple: 'It's not safe here. We have to go.'

Without saying a single word in response, she'd grabbed her coat and shut the door, leaving behind what little of value lay in the apartment, which Logan guessed had been as much a prison as a home. Then they'd been on their way. She hadn't asked any questions. He hadn't volunteered any answers. It was as though she'd fully understood the perilous situation she'd been in, that she hadn't really expected the Russians to hide her from the Americans, keep her safe, for good.

'Are you going to tell me what's happening?' Grainger said eventually.

'What do you think is happening?' Logan responded after a few seconds of trying, and failing, to find words to answer the question.

He looked over at her. There had been something close to disgust in his voice. He wasn't sure whether that was with herself or the Russians who had pretended to be her saviours but then played their hand and dealt Grainger straight back to the people she had run from: the Americans. The CIA.

She looked down and he couldn't help but feel bad for having used such a harsh tone of voice.

'A deal was struck,' Logan said. 'The CIA found out where you were. They want you dead. The Russians were happy to give you up.'

She didn't respond. He thought he saw a tear escape her eye, but it was difficult to tell in the near-darkness of the car.

'Why did you come for me?' she asked.

'What else could I have done?'

'I knew something would happen eventually. They took me in but I meant nothing to the Russians. I knew I'd just become a bargaining chip for them.'

She wiped her face with her hands.

'When I saw you standing there,' she said, 'outside the door, I thought for a moment it was you who'd been sent. I thought it was you who was going to kill me.'

As much as Logan still wanted to hate her, his heart went out to her. He'd been through his own hell plenty of times, when it felt like he'd been abandoned by the world. He could well imagine the torment she must have gone through over the past year – alone in a foreign country, no one to turn to, not even able to trust the very people who had been claiming to provide her safe haven. And she was right to have felt that way. The Russians had never taken her in for her benefit.

'If you thought I was going to kill you, why did you just stand there? You didn't try to hide from me, or attack me.'

'Because I know I deserve it. And really, it's inevitable. They're never going to stop looking for me.'

After what she'd done, it was hard to argue with that. And yet he wasn't going to let them kill her. Not the Americans, not the Russians, not anyone.

He just couldn't.

'I'll protect you,' he said.

'Why?'

'Because I was part of their dirty deal too. The FSB, the CIA, even my own people were in on it. And right now, you're just about the only person in the world who doesn't want me dead.'

Chapter 4

London, England

Peter Winter sat on the soft leather chair behind his desk in the JIA's London office. Until three days ago, the office had belonged to Charles McCabe, his former boss, who'd been shot and killed outside a cafe in the Russian city of Omsk. Mackie, as he was more affectionately known, had been a charismatic leader. Someone whom Winter, despite his vastly different personality traits, had long aspired to be like.

Following Mackie's untimely demise, Winter had immediately taken over day-to-day management of his boss's portfolio of agents. It was the step up that Winter had craved for the last five years working for Mackie. It should have been a moment of happiness, of satisfaction. In some ways, despite the circumstances, it was – or at least it would be in time. In a few days, maybe a few weeks, he would open the bottle of champagne his girlfriend had bought him for his thirtieth birthday two years ago that he had been saving for the day when he was finally promoted to commander within the JIA.

But not yet.

Not while there was still so much turmoil, not just in the JIA but in his own mind.

And not while Mackie's killer was still on the run.

In many ways, the unexpected promotion hadn't been easy on Winter, despite it being a position he'd long craved. He noticed the looks from other people within the organisation. He knew they saw him as the young whippersnapper, promoted above his level of experience and aptitude, commanding agents who in some cases were many years older than him and had many more years' experience. Not that he felt he wasn't up to it. He knew he was. But knowing the doubts that others were surely feeling only added to the weight of expectation on his slender shoulders.

'So what news do you have for me?' Winter asked, looking over his desk at Paul Evans.

Winter and Evans were similar. Both tall and wiry, both of a similar age and service span with the JIA. Both were tech-savvy thinkers, puzzle solvers, brains rather than brawn. And yet they were leading very different lives. Evans was a field agent, much the same as Carl Logan, albeit with very different characteristics. Winter, on the other hand, was essentially a paper-pusher. He commanded a group of agents but rarely had to get his hands dirty. Yet he was now considerably more senior in the hierarchy than Evans would ever be – a specialised field agent really had nowhere to climb to.

'We have nothing on Logan,' Evans said. 'If that's what you mean.'

'He's just disappeared?'

'It would seem so. It doesn't help that there's no way of tracking him now. No IDs, no bank accounts, no phone.'

Winter wasn't sure whether Evans's comment was a dig at him. It was Winter, in his new role, just hours after Mackie's death, who had proposed to the JIA committee that they clear Logan's bank accounts, wipe away any record of his time with the JIA, his identification, essentially his entire life. To the outside world, it was now like Carl Logan had never existed.

In many ways, to the outside world, he never really had.

The committee had approved the request almost without question. Somehow, after being held captive by the Russians for three months, Logan had escaped and had wound up at the scene of Mackie's murder. Even worse, he had fled the scene with the Russians. Exactly what was happening wasn't clear. But Logan was now on the JIA hit list. A rogue agent.

The idea of deleting Logan's identity and taking his belongings, his money and everything he had was to make it impossible for Logan to continue operating as much as it was to protect the

JIA's position. But Winter was now starting to wonder whether the decision had been too hasty. Whether he'd actually acted with his heart – angered by Mackie's death – rather than his head. In deleting all evidence of Logan's existence, had Winter in fact handed Logan exactly what he needed to disappear for good?

For years, Logan had operated like a ghost, in the shadows. Now he was a ghost even to the JIA.

There was a knock on the office door and Winter's secretary opened it and stuck her head around.

'Jay Lindegaard is here to see you,' she said.

'Shit,' Winter muttered.

He really didn't want to speak to Lindegaard, the most senior of the JIA's committee members and a long-time CIA agent and pain in the arse. Winter was surprised the man hadn't just blasted his way into the room. That was certainly his usual style.

'Okay, send him in,' Winter said.

Moments later, Jay Lindegaard, wearing a light-grey suit that bulged in all the right places, strode into the office and right up to the desk, eyeballing Winter all the way.

Winter got to his feet, coming a few inches short of Lindegaard's height and a few inches narrower than his muscular physique.

'Jay, this is Paul Evans. I'm not sure whether you two have met?'

Evans stuck his hand out toward Lindegaard.

'Yes, I know who he is,' Lindegaard snapped, ignoring the offer of a handshake. 'Have you found Logan yet?'

'We were just talking about that actually.'

'And?'

'And we're at a bit of a loss,' Winter said, sitting down.

'A bit of a loss?' Lindegaard barked in his thick American accent. He remained standing. 'Do you have anything at all? We have a madman out there killing all and sundry. He's now running around with one of the most wanted criminals in the world. Do you know he could bring down this entire organisation if we don't stop him?'

'We're trying,' Winter said, doing his best to remain composed. He looked over at Evans and tried to gauge his response to Lindegaard's reference to Angela Grainger. Evans hadn't been brought into the loop yet about that. But there was nothing. Not even a twitch. 'As it is,' Winter continued, 'we haven't got any agents left on the ground in Russia.'

'And yet you two are still sitting here,' Lindegaard said. 'How do you expect to get anything done if you're three thousand miles away from the action?'

'That's my point,' Winter said. 'I don't think we can. We need to get feet into Russia and tap up our sources from there.'

'So why is Evans still here then?' Lindegaard blasted. 'Why isn't he in Moscow already?'

'Actually, that was why I called Evans in,' Winter said, hearing his voice becoming weaker in the face of Lindegaard's bombarding manner.

As much as he wanted to fight back, Winter knew that entering into a shouting match with Lindegaard wouldn't help matters. With Mackie gone, Lindegaard was now technically Winter's immediate boss, along with the other three committee members. He had to at least try to keep Lindegaard at bay. Which sounded infinitely easier than it was.

'We were just about to go over the arrangements,' Evans chimed in.

Lindegaard turned his steely gaze to Evans and stared down at the young agent. After a few seconds, he huffed and spun around, then headed back to the door. He stopped when he reached it and turned again to speak.

'This is not a strong start you're making, Winter. I might not have seen eye to eye with Mackie at all times, but he was good at his job. You've got some big boots to fill. So start filling. I want Evans in Moscow now. And I want daily updates from you. We need to keep moving before Logan causes any more damage.'

'Yes, sir,' Winter said.

'And if you get even a sniff of where Logan is, you come to me immediately. He's a threat to you, me, everyone in this organisation. The longer he stays on the run, the bigger that threat becomes. Got it?'

'Yes, sir.'

'I've got to head out of the country but call me anytime to update me.'

As soon as Lindegaard slammed the door behind him, Evans began to get up from his chair.

'Where are you going?' Winter said.

'He just said–'

'Sit down! We're not done yet.'

Evans gave a sour look but did as he was told. Winter was surprised at himself for his authoritative tone. Perhaps Mackie had rubbed off on him more than he'd realised. Or maybe he was just riled by Lindegaard's unnerving presence.

'Before you go, there's something we need to discuss,' Winter said.

Evans stared at Winter sullenly.

'We lost a good agent out in Moscow,' Winter said.

He was referring to Jane Westwood, who'd been operating under the alias Mary White. The reports coming back from Russia were that Logan had taken Westwood hostage in Omsk after she'd been sent to bring him back in following his apparent escape from the FSB. She'd wound up dead in a back alley in Moscow. Logan was the obvious culprit, but the picture of exactly what was happening in Russia was becoming less clear by the hour.

'I know,' Evans said. 'I worked with her on her first assignment. She was a real asset.'

'She was. But I'm more than a little suspicious about how she was killed. Just what went wrong out there?'

'Logan's gone rogue. It's simple, isn't it? The Russians have turned him. He's working for them now.'

'Then why did his killing spree involve taking out numerous agents from the FSB too? It doesn't look like he's the best of friends with anyone anymore.'

Evans didn't respond.

'I spoke to Logan,' Winter said. 'Not long after Mackie was killed. And I spoke to Westwood too. There was something bugging her. She was telling me about the CIA agent she'd been teamed up with out there. I didn't think much of it at the time. I knew the CIA had been brought into this mess to help find Logan when he'd first been captured in Russia – against the wishes of Mackie, I would add – but it's the CIA's involvement that doesn't sit easy anymore.'

'In what way?'

'Angela Grainger,' Winter said. 'You remember her?'

'Of course,' Evans said, his face deadpan.

Winter knew Evans and Grainger had never met face to face, but Evans had been involved, along with Logan, in the mission to rescue Frank Modena – the US Attorney General – after he'd been kidnapped in Paris. A kidnapping plot that Angela Grainger had orchestrated. So Evans knew of her. Everyone knew of her. What Evans didn't know, though, was that since Grainger had escaped from Logan, from everyone, she had fled to Russia to be sheltered by the FSB.

'And you know that's who Logan's with now?' Winter said.

'I do,' Evans said. 'Because Lindegaard mentioned it and now you have too.'

'We didn't know the Russians had been harbouring Grainger. She'd been on the run for over a year. Her presence in Russia only became apparent when we were negotiating for Logan's release. The Russians, clearly, were using her as a massive bargaining chip.'

'I can imagine,' Evans said. 'And I'm guessing that's why the CIA took an interest in Logan's imprisonment.'

'Exactly. But that's when things started getting muddy. The CIA took over. After that, I'm not sure what deals were done with whom.'

Winter knew the CIA had been working with Mackie. The JIA was jointly funded by both the American and British government, and working side by side with the CIA and MI6 wasn't unheard of. When Logan had first been apprehended in Russia, Mackie had been desperate to arrange a deal to get his man out alive. After weeks of making no headway, the CIA had come into the fold to help negotiations. But the deal had never been struck. Logan had escaped – or at least claimed to have escaped – from the clutches of the FSB, only to later draw Mackie out into the open, allowing the Russians to murder him. On the face of it, it appeared Logan had been turned and was now working for the Russians.

But Winter was increasingly getting the feeling that wasn't the whole story.

'Something was happening in Moscow,' he said. 'Something

that got a number of people killed. I'm pretty sure the CIA didn't come into this to help Logan. They wanted Grainger – I'm certain of that. But what were they offering in return?'

'Maybe it was Logan.'

Winter raised an eyebrow. 'Mackie would never have allowed that. He wouldn't have given up on Logan to score points with the CIA.'

Winter wanted to believe his own words, but then he'd been asking the same question himself. If Logan had been the other part of the deal – a swap, his life for Grainger's – then just who had sold him out? Winter certainly wasn't aware of Mackie having done so.

'I'll get on the next flight to Moscow,' Evans said. 'Whatever's happening, I've got more chance of uncovering it if I'm on the ground.'

'Of course. You do that. It's a start at least,' said Winter. 'But I don't think you'll find the answers there.'

'Why not?'

'Because Logan isn't in Moscow. If I were to bet, I'd say he's not even in Russia anymore. Wherever he is, you need to follow him.'

'Do you know where he'd go?'

'No. But you have to find him. And quickly. Get to him before the CIA or the FSB do. Because Logan is one of the only people who knows what's really happening here. And unless we find him first, we may never find out the reason Mackie was killed.'

Chapter 5

Volgograd Oblast, Russia

Logan stared into the distance, squinting his eyes as though it would help him make out the dark road ahead. They were travelling on a single track lit only by the headlights of the car and the dim moonlight reflecting off the snow on the pine trees and in large mounds at the side of the road.

Traffic was sparse and they had gone for miles at a time without seeing another vehicle. Every time a car approached in the opposite direction, both of them would hold their breath, the tension in the car rising to bursting point as they waited for an attack to come. So far, every car had simply disappeared into the blackness behind them.

'Where will we go?' Grainger asked.

'I don't know,' Logan responded, not taking his eyes off the darkness in front. 'We have to get out of Russia first.'

'Is there anywhere safe we can go? Anybody or anywhere in Russia you know that you could take us to?'

'Right now, I don't think there's anyone, anywhere I could trust.'

'There must be someone.'

Logan had been racking his brain for hours. He'd been on missions to Russia before. To many of the surrounding countries too. Along the way, he'd worked with various people: a small number of other JIA agents, with double agents, informants. But there was no one he'd become close to, or stayed in contact with.

That just wasn't the way the JIA worked, and it certainly wasn't the way Logan worked.

But he knew he needed help. They were being hunted on multiple fronts. Following his escape from his prison cell in Siberia, Logan had been tricked into luring Mackie to his death. He'd been set up for murder. Someone had betrayed him and there was no one left he could trust, it seemed. Not long after Mackie had been killed, the JIA had stripped Logan of his identity, his possessions. Now, neither he nor Grainger had anything in the world except the clothes they were wearing, the car, the gun stashed in Logan's waistband and the wallets he'd stolen from the bodies of the dead CIA agents outside Grainger's apartment. What they had was enough to keep them safe and on the run for a few days if they kept their heads low and stayed in the shadows. But then what?

A thought struck Logan, a saying that had come to mind when he'd first learned of the deal the FSB and the CIA had struck to kill Grainger: the enemy of my enemy is my friend.

He didn't need to find someone he could trust. All he needed was someone who was willing to work against his enemies.

And in his time, he'd certainly come across a few people who fitted that criteria.

Logan looked down. The fuel indicator on the car was edging closer and closer to empty. They had no map, no GPS, but Logan knew they were still bearing south because of the position of the moon and stars he glimpsed every now and then through the thin clouds. There were also sporadic road signs that gave the names of larger towns many hundreds of miles in the distance. Volgograd – one of the largest cities in Russia and the site of famous battles during World War Two when it was known as Stalingrad – was a little under two hundred miles away.

Logan didn't want to go there, but he knew that as long as they were closing the distance to the city, then they were still heading south, away from Moscow and edging closer to the border. But there couldn't have been more than fifty miles left in the tank. So when they spotted a sign indicating a petrol station a mile further ahead, Logan was both relieved and suddenly filled with tension.

'We have to stop here,' Grainger said. 'We'll not make it to another one.'

'I know,' Logan said. 'Let's just hope it's still open.'

The time was just short of two in the morning. Given how quiet the road was, Logan thought it likely that the place would be shut. As it was, the service station was positioned just off a junction with a larger carriageway running overhead and so was open twenty-four hours a day. Despite its proximity to the other road, it was just a solitary petrol station with a small, plain building – no shops or other amenities like you would find on a major motorway. Logan was pleased about that.

He drove the car up to one of the pumps and turned off the engine, then opened the door and stepped out into the bitter night. A blast of cold air smacked against his face and he shivered as he looked up at the pump's display. When the numbers were set to zero, he began to fill up. By the time the tank was full, he was shivering vigorously. He put the nozzle back onto the stand and walked toward the building, where he could see a solitary worker standing on the other side of the window.

Inside, Logan grabbed some refreshments before heading to the teller. Behind the desk, both detailed road maps and GPS units were for sale. The maps would be cheaper but they only covered certain parts of Russia. And he wasn't planning on staying much longer.

'How much is the GPS?' Logan asked in Russian, which he could speak fluently, albeit with a slight accent that would tell any native that Logan wasn't.

The man turned and pointed to the three choices in turn, giving Logan a brief description as to why one was more expensive than the other. It was the mid-priced one that Logan wanted. The one that had the most extensive pre-loaded maps. But he wasn't sure the paltry cash he had would stretch.

He took out everything he had and began to count out the notes onto the teller's desk. By the time he got down to coins, he was still two hundred roubles short. He'd hoped the cash he had would last a few days. He was hungry and thirsty, but he knew over the coming days the GPS unit would be more valuable than snack food. And he would just have to hope that the full tank of petrol would take them at least over the border, because they wouldn't get the chance to fill up again before then unless they came across more money.

In the end, Logan put back some of the food and settled the balance with the teller, leaving the shop with less than a hundred roubles in his pocket.

As he approached the car, Grainger wound down her window, a questioning look on her face. Logan didn't say anything, just dumped the goods down onto her lap through the open window.

'Take a look back where we came from,' Grainger said, peering into the wing mirror next to her, her warm breath clouding around her face as she spoke.

Logan didn't respond. He continued around to the front of the car, eyes fixed down the dark, unlit road. His hand was on the door when he spotted a glint in the distance. He stood still, searching the darkness. He spotted it again when a large truck thundered past on the overhead carriageway behind him, its wide beams catching and reflecting off the distant metallic object.

He looked through the car window at Grainger, who nodded at him.

It was just as she'd said it would be.

And that was why he'd already guessed what the object was when the bright white headlights of the vehicle were turned on and the growling engine of the four-by-four was brought to life.

Logan stood motionless, waiting, calculating, as the vehicle, fifty yards in the distance, lurched away from where it had been hidden, heading toward him.

When it was caught in the light of the petrol forecourt, Logan wasn't at all surprised to see what type of vehicle it was: a gleaming, black BMW X5. The exact same type of vehicle that Lena and her men had driven to the exchange with the CIA in Moscow.

Logan knew even before the car came to a screeching halt just five yards from him, the front passenger opening his door, gun in hand, pointed toward Logan, that the occupants had been tailing them. And that they were from the FSB.

Chapter 6

'I don't think they'll make a move straight away,' Grainger had said some hours earlier. 'They'll wait to see what we do.'

She'd explained to Logan that the Russians had planted a tracking chip in her right shoulder. Having felt around inside his jumper, she'd found a similar lump on his shoulder too. They had both been tagged by the FSB.

'They did it the first day I arrived in Russia,' Grainger said entirely casually, the emotion and sadness she'd expressed earlier replaced with a steely determination. 'Lena said it was for my own protection. So they'd know where I was even if the Americans tried to take me away.'

'Yeah, she's full of kindness that one,' Logan said.

He was surprised he hadn't found the chip in his shoulder before, but then he had been held captive by the Russians for three months. For much of that, his mind had been distant and detached from his body. The chip could have been planted in him at countless points during his ordeal without his being any the wiser.

'Why didn't you tell me at the apartment?' Logan had asked. 'We could have removed the chips then.'

'I wasn't sure we'd have time. I saw the look on your face. I knew we had to leave immediately.'

She was right, but the answer wasn't quite good enough.

'Then why not tell me as soon as we were away from there?' Logan asked.

'I wanted to wait and see what their response would be.'

Logan frowned, perturbed that she seemed so nonchalant about the whole thing.

'And was their response what you expected?'

'Absolutely. They're tailing us – I have no doubt about that. Remember, if what you told me is right, it's not the Russians who want me dead. It's the CIA. So perhaps the FSB still think I, or even both of us, have value to them. Or maybe they just want to see what we'll do next.'

Logan mulled over her words. Despite his wariness, it made sense. The fact the FSB agents hadn't shown themselves spoke volumes. Maybe they were simply awaiting a command to kill from their superiors. But more likely they were stalking, waiting for an opportune moment to recapture their prey. Killing Grainger was of no benefit to them – nor was them killing him, for that matter, now that he was a wanted man himself – unless revenge was the only thing on their minds. They wanted both of them back under their control.

'We should just cut the chips out and be done with it,' Logan said. 'It would only take a few minutes.'

'You want to run forever?'

'No. I want to stand and fight. But on my terms. Right now, it wouldn't be an even fight. We don't know where they are, how many of them there are.'

'Then I say we lure them in. Let them think they've won the race.'

Logan considered the idea. 'They'll have weapons. Money. IDs,' he said.

'My thoughts exactly.'

He had forgotten just how savvy Grainger could be. She was an experienced agent after all. At a moment when most people would be panicking about how to lose the tail, wanting to run as fast and as far as they could, she was plotting a way to tackle the hunters in order to strengthen their own hand.

'Okay, we'll have to stop soon anyway,' Logan said. 'Whenever we see the next petrol station, I'll make myself busy and you keep a lookout for them. As long as we're on the move, it's unlikely that anything will happen. When we stop, they may take the opportunity to confront us. Much easier for them to do it then than tackle a moving target.'

'Unless their only interest is in tailing us. To see where we're going and what we'll do.'

'Maybe. But they won't do that forever. And there's only one way to find out.'

Logan reached down.

'You have this,' he said, handing Grainger his gun. 'I want them to think they've caught us by surprise. You keep that in the car, out of view.'

And that was why when the man stepped out of the black BMW, weapon drawn, Logan didn't panic. He stood and waited.

Logan didn't recognise the man at all. He was dressed in a thick black overcoat and shiny black boots, a hollow look on his hard and weathered face, the hand pointing the handgun unwavering.

A moment later, the rear door opened and a woman stepped out, gun in hand. Logan didn't recognise her either. The steely, calculating look in her eyes reminded him of Lena, though with her pointed features she wasn't nearly as attractive.

As she moved aside to shut the door, Logan managed a glimpse inside the vehicle. There were no other occupants in the rear. So a total of three people to contend with. The driver was the only one not yet joining the party.

'Put your hands in the air,' the man said in heavily accented English. 'Then slowly move down onto your knees.'

Logan did as he was told. He was pretty confident these people didn't want to kill him here. But he didn't want to test that theory. Nor did he want to risk them shooting him in the leg or somewhere else non-fatal.

The woman began to move forward.

'Is she in there?' she said to Logan.

'Who?' Logan said.

'Angela Grainger.' The woman gave Logan a stern look. 'She belongs to us now. Is she in the car?'

Her words sent a cascade of thoughts through Logan's mind. Grainger was still of value to them – that was clear. Maybe the Russians thought they could do another deal for her life with the Americans. But what about Logan? Was he simply expendable? Maybe the fact he had caused them so much trouble already had brought them to that conclusion.

'Yes. She is,' Logan said.

The woman took another two paces forward, craning her neck to try to get a view into the front of the car. The man was also moving forward, toward Logan.

'Miss Grainger,' the woman said, not shouting but louder than before, 'please come out of the vehicle.'

There was no movement from within the car.

'Do it now or I'll shoot your companion,' the man shouted.

He was now just three steps from Logan.

The lady took one more step toward the car and then a gunshot rang out, loud and clear, the sound travelling and echoing off the mass of concrete of the raised highway behind where Logan was kneeling.

Logan didn't need to look to see what had happened. But the man pointing the gun at him did. That was his fatal mistake.

Logan leaped up and, using his momentum, thrust a knee hard and fast into the man's groin. The man recoiled, shouting out in surprise and pain. Logan grabbed the man's gun arm and twisted it around. He thrust it down at the same time as hauling up his other knee, crashing the man's arm down against his thigh and snapping both the radius and the ulna.

The man screamed and reflexively released his grip on the gun. Logan grabbed it, turned it around and fired three quick shots, each hitting the man in his chest only an inch apart in a neat cluster.

As the body was still falling to the ground, Logan heard screeching tyres and looked up to see the BMW reversing, swinging around to head back where it had come from. Clearly the driver didn't fancy his chances on his own.

Logan quickly readjusted his aim as the driver righted the car and it began to veer away. Before he got the chance to fire, another two gunshots blasted. Logan looked on as one of the vehicle's back tyres exploded, shards of rubber flying into the air. The car careened left and right, the driver unable to keep it under control. It plunged through a mound of snow, which burst into the air, then came to a crashing halt in a ditch at the side of the road.

Logan looked over and saw Grainger, standing up out of the car, gun resting on its roof. A few feet away lay the body of the woman, entirely motionless. There was a black hole, seeping blood, where her left eye used to be and where the bullet from Grainger's gun had penetrated her brain.

'You take the left side, I'll take the right,' Grainger said, moving her gun off the roof. Crouching down, she moved toward the stricken vehicle.

Without saying a word, Logan immediately followed suit, moving out toward the left to come around the BMW on the driver's side. As he approached the crumpled heap, steam rising from the bonnet, he saw the driver's door was already open.

His first thought was that the driver may have already bailed out and was either running or hiding. As he moved closer, though, he saw the man's arm hanging down, flailing around by his leg, which was trapped in the crumpled footwell.

Logan kept his gun out as he moved right up to the man. When Logan reached him, the man turned his head to face him.

The airbag had deployed in the collision and was draped over the man's waist. He had a gash on the side of his head from which a thick trail of blood was working its way down his face. It looked as though he had cracked it against the side of the car at impact, the airbag ultimately providing little protection.

The man was alert but panting heavily. He looked to be in pain. Logan stared past him and spotted Grainger through the passenger side window. She opened the door, gun held out toward the man.

'Are you armed?' Logan asked him.

The man nodded and looked down at his chest, indicating that his gun was there. Logan reached out and undid the man's coat, then took the handgun out of its gun strap.

'I'll stay on him,' Logan said to Grainger. 'You check the car.'

Without saying a word, Grainger put her gun away and quickly searched the car, opening each of the doors, checking the glovebox and boot, taking away anything that was of use. When she was finished, she headed back to the two bodies on the petrol forecourt and searched them too. She called over to Logan when she was done and he took two cautious steps backward, his gun still pointing toward the driver, before he turned and ran back to the car.

When he reached it, Grainger was already inside. He jumped

into the driver's seat and fired up the engine. As he drove off, he looked at the petrol station window, where the worker had been standing when they first arrived. There was no sign of him now. No doubt he was hiding somewhere. And no doubt he had called the police. That didn't overly worry Logan, though: he was already a wanted man.

Grainger rummaged through the takings as they sped away down the dark single-track road. As expected, the FSB agents had been armed. Logan and Grainger had now acquired three more handguns together with numerous magazines.

Although the agents had been thin on personal items, they did have on them some cash and two credit cards. Grainger had also found passports stuffed in the glovebox of the BMW, but no other identification such as driving licences or documentation to say whom the agents worked for.

Logan could guess why. He generally travelled with little ID unless it was necessary. The passports the Russians had been carrying would be fakes. They were to allow the FSB agents to track Logan and Grainger over the border of Russia, to wherever they were heading. They would all be cover identities.

What the possessions did suggest was that the Russians had been willing to play the long game if necessary, travelling across countries to keep on Logan and Grainger's tail. He didn't know why they would do that, or why the trackers had taken the opportunity to confront them at the petrol station.

Logan did know one thing, though: the passports the agents had been carrying were exactly what he and Grainger needed.

'So what now?' Grainger asked.

'We need to get these chips out,' Logan said.

'And then?'

Logan smiled. 'And then we're leaving Russia for good.'

PART 2

The forgotten enemy

Chapter 7

February 1997
Highlands, Scotland

Logan awoke when he felt pressure on his wrists. He opened his eyes, slowly at first, but then was suddenly alert when he saw the men crowding around his bunk. He tried to jump up, only realising then that his wrists and ankles were shackled with ropes. Each was wound tightly and held firmly by the four men hovering over him. A fifth man, standing right next to Logan, half-smiling, half-snarling, was the leader of the pack of army grunts: Fleming.

'Wakey-wakey,' Fleming cackled. 'If it isn't the boy wonder. Do you fancy heading out to the mess for some chow or are you a bit tied up?'

Fleming's men laughed at the lame joke. Logan's tense limbs relaxed some and he laid his head back down on the bed. He wanted to fight back, but he knew that with the position they had him in, there was little he could do.

'Okay, lads, get him off the bunk.'

The two men to Logan's right tugged on their ropes with force and hauled Logan from the bed. He landed on the cold, hard floor with a heavy smack that sent a shock all the way up his spine. The two men on the other side climbed across the bunk, and once in position, all four men pulled tight on the ropes, stretching Logan's limbs out like he was performing a star jump.

Fleming walked up to Logan and stood right over his face.

'You still want to be one of us?' he said, smiling but with anger in his voice. He unzipped his trousers. 'Then drink up, soldier boy.'

'No. Come on, please!'

Warm, thick urine cascaded onto Logan's face and he spluttered and then squeezed shut his eyes and his mouth. The other men groaned in mock disgust and then laughed and then groaned as Logan was covered in the sickly yellow liquid. He held his breath but the ammonia stench still got through, making him gag and retch.

'You want to be just like us?' Fleming shouted. 'Then drink my fucking piss, you piece-of-shit civvy!'

Logan began to writhe, his torso bucking up and down, his head lolling from left to right. Moving his arms and legs was impossible; each was outstretched and secured in place by the strength of a fully grown man. It was hopeless. He simply had to lie there and take it, the ghastly sound of the men's laughter filling his head.

When it was finally over, Logan opened his eyes. He saw Fleming zipping up and immediately took a deep breath, filling his starved lungs with air. Urine on his face rolled into his mouth and he coughed and spluttered, trying to force it back out, much to the amusement of the men.

'Get your shit together, Logan,' Fleming said, turning away. 'We're heading out in fifteen minutes.'

The four men let go of the ropes and Logan's arms and legs slumped down. He instinctively rolled onto his side, curling his legs up into his chest, still coughing, trying to remove the foul smell and taste from his nose and mouth.

'Yes, Captain,' he choked.

Twenty minutes later, the six men were flying in a Westland Puma helicopter high up above the Scottish Highlands. Logan hadn't uttered another word to the men since the latest hazing incident.

Was it really hazing, or just outright bullying? He wasn't sure anymore.

He did know that he'd been made about as welcome as a rat in a kitchen. For the past month, he'd been teamed up with the small patrol of SAS men, taking part in their gruelling exercises.

He'd expected a frosty reception from the army men, but in fact what he'd had was even worse – he was, after all, an outsider being let into their secret world on the say-so of some unseen person they knew nothing about.

They had no idea who Logan was, what his life had been like as a troubled teen, or what he was now being trained for at the JIA. All they saw was a civilian, a young man some ten years their junior, someone who'd never seen war or combat and who didn't understand the first thing about the military, being thrust into their world to be trained up just like them. And they resented him. Resented who they thought he was.

The men had been staying at the remote base camp in the far north of the Highlands for two weeks, carrying out various exercises and training missions, building up for the final escape and evasion exercise that would last for the next five days.

The five army men were already fully fledged members of the UK's most prestigious special forces unit, the SAS. They were there to keep themselves fresh in between active missions. Logan was an early twenty-something civilian with plenty of recent combat training but zero real-life experience.

He'd been thrown in with the sharks.

Logan had already been around the world to train in various skills – survival, combat, arms, interrogation – and on many of those stints, he'd been teamed up with battle-hardened military men. The JIA was a small operation and ran few training centres of its own. For virtually all of the long and tiring training period, the JIA shipped recruits out to a combination of the army and the mainstream intelligence agencies, the mix depending on the exact skill set and training regimen of the particular candidate.

So far in Logan's experience, few of the groups he had been sent to had welcomed him, the outsider. But none of them had been so filled with hate and anger as Fleming and his grunt patrol.

Logan guessed Fleming was in his late thirties. He was six inches shorter than Logan and not as thick in his frame, but he had the grizzled appearance of an experienced warrior and he was lean and strong, fast and agile: everything he needed to be to carry out his gruelling job. There was a lot that Logan admired about the man – his skills at least – but absolutely nothing that Logan liked or respected.

Fleming was a captain, a commissioned officer. The other four men were sergeants and corporals. They obeyed Fleming's every word, his every command. They were like his little pets. Even when Fleming wasn't in the room, Logan had never heard one of the others say a single derogatory word about their captain. Logan hadn't yet figured out whether that was because Fleming had somehow won them all over or because they were simply so shit-scared of him that they didn't dare say a bad word about the man even when he wasn't there.

While training with the men, Logan was supposed to act and live like them. But Logan wasn't in the army. They could give him a hard time while he was with them, but after next week he would no longer have to abide by their outdated hierarchy and petty rules. And there was only so much bullying he would take before he snapped.

Logan guessed this was one of the reasons he had already completed extensive mental conditioning. A few months ago, he would have tried to tear Fleming's head off the first time the captain laid a finger on him. Logan was headstrong and seldom scared of anyone or anything. And while on the outside he was mostly calm, placid, almost emotionless, an angry outburst was always bubbling under the surface.

Since the training had started, he'd become more in control of his fiery temperament. Even though he could still feel the anger boiling inside him day by day, he had so far kept it under wraps, playing along with Fleming's hateful games. But he hadn't forgotten any of the torment, and he enjoyed thinking of the different ways he could wipe the smirk off Fleming's face for good.

All he had to do now, before he left this rotten place for good, was make it through the final exercise. Five days stranded and cut off from life in the frozen Highlands of Scotland.

A foreboding and deathly place.

A place where all sorts of accidents could befall even the most experienced survivor, mountaineer, orienteer. Where even the smallest slip could cost someone their life.

'You ready for this, Boy Wonder?' Fleming shouted over the din of the helicopter's rotor.

Logan gave him a cold, hard stare.

'Yes, Captain. More ready than you could imagine.'

Chapter 8

The helicopter dropped Logan and the SAS men in a small clearing in a pine forest high up in the mountains. They had been shown on a map the night before the drop location and the extraction point some fifty miles away, but they had no luxuries such as maps for the exercise itself.

They had five days to reach the extraction point. But the exercise wasn't just about orienteering: it was about escape and evasion. The six men would be hunted. The trackers were another group of trained SAS soldiers. Starting from the same drop point as the evaders, the trackers would have simply their wits and their training to figure out where to go. The evaders would have a few hours' head start and would have to use all their training and guile to stay one step ahead.

As soon as Logan's feet touched the ground, he sprang into action and followed the other men into nearby wooded cover as fast as he could, cold air blasting into him from the helicopter's rotors.

When all the men were on the ground, the helicopter ascended and moved off into the distance, its racket fading, replaced by a foreboding silence. Logan crouched down, huddling with the others.

The temperature was well below freezing. It likely would be for the duration of the exercise. Although the helicopter had been unheated and cold, Logan was already shivering from the sudden temperature drop now that he was outside. He knew it would pass as they began to march on, but it was a chilling early reminder of just how tough the next five days would be.

Each of the men had on basic army fatigues and overcoats. No rucksacks, tents, sleeping bags. Just their clothes and a survival tin each that contained little other than a basic penknife, a pocket mirror and a mini compass.

'Okay, lads,' Fleming said, 'we move out quickly. They'll be tracking us within a few hours so let's move as far and fast as we can for now, make it difficult for them. Extraction point is south-east. Jones, Medway and Lewis, you head out twenty degrees east of that. Butler and Logan, you come with me – we'll head out twenty degrees south of extraction.'

'Yes, Captain,' the five men chorused.

'Always remember the basic rules. And we'll try to align paths after forty miles, some point during day four probably if we keep progress steady.'

'Yes, Captain,' the SAS men said. Logan kept his mouth shut this time.

'And if you get caught, they're not going to be giving you a nice warm mug of cocoa. It's straight to interrogation. And they won't be holding back. So don't. Get. Caught.'

'Yes, Captain.'

'Now let's go.'

With that, the men stood up and split off into the two mini groups. Each of them, including Logan, understood the basic rules Fleming had mentioned. In fact, everything Fleming had said was as expected. The trackers would be using all of their skills and experience and would have dogs too. And Logan was sure Fleming was right when he'd said the trackers wouldn't be holding back. They were all trained SAS soldiers. They had as much to prove as Fleming and his team.

Splitting into smaller groups was essential to make the trackers' job harder from the start. Going off at a tangent to where they wanted to be would further complicate matters for the trackers and meant that within a few hours, the two groups of evaders would be some distance apart.

Logan adopted the rear position as he, Butler and Fleming began their march through the pine woods. He wanted to keep the others in sight at all times. It wasn't just the trackers he was concerned about. It wouldn't surprise him at all if Fleming brought his bullying out into the wilds.

The woods were dark and sinister. Easy to get lost in, to disappear for good in, Logan thought with both promise and anxiety. The ground underfoot was mostly frozen with just small, boggy patches of mud. It did at least feel warmer in the woods than out in the blustery open.

The three moved on for close to six hours, taking five-minute rests every hour. The pine forest opened out along the way, leaving them in an icy wasteland with only the natural crevices and undulations of the mountains to keep them in cover. The ground all around was white. Even though it was riskier from a safety point of view, they tried their best to stick to the slippery ice patches rather than the deep snow, which would leave an obvious trail. It wasn't always possible to do so, because the ice patches came and went at random, but it at least meant the trail left in the soft snow was patchy and erratic.

Rather than heading in a straight line, they zig-zagged across the terrain in order to map out a route that didn't require never-ending ascents and descents, but also to further complicate their trail. It meant forward progress was slower, but was a necessary technique to aid evasion.

With darkness quickly descending, they finally stopped for a prolonged break. They found a large rock whose overhanging edge created a mini shelter that the three could all fit under if they sat tightly together with their backs to the stony surface. The rocky crevice also provided cover in just about every direction.

'We'll rest up for two hours,' Fleming said. 'Then get on our way.'

'Shall we build a fire?' Butler asked.

'We're going to need one out here,' Logan said, huddling down into the neck of his coat. The shivering had already kicked in even though they'd only stopped moving for a few seconds.

'It'll take too long to make,' Fleming said, 'foraging through this crap. There's not exactly an abundance of wood out here.'

'We'll get enough from the gorse,' Logan said. 'There's plenty around.'

Fleming glared at Logan, clearly not liking being challenged even if what Logan had said was valid.

'Plus we need water,' Logan said. 'We haven't passed a stream or a tarn that wasn't frozen solid in hours. We can use the fire to melt some snow.'

'Fine,' Fleming said. 'Butler, go and find some stones. Logan, get the gorse. I'll dig a pit up against the rock.'

It took Logan the best part of twenty minutes to collect the gorse. It was thick and frozen and full of thorns. His hands were blue from cold and covered in nicks and scratches by the time he'd finished. When he headed back to the rock, he saw that Butler and Fleming had already prepared the pit, over a foot deep, neatly lined with large grey stones.

'What took you?' Fleming said, sounding pissed off.

Logan ignored the question, just threw down the pile of branches and twigs he was carrying that would act as kindling and tinder. 'This should be enough to get it started,' he said. 'But I'll need to find some thicker branches if we want it to last.'

'Okay,' Fleming said. 'But be quick.'

Logan headed off again and it took another twenty minutes of foraging to collect some thicker wood. He tried to remain alert to the sounds and sights around him as he searched – looking, listening, for signs of the trackers – but his senses were waning and he was quickly becoming groggy and listless from the combination of exhaustion, lack of nourishment and cold.

Eventually he found some dishevelled gorse that may or may not have been dead and snapped off the thorny branches, then used the penknife to cut the thicker base stems close to the ground. He took the pieces back to the rock.

Fleming and Butler were squatting in front of the pit, where they had already set the tinder and kindling alight. As Logan approached, he could hear the two men talking, but they stopped as he neared and stood up, facing him. Logan dropped the wood by Fleming's feet.

'Everything okay?' Logan asked.

'Just discussing tactics, that's all,' Fleming said, smiling.

'Anything you want to let me in on?'

'Guys,' Butler said, holding up a hand, 'I think I hear something.'

The three men stopped talking and instinctively crouched. Logan looked around in the darkness for any sign of movement.

'Cover the fire up!' Fleming hissed in a whisper.

'It can't be them, surely?' Logan said, unable to see or hear any sign of the trackers. 'We were moving too fast. Trying to follow our trail and with the tracker dogs sniffing around here, there and everywhere, they can't have been going even two-thirds of our pace.'

'Well, there's something out there,' Fleming said.

'Shhh. There it is again,' Butler whispered.

'Probably an animal. An owl or–'

'Just put the goddamn fire out!' Fleming said, more loudly but still at a whisper.

Butler and Logan began to throw clumps of snow onto the newly lit fire. It crackled and fizzled, fighting for its life, but was soon buried deep.

'There it is again,' Fleming said. 'Over there.'

He pointed off into the distance but it was pitch black. Logan couldn't see a thing. He was squinting, straining his senses for any noise or sign of movement. But there really was nothing.

Then he heard Butler shuffle in the snow behind him. He started to turn to look, but fell forward when he was suddenly shoved in the back. Logan landed face first in the soft, cold snow. He tried to spring to his feet to stave off whatever attack was coming, but before he could, a boot was thrust into his back, pinning him down.

Logan turned his head and looked up at the shadowy figure of Fleming, his grinning face caught in the dim moonlight.

'Sorry about that, Boy Wonder. Had you going there for a second, though, didn't I?'

Fleming's gaze turned to a point behind Logan and he nodded. Logan followed his line of sight, but the only reaction he could manage as he saw the rock swinging toward his head was to squint and turn his head away.

The stone cracked against the side of Logan's face, sending a shock wave right through him.

'See you at the finish line,' Fleming cackled, just a few seconds before Logan passed out, face down in the powdery white snow.

Chapter 9

Jay Lindegaard stepped into the hospital room and closed the door softly. He turned around and looked at the young woman lying on the bed in front of him. Her eyes were shut. White sheets were draped neatly over her body, covering her all the way up to her shoulders, her arms resting on top. There was a cannula in the top of her hand, the connecting tube winding up to the clear plastic bag suspended high above the bed. The heart monitor on the opposite side beeped away, the blips regular and calm, the peaks on the machine's screen shallow and consistent.

Lindegaard stared at her. He couldn't help but think how stunning her face was, even without make-up, even after the ordeal she'd been through. He was a proud man. Proud of her. He had his faults, sure. Who didn't? He knew he was crass, arrogant, a bully if truth be told. He got all that. It was, in his eyes, what made him so effective at his job. But he was also fiercely loyal. To his country. To his family.

All he'd ever wanted to do was work hard making a living to protect those interests. The CIA was of course where he could put his strengths and values to best use. He'd worked for the CIA for God knows how many years – his first and only employer. Lindegaard saw it as a mutually beneficial relationship. His role at the JIA? That was something else.

The JIA's existence was a necessity. In the modern world, the secrecy of the CIA was no longer secret enough. There were too many laws and rules by which its employees needed to live, and too much scrutiny from government, the press and the outside world for it to operate freely like it had done in the past. The JIA was a step further removed. A step further from prying eyes. In many ways, it was exactly the organisation Lindegaard wanted to be involved with.

Yet he'd always felt uncomfortable about his role as one of the four members of the JIA committee – effectively the four men who had the final say over everything that happened at the organisation. There was something about the way the JIA worked that didn't quite sit well with Lindegaard.

Perhaps it was the fact that control of the JIA was shared between the US and its biggest ally, the UK. Maybe it was simply the people he had encountered since working with the JIA. They were … well. Just not CIA. Just not quite American enough for him.

Lindegaard snapped out of his thoughts and moved over toward the window. He pulled the thin blue curtains together, blocking out the bright sun that had been shining through and had heated the room to a beyond comfortable temperature. Then he turned and headed to the simple armchair next to the bed. As he slouched down onto the seat, she murmured and wriggled, then opened her eyes.

He continued to sit, staring at her face, waiting to see whether she would drift back off or come around. After a few moments, she turned her head toward him, grimacing with pain as she did so. Her eyes registered surprise when she saw who her visitor was.

'Uncle?' she said.

'Hi, sweetie. Sorry. I thought you were sleeping.'

He spoke to her in English. His Russian was patchy at best. Her English was perfect. Better than his even and yet it was his first language.

She shifted her position, trying to sit up. Her face wrinkled in pain. It didn't appear to him to have been worth the effort – she only managed to move herself a few inches before she gave up.

'Put me upright, will you?' she asked.

Lindegaard nodded and leaned forward. He pressed the button on the side of the bed and there was a whirring noise as the back third of it began to creep up, lifting her head and torso.

'How are you feeling?' he asked.

'How do you think?' she responded, managing a half-smile.

'I know, silly question. The doctor said there hadn't been any complications in surgery, though. You're going to be fine.'

'To be honest, that really doesn't make me feel much better right now.'

'So, tell me what happened?'

She tutted and closed her eyes for a couple of seconds. 'I was wondering how long it would take for the pleasantries to wear off.'

'What are you talking about?'

'Oh, come on,' she said. 'You're not here because you're concerned about me. You're just concerned about what might have happened. Concerned about yourself.'

'Can't I be concerned about both?'

'You could be, but I don't think you are.'

'Maybe you don't know me as well as you think then.'

'Quite frankly, I don't really care.'

'I know you don't mean that.'

She huffed and turned away from him, staring up at the ceiling.

'Please, just tell me what happened,' he said, trying his best to sound sincere. 'We can still get through this. But I have to know what we're working against.'

'Logan doesn't know!' she snapped.

Lindegaard didn't say anything for a few moments, waiting to see whether she would add to her blunt answer. She didn't.

'You're sure about that?' he said.

'I can't be one hundred per cent, how could I be? But I can't believe he wouldn't have told me, used it against me, if he'd known.'

'Why do you think he let you live?'

The question hung in the air, the room falling deathly silent except for the hum of the monitor and the bleeps coming from it with every beat of her heart – they were noticeably faster now.

Lindegaard stood up and moved over to the bed. He sat down by her side. The bed was set high and his legs dangled off the side, his feet barely touching the floor. He reached out and pushed a wave of silken hair away from her face.

She'd been shot twice. Once in the shoulder, once in the gut. She'd suffered terribly. She'd very nearly bled to death before the paramedics had got to her. And yet, despite what had happened, her skin and features remained sublime. He gently brushed the back of his hand across her cheek, feeling the warmth and softness of her skin, noticing the look of unease in her eyes.

'I don't know,' she answered eventually, almost a whimper, her usual confidence and bravado non-existent.

'Are you sure about that?' he said.

His hand moved slowly down to her neck, almost caressing. But then, suddenly, he clenched, pushing down hard. His fingers squeezed around her windpipe.

'Are you absolutely sure about that?' he said through gritted teeth, pushing his face down only inches from hers.

She began to writhe, slow, awkward movements. There was little strength in her small frame – a combination of her ordeal and the drugs she'd been given. He knew he could quite easily crush the life right out of her. She was entirely helpless. He squeezed harder. Her eyes bulged; her face contorted and turned red.

'How did you fuck it up?' he said, feeling the anger building up, channelling it down into his clenched hand.

'I'm sorry!' she managed to say through panicked, pained breaths.

'You can see how this looks, surely? You can see why I've got to do this?'

'Please! Please, stop!'

He ignored her feeble protests, focusing on her cringing and crinkled face as he steadily choked her. He was almost enjoying the moment. But after a few more seconds, he pulled his hand away and then watched curiously as she slowly regained her composure.

As if a switch inside him had suddenly been flicked, Lindegaard's features quickly softened and he once again began to gently brush her hair with his hand.

'You look so much like your mother,' he said, smiling at her.

She sank her head down lower, as if trying to get away from his touch.

'You're my niece and I love you,' he said.

'I know. I'm sorry,' she said.

'And we can still get through this. But you have to tell me if there's anything that could threaten my position. If there's anything at all that could get in the way.'

'I would,' she said. 'You have to believe me.'

'I believe you,' he said, leaning in close. 'But don't think for a second I won't kill you if you're lying to me.'

She looked away from him and he could see tears forming in her eyes. He wasn't sure whether they were from sadness or fear. It was unusual to see her so vulnerable, so weak. So emotional. She was usually so strong and in control.

But rather than feeling for her, her weak and emotional demeanour worried him.

He had meant what he said. He did love her. And he wanted to protect her, just as he had vowed to his sister, her mother, that he would all those years ago.

If she had been anyone else, he would have killed her already. For now, he would give her the benefit of the doubt.

But he knew he would have to keep a careful watch on her. She had failed once and who knew what damage that had already caused. And as long as she was stuck in here recuperating, and Carl Logan and Angela Grainger were still out there alive, Lena Belenov, the FSB's finest, was nothing more than a loose end. A complication.

Without saying another word, Lindegaard got up and headed for the door.

Chapter 10

Highlands, Scotland

When Logan came to, his entire body felt numb from the cold. It took him a few moments to find the strength to get his limbs working again. He hauled himself to a sitting position and pulled his hand up to the spot where the rock had crashed into his skull. There was a gash that was sticky with blood. The area around it was lumpy and sore. The cut wasn't deep, though, and the flow had already stopped.

Logan grimaced as he got to his feet. Pain shot through his head. His legs felt dull and heavy. He didn't know how long he had been out for. Minutes at most. Any longer and he probably wouldn't have woken up at all, given the freezing temperature. As it was, he was shaking violently from the cold, his whole body spasming.

He felt over his body, patted himself down, looked around the ground, realised that Fleming and Butler had taken everything but the clothes off his back. He had no knife, no compass, no watch on his wrist. He cursed loudly and kicked at the soft snow, sending plumes of white into the air.

If he'd thought the task ahead was arduous before, it would be even more so now. He was out in the wilds all alone with nothing but his wits.

But as daunting as the situation was, something else entirely was filling his thoughts. This was the last straw. He wasn't going to sit back and take Fleming's shit any longer. It was time to fight back. Despite the perilous position he found himself in, Logan's mind was already racing, alert, focused.

Fleming would have to wait, though, if only for a few hours. Logan knew time was on his side. He guessed he was still a couple of hours ahead of the trackers. Before he set off again, he needed to get warmed through and find some water and food to fuel his body. After that, he was going to become the hunter.

It was supposed to be an escape and evasion exercise, but Logan knew at that moment the game had changed. It was time to put everything he'd learned to the test. He no longer cared if the trackers found him. Getting Fleming and Butler was the goal now.

He set about rebuilding the fire, first removing the covering of snow and then re-digging the pit. It took some time to gather enough kindling and tinder, particularly as he no longer had the knife to cut away the branches. But it was worth the effort. The warmth from the fire when it was finally ready quickly made him feel revitalised.

Perhaps more importantly, it made it possible to melt some of the snow for water, which he desperately needed. It would have been a whole lot easier if he'd still had a survival tin to use as a receptacle for the water. As it was, he had to hold the snow above the fire a handful at a time, lapping up the small amount of liquid that pooled in his hand with each fistful. It was a lot of effort for a small amount of water, but he knew it was better than simply eating the snow, which would deplete his energy supply as a result of further reducing his core temperature.

Logan thought he would be about an hour behind his foes. If he'd set off after them as soon as he'd woken up, he might have caught them in minutes, but he just hadn't had the energy. And he knew they would have to stop eventually too. That should prove to be his opportunity to snare them.

Provided he could actually find them.

When he felt able enough to get on the move again, Logan covered the fire with snow, completely burying it, and then set off along Butler and Fleming's sporadic trail. Initially it was clear which way the two soldiers had headed, but the trail didn't last long. Logan's progress was soon slowed as Butler and Fleming's tracks became almost non-existent, with nothing more than a few yards of prints and spoor at a time.

After a while, Logan began to doubt whether the snippets he was finding were even from Butler and Fleming at all. As adept as Logan had shown himself to be so far in his training, Butler and Fleming were seasoned evaders and knew every trick in the book for covering their tracks.

The terrain certainly wasn't helping either. Logan had crossed two small bodies of water already, which somehow or other were unfrozen. It had given him the opportunity to drink but crossing water made it notoriously difficult to track. Even with dogs, water would have been a huge hindrance. Depending on how far the evader moved in the water before emerging, the scent trail could disappear entirely.

To add to that, the further Logan went, the harder he found it to figure his direction of travel. He was good at telling his orientation from the position of the stars, but it was a dull and overcast night with the glare of the moon only barely visible behind the clouds. That at least gave him some idea as to where he was going given his understanding of lunar movements, but it was nowhere near as accurate as the soldiers could be, given that they had compasses.

After a few hours, Logan began to realise that following the trail was near-impossible. He couldn't have moved more than a few miles since he'd left the rock. The cold night and tiring exercise were quickly sapping his energy and motivation.

A doom-and-gloom feeling began to slowly creep over him and it wasn't much longer before Logan lost the trail altogether. Some two hours before, he had entered a forest, which varied from expanses of fir trees to patches of thick undergrowth. There was little snow, just frozen-solid ground, and he hadn't seen a footprint or any signs of life since he'd walked past the first looming tree.

It was easy terrain to stay hidden in, especially at night. Perhaps Butler and Fleming had already stopped for rest and Logan, lost in the woods, had simply carried on past them. It would explain why there was no evidence at all of where they had gone.

Logan was at a loss. With only sporadic glimpses of the dim moonlight coming through the tree canopy, his already diminished sense of direction was now all but gone. He stopped moving and slumped against a thick tree trunk, his legs exhausted, his stomach aching with hunger, his hands blue with cold.

After a few seconds of unsatisfactory contemplation, Logan moved onto his knees and began to root around the trunk of the tree, scraping off the moss with his fingers. It was reindeer lichen, a staple food for survivors in cold climates. It didn't taste great and its nutritional content was poor at best, but it was a lot better than nothing. It would have been better heated through, boiled or fried or roasted, but he stuffed it into his mouth frozen, almost past caring about the possible consequences of ingesting the ice-cold food. Instead, his mind raced with thoughts of how he would get his own back on that bastard Fleming.

After a few soggy, cold mouthfuls, Logan's insides began to cramp, a natural instinct warding him off eating any more of the frozen moss. He cursed himself for having been so nonchalant.

The paltry amount of food inside him would give him a little energy, but Logan determined there was little benefit of moving any further in the night. If he could wait until morning, he would have a much better sense of where he was and where he was going. Plus, he badly needed rest and more food.

Feeling somewhat dejected at the prospect that Fleming could be moving further away, Logan got to his feet to begin another fire. If he was stopping, he would need a way of staying warm. And he needed more food too – the fire would be essential for warming through any more moss or other food he could find.

Then, suddenly, something caught Logan's attention. At first he thought it was an animal sound. A call maybe. He strained his hearing, holding his breath so that the only sound around him was the gentle rustling of foliage in the cold breeze. He heard it again. It was distant and quiet, dispersing in the freezing air. But the sound was unmistakable.

A human voice.

And not just any voice. A deep, growly bass voice.

Fleming.

Chapter 11

London, England

Peter Winter walked up the six front steps of the townhouse and stopped at the entrance as he fished out his keys. The building, in Islington, contained the flat where he and his girlfriend lived. Like many others in the area, it had once been a single home for the well-to-do owners, but many years previously each of the four floors, including the basement, had been split into separate dwellings.

Islington was still a relatively prosperous area with small enclaves of real wealth, but like many parts of London, it was never far away from poverty either. Still, it was a vibrant neighbourhood that had a bustling atmosphere and to Winter it was home.

It was almost nine p.m. and although he hadn't called home to say he would be late, he guessed his girlfriend wouldn't have bothered to cook any food for him; his working late was becoming an entrenched habit. Like it or not, his girlfriend seemed to have got used to the idea that he wouldn't be back until well into the evening each weeknight. He'd tried his best to at least shut himself off from his work at weekends but that too had become harder and harder recently.

The set-up that the young couple had was far from ideal, but Winter guessed it was probably no different to that of many professional couples: lawyers, accountants, doctors and the like. Scratch that, people in just about any walk of life had to work long hours if they ever wanted to get anywhere.

Working hours aside, though, Winter realised his job was hardly comparable to most other professions. For the past few days, he had been trying, to no avail, to figure out why it appeared one of the most experienced – and certainly the most deadly – secret agents the JIA had ever seen had gone rogue and was now working for the enemy. It was a matter of urgency. Of national security. The information Logan knew, if it fell into the wrong hands … no, Winter didn't want to think about that. He just knew he had to find Carl Logan. And fast.

So far, though, he was at a complete loss.

'Honey? It's me,' Winter shouted as he unlocked the front door and stepped into his flat.

He shut the front door, took off his shoes and walked along the bare oak floorboards toward the kitchen. The lights in the hall were on but the kitchen was dark. As he proceeded further down the corridor, he noticed too that the lounge, bathroom and bedrooms were in darkness.

He took his phone out of his pocket and saw he had two text messages and two missed calls from Claire, his girlfriend, as well as a voicemail.

'Shit,' he said.

He put the phone to his ear and listened to the voicemail she'd left him almost two hours ago. He had heard the call at the time but had been in the middle of something and had ignored it, planning to call back soon after. He never had.

Winter moved the phone away from his ear as he heard Claire's voice blasting down the line.

'Shit,' he said again.

It had completely slipped his mind. They were supposed to be going on a night out to celebrate her friend's birthday. Claire was pissed off, and rightly so. As he looked at the text messages, he could well imagine her temperature rising with each angry word she had typed.

But actually, the more he thought about it, although he knew he was well and truly in the bad books and would have a lot of making up to do, he was pleased he had messed up this time. Spending the night socialising hardly seemed appropriate, given the turmoil he was dealing with. While Claire and her friends were busy having a social drink and gossiping about the latest dumbed-down reality TV series, he'd been dealing with what was potentially a threat to just about every intelligence service the JIA had ever worked with. Plus, he couldn't stand most of Claire's friends anyway. They were whiny, self-important brats who had no clue just how insignificant they were.

After grabbing a bottle of beer from the fridge and a giant packet of chilli-flavoured crisps from the cupboard, Winter went to the lounge and sat at the desk. He fired up the computer and logged on to his JIA account. He took a long swig from his beer and enjoyed the taste and the feeling as the chilled liquid slipped down his throat.

He opened up the files he had been busily scanning earlier at the office. The files he had been pulling together on Jay Lindegaard.

Winter's first real run-in with Lindegaard had come many months ago now, during Logan's ultimately successful mission to rescue Frank Modena, the American Attorney General, after he had been kidnapped in Paris. That case had come at a time when Logan was still, in all honesty, a bit fucked up from his previous mission, which had seen him captured and tortured by a sadistic terrorist, Youssef Selim.

Lindegaard had been gunning for Logan from the start of the Modena case, wanting him removed not just from that assignment but from the JIA altogether. Winter and Mackie had stuck by their man, albeit reluctantly at times.

During that mission, Winter had been tasked by Mackie with finding dirt on Lindegaard to use against him. In the end, the task hadn't been hard. Lindegaard had sent some heavies after Logan – used his own CIA assets – following Mackie's constant refusal to remove Logan from the case. An underhand tactic, but one that was ultimately of little surprise to Mackie and Winter. They operated in a secret and dark world, and Winter knew full well that what you dished out to others was ultimately going to be dished out to you. There really was no such thing as an ally.

Never trust anyone. That was one of the first lessons Mackie had ever hammered into Winter. And yet, despite Mackie's insistence about that unbreakable rule, Winter had never truly abided by it. Because he'd always trusted Mackie one hundred per cent. You trust someone based on their values, the way they deal with you and carry themselves, and the way they treat other people.

To Winter, trusting was a natural instinct, only broken when there was positive evidence to do so. He'd trusted Mackie from day one. He'd trusted Logan too, despite rarely getting along with him. Or at least he'd trusted Logan to do the right thing by Mackie. And yet look how that had turned out. Logan was now the key suspect in Mackie's death.

But Lindegaard? Winter had never trusted him. He'd never liked him either.

Logan had, as ever, dealt with Lindegaard's sucker blow with ease, and Winter and Mackie had used that act of treachery, of desperation, to their advantage – they'd essentially blackmailed Lindegaard to allow them to operate away from his scrutiny and challenge. That had carried on right up until Mackie's murder. They'd never felt the need to take their knowledge of Lindegaard's betrayal outside the circle of three men, even though, if they'd wanted to, they could have used it to ruin Lindegaard's JIA career.

No, dirt like that didn't come along very often and it was best to keep it under wraps and wait and see just how valuable it might become.

Winter still had the leverage over Lindegaard because of that incident, but he sensed the older man would put up a hell of a fight if Winter ever tried to use it against him again – particularly now that Mackie was no longer on the scene. And so, ever since that day, Winter had kept on top of Lindegaard, looking for anything fresh that he could use against him.

Even before Logan's recent capture in Russia, his subsequent release and Mackie's death, Winter had had Lindegaard's email accounts hacked – his phones too where he could. He'd placed bugs in Lindegaard's London home, though he knew that Lindegaard, as with every JIA staff member, regularly had his house swept for such devices and it was a constant challenge to keep eavesdropping channels active. Despite all of that effort, so far Winter had no new dirt.

He knew the fruitless search was at least in part because Lindegaard had already been spooked once. As cautious a man as he always had been, it seemed Lindegaard was now ultra-cautious. Emails were almost non-existent. He used the mobile phone that had been supplied to him by the JIA only for rudimentary business. He had a second mobile phone, for his CIA business, but Winter had struggled to get any kind of trace on it.

He knew that Lindegaard had also taken to using pay-as-you-go SIMs regularly, for just a few days at a time, a few weeks maximum, in order to further limit the ability of anyone to keep track of his calls. And it seemed Lindegaard never spoke about business in his London apartment, or at the very least he spoke so vaguely that it was impossible to glean anything of interest.

On the face of it, Lindegaard's secretive behaviours were outwardly suspicious. But then Lindegaard had worked for the CIA for something like thirty years, so being clandestine was second nature to him. The problem for Winter was that Lindegaard's renewed caution meant he was getting nowhere in finding further collateral, which he was sure he was going to need to survive as a commander at the JIA. Lindegaard had hardly given him a warm reception since Mackie's untimely demise and it wouldn't be long before the CIA man was gunning for Winter – he was sure of that.

Winter's phone chirped on the computer desk, shaking him from his thoughts. He hoped it wasn't Claire; he really didn't want to speak to her now. He looked at the caller ID and raised an eyebrow when he realised the call was coming from his office.

'Yes?' he answered with just the faintest hint of suspicion.

'It's me,' said Pam, his secretary.

'I thought I told you to go home?'

'I know, you did. I was just about to. But you really need to see this.'

Winter's suspicion quickly switched to intrigue.

'What is it?' he said.

Pam was in many respects a traditional secretary. She had worked for Mackie for years, taking care of admin and expenses, managing his diary, doing all of the things that Mackie had believed himself too busy to do. With Mackie gone, Pam was now Winter's secretary. It was the first time in his career that he'd had someone there to look after him, and so far the relationship had been somewhat awkward. Many of the things that Pam was there to do, Winter was just too used to doing for himself.

But what Winter had quite quickly come to realise was that

Pam truly was a traditional secretary. She wasn't just there to take care of admin; it was abundantly clear to Winter that she had known every facet of Mackie's working life: his movements, his relationships, his agents, their missions. And she understood the politics of the JIA organisation as well as anyone – probably more so than he did, in fact.

Because of that, for the past few days, rather than have her organise his diary, he'd been picking her brains, using her as a sounding board, finding out what she knew about Mackie and what he needed to know about his new role. It had been a big education for him.

'I've found something that you need to see,' Pam said. 'About your good friend.'

Winter could feel his heart thud in his chest. He knew she was referring to Lindegaard.

'Go on.'

'Probably best you see for yourself. I've saved the file in your server area. You'll spot which file it is, I'm sure.'

'Okay, thanks,' Winter said.

Pam ended the call and Winter immediately began to click through to where Pam had indicated. He wasn't surprised by her vagueness on the phone. Being discreet was part and parcel of the job. But it did raise his interest all the more that Pam had been so wary not just of telling him what she had found but of saying Lindegaard's name aloud.

He opened the folder in which he guessed Pam would have saved the document and spotted the file almost straight away because of its unusual name. It was called 'read then delete'.

Winter felt his heart pound in his chest even harder as he double-clicked on the file icon. He felt like a naughty child doing something his parents had forbidden.

The file opened on his screen and he scanned the text inside. And he saw exactly why Pam had been so cautious.

Winter quickly closed the file, highlighted and deleted it, then went to his recycle bin and deleted it from there too. He then sat back in his chair and swigged the remainder of his beer. As he set the empty bottle down on the table in front of him, he couldn't help but break out into a wide grin.

It looked like he had some more collateral at last.

Chapter 12

Highlands, Scotland

Fleming's voice had come from the right. The opposite direction from where Logan had approached the area. He crouched low, peering into the dark distance for any sign of movement, listening for any other noise, voices.

Logan began to wonder whether he'd imagined the voice. But it had been so clear. Perhaps his senses were fooling him, though, as to which direction it had come from?

Then, a few seconds later, he heard the distinct sound of Fleming's voice once again. And it was near. Logan remained as still as he could, his breathing slow and shallow, his body solid and unmoving. His mind was in overdrive.

For hours, Logan's thoughts had been filled with ways to get his own back on Fleming, Butler and the others. Not just for what they'd done on this exercise, but for the abuse they'd so readily inflicted on Logan for weeks. He wanted to make them pay, even if harming the men at all, never mind out in the middle of a frozen wasteland where they had no way of contacting base camp, would likely be a really bad career move. The JIA were training him to be a fighter, weren't they?

So he would fight.

Logan began to move forward, still crouching low. His steps were slow and soft, his eyes darting back and forth between the ground and the area in front of him.

He caught a glimpse in the near distance, lit up in the dim

moonlight, of the familiar grey and white fatigues that he and each of the SAS men were wearing. He inched further forward, even more slowly than before. Finally he came to a stop at the base of a thick pine tree. He spotted two figures hunched over in a small clearing just yards in front of him.

Fleming and Butler.

They were huddled over a fire. Although Logan couldn't see the flames as the fire was sunk into a pit, the ember glow emanating from the hole was clear and was lighting up the two men, the orange illumination cutting a stark contrast to the near-darkness surrounding them.

They were talking but their voices were too quiet and muffled for Logan to make out any words. He guessed they'd stopped for a longer rest; a neat pile of twigs and logs next to them suggested they were planning on keeping the fire going for some time.

Logan began to creep forward again, staying low. The clearing that Fleming and Butler were in was only about ten yards wide. There was now just one more tree between them and Logan. He edged up to it and came to a stop once more.

Keeping his eyes on the two soldiers, he felt around on the frozen ground beside him, looking for a stone or a loose branch. Anything he could use as a weapon. He found a small fallen log, about a foot long, three inches in diameter. Exactly what he needed. He turned it over in his hands, ignoring the ice-cold that seeped from the log into his bare hands, thinking through his attack. Part of him felt like a coward for even contemplating what he was about to do.

But they had it coming, didn't they?

Logan was about to leap into action but then he stopped suddenly. A crunching noise somewhere off to his left. His gaze shot in that direction and his body froze.

Was it the trackers? Or the rest of Fleming's men, perhaps?

Logan held his breath and waited, staring into the darkness, aware that Fleming and Butler had stopped talking and must have heard the noise too. He risked a glance over in their direction. Butler was on his feet, peering over to where the noise had come from. Fleming had turned too, though he remained sitting on the ground. Logan followed their line of sight and a moment later there was more noise, rustling.

Logan's heart was thudding in his chest. He gripped the log tightly. His whole body was tense.

A second later, a small grey squirrel darted out into the clearing, sniffed the air, then bounded straight back into the darkness.

Logan exhaled slowly, feeling his nerves calm. He began to caress the log again, feeling its icy surface with his fingers. But then he turned his gaze back to Fleming and Butler and his eyes widened.

Fleming was staring right at him.

Logan froze. He held his breath, his body solid, completely still except for his thumping heart. The noise seemed to fill his head and make the world before him jump with each beat.

As Logan continued to stare at his foe, Fleming's face showed no visible reaction or emotion. No surprise or fear or anger. After a few moments had passed without so much as a blink or a twitch from Fleming, Logan could only assume that he hadn't given his presence away and Fleming was merely staring into the black forest around him. Logan's body was, after all, obscured by the tree that he was hunched behind and the glow from the fire didn't reach as far as where he was.

Catching Fleming's glare had startled Logan nonetheless. It was clear that Fleming and Butler were on high alert. Both because the trackers were somewhere out there and because they would surely assume Logan was following them.

Maybe it was more than that even. The feeling of isolation and the eerie blackness must affect even the most hardened and experienced soldiers, Logan guessed.

After a few more seconds, Fleming returned his attention to the fire pit and he and Butler began talking again, though their voices were noticeably quieter than before.

With them both distracted, Logan took two deep breaths and then sprang into action. He leaped to his feet. He darted forward, aware that his approach would be anything but silent, but banking on his speed over the short distance giving him the element of surprise.

When he was three steps away, he swung the log back and began to bring it forward, aiming for the back of Butler's head. It was a cheap shot. Taking the solider out from behind. Butler had shown no qualms, though, when he'd done the same thing to Logan earlier. In the moment, Logan really didn't care what the consequences would be. Butler had it coming. Fleming too.

But when the log was just a few inches from making contact, Butler suddenly reacted. Logan knew his foe's movement, his speed of thought, was too quick and deliberate for him to have been alerted by Logan's approach. There simply hadn't been enough time.

Which meant Butler had known the attack was coming.

Which meant Fleming had likely spotted Logan after all.

All of this dawned on Logan in the split second that he was in mid-swing with the log. By then, it was too late to do anything about it.

Butler twisted his body. He brought up his arm to protect himself from the incoming blow. The log smacked against Butler's forearm. The contact was solid. It sent a judder through the log and all the way up Logan's arm, into his shoulder.

But the force of the blow wasn't enough to stop Butler's counterattack. He was already shooting up, his other fist balled and hurtling toward Logan's midriff.

Butler's fist caught Logan in his kidney and sent him reeling back in pain. He slouched down, fighting against the haze that suddenly clouded his vision. He lifted his head. He caught sight of Fleming, already on his feet, moving fast around the side of him.

Logan instinctively turned his body, following Fleming's movement. He was completely oblivious when Butler's fist came toward him again, an upper-cut that caught Logan right on the edge of his chin, snapping his head back painfully.

He was on the ground in a heap before he knew it.

Logan heard Fleming laugh.

'Great shot, Butler!' Fleming said. 'Jesus, I thought that one was going to take his jaw clean off!'

Logan opened and closed his eyes, waiting for the stars to disappear. His body felt distant.

'Get him up on his feet.'

A thick hand wrapped around Logan's arm and began to tug at him. Then there was a shout of pain.

'Fuck!' Butler screamed, letting go of Logan and falling backward. 'I think my arm's broken. That little piece of shit!'

He thrust a heavy boot into Logan's side. Logan winced in pain, though he couldn't help but crack a wry smile once the throbbing from the blow began to subside. He knew the contact with the log had been good. Certainly enough to smash the thin bones in the lower arm.

'Hey, Butler. How's that arm?' Logan murmured through laboured breaths.

'I'm going to fucking kill him!'

Butler lunged toward Logan but Fleming leaped up at him, holding him back.

'Not like this,' Fleming said, his hard stare fixed on Logan.

Fleming held on to the raging Butler, keeping him at bay, waiting for the red mist to dissipate.

Logan was still dazed but he was beginning to feel some focus returning. He lifted his torso, placing his weight onto his elbow, grimacing from the pain in his side and jaw.

'Help him up,' Fleming said, releasing Butler.

Butler stood staring daggers at Logan. His left arm, the one Logan had struck, was dangling uselessly down by his side. Butler grabbed Logan with his good hand and hauled him up onto his feet.

'So what was the plan, Boy Wonder?' Fleming spat. 'Take us out with our backs turned, then leave us out here to die?'

'No worse than what you did to me,' Logan slurred.

He felt around his jaw. It had seized up and was painfully sore to touch but didn't seem to be broken.

The fog in his mind from the initial kidney blow was fading and, despite the odds, Logan began to plan his next move. But he was caught unawares when Fleming hurled a fist into his stomach and he doubled over in pain again.

'You forgot one thing, though, didn't you?' Fleming said. 'You're not dealing with dumb civvies out on the streets of London here. We're better than you. We're trained for this shit.'

Fleming wound up for another hit, but this time Logan was ready. Adrenaline was surging through his body. He was way past the pain. Anger and hatred were boiling up inside him. He dodged Fleming's fist and the soldier's momentum sent him stumbling past. Logan twisted and threw a hook into Fleming's back, sending him to the ground.

As Logan tried to reset, he spotted Butler lunging toward him. Logan stooped down and charged forward, catching Butler below the waist and sending him up into the air. The soldier somersaulted over Logan and landed in a heap on the ground, head first.

These soldiers were tough, trained fighters. The best the army had to offer. Logan might have been less experienced, less gnarled and slower too, but he was bigger. The soldiers lacked the brute strength that Logan had. He knew that his hits could make the difference in this fight.

But what the SAS men lacked in sheer strength, they made up for in speed and cunning and pure fighting instinct. When Fleming next came forward, Logan tried again to dodge him, winding up for a killer blow. But he never saw the feint from Fleming coming.

Fleming spun around in an arc, completely flummoxing Logan. As he completed the turn, Fleming's elbow caught Logan just below the ear. The jolt of pain caused him to stumble sideways. Before Logan could do anything to react, to defend himself, to offer up any kind of response, Fleming crashed the sole of a thick boot against Logan's lower leg.

It was a perfect shot. Full of power and purpose. Timed and placed with absolute accuracy. Logan's weight was planted, his leg stiff, making the impact worse. If his leg had been relaxed, bouncy, the strike would have taken his foot off the ground, the moving limb cushioning the blow. As it was, his foot didn't budge and his lower leg simply caved in, the tibia and fibula snapping like they were nothing more than dried twigs.

Logan screamed in pain and fell to the ground, immediately clutching at his stricken limb.

'You just don't listen, do you?' Fleming growled, righting himself, then crowding over Logan. 'You're not like us, Logan. You're just not good enough. You never will be. The sooner you stop fighting it, the better for everyone.'

Logan heard the words but he didn't respond. He was still screaming in pain, his body tumbling this way and that as he fought against the agony. He looked down at his leg. The white of broken bone protruding awkwardly through a tear in his fatigues was clear even in the dull light. There was already a large, dark, wet patch from the blood that was flowing out of the open wound.

Logan's eyes rolled at the sight and from the pain coursing through him. He felt like he would pass out. He hoped he would, to escape the pain.

He caught sight of Butler on the ground just a few feet in front of him. He was sitting up, nursing his neck.

'Butler, come on, get up,' Fleming said. 'It's time to get going.'

Butler looked over at Logan, at his injured leg, then into his defeated eyes.

'Shit, Captain. What are we going to do?' he said.

'What do you mean? We're going. This prick got what he deserved.'

Butler clambered to his feet, grimacing, his broken arm hanging like it was merely an attachment to his clothing rather than one of his limbs.

'We need to get you out of here,' Fleming said to Butler. 'Get you back to camp so they can get your arm seen to. Fuck knows what damage's been done.'

'He'll die out here,' Butler said. 'I can still walk but Logan's completely screwed now.'

Fleming looked over. Logan, panting heavily, caught his gaze and fought hard to keep his stare on Fleming. He wanted to get up and rip the captain's head off, even though he was absolutely certain that his opportunity had now gone.

This fight was over.

'He brought it on himself,' Fleming said.

'Captain, I–'

'Soldier, move out! That is an order.'

'Yes, Captain.'

Butler glanced at Logan one last time, a sorry look on his face. But he didn't question Fleming's orders again. He hung his head and turned around, then he and Fleming walked off, back into the dark treeline, without saying another word to Logan or to each other.

Within a few moments, they were gone, out of sight.

And Logan finally closed his eyes.

Chapter 13

It was Evans's second day in Moscow. The first had been pretty much a complete waste of his time. He understood why both Winter and Lindegaard had insisted he come here – it was the last place they had been able to pinpoint Logan. The problem was that everyone who had seen Logan or been with him was now dead.

All except one, that is. Lena Belenov. The FSB agent who had been central to the deal that Mackie and the JIA had been trying to broker for Logan's release following his capture on Russian soil, back in the autumn. She was still alive. A gunshot wound to the stomach. Another in her shoulder.

She was one of the few people who really knew what had happened in Moscow. And what had happened to Logan not only during his captivity but in the days following his escape from the FSB's jail cell.

The problem now was that she was holed up in a private hospital clinic near Taganka Square in central Moscow. Evans had done his best to scope out the facility the day before, but there was no way he was getting in there on his own. The clinic took up the far end of a sprawling four-storey building, a nondescript structure with block-like features and pale-yellow rendered walls – part of the 1930s' constructivism architecture still seen throughout central Moscow.

Evans had walked past the clinic three times the previous afternoon. Each time, the same police patrol car had been stationed across the street from the hospital's entrance. And each time other men had been conspicuously hanging around the entrance, either plain-clothed police or FSB, Evans guessed. Either way, it was clear the clinic wasn't used by your average citizen and Evans could only assume that the security inside would be greater still.

So at the moment speaking to Lena Belenov was a no-go. At least until he found a friendly way in.

Belenov wasn't Evans's only lead, though. He hadn't been sent to Moscow entirely without direction. He looked down and lifted the sleeve of his thick black windbreaker to check the time. Five to eleven. Five minutes before his planned rendezvous with Nikolai Medvedev.

Evans stuffed his hands back into the fleece-lined pockets of his windbreaker. When he'd left England the day before, the weather had been sunny and warm. In Moscow, it was grey and dull. Although it wasn't cold by Moscow winter standards, there was a chilling wind that was all the fiercer for the open position where Evans was sitting: on the bank of the Moskva River, not far from the Borodinsky Bridge.

The spot that had been chosen for the meet was neither the quietest nor the busiest area around. There was always a careful calculation to be made for the location of meetings with informants. Each had its advantages and disadvantages.

To a large extent, the choice depended on how likely it was that either you or the informant would be under surveillance. The quieter and more secluded the meeting place, the easier it was to spot any lurkers. But it also made the meeting so much more obvious. Not a problem in some cases; for example, a very brief exchange or where the threat of surveillance was very low, such as meeting a low-ranking official or a simple civilian informant. Conversely, very busy places – tourist traps and the like – were much easier to get lost in, but it was also harder to spot anyone watching.

The location that Medvedev had chosen was something like middle ground. It certainly wasn't deserted – there were plenty of pedestrians and even one or two eager tourists dotted about – but it wasn't exactly thriving either. All in all, it felt like a comfortable spot for the meeting that was to take place. Evans, who had only been in the country since the previous day, had no reason to suspect he was being surveilled. The fact Medvedev had agreed to meet at all led Evans to assume the FSB agent felt he was in the same boat.

At the very least, the UK embassy was only a mile up the riverbank. If the meeting didn't go to plan, if Evans needed to run, he could head there. He wasn't sure what Medvedev's exit route would be if he became spooked, but could only assume the experienced agent had one.

Evans looked down and checked the time on his watch again. One minute to eleven. Medvedev had never yet been late for a meeting and thoughts began to creep through Evans's mind as to what it might mean if this time the FSB agent weren't on time. But as he looked back up, a figure walking toward him caught his attention. Medvedev.

He was wearing casual attire: jeans and trainers, a bulky brown leather jacket, matching cotton gloves and a scarf and baseball cap. The cap was pulled down, obscuring his face, but Evans knew it was Medvedev. If nothing else, the thick white stubble covering his wide jaw was a dead giveaway.

Medvedev put his hands in his pockets as he reached Evans, who was still seated. 'Let's take a walk,' he said in Russian.

His voice was husky and dry and monotonous. But Evans thought that even in the brief introduction, he had detected tension. Not unusual, given the circumstance of their meeting, but it made Evans feel anxious.

Evans said nothing but got to his feet, looking left and right. Several people were walking in each direction across the riverfront, but no one caught Evans's eye as being out of place. No signs of surveillance. And if they kept moving, it would give them the chance to keep an eye on the people and vehicles following their direction.

'Okay, this way,' Evans said, turning to his left.

No other preamble, no pleasantries, no shaking of hands. In fact, in all of their meetings, they'd never once had any bodily contact or hand-to-hand exchanges at all. Unless passing documents over, a feat not undertaken lightly, the lack of contact was an absolute necessity. It had been standard protocol for years, ever since the revelations in the 1980s that the Russians were using the chemical compound NPPD to mark Americans they suspected of spying.

NPPD, routinely referred to as spy dust, had been used to identify Russian officials who had been in contact with the marked Americans. Any kind of bodily contact – a handshake, an arm on the shoulder, passing of documents or disks – would spread the dust. A Russian official who exhibited the telltale glow under fluorescent light, either on his hands, his clothes or his belongings, must have been in contact with one of the marked people.

And it was the gulag or worse for them.

In truth, many spy agencies had used similar marking techniques both before and after the use of NPPD hit mainstream media attention in the 1980s, but the implications remained the same.

'Is something the matter?' Evans asked.

He could sense by the edgy way Medvedev was walking, glancing here, there and everywhere, that he was on high alert.

'There's a lot of heat out there. I can feel it.'

Evans remained calm. 'Heat on you or me?'

'There's heat on everyone right now.'

They carried on walking, slow steps, both aware of everyone around them, but Evans doing a better job of hiding his spying.

'Were you followed?' Evans said.

'Usually I'd say no, for sure. Today, the answer is: I don't think so.'

It was an unusual response. And one that drained any remaining confidence Evans had.

'Okay. Then let's keep this brief. We'll walk to the next bridge and then head off.'

Evans calculated that at a slow pace, it would give them somewhere between five and ten minutes.

'Agreed,' Medvedev said.

Medvedev, who was in his late forties, had been an FSB agent for his entire career. He was a classic intelligence agent, the matters he dealt with largely to do with politics and diplomacy. But like many long-serving agents, he'd grown disillusioned some time ago over the shades of grey in which he found himself living.

Evans's role at the JIA was about as close to traditional espionage as there was. Even with only a few years of field experience, he could already see how someone could be turned. After a while, the monotony of lying, deceiving and forever playing games simply grinds people down and it becomes hard to remember exactly who you really are, whom you're working for and why.

Plus, the longer you're an agent, the more baggage you generate, and with that baggage comes leverage that others will inevitably use against you. A combination of these factors had led to Medvedev first becoming an informant for the JIA more than five years ago.

It was MI6 who had first tapped him up. They had been profiling the FSB agent, as they did with all senior foreign officials. One day MI6 had caught Medvedev in the act of passing information to the Chinese in exchange for a not-insubstantial amount of money. That was enough leverage to bring on board an agent who was clearly already disillusioned with his own people, or perhaps just greedy. Either way, after that incident, he had been passed along the food chain to the JIA, who had been milking him ever since.

Evans had so far been the sole agent from the JIA to have met Medvedev face to face. He was Evans's first informant and continued to be his most important, which as a result had seen Evans spend much of his time with the JIA in Moscow, deciphering and following up on the information Medvedev had provided.

That said, over the course of five years, he had only met with Medvedev seven times. Although theirs was an important relationship, it was nevertheless a fraught and dangerous game they were playing, and each of their meetings had been carefully planned and orchestrated.

All except this one, that is, which had been much more spur of the moment. Perhaps that was the reason Medvedev seemed so tense.

'I need to get to Lena Belenov,' Evans said.

Medvedev stopped and turned to face Evans, who stopped too. 'Impossible,' he said.

'Impossible for you or for me?'

'Impossible for you.'

Medvedev began his slow walk again and Evans followed.

'But surely someone's spoken to her? I need to find out what happened to her.'

'It's too difficult right now. Even for me.'

'Even for you? I'm not sure how that could be true for someone in your position.'

'It's hard to explain. I've never seen the FSB like this. There's just so much confusion right now. Trust is a word that doesn't really exist anymore. Every move, every conversation is being scrutinised. And the FSB ... we've lost many agents over the last few days. All because of one man.'

'Carl Logan.'

'Yes. He's still the focus, as I'm sure you can imagine. They'll ... we'll do anything to capture him again.'

'The FSB aren't the only ones on his back, that's for sure. So what's happening now? What are your leads?'

'The whole FSB is on lockdown,' Medvedev said. 'The SVR too,' he added, referring to Russia's external intelligence agency.

'I'm not sure I understand why,' Evans said, raising an eyebrow. 'Why isn't this just a simple manhunt?'

'It seems Lena Belenov wasn't entirely forthcoming about her dealings with your people. At the moment, nobody knows just what deals were struck by whom. Or what damage might have been done.'

'They could ask her.'

'They have. But everyone is keeping tight-lipped. At least with me. And whatever answers she's given probably don't carry much weight. Like I said, trust is a word that doesn't exist anymore.'

Alarm bells were ringing in Evans's mind at Medvedev's unusually vague answers. Evans knew that Lena Belenov had been central in the dealings between the JIA and the FSB over Logan's release. He also knew that somewhere along the line the CIA had become involved in those negotiations. From there had sprung the catalogue of events that had led to Mackie being executed and Logan going on a gung-ho rampage to rescue Angela Grainger from under the noses of the Russians.

So Evans could understand why the FSB and SVR would be on high alert. But there was clearly more at play than this simply being the Russians out to track down Carl Logan.

What worried Evans most was that Medvedev was being so cagey as to exactly what was happening, what information they'd got from Belenov, and the theories and leads the Russians were now working on. Evans couldn't believe that such a senior agent as Medvedev would be so completely in the dark.

Just how much did Medvedev know that he wasn't telling?

'Who killed Charles McCabe?' Evans asked.

'I don't know. Not the FSB. We had no reason to.'

'And not Carl Logan?'

'No, I don't think so. Which doesn't leave many other options.'

Medvedev's clear response surprised Evans. The picture of exactly who had killed Mackie and why was certainly muddy. Although Logan had initially been the prime suspect, and officially, at least, still was, Evans had got the impression from his talks with Winter and now Medvedev that all sides were now coming to a different conclusion. And Evans knew Medvedev was, rightly or wrongly, pointing the finger at the Americans. The CIA.

'But why?' Evans said.

'That's what we're trying to find out.'

'And what about Carl Logan? Where is he now?'

'You're asking me? He's your agent, isn't he?'

'At the moment, we're not quite sure about that. And he's in your country. He escaped your custody.'

Medvedev winced at Evans's words and then sighed.

'We were tracking him. Him and the girl, Angela Grainger. But they've gone.'

'Gone?'

'They were both chipped, but the last we saw of either of them was a few hundred miles from Volgograd.'

'What happened?'

'We had a car following them. But when our people took a chance and confronted them, Logan and Grainger attacked them. They got away.'

The situation was a complete mess. Logan was highly trained, sure, but was it really so hard to capture one man? Or were the FSB playing their own little game here? Maybe Logan really was an asset of the Russians now and they were simply protecting their man. There seemed so many possibilities and yet none of them made full sense.

'You said they *were* chipped?' Evans queried.

'We had a second surveillance vehicle a few hours behind the first. When they eventually caught up with the signal from the chips, the team were following a flatbed truck past Volgograd. We found the tracking chips in the back of the lorry. There was no sign of Logan or Grainger.'

Evans shook his head at the cheap trick. He'd like to think the JIA wouldn't have so easily let Logan get away. And yet, he supposed, if what Medvedev was saying were true, the Russians had at least been following them. The JIA had literally no clue as to Logan's movements.

'And since then?'

'Nothing.'

Evans wasn't sure what to believe. Medvedev definitely knew more than he was letting on. Which worried Evans. Because the Russian agent was supposed to be his asset.

'He's running,' Evans said, more to himself than to Medvedev.

There were only a small number of possibilities of where Logan was running to, given his last known location and where he had started. One thing Evans knew with confidence: by now, Logan was no longer in Russia.

After walking in silence for a few strides, Evans looked down at his wristwatch. The time was seven minutes past eleven. They were nearly upon the next bridge along the riverfront – the Bogdan Khmelnitsky footbridge, a unique glass-covered walkway across the Moskva River.

'I'll carry on going,' Medvedev said. 'You can head off here.'

'Okay,' Evans said, disappointed.

It felt strange to come away from a rendezvous with Medvedev with so little of value. He wanted more time. Wanted to ask more questions.

Just a few seconds later, as Evans was preparing himself to head onto and over the bridge, two men up ahead caught his eye. They were walking a few yards apart from one another. Nothing in particular was distinguishable about them – they wore plain clothes and were neither tall nor small, neither skinny nor fat. Just two very normal-looking guys. Yet something about the way they moved, ghosting along, almost without purpose, suggested they were in fact together. Trying just a bit too hard to blend in.

As soon as he laid his eyes on them, Evans had no doubt.

It was a surveillance team.

And Evans knew this would be the last meeting he ever had with Nikolai Medvedev.

Chapter 14

Glasgow, Scotland

The tracker team found Logan five days later. At first they believed he was dead. His body, lying in the snow, was lifeless, blue and frozen – like it had been in cold storage for weeks. But the small movements in his chest, his shallow breaths coming from his cracked lips, told them he was alive. Just.

By that point, Fleming and his men had already safely reached the rendezvous point. Knowing they'd lost the game, the trackers had been making their way back to camp to debrief when one of them spotted Logan's unconscious form completely by chance, just four miles from the rendezvous point – he had somehow dragged his injured body across miles of barren land.

He was suffering from severe hypothermia, his core body temperature having dropped dangerously low to barely twenty Celsius. He remained unconscious for two days after rescue, by which point Fleming and Butler and the others had moved on to a different location and Logan had been flown to a private clinic near the centre of Glasgow to recover.

All this was explained to Logan by his boss, Mackie, who came to visit the day after Logan woke up. By that point, Logan's core temperature was almost within the healthy range, but he was still a groggy mess. His body was leaden and useless. His broken leg was heavily plastered and would be for weeks to come. Full rehabilitation would take many months, if he recovered at all.

'You're a lucky guy, Logan,' Mackie said.

He was sitting on a chair next to Logan's hospital bed. His facial expression was sympathetic but his tone was almost indifferent.

'You think?' Logan said.

'Yes, I do. I don't know how you managed to stay alive. Not with your leg like that.'

Logan closed his eyes. He couldn't remember exactly what had happened after Fleming and Butler had left him. His memory was a blur; he was only able to grasp snippets of his time out in the Highlands. But even those snippets were a jumble with no sense of the order in which the events had occurred.

'The splint you made saved your leg. Probably saved your life.'

'The doctor said he can't be sure yet. About the leg.'

'I've seen worse, Logan. That leg will be fine. Believe me. You're a survivor. You're a fighter. I knew my instinct about you was right.'

Logan wanted to take Mackie's words as a compliment and yet it was hard to feel positive. He'd questioned many times during his short spell under Mackie's wing why he was bothering with the charade at all. He wasn't cut out for this. He didn't care about the greater good. He'd been lured into the secretive world of the JIA by his own misconceptions of the glamour and reward to follow. There was no sign of any of that yet. All he'd seen so far was torment and misery. Was this life really any better than the shit he'd left behind?

And look at the mess he was in now. If he couldn't even make it through the training, then how could he ever be the agent Mackie wanted him to be? He was surprised Mackie had bothered to show up at the hospital at all. Out in the wilds, Logan was sure that if he survived, then the least he could expect was for them to throw him back out onto the streets, to continue living the crappy life he'd been trying to run from.

'I couldn't die out there,' Logan said, sounding more resolute than he really felt.

The truth was he had no idea how he had survived. Surely it was down to luck as much as anything else.

'Tell me what happened,' Mackie said, pulling his chair closer. 'I mean, tell me what really happened. Not the bullshit that Fleming told his squad leader.'

On hearing Fleming's name, Logan closed his eyes and clenched his fists as tightly as his weak body would allow. After a few moments, he found the strength and focus to recount to Mackie what had happened. At least what he could remember. He went from the hazing on his very first day with Fleming through to the fight in the Scottish Highlands that had left Logan on the brink of death. He stopped then, unsure which memory came next.

Mackie didn't push for any more. Clearly the part of the story Logan had told was the part Mackie had wanted to hear.

'I guessed as much,' was all Mackie said.

No shock, no excuses, no apologies. No commitment to having Fleming reprimanded or court-martialled or discharged or whatever the hell it is that happens to SAS soldiers when they break someone's leg on a training exercise and leave them for dead.

Not that Logan cared much for any of those trivial punishments. Whatever had happened to Fleming, Logan's business with him was unfinished.

'So what did Fleming say then?' Logan asked.

Mackie shrugged. 'That they lost you in a blizzard. That they searched for you but then deemed it safer to carry on to the extraction point to raise the alarm than risk all three of you dying out there.'

'But you didn't buy it?'

'You with a broken leg, the bruises on the rest of you? Butler's arm had been smashed – the bones were in pieces. He said he fell, but I'm not stupid. And I knew you lot wouldn't be getting along like a house on fire. So no, I didn't buy it.'

Logan could feel anger bubbling up inside of him at Mackie's words.

'Why did you send me out there with them in the first place, if you thought something like this might happen?'

'Because this is what your training entails. This is how we're going to mould you into the agent we need. You've got to expect to be taken to the brink mentally and physically. It's how you deal with it that counts. It's how you move on and get stronger and more resilient that I'm interested in. I never said this would be easy for you.'

'No. You didn't.'

'You're a natural fighter, Logan. I can see it in you. You're fierce and you're unrelenting. That's why I picked you for this. But you're also naive and stupid.'

'Thanks. That makes me feel much better.'

'What I mean is, you're not a smart fighter. You fight with emotion. Hatred. Anger more than anything. That thirst for revenge that I can see in your eyes now, that I saw in your eyes the day I met you, it clouds your judgement. You can have all the combat skills in the world, but when you're up against a man like Fleming, you need more. You need to be able to control yourself. You can't let emotions get in the way.'

'Revenge is a dish best served cold,' Logan said, knowing full well that it was a concept his fiery temperament struggled with.

'My point exactly. Everyone knows it but few can actually stick to it. Now, I want you to forget about Fleming altogether. He's gone – a lesson learned and nothing more. Revenge is not what we're about. It's not what you're about now. Emotion doesn't come into what we do. It can't. And that's all revenge is. It's a basic human reaction. Largely a mixture of anger and shame. It's useless. You need to look past it. Forget you ever met Captain Fleming.'

'And how do I do that?'

'We'll help you to do that. We'll train you to fight like that – with no emotion. To live like that. You've already started down that road. There's a way to go still, but we'll help you. *I'll* help you. When you can do that, this whole mess won't even seem like a distant memory. It will be like it happened to someone else.'

Logan heard Mackie's words and decided: he would have the training. They could mould him however they wanted. Despite his melancholic feelings as he lay in the hospital bed, deep down he knew that every step with the JIA was making him stronger, more able to handle what the world threw at him.

But he also knew he wouldn't forget Fleming. For his entire life, Logan had kept true to a single principle: that people who wronged him got what they deserved.

It didn't matter what the JIA did to Logan, Fleming was going on the list.

He'd get his comeuppance one day.

Chapter 15

Moscow, Russia

'Two men up ahead,' Evans said. 'One with a black jacket, the other a parka.'

Medvedev didn't respond. Evans gave him a few seconds to clock the men before he carried on.

'Are they FSB?' Evans asked.

'If they are, they certainly weren't invited by me.'

'Come on. Follow me,' Evans said.

He moved off to his left, toward the traffic, and without looking, dashed across the road to the buildings on the other side. The road was crowded, which meant the vehicles were slow moving, and Evans's sudden traipse through the traffic drew nothing more than a solitary honk of a horn from a compact car.

Evans glanced quickly behind him and saw that Medvedev was still with him. He knew that to evade surveillance, the best course of action was to split up. But not today. There was very little left in him that trusted Medvedev. He wanted the Russian right where he could see him.

'This way,' Evans said, increasing his pace and taking a turn down the first side street he came to.

He looked behind again as he rounded the corner to see the two men from the river crossing the road. They were staring over in his direction now, moving with more purpose. Both had their hands in their pockets. Evans wondered whether they were armed. He wasn't.

'Shit,' Evans said, picking up his speed even more. 'We need to lose these two.'

'Just keep going,' Medvedev said. 'Once we get past the next junction, the streets are less open. It won't be too difficult.'

'Unless they're not too concerned about making a scene.'

'You're suggesting they might attack us? Shoot us? Never. Not out in the open. Not two unarmed civilians.'

Evans wasn't feeling quite as confident as Medvedev about that.

'Do you know how to get away from here?' Evans said.

'Of course,' Medvedev responded. 'Once we lose them, I'll circle back and head west, back across the river.'

His speech was becoming stilted as a result of the quickening pace of his breathing.

Evans didn't respond. But he certainly wasn't going to let Medvedev go anywhere without him. Evans looked behind again. They were putting distance between themselves and the two men, who were still trying hard to blend in. For just a fleeting second, Evans felt a little more confident again.

But then, as they neared the end of the street, a large four-by-four came careening around the corner. Evans guessed even before the vehicle came to a crunching halt just twenty yards in front that it was more heat. As the body of the car rocked back and forth on its high suspension, a man and woman whipped open their doors and jumped out. They immediately began walking toward Evans and Medvedev.

'Fuck's sake,' Evans said. 'Who are they, Nikolai? Who was following you?'

'They weren't following me!'

'This isn't normal surveillance,' Evans said. 'This isn't how it's supposed to happen. They're not just spying on us. They're here to snatch us. What did you do?'

'I don't know who they are!' Medvedev protested.

'Come on, back this way,' Evans said, spinning on his heel and heading back toward the river. The two men who had followed them from the riverfront were at least without a vehicle.

Medvedev followed, but just a few seconds later another car, a black saloon, turned into the road up ahead. It crawled just a few yards before turning lengthways and stopping, blocking the road. There was now a vehicle and two people on foot blocking each end of the street.

'What the hell is going on here?' Evans bellowed. 'You set me up?'

'No, I didn't!'

'Come on. I'm not getting caught today.'

Evans sprinted over toward the entrance to an alley that ran parallel to the riverfront road. Medvedev followed. This wasn't how Evans had planned the rendezvous to end. Not at all. Something had gone badly wrong. There were multiple patrol teams on them. That kind of heat didn't happen by chance. Even if Medvedev hadn't set him up, it was clear the FSB agent's cover had been blown. Medvedev certainly wasn't an asset anymore.

Evans ran as fast as he could down the alley, looking back every couple of seconds to check Medvedev was still with him and whether the tracker teams were following. His mind was in overdrive, his body too, his limbs pumping away. The alley was dark and dingy, only just wide enough to fit a vehicle. As Evans turned his head again, he spotted the saloon car behind him, just entering the alley. The glare from the beam of the bright headlights caused him to squint.

'When we get to the end, we have to split,' Medvedev shouted.

Evans didn't say anything. He just hoped they would make it that far.

'You go right,' Medvedev added.

The end of the alley was now only twenty yards away. Evans took one last glance behind, hoping the progress of the car was being hampered by the narrow passageway, which was obstructed here and there with industrial bins and fire escapes. But the car was nearly upon them. The growl of its engine filled his ears.

Was the driver just going to mow them down in the alley? Surely that wasn't protocol. But the car certainly didn't seem to be letting up.

Evans tried to pump his arms and legs faster. Medvedev, who was a good few years older, was already fading and falling behind. Evans ignored the daggers he was feeling in his legs. The pain in his lungs, which felt like they were about to explode. His legs pounded away. He pulled closer and closer to the end of the alley. The groan of the saloon car behind him became louder with each step he took. He wondered whether Medvedev had already been run down, not that he dared look.

Just as he came to within touching distance of the end of the alley, to safety, a battered grey van appeared from nowhere and screeched to a halt, blocking the opening up ahead. Evans had to throw on his brakes to avoid running slap bang into the van.

He stumbled forward, coming to a stop just in time to avoid a collision. Behind him, he heard screeching tyres as the driver of the saloon car tried desperately to do the same. Before Evans could catch a breath, or turn to look behind to see just how close the car had come to crushing him, the side door of the van slid open.

The first thing Evans saw emerge from the van was the barrel of a gun. He noticed it just a split second before he saw the leather-gloved hand that was wrapped around the trigger. The hand belonged to a figure decked in black, a woollen balaclava obscuring the face.

Despite the ominous scene, it was the distinctive shape and contours of the gun barrel that drew Evans's attention. It was a German-made Walther PPK. One of Evans's favourite guns. A much better gun, in Evans's eyes, than the more recent American PPKs that were manufactured under licence in the US. The German Walther PPK was famous as the gun that Adolf Hitler shot and killed himself with. It had been used in service since 1935. It was a stalwart. A true legend.

Evans should have been terrified to see the barrel of the Walther protruding from the van. But he wasn't. Because the gun wasn't pointing at him. It was pointing at Medvedev.

Evans looked over at the Russian, who caught his gaze. He was panting heavily. His warm breath billowed into the cold air. A look of bewilderment was on his face. Just a few yards behind Medvedev was the saloon car – at a stop but with its engine still rumbling. Clearly the chase was over now.

Evans's whole body jolted when the deafening bang rang out. He saw the neat, circular hole appear in Medvedev's forehead and watched, frozen to the spot, as Medvedev's body crumpled to the ground in slow motion, the perplexed look still etched on his face.

Evans turned to where the shot had come from. His brain again registered surprise when he noticed that the barrel of the gun was no longer pointing out of the van's open doorway. In fact, there was no sign of the figure who had been there before at all. But then, as he was determining what he should do next, he felt a sharp stab in his arm. He recoiled and looked down to see a long syringe being pulled from the sleeve of his windbreaker.

Cold liquid from the syringe surged through his arm, up his shoulder and into his core, sending a sinister shiver right through him. With the drugs pumping through his blood immediately taking hold, he was only partially aware of the gloved hands that grasped him and thrust him aggressively into the waiting van.

Chapter 16

Aktobe Province, Kazakhstan

Ultimately, crossing the border out of Russia had been simple. Even without the acquired passports of the Russian agents, Logan's plan had always been to exit Russia into one of the neighbouring ex-Soviet countries. He knew that Russia's borders with these countries were extensive and, road and rail network aside, largely unmarked and unguarded.

Kazakhstan alone, the country to which Logan and Grainger had headed, had a border with Russia that stretched more than four thousand miles. Although border posts were in place on major routes, some multilateral, allowing internationals to pass through, and others bilateral, only allowing nationals from the two countries to pass, keeping full control of such a vast stretch of land was impossible. And entirely unnecessary for two such closely allied countries.

As it was, with the Russian passports in hand, there had been no need to abandon the vehicle and traipse over frozen ground to leave Russia. Logan had simply driven up to the bilateral border post near to the tiny Kazakh village of Zhanybek, shown his and Grainger's IDs and passed through into the vast Central Asian country of Kazakhstan. The fact they only barely resembled the pictures on the passports didn't matter. A couple of Russians passing into the ex-Soviet state was hardly worthy of a raised eyebrow even.

Being in Kazakhstan was a means to an end. Logan wasn't

planning on staying in the country any longer than necessary. It was simply a stepping stone. The problem was it wouldn't be quite so easy to leave Kazakhstan, unless he was simply going to head back into Russia, which he had no intention of doing. That meant he needed help.

Which was why he and Grainger were heading along the twisting roads of western Kazakhstan, through the barren, frozen deserts and grassy steppes toward the city of Aktobe.

Logan had a basic understanding of the country's geography from previous assignments there, but he was glad to have the assistance of the GPS unit. The drive from where they crossed the border to Aktobe was more than six hundred miles, yet wouldn't even take them halfway across the vast country – one of the world's largest and most uninhabited places. Kazakhstan was the ninth largest country by land area in the world, but its population, largely clustered in the larger eastern cities, was just seventeen million.

Logan had never been to Aktobe before, but he knew exactly the address to head to. With the aid of the GPS unit, he knew they were now only twenty miles from their destination.

They had stopped twice since leaving Russia: the first to rest and refuel themselves, the second time to refuel the car. They had both taken turns driving, giving the other a chance to sleep and meaning they had been able to keep going through the night. The drive to Aktobe had taken more than twelve hours and it was now mid-afternoon.

'Do you really think he'll be here?' Grainger asked.

She had woken up about ten minutes before, after sleeping for the best part of the last two hours, but had so far not spoken.

'He certainly was last time I checked.'

'Which was when?'

Logan didn't answer immediately. Not because he didn't know the answer, but because he knew the answer wouldn't instil much confidence in Grainger.

'About two years ago,' he said eventually.

Out of the corner of his eye, he saw her shaking her head.

'About two years? So is it two or is it more or less than that?'

'More like three,' he admitted.

Grainger tutted. 'So we could just be greeted out here by some local farmer and his flock. That's really going to help, isn't it? Maybe he can sell us a cow.'

'That could be quite useful actually,' Logan gibed. 'Would feed and clothe us for a while.'

'So you know how to make leather goods now? You really are a master of all trades.'

They both smiled before Grainger returned to her point.

'But if he is here, do you really think he can help us?'

'It's got to be worth a shot. Unless you have any better ideas.'

He certainly wasn't entirely comfortable with the idea, but they needed somewhere to stay away from watchful eyes. With someone who would have the means or at least the connections to help them to keep travelling away from Russia and onwards to safer ground. The more respite they had and the closer to safety they got, the more opportunity Logan would have to determine exactly what to do next. When it came down to it, there were really only two options: run away and hide, or fight back. His natural instinct preferred the latter but he had no clue yet where to start.

'Carl, I just hope you know what you're doing.'

'Me too.'

He'd told her why they were going there. Whom they were going to see. Not a friend. Someone he knew. From a long time ago. So long ago it almost felt like a different life. Until recently, Logan would never have thought to turn to this man on whom he had kept a careful eye for much of his adult life.

As they neared the destination, the GPS took them on a route that circumvented the city of Aktobe, taking them further north, back toward the Russian border. Over the course of the six-hundred-mile journey, they had snaked back and forth toward the border numerous times, coming within just a few miles of it as they bypassed the northern city of Oral, the capital of the West Kazakhstan Province. The mood in the car had become strained and somewhat awkward each time they had come closer to Russia, as though they were fearful of a sudden onslaught from hordes of Cossacks.

Whatever the outcome of their visit to Aktobe, they would need to look for alternative transport from here on in. They had to believe the Russians would follow them over the border at the least and would probably already be in touch with the Kazakhstan NSC – the National Security Committee, successor intelligence agency to the KGB – to ensure Logan and Grainger were on their wanted list. Although they had made hours of solid progress, now was a good time to lay low while they figured out their next steps.

They passed the small city of Aktobe and the landscape soon returned to largely uninhabited hinterland. In the summer months, temperatures in this part of the country would soar – much of the area was sandy desert with just small pockets of grassland and vegetation. In the winter, it was cold and dark, icy and foreboding.

Through the night, the temperature had dropped to below minus twenty. It was currently a more balmy minus five, but the cloud cover of the day had also brought with it heavy snow, which was making driving almost impossible. The main roads they had travelled on from the border had been well gritted and clear of snow and ice, but now they had moved onto a smaller, twisting singe-track road and the conditions were worsening by the minute.

Logan slowed the car to less than ten miles an hour, squinting as though it would help him see through the sheet of white hitting the windscreen. The wipers vibrated and shuddered as they whizzed across the glass as fast as they could go, but the snow was falling so quickly that it made little difference.

They took a left onto a narrow lane that rose into the distance and had deep cuts in the snow from the wheels of previous vehicles. Snow, piled up on the side of the road, towered over them.

As Logan edged the car up the track, he felt the back end lose grip and begin to fishtail. He pressed down hard on the accelerator. The engine whined and the tyres spun and skidded but eventually found traction and the vehicle shot forward suddenly. Logan eased off the accelerator momentarily while he restored control, then pushed down again, slowly building up the power, willing the inadequate vehicle to keep going up the hill.

After another hundred yards, the GPS unit showed they had reached their destination.

'I don't see anything,' Grainger said. 'There's nothing here at all.'

She was right. But this had to be it, Logan thought. They had to be near.

'Those things aren't always accurate, you know,' Grainger continued. 'I mean, we could just be driving aimlessly here. Wouldn't we be better sticking to some semblance of civilisation?'

'No,' Logan said. 'This track isn't here just for the hell of it. The house must be here somewhere. We'll keep going.'

'I can't see a thing out of the windows. It's just snow everywhere.'

Logan huffed in agreement but didn't otherwise respond. Visibility couldn't have been more than a few yards. But then, as they rounded a bend in the track, the view in front began to clear. Logan wasn't sure whether the snow was dying down or the change of direction, which meant the snow was now coming at them from behind, had helped give them a better line of sight.

Not long after, in the near distance, Logan caught sight of what they were looking for and felt a wave of relief wash over him.

In front of them was a large, sandy-coloured wall with thick snow sitting on it like icing on a cake. Within the layer of snow, there were flashes of metallic grey here and there: barbed wire. Beyond the wall was a house. It was huge: three storeys tall, many windows wide. But it was also plain, box-like, much of it with a flat roof. It was unassuming and unattractive. The walls were white-washed but their colour against the bright white snow made the house look stained and yellow and dirty.

The track led to a set of sliding metal gates at the front of the property. The gates were a simple structure. Functional. Security rather than decoration. There was a small wooden guard post in front of the gates.

All in all, the building and its security-driven trimmings didn't look like a residence. More like a small barracks or army outpost. Logan wondered whether that had indeed been its original purpose. The city of Aktobe had long been a strategically important position and had played a large part in many Central Asian conflicts over the years.

'Are you sure about this, Carl?' Grainger asked. 'Just what the hell is this place?'

'It's nothing more than I expected,' Logan said. 'And it at least tells me that he's definitely still here.'

'Right now, I'm not sure if I'm happy about that or not.'

'Well, we're here now. What have we got to lose?'

'Out of the frying pan, into the fire.'

'Something like that,' he conceded.

'I think we can at least safely say that we're not going to be buying any cows today.'

Chapter 17

Logan pulled the car to a stop at the guard post. A man emerged wearing a thick green overcoat that reached down almost to his ankles. On his head he wore a military-style ushanka, the flaps tied under his chin so that much of his face and head was protected from the bitter elements.

'I certainly don't envy him,' Logan said to Grainger, 'sitting out here in this.'

Logan spotted an assault rifle inside the wooden hut, propped up against the back wall. It wasn't clear whether the man had any other weapons on him. Logan wound down his window and squinted as a blast of ice-cold air hit his face.

The man – who was a similar age to himself, Logan thought, and who had distinctive Kazakh features, the epicanthic folds on his eyes that all Mongoloid peoples have – bent down and stuck his head toward the open window. He said something that Logan didn't understand. Logan guessed it was Kazakh, a language of which he could remember only a small number of words. The man's tone was brash, his look suspicious.

Logan spoke back to him in Russian. Although Kazakh was the national language, he knew almost everyone in Kazakhstan also spoke or at least understood Russian – although many of the inhabitants spoke a hybrid of the two languages, throwing in random words from one or the other tongues almost subconsciously. In any case, it was clear this man understood Logan's words by the change in his facial expression. Even so, he didn't make any move to accommodate his guests.

'Just tell him it's Carl Logan,' Logan added. 'I'm sure he'll remember me.'

The man huffed and stood tall, taking a walkie-talkie out of his pocket. He spoke quickly into the receiver. The howling of the wind drowned out his voice but Logan could tell the man was again speaking in the unfamiliar language. The only word Logan made out was his own name as it was repeated to whoever was on the other end. When the guard finished speaking, there was a short pause and then Logan heard a distorted voice give a response. The guard listened and when the voice finished, he put the radio back into his pocket and bent down again.

'Drive through and park on the left,' he said, now speaking in Russian. 'Park behind the other vehicles. Someone will come and meet you there.'

The man trudged over to his hut and sat down on his chair. A few seconds later, there was an electronic whir as the metal gate began to open, sliding on its rollers, across to the right. The man on the outside certainly hadn't activated it, so it must have been controlled by another guard on the inside.

As Logan drove the car through the open gates, he spotted the small parking area on the left. Three other vehicles were there – two large four-by-fours and a pickup truck. All silver, all virtually new.

A man appeared, as if coming from nowhere through the wall of snow that was still falling. He was dressed similarly to the guard at the front gate but was noticeably taller. He waved Logan in behind the pickup truck.

Logan switched off the engine and looked over at Grainger. She looked uncomfortable. But it was too late to change their minds now.

'Come on,' Logan said. 'Just follow my lead.'

Logan opened his door without waiting for a response. He stepped out of the car, a shiver running through him. It served as a chilling reminder of the last time Logan had seen his host. Snow smacked against his face and he reached up with his arm to protect himself from the blizzard as he turned toward the approaching guard. Logan was caught by surprise when he saw the man was wielding an AK-47 assault rifle, the barrel of which was pointing at Logan's chest.

'Put your hands in the air,' the man said in Russian, coming to within inches of Logan.

Logan did as he was told.

'Are you armed?' the man said.

'Yes,' Logan said.

'Where?'

'In the car.'

'And your friend?'

'Why don't you ask her?'

'Get her out,' the man shouted, off to his left. Another guard came into view and met Grainger as she emerged from the car.

Logan looked over and was pleasantly surprised to see that the expression on her face had changed to one of steely determination.

'Can we get inside?' Logan said to the guard. 'I'm freezing my balls off out here.'

He jumped when he felt hands on him from behind. It was another guard, he assumed, patting him down. Satisfied, the man went over to Grainger and did the same.

Neither he nor Grainger had a gun on them. Logan hadn't wanted to complicate matters and had insisted they both leave their firearms in the car. The idea wasn't to come here to fight, even if the guards didn't quite believe that yet.

'Okay, follow me,' the tall guard said after his colleague had finished patting down Grainger.

He lowered his weapon and turned on his heel.

Logan followed after him, Grainger behind, the other two guards at the rear. A total of four guards had welcomed them thus far. And Logan assumed that each of them was armed. Heavy protection for sure.

The guard led them into the expansive building through a side entrance that opened out into a kitchen. Logan sighed with relief as he stepped inside and the snowy air disappeared, replaced by warmth and comfort and the smell of freshly cooked food.

They walked from the kitchen into a hallway and across into a lounge area. The building on the inside was only marginally more attractive than the outside. Although it was clear now that this was indeed a home, the decor was still simple and functional – no elaborate art or ornaments or decorations. The furniture was stoic and dour and purposeful. It almost looked like whoever lived here didn't fully believe this was their true home – just somewhere to eat and sleep. Temporary accommodation. But it was certainly better than what Logan had become used to recently.

As they entered the lounge, Logan spotted the man they had come to see. He was sitting in an armchair, a thick cigar stuck between his lips.

A wave of emotions coursed through Logan. The man was noticeably older than the last time Logan had seen him, his face even more hardened than before. But he retained a look of power and confidence that told Logan he hadn't lost any of his appetite for life. He stood as Logan approached.

'Carl Logan. Well, I have to say, this is certainly intriguing.'

His voice was loud, deep, gravelly. It had taken on a huskiness too since the last time Logan had seen him, but it was still unmistakable. Logan reached out his hand and his host hesitated for just a second before taking it and giving it a bone-crushing shake.

'You know, I always wondered whether you'd turn up one day. But I have to say, I'm still very surprised you did.'

'Fleming,' Logan said, 'you're looking good.'

'It's Captain to you,' Fleming responded, smirking.

Chapter 18

London, England

Winter was fast asleep in his bed when the phone call came. It was eight a.m., far later than he'd normally be asleep on a working day. He usually set his alarm for six and was at his desk at the JIA office for half seven, unless he was off on one of his many trips around the world.

The previous night had been anything but usual, though. Having found the startling intelligence on Lindegaard that the Russian FSB agent Lena Belenov was his niece, Winter had at first been on a high. The high had quickly faded, though, as he'd contemplated exactly what it all meant. That was when the anxiety had started to build.

What Winter had found meant a lot of the unexplained events suddenly made more sense. He'd never warmed to Lindegaard, and finding that he had a close family connection to an FSB agent was astonishing. Sure, such a connection was entirely legitimate if appropriately disclosed and if their work for their respective organisations was correctly siloed. But Winter didn't believe that to be the case at all. Certainly he could see no disclosure of the relationship in JIA records – not that he was privy to the committee's official papers, although he had managed to hack into the archived databases to check.

He had no way of knowing what disclosures Lindegaard had made to the CIA, but if Winter were a betting man, he'd say there had been none. And given Lena Belenov's connection to Logan's imprisonment in Russia and the subsequent negotiations with the JIA and the CIA for his release, finally some answers were falling into place.

Just how far did Lindegaard's role in this sordid mess stretch?

After some hours of quiet deliberation, Winter had ultimately decided that perhaps what he'd found, rather than being a help, may in fact be a huge hindrance. Because he now knew that he, the JIA and everyone else involved were playing one huge game of cat and mouse, and Jay Lindegaard seemed to be at the centre of it all.

Winter was at a loss as to whom exactly he could trust with what he'd found. In the end, he decided there wasn't a single person he could share the information with. Not until he'd figured out more of the story on his own.

Winter had spoken to Paul Evans twice in the small hours of the night. Winter had said nothing to his agent about Lindegaard and Belenov. It wasn't something he could just blurt out over a phone line to someone a couple of thousand miles away. Instead, the two men had discussed at great length Evans's plan for the following day – the meet with Nikolai Medvedev.

It was Evans who had proposed the meeting; he was Medvedev's handler after all. Winter had okayed it even though he wasn't one hundred per cent comfortable with the rushed nature of the organisation – despite his reservations, the time was hardly right to be causing needless delays. Evans had been resolute, calm on the phone. Nothing amiss, as far as Winter had been aware.

He wasn't sure what time he'd finally fallen asleep, in his chair by the computer. Claire had found him like that when she'd returned home sometime after three a.m. A half-hearted argument had followed over just how much of an arsehole he was. His reluctance to fully defend himself against her drunken onslaught had only seemed to make her angrier, culminating in her giving him a ferocious slap across his face. He'd said and done nothing in response.

As angry as she'd got, as close to the brink he could feel their relationship was coming, his mind was too clouded by the task at hand. In the end, Claire had skulked off to bed and he'd followed not long after, passing out within seconds from mental exhaustion.

When the phone rang at eight a.m., Claire had already upped and left for the day without saying goodbye or attempting to wake him. Winter knew he was in the doghouse. He hoped in time he would get the chance to make it up to her. But as he listened to the voice on the other end of the phone, any thoughts he had about Claire and the work he needed to put into their strained relationship were quickly forgotten.

Something had gone badly wrong. The man calling Winter, an asset who was a British expat making a living in Russia as a language tutor to the rich, knew little of the details of what had happened. He'd simply gleaned what he could from news reports about a shooting that had taken place in central Moscow, and from making a few phone calls to his own well-connected contacts. Two things were abundantly clear, though: Nikolai Medvedev was dead, and there was no sign of Paul Evans.

After putting the phone down, Winter immediately tried contacting Evans. No response. The early news reports coming out of Moscow were vague and spurious, simply stating that there had been a shooting incident. No identification of the victim or any perpetrators. Certainly no mention of a missing British spy.

The vagueness wasn't unusual, given the identity of the dead man – a senior official for the FSB. The Russians would be keeping tight-lipped about that for as long as it suited them. In fact, by the time Winter had left his flat, the news channels in the UK weren't carrying the story at all. What interest was there in the shooting of a single unknown person in a foreign city?

Once Winter had fought his way across London to the JIA office, though, a whole new mess awaited him. By that point, some three hours after the meet that Evans had planned with Medvedev, the shooting was making headlines not just in Moscow and Russia but on every major TV network in the Western world. And the reports coming from Moscow changed the landscape significantly: Carl Logan – identified by the Russians as a British spy – had been named the number one suspect in Nikolai Medvedev's murder.

Chapter 19

Aktobe Province, Kazakhstan

Many years ago, Logan had vowed revenge against Captain Fleming. Logan's desire to get his own back on the man who'd left him for dead with a broken leg in the wilds of Scotland had never been fulfilled.

Fleming had dodged a bullet, there was no doubt about that.

For months after the incident in the Highlands, Logan's hatred for Fleming had remained sharp and front of mind. On an almost daily basis, he cringed as he recounted the many times that Fleming had got the better of him, and he filled his head with thoughts of how he would punish Fleming when he came face to face with him again.

That day had never come. Ultimately, Mackie had been right. The JIA had trained Logan to ignore his emotions. To live, work and fight with a clear head. They had turned him into a robot, a machine, something that on the outside resembled a human being but on the inside was a vast nothingness. Living like that had seen Logan through many years of gruelling and deadly missions for the JIA. And it had eradicated the thirst for vengeance that had clouded his formative years.

In fact, his vengeful streak had only truly been resurrected following his fateful assignment to capture Youssef Selim almost two years ago.

Although Logan had never sought his revenge on Fleming, he'd certainly not forgotten about the army captain. Logan had kept abreast of Fleming's every move since that day in Scotland.

At first, Logan had been plotting, planning his moment of retribution. But he had never gone through with it. The need to exact his revenge on Fleming had dwindled along with every other emotion. Over the years, checking up on Fleming had merely become a habit, one last remnant of his previous life – a feat of curiosity as much as anything else, rather than part of a master plan to track down and punish the ex-soldier.

Right now, though, as odd as it seemed to Logan, Fleming was the only man he could think to turn to. Did he trust Fleming? No. Logan didn't truly trust anyone anymore. He'd learned to live like that a long time ago and recent events had only further cemented that belief. Could Fleming help him? Yes, he could. The only question was whether he *would*.

'I'm assuming you're not here to assassinate me?' Fleming said, sitting back down in his armchair.

'Why? Have you done something that would warrant it?'

Fleming shot Logan a look of disdain. Clearly whatever had happened to Fleming in the years since Logan had last met him, he still had the same air of superiority. He didn't like to be challenged and he didn't like people answering back. Once an army captain, always an army captain.

'That's your job, isn't it?' Fleming said. 'The super spy. The deadly assassin. The boy wonder.'

'If you say so.' Logan shook his head and went and sat down on one of the two brown leather sofas. Grainger timidly followed and sat next to him. 'I'm not sure I'm exactly in a job right now,' Logan added.

Fleming took a big puff on his cigar and smiled as he exhaled, tilting his head back so that the cloud of smoke billowed up into the air.

'Ah, I get it. So that's why you're here. They booted you out. What, did you start to enjoy it just that little bit too much? Enjoyed the adrenaline rush of seeing our fellow humans suffer at your hands?'

'Not even close,' Logan said.

'No? But you're here because you need my help, aren't you?' Fleming quizzed.

'Yeah. I do need your help,' Logan said, looking down at his feet and then up at Grainger. 'We both do.'

Grainger simply nodded. She was gazing over at Fleming, her face betraying no emotion.

'Well, this really is a turn-up for the books,' Fleming said. 'The boy wonder needs my help. Again.'

'I didn't need your help back then. And I certainly didn't get it.'

Fleming smirked. 'You're saying I didn't make you stronger?'

'You didn't.'

'Ah, well, it depends exactly how you look at these things. But you need my help now. You know I'm not in the army anymore?'

'I heard.'

'So you've been keeping tabs on me?'

'I keep tabs on a lot of people.'

'Of course you do. You're a proper James Bond, aren't you?'

Logan didn't respond.

'I'm surprised you just can't see that I helped you back then,' Fleming said. 'I helped that agency of yours mould you into exactly what they wanted you to become.'

'Maybe the end product was what they wanted, but I'm sure I've nothing to thank you for.'

'No, you're just bitter because you thought you could beat me.'

'I'm sure I could have.'

'Ha, just because I'm a bit older and a bit rounder now, don't think for a second I'm not just as capable as I was back then.'

'I'm not here to compare dick sizes.'

'Then what are you here for?'

Something caught Fleming's attention over by the doorway. Logan glanced over and saw a man entering. The man did a quick double-take and stopped just a few feet into the room, staring coldly at Logan.

'What the fuck?' the man said. 'I don't believe it.'

'Butler, you remember Carl Logan?' Fleming said.

'Of course I do.'

Butler walked over to the empty sofa, one eye on Logan the whole time, and then sat down. Logan wasn't at all surprised by his presence. What he had said to Grainger had been true – he hadn't checked up on Fleming in almost three years – but he knew all about these men.

Fleming had left the army five years ago. A dishonourable discharge was the official line, though Logan knew there was a lot more to the story than that. Since then, Fleming had set up shop as a security consultant in Kazakhstan. Butler, who'd long left the army for capability reasons, something about his weak left arm, had tagged along.

Fleming operated as a freelancer, working for the many foreign companies – Chinese and Western – investing in the region to exploit the money-making potential of the country's vast energy reserves. From the look of his residence, armed guards and all, Logan could only guess that Fleming's business enterprise was earning him a not-insignificant amount of money.

Butler too had noticeably aged since Logan had last seen him, but the years hadn't been as kind to him as they had to Fleming, even though he was younger than the captain. He had a defeated look in his eyes, like many ex-military do. Usually it comes from a combination of the troubles seen in battle and the difficulty in assimilating back into a normal life. For Butler, though, Logan guessed it was the fact his military career – his lifeblood – had been cut short so abruptly. Butler's facial features had softened and become puffy and his body had also filled out some. Judging by the changes in Butler's face, the additional weight appeared to be mostly fat, though with the thick clothes Butler had on, Logan couldn't tell for sure.

'What's he doing here?' Butler said, looking from Logan over to Fleming. Butler's acidic tone didn't surprise Logan at all. He was certain that Butler was holding a grudge for his untimely exit from the SAS.

'We were just getting on to that,' Fleming said, still exuding calm and arrogance, in stark contrast to Butler's anger and suspicion. 'Perhaps you could start, Logan, with who your friend is. It's a tad rude that you haven't introduced us yet.'

'I know who she is,' Butler said, eyeing Grainger up and down.

'You do?' Fleming queried.

'Angela Grainger. Pretty much the FBI's most wanted.'

Logan glanced over at Grainger and noticed her cheeks redden. She looked down, as though embarrassed by her notoriety.

'Then I guess you'll know why we're here,' Logan said to Butler.

'He might, but I certainly don't,' Fleming interrupted.

'They're on the run,' Butler said. 'They're on the run from the CIA – the FBI too. And the boy wonder thought maybe you could help him.'

'Is that so?'

'You ask me,' Butler continued, 'we should feed them to the wolves. We don't owe this guy anything.'

'But I didn't ask you,' Fleming said to Butler, before directing his attention back to Logan. 'So is it true? You're on the run from your friends at the CIA?'

'I don't have any friends,' Logan said. 'I never had.'

'What did you do?' Fleming said, his tone suspicious but his look one of intrigue.

'It's a long story.'

'And it's a long winter. There's not much to do in Aktobe when the temperature's minus twenty and there's fifteen feet of snow. I've got plenty of time. So try me.'

'Let's just say Butler is right. I need your help.'

'You've got some balls coming to me for help.'

'The way I figure it, you owe me.'

'You broke my arm, you piece of shit!' Butler shouted. 'I never made it back into the field because of you. You ruined my life. I should kick the living shit out of you. I'm not going to help you.'

Logan glared over at Butler but said nothing.

'It's true,' Fleming said. 'I'm not sure why you think you're welcome here.'

'I think you'll find I suffered more than either of you.'

'Perhaps we'll have to agree to disagree on that,' Fleming said. 'What exactly do you need from me? Tell me that and then let's see.'

'We need somewhere to stay. Just for a few days. This place is secluded and off the grid.'

'And yet you managed to find it.'

'I'm good at that sort of thing.'

'So that's it? You need a place to stay?'

'And I thought you might know some people who can help us get to our next destination.'

'And where's that?'

'China.'

Fleming humphed. 'China? I can't stand that fucking place or its squinty-eyed people. They might be pumping money into Kazakhstan but they pay peanuts and expect the world.'

'I wasn't inviting you to come with us. We just need help getting there.'

'And why the hell do you think I'll help you?'

'Because you do owe me. And because the people who are after me, who screwed me over – they screwed you over too.'

Chapter 20

'This is some weird shit, Captain,' Butler said to Fleming.

They were standing in Fleming's kitchen, each drinking a cup of tea. Fleming had made it. As usual, it was weak and yellow like piss-water. Even though it tasted like crap, it was at least warming and soothing.

Bulat, one of the guards, had taken Grainger and Logan to a guest bedroom upstairs so they could shower and rest. Fleming hadn't exactly agreed yet to help them, but he was accommodating them for now. Albeit Bulat had been ordered to stand guard outside their room and not let them out until instructed to do so.

'You have to admit, though,' Fleming said, 'them showing up out of the blue, in the middle of this damn awful winter of all things, does pique your interest.'

'Not really. It piques my suspicion. I'm not sure that's the same thing.'

'You worry too much. You always have.'

'I didn't say I was worried,' Butler said, offended. 'Just that I don't trust them. Especially Logan. Don't forget who he works for.'

'What harm could he do? If the JIA or someone else wanted us dead, or even if they were just trying to snare us, why would they send Carl Logan here under this pretence?'

Fleming had a point. Butler knew about the JIA. As secretive as it was to the outside world, the SAS had worked closely with it more than once in Butler's time. The JIA served a purpose – much like elite combat units of the army – but Butler couldn't think of a reason that he or Fleming would be on the JIA's watch list. Unless Logan was just there on some personal mission. But like Fleming said, if that was the case, why the pretence?

'And anyway,' Fleming added, 'didn't you say you knew who the woman was?'

'Of course. Don't you remember all that fuss about Frank Modena, the American Attorney General, being kidnapped in Paris?'

'Yeah. They found him, didn't they? That mad terrorist was behind it.'

'Kind of. Youssef Selim was involved, yes, but Angela Grainger is the one the Feds are pinning the kidnapping on.'

'You know as well as I do how the Feds and their ilk like to pin things on the wrong people,' Fleming said, the disgust in his voice clear.

It was the American intelligence services who had cynically brought Fleming's army career to an end. At least, that was how Fleming had portrayed it to Butler. He'd been made a scapegoat following what had been labelled a botched hostage rescue mission in Syria. Botched meaning that details of the mission had somehow come into the public domain, leading to the Americans swiftly denying their involvement in Fleming's apparently gung-ho tactics that had resulted in the deaths of two civilians but seen ten others safely rescued.

'Either way, she's wanted,' Butler said. 'And that means there's heat following her. Do you really want that brought to your door?'

'The Feds and the CIA aren't interested in us or what we do here. They got what they wanted from me when they had me turfed out the army.'

'The CIA may no longer care, but the NSC do.'

Fleming shrugged. 'I don't think Carl Logan has the slightest idea of what we're doing here,' Fleming said. 'And even if he did, why would it concern him?'

Butler did agree on that. He knew that the US and UK intelligence services posed very little threat to Fleming's operation. In reality, the Kazakh NSC didn't either. They were easy to pay off. Experience had already shown that. After all, the agents at the NSC were gaining from Fleming's business enterprise too. In fact, there really weren't any losers. Except for Fleming's competitors.

What had started out for Fleming as an entirely legitimate security operation had morphed somewhat over the last few years. It always did in that part of the world once the big C took hold – corruption.

After leaving the army, Fleming had quickly made a name for himself in the local market, providing security services to foreign nationals and to the large foreign oil and gas companies. They paid top-end for simple services like transporting delegates and maintaining personnel at important sites.

There was even more money to be made if one had a little more guile. And the Chinese, American and European companies had no problems in passing over big bucks for little in return, as long as it meant they got to keep hold of what was coming out of the Kazakh ground.

The foreign companies poured billions of dollars into the region. All Fleming had to do was skim a little off the top, entering into bogus service contracts – the larger and more complex, the better – and, as long as everyone involved in the scam got their cut, the money flowed for doing next to nothing and everyone was happy.

Well, almost everyone.

The armed guards at Fleming's house were a necessity in his line of work for two very good reasons: to keep competitors at bay, and to keep the NSC at bay.

The NSC were easier to deal with. Usually a back-hander here and there was all that was needed. Whenever things got more heated, on the odd occasion the NSC had tried to rough up Fleming or Butler or their men, a little more money was always a deal clincher.

It was with the competitors that the real dangers lay. The problem was only so much could be skimmed from each master contract. Get there first and there was always an angry line of people behind wanting their slice too.

Fleming's largest contract was worth fifty million dollars over three years. For that, he'd provided just a handful of man days of security work to a local gas venture operated jointly by the Kazakh government and Chinese investors. His competitors hadn't got a cent. Fleming had used all his charm, bravado, arrogance and scare tactics to get rights as the sole security provider to the venture. And that had led to an armed stand-off with his closest rival, a Georgian named Tamaz Graneli, at Fleming's house.

Graneli had turned up drunk in the middle of the night with three of his men, all armed with sub-machine guns and assault rifles. It hadn't been his wisest move. Unprepared for the attack, Fleming and Butler had nonetheless quickly gained the upper hand and had shot dead two of Graneli's men before he and his last guard had hastily fled the scene.

In fact, as far as Butler knew, Graneli had fled Kazakhstan altogether in order to reignite his flailing business. The last anyone had heard he was now in Uzbekistan, trying to sweeten up the local oil and gas ventures there.

That day had shown Fleming he could no longer rely on himself and his own training to keep safe. Not long after, he'd begun to employ security guards around the clock at his house.

'What if Logan isn't working for the JIA anymore?' Butler said. 'You've moved into consulting. Perhaps Logan has taken his skills into the private sector too.'

'If someone had hired Carl Logan as a hitman to take me out, then I don't think we'd be having this conversation. And if someone had hired Logan, why the hell would he be running around with the FBI's most wanted?'

Butler shrugged again. It was a fair point.

'I believe what he said,' Fleming said. 'Logan's in trouble. He needs my help.'

'And you're going to give it to him?'

'Maybe. Or maybe there's another angle to all this. For us.'

Butler raised an eyebrow, then finished his cup of tea before responding. 'What angle?'

'The way I see it,' Fleming said, smiling, 'we've got ourselves one hell of a prize here. What would the Feds pay if we gave them Angela Grainger on a plate?'

'How do you suggest we do that in a way that doesn't give away who we are and the fact that we already have her?'

'I don't know yet,' Fleming said. 'I'm still trying to figure that one out. But there'll be a way.'

There was a knock on the kitchen door and Fleming shouted for whoever was on the other side to come in. The door opened and in walked Maksat, Fleming's most experienced and most reliable guard. He was six foot seven and built of pure muscle. Before coming to work for Fleming, he had spent many years as part of Kazakhstan's Republican Guard. While he'd not seen action in the field to anywhere near the extent Fleming or even Butler had, he fit the mould of security guard perfectly. No one in their right mind would mess with a giant like him.

'I've finished searching their car,' Maksat said in as close to Russian as he could manage.

Fleming could speak Russian fluently. Butler's Russian was getting better by the day. While he couldn't speak it with much confidence, he could usually understand what others were saying as long as they didn't speak too quickly and their accents weren't too strong.

'And?' Fleming said.

'And this.'

Maksat slapped down onto the table three handguns. One was a Glock. The other two were an MP-443 Grach and an SR-1 Vector. Butler could guess even before Maksat continued what this might mean.

'The MP-443 Grach and the SR-1 Vector are Russian-made guns,' Maksat said. 'Standard issue for the Russian military. Also very common for the special forces and the FSB.'

'I know that,' Fleming said. 'I know my guns.'

'You think Logan and Grainger are working for the Russians?' Butler asked.

'That's crazy,' Fleming snapped, though the frown on his face told Butler he was thinking through the possible implications nonetheless. 'Those guns are Russian made, but they're standard military issue for just about every ex-Soviet state. Kazakhstan included. It doesn't mean anything.'

'Maybe,' Maksat said. 'But either way, I don't think those two are working for the Russians. I also found these.'

Maksat took from his pocket two Russian passports and placed them on the table next to the guns.

'Look at the photos. Those aren't of Logan and Grainger. Think about where they are. Where they might have come from. How did they get these guns and passports? And how did they get into Kazakhstan?'

'What are you suggesting?' Butler said.

'He thinks Logan and Grainger aren't just running from the Americans,' Fleming said. 'They killed, or at least attacked, some FSB or SVR agents to get hold of that gear. They're running from the Russians too.'

Fleming rubbed at the stubble on his chin and raised his eyebrows.

'Well, Butler, my dear friend, it looks like the stakes are even higher than we thought. And the rewards too.'

Chapter 21

Grainger sat on the bed and looked out of the dirty window at the endless white outside. The snow had stopped falling but there were still wisps and flurries of flakes in the air from the wind, which was whipping fiercely across the wide, open plains. There was no sign of any town, village or even other buildings outside the walls to Fleming's compound. No sign of life at all. Which, in a way, was a good thing, Grainger realised.

She'd finished in the shower and was now dressed. Having been stuck in the car for the best part of twenty-four hours, her body was aching all over. Even though they'd kept the temperature in the car at a steady sixteen degrees, it felt like she'd caught a chill. Or maybe it was just her mind imagining the cold as she stared at the snow outside. Either way, her body was slowly thawing now and the hot shower had certainly helped.

Logan had headed into the bathroom as soon as she had finished. There was a strange awkwardness between them. Grainger guessed it was as much to do with the unease that she was feeling at their current location than anything else, but she couldn't help but feel disappointed by their tepid reunion.

But then what had she expected? Until Logan had turned up at her apartment, she hadn't been sure she would ever see him again. She was on the run from him, from the world, and after what she'd done to him, the least she'd expected was that he was probably there to turn her in. In fact, she was still trying to get her head around why that wasn't the case.

He said he wanted to protect her. She didn't feel she needed protecting. She never had. She'd always been able to take care of herself just fine. Yet she was still drawn to Logan and couldn't deny that from the moment she had seen his face on the other side of the apartment door, all of the strong emotions that she'd once felt for him had come rushing back.

Did he still have feelings for her too?

Regardless, now was hardly the moment for her to jump into his arms and plant kisses all over his face. Whatever strong connection they had once had, a unique bond that had brought them so close together, Grainger wasn't sure they could ever forge a real relationship now. Not after what had happened. And not while their lives were still in so much turmoil.

When Logan emerged from the bathroom, he was fully dressed but looked noticeably fresher than he had minutes before. Grainger couldn't help but think how great he looked, how secure she felt in his presence, and that only made her feel worse.

'That's so much better,' he said. 'I can actually feel my toes again. How anyone can live through these winters I really don't know.'

He sat down on a chair at the desk by the window. Both the chair and the desk were old and battered. Everything in the house felt un-homely and plain. Grainger wondered whether it was a deliberate attempt by Fleming to make the house not feel like a real home or whether he just didn't care. Logan had told her that Fleming had been in the SAS for more than twenty years, always on the move, so maybe he'd simply become accustomed to living in less-than-salubrious surroundings.

In some ways, she was the same. She'd spent so much of her FBI career working away that the house she'd shared with her ex-husband – Tom, a fellow agent – had rarely felt like a true home. Just another stopping point. Perhaps that was one of the reasons their marriage had been doomed to failure from the start.

'What do you think Fleming is doing here? In this place?' Grainger asked.

'He's a security consultant,' Logan said. 'For the oil and gas companies.'

'Yeah, right. So he just likes to bring his work home then. Is that the explanation for the barbed wire and commandos?'

'It's not so unusual in this part of the world to have armed guards. Believe me, I've seen it before.'

'Surely you're not telling me you think he's legit? No one who's legit lives in an armed fort.'

'No, I'm not saying that at all. But I don't think he's some sort of master criminal kingpin either. Money is so easy to come by around here and that brings its own dangers. I'm betting he's taking the multinationals for a ride. That's how he's making his money.'

Grainger had never met Fleming before, but she wasn't a complete novice when it came to corruption. The world's large oil and gas companies sprayed money around in the cheap, underdeveloped, mineral-rich countries that they plundered. Wherever they went, there were always the telltale signs of their destruction. Governments and politicians got rich. Keen and lucky businessmen got even richer. They were the ones you read about in the papers, the multibillionaires who made their money overnight.

Others, like Fleming, were happy to skim what they could. Most of the population got nothing from the involvement of the multinationals, or at best a low-paid, back-breaking labour job. That, unfortunately, was the way of the world. Having said that, embezzling money was one thing. Armed guards? That was a new one for her.

'You really think Fleming would have all those guards if that's what he's up to? Just a common fraudster?'

'Yeah, I do. It's like the Wild West out here. The same in many countries. It's the power of money.'

'You know there's a guard right outside our door?' Grainger said. 'We're basically prisoners in this place.'

'For now. But it's better than any other option I can think of. Would you rather be in here or out there in the car? Fleming will come around eventually. And until then, we're safe and warm at least.'

'I don't know why you're so sure about him.' Grainger stood up and took the towel she'd had wrapped around her hair back into the bathroom. When she came out, she stood in the doorway, hands on hips. 'It doesn't strike me that you two, or you and Butler for that matter, ever got along too well.'

'That's probably an understatement,' Logan said, getting up and moving over to the bed.

'So why are we here?'

'Fleming hates the authorities. He also hates the Americans with a passion. In the end, he'll be happy to help get one over on them.'

'You're playing a risky game, Carl. And it's our lives you're playing with.'

'I can handle Fleming. If our being here goes awry, I'll get us out.'

'You really think you can take on the world, don't you?'

'I've never failed yet.'

Grainger humphed. 'You really think so?'

Logan stared at her but made no reply to her sarcastic comment. She walked over to the bed and sat down next to him. Her shoulder brushed against his and her heart jumped in her chest.

'Why did you come for me?' Grainger asked.

'I couldn't let them kill you. And I had to know.'

'Had to know what?'

'I had to know how I'd feel if I saw you again.'

'And how do you feel?'

'I'm not sure I know the answer to that yet.'

'How do you want to feel?'

'I want it to feel like it did before.' Logan looked up at Grainger, looked deep into her eyes. 'But it just doesn't.'

Grainger tried her best to show nothing in response to his cutting words, but she felt her bottom lip quiver. After a few seconds of fighting it, her composure returned and she gave a meek smile.

'It might do again. I hope it does.'

'Me too.'

'When I was in Russia,' Grainger said, 'I always wondered about us. About what could have been. I expected you would come to find me, even if it was just to turn me in.'

'Believe me, I tried to find you.'

'You know, your knock on the door wasn't the first unexpected visitor I had.'

Logan raised an eyebrow. 'No?'

'No. About four months ago, I had a visit out of the blue.

Someone I really didn't expect to see again. My ex-husband, Tom.'

'You're kidding, right?' Logan said, a sour look on his face.

'It's not what you think. He's an FBI agent too, remember. He's good at finding people.'

'I thought I was, but apparently not,' Logan said, looking embarrassed, though Grainger wasn't sure why.

'He said he was there to help. That he wanted to be with me again. It was such a bullshit situation. Ever since we split, he's wanted me to come back to him. This time, I felt like he was blackmailing me. That if I didn't let him back into my life, he'd turn me over to the FBI.'

'So what happened?'

'He stayed a few days. I hadn't had company from someone I knew for months. It was nice to have someone to talk to and be with. In a way, I wanted it to work. But it just didn't. In the end, I think maybe he realised that too. He left for America, not wanting the agency to get suspicious about his whereabouts. I haven't heard from him since.'

'Clearly he kept true to you, though,' Logan said. 'I mean, you'd know if he'd given you up. Given the ploy that the CIA had to follow to get to you, it looks like they were in the dark about where you were until only a few days ago.'

'I know,' Grainger said, smiling. 'There aren't many people in the world I can trust. But it seems Tom's one of them. He might be able to help us?'

Logan shrugged and Grainger took that as a sign that he didn't agree. Actually, she wasn't so sure what Tom could do now either. She was certain he would jump at the chance of coming back into her life, but could Tom really offer anything that Logan couldn't in their current situation? More than anything, her reason for bringing up Tom's name was to test the waters with Logan. To gauge how he would react to knowing that Tom hadn't yet given up on her. Would it make Logan back off even further from her, or would it act as a prompt for him to show his true feelings?

There was an awkward silence for a few moments and Grainger waited it out, waiting for Logan to offer up a response.

'Before you shot me,' he said eventually, 'you told me you loved me. Did you mean it?'

'I think so.' She looked down at the floor. 'I think I could have done.'

'If things hadn't ended like they did.'

'Exactly. Maybe we just weren't supposed to happen.'

'Maybe.'

'But we did happen, Carl.' She turned back to face him and reached out, lifting up his chin so that he was looking at her. 'We did happen.'

Shutting away the elements of doubt in her mind, she moved closer to him and wrapped her arms around his neck. She clung on and closed her eyes, feeling his chest move in and out against hers as he breathed slowly and calmly.

She didn't let up – just held him tight. Eventually he moved his arms around her and squeezed, and she nestled into him further. Then they were both still for a while. And as they sat there in each other's arms, just a sliver of the sadness and confusion that Grainger had been feeling disappeared.

PART 3

Know your enemy

Chapter 22

Moscow, Russia

He opened the door to the hospital room and quietly stepped inside. It was dark out and the curtains in the room were drawn. The bedside light was on, gently illuminating the room and casting a pleasant glow on the face of the woman lying in the solitary bed.

He closed the door softly, then looked over at her and waited a few seconds. Her eyes were shut, her face calm and content. Her arms were on top of the covers, draped alongside her body.

Satisfied that she was asleep and wasn't stirring, he slowly and silently crept toward her. The only noise in the room came from the heart monitor that stood by her side, its blips steady. When he reached the bed, he looked down at her. He could see the small rises and falls of her chest but could hear no sound escaping her lips. The rich smell of the flowers by her bedside filled his nose. He recognised the scent but couldn't place why. Regardless, it fired pleasant memories in his brain and, looking down at the helpless figure before him, he couldn't help but feel the rumblings of arousal.

After a short wait, without so much as a stir from her, he carefully reached into the pocket of the white laboratory-style coat that he had on over his clothes and took out the still-packaged syringe. Carefully, he took the syringe from its wrapping and stuffed the paper and plastic waste into his other pocket. He then took out the vial, which contained a solution of thiopental, and stuck the needle through the lid. He slowly drew out the syringe's plunger, taking in five millilitres of solution. For good measure, he kept going one more notch, another fifth of a millilitre.

He had never done this before, but he was performing the role with ease, each of the steps coming in succession like he had perfected the routine by rote. While he was stepping into new territory today, it wasn't like he was completely unschooled. In fact, he knew everything there was to know about the drug he had just loaded into the syringe.

Thiopental had previously been commonly used as a general anaesthetic. In small doses, it caused unconsciousness within less than a minute. But for administration in even smaller doses, it was more widely known by another name entirely: truth serum.

Long the thing of fantasy, of fiction, thiopental's effect as a truth serum was little different to that of alcohol, decreasing inhibitions and making subjects more likely to be caught off guard when questioned, and increasing the possibility of the subject revealing information through emotional outbursts.

Today, though, he wasn't using thiopental for either of those purposes.

As he put the vial back into his pocket, he suddenly froze when the woman murmured and started to wriggle under the covers. He held his breath, held his pose, waiting to see whether she would wake up. She went still again after a few more seconds and he reached out and took her wrist in his hand.

Her skin was soft but clammy and cold. He turned her arm over, then gently tapped on her forearm, trying to coax a vein. The pressure stirred her again and this time she opened her eyes. She didn't move at first, just fixed her gaze on him, the syringe in his hand. It only took her a second to figure out what was happening. Maybe it was the unfamiliar face that tipped her off. Or maybe it was just instinct.

Regardless, there was really nothing she could do to stop him.

He gripped her arm hard – his strength easily enough to overpower her weak squirming – and thrust the needle down, piercing her skin and the throbbing vein just underneath. He pushed his body down onto the bed, putting his weight onto her to prevent her from writhing, then slowly but assuredly squeezed all of the liquid into her bloodstream. When he was done, he calmly withdrew the needle and placed the syringe back in his pocket, then cupped his hand over her mouth to muffle her pathetic cries.

Thiopental's uses were wide and varied. But its most common application in recent years was far less salubrious than its origins as an anaesthetic. Most recently it had become the drug of choice for lethal injections. Its potent coma-inducing properties were perfect to render a subject defenceless while the cocktail of drugs injected in combination set to work inducing paralysis and then, eventually, stopping the heart.

And yet thiopental's potency was such that it was also increasingly used for single-dose lethal injections, eliminating the need for those other drugs which, in America at least, had drawn the ire of certain public bodies for their supposed horrific effects on death row inmates.

In that sense, thiopental truly was a unique drug.

That was why when she had woken up, he hadn't panicked. Because he knew the dose he was giving her was huge. Much greater than would be needed for analgesia alone, or even for inducing a coma. The dose coursing through her blood would take effect within seconds. Once it had, nothing could save her.

He looked deep into her eyes as the realisation of the situation dawned on her.

He had never met this woman before. Until recently, he hadn't known about her at all. She had played an important role in events thus far. The problem for her was that there was little else she could offer now. Despite her apparent strengths, she had become a liability. She must have known that.

Thankfully, the problem had now been resolved. After just a few more seconds, she closed her eyes. He knew she would never wake up. He stood up off the bed and looked down at her unmoving body, deep in thought but entirely lacking in emotion over what he had just done.

What he had heard about her was right. She was pretty. Very pretty. But when he had looked into her dark eyes, he had seen something quite different: a devilishness that he was sure had been used to wicked effect. Certainly a great talent. In a way, it was a shame to lose her.

But needs must.

Not wanting to dwell any further, he turned to leave.

Lena Belenov was the first person he had ever killed. It wasn't a proud moment or a sad moment. He wouldn't celebrate tonight but he wouldn't lose any sleep either. This was just his job.

He had many talents but he'd never seen himself as an assassin, despite having carried out the duty with such ease today. Desperate times called for desperate measures.

Regardless, it was over now. One less problem to worry about.

And as he opened the door to leave, he couldn't help but smile about that.

Chapter 23

Aktobe Province, Kazakhstan

Logan woke up when there was a sharp knock on the bedroom door. He lifted his head and pushed his torso up with his elbow, then rubbed his eyes and glanced at the clock on the bedside table. It was almost seven p.m. and was now dark outside.

He looked down at Grainger. She was still sleeping, nuzzled against his side on the single bed. They'd fallen asleep in each other's arms without saying another word.

There was another knock on the door, louder this time. Grainger stirred and opened her eyes.

'I'll get it,' Logan said as he slipped away from Grainger.

He stood up off the bed and moved to the door. Opening it, he was greeted by the guard who had brought them up to the room earlier. He was still armed, lazily holding his sub-machine gun by his side, the strap slung over his shoulder. Butler was standing behind him, an angry look on his creased face. Logan wondered whether the look was reserved only for him or whether it was just Butler's natural demeanour now.

'We've cooked some food,' Butler said. 'We thought you might want some.'

He spun around and marched across the landing toward the stairs without waiting for a response.

'Sounds good,' Logan shouted after him.

He turned around and saw Grainger standing up groggily.

'What time is it?' she groaned.

'Just gone seven.'

'Really? I thought it would be later. I think I could have slept right through the night.'

'Yeah, I'm pretty whacked too. They're having dinner downstairs. The food will do us good.'

'I guess so. I'll just go and freshen up. I'll see you down there.'

'Okay,' he said, smiling at her. She reciprocated and he felt his own smile broaden.

Grainger headed over to the bathroom and Logan turned and walked out of the room and made his way down to the kitchen. The smell of food – cooked meat and vegetables – got stronger with each step he took. By the time he reached the kitchen, his belly was growling and his mouth was watering.

'Ah, glad you could join us,' Fleming beamed with over-the-top niceness. 'Where's your friend?'

'She's coming,' Logan said, sitting down at the rustic oak dining table. Logan didn't think it was deliberately rustic, just old and worn.

'You two have some fun up there?' Fleming gibed.

'Of course,' Logan said. 'A real party.'

Fleming laughed and shook his head. Logan raised an eyebrow at Fleming's unusually upbeat manner. It wasn't the Fleming he'd come to know and it made him nervous.

Fleming was sitting at the head of the table, Butler to his right. Two guards sat at the table too, the one who had taken Logan and Grainger to their room earlier and the taller guard. A third guard stood over by the stove, spooning out what looked like some sort of meat stew. No sign of the one who had been at the hut outside the gates. Perhaps he wasn't allowed to come in for dinner.

'Help yourself to bread and wine,' Fleming said, pointing at the sliced French stick on the table and giant carafe of red wine.

Logan reached over and took the carafe, then poured wine into his glass right up to the brim. He took a large chunk of bread, half of which he stuffed straight into his mouth.

Grainger came into the room a few moments later.

'Hello, Angela,' Fleming purred. 'Glad you could join us. Please, take a seat.'

Grainger didn't respond but sat next to Logan, at the opposite head of the table to Fleming.

'Now that we're all present and accounted for, I'll do some intros,' Fleming said. 'Obviously you know me and Butler. We also have six men working shifts at the house through the day and night. This here is Maksat.'

Fleming tapped the big man to his right on the shoulder. Maksat looked over at Logan and nodded.

'Ex-Republican Guard,' Fleming said. 'Not one to be messed with.'

Maksat shrugged and took a piece of bread from the bowl on the table.

'This here,' Fleming said, standing up and putting an arm around the neck of the man serving dinner, taking him by surprise and almost causing him to lose his balance, 'is Vassiliy. His father was a general in the Russian army. Vassiliy is an excellent chef, I'm sure you'll agree.'

Fleming sat back down at the table and pointed over to the last guard.

'And this guy is Bulat. If you don't know him, you don't know anything. Bulat won a bronze medal at the Olympics when he was only seventeen. After that, he broke two world records in his weight class. One of the best weightlifters this proud nation ever produced.'

Fleming spoke with genuine pride, as though each of the men in the room were his son. It left even more bitterness in Logan's mouth to know that this man, who quite clearly cared for his workers, had passed up the opportunity to coach and mentor Logan all those years ago. Instead, he had chosen to bully and humiliate him, and ultimately leave him for dead.

What did these men have that Logan didn't?

'Quite a crew you've got,' Logan said.

'They really are the cream of the crop,' Fleming responded.

'What about the guy outside. By the gates? Is he not part of the A Team?'

'Of course he is. They all are. Every single guy who works here is the A Team. But everyone has to put their shift in too. It's his turn to guard the gate tonight. Simple as that. His name's Ilya.'

'So what's his tagline?' Logan asked.

Fleming raised an eyebrow as if offended by Logan's nonchalant question.

'He was special forces,' Fleming said. 'All of the men are here because they're the best, one way or another. I have the utmost respect for all of them. They deserve it.'

Logan knew that Fleming's final comment was a gibe at him. Fleming had never had any respect for Logan. That was clear. Though Logan knew it wouldn't have mattered how good he was at his job or the exercises he was put on with the SAS squad twenty years ago – for some reason, Fleming had taken a dislike to him and that was that.

'Please, Angela, help yourself,' Fleming said, pointing to the bread and wine.

'No. I'm fine, thanks,' she said.

Vassiliy began to hand out large, plain white bowls that were filled to the brim with piping hot stew. The intense smell as the bowl was placed in front of Logan made his belly grumble even more loudly and he saw Grainger smirk at the noise. He took a spoonful of the brown soupy mixture and chewed a large chunk of meat that he guessed was beef but could equally have been horse or some other kind of large animal. Either way, it tasted good and was tender and sweet.

'What did I tell you?' Fleming said, smiling at Logan. 'It's good, isn't it? Bet you wish the British army had served food as good as this.'

'It's good,' Logan said.

He took another large swig from his glass of wine, which was now close to empty.

'Help yourself to more,' Fleming said. 'There's plenty of everything.'

Logan noticed that both Fleming and Butler were drinking the wine but the Kazakh guards weren't. Clearly they were still on duty and Fleming's niceties only stretched so far. He poured himself another glass.

'What happened to the rest of your squad?' Logan asked. 'From the army.'

The smile on Fleming's face faded somewhat at the question. Logan knew Fleming's discharge from the army had been anything but honourable. He'd been publicly shamed. It was little wonder that a man with the sense of pride that Fleming had could see no better response than to flee the country for good.

Logan did have some sympathy for Fleming in that regard.

From what he'd managed to find out about Fleming's discharge, it was the CIA who had messed up on the details of the mission they'd sent Fleming on. Then they'd hung him out to dry when the heat on them had got too strong. He could only assume that Fleming – an undoubtedly proud man – now had a deep-seated hatred of the Americans and the CIA. Which was exactly the reason Logan believed Fleming might help him.

'Mixed bag really,' Fleming said. 'Jones is still in the army. He's the only one of the old team that's left. It was nearly twenty years ago when you were with us, remember. A lot has changed since then. The world has changed. Risks and terrorism have changed. Politics too. More than anything, a lot of us had just had enough. That kind of job saps your soul after a while.'

'I know how you feel,' Logan said.

Butler grunted and Logan flicked him a stare.

'But Butler's the only one you've invited out here,' Logan said.

'No,' Fleming said. 'Actually, I invited all of them here. But most have families or just wanted to retire quietly. Butler was the only one who said yes. And I'm glad he did. He was my wingman in the army for years before they booted him out.'

Logan resisted looking up at Butler, but he could well imagine the ex-soldier was giving him the death stare. He finished his stew and grabbed another piece of bread to mop up the remnants in the bowl. Looking around, he saw the others had barely got through half of theirs.

'I like your style,' Fleming said, nodding at Logan. 'Just like in the army. When the food's in front of you, eat like you've never eaten before and like you never will again.'

'I wouldn't know,' Logan said, after he'd downed the last of his second glass of wine. 'I was never in the army.'

'You don't say,' Butler chipped in.

Logan reached out again for the carafe of wine.

Fleming laughed. 'I said help yourself, but it's not quite a bottomless pit.'

Logan pulled back, not sure whether Fleming was being serious or not.

'I'm kidding,' Fleming confirmed. 'Go for it.'

'I'm just relaxing, that's all,' Logan said, grabbing the jug and pouring himself and Butler, who had finished his, another glass.

Grainger tutted and Logan looked over at her. She was scowling at him.

'It's hardly the right time to be getting wasted,' she said.

'Ouch, that's you told,' Fleming remarked. 'Bulat, go and fill up the wine, will you? Looks like we're going to have a busy night.'

Bulat dutifully did as he was told. Grainger finished her stew and pushed the bowl away.

'Vassiliy, that was very nice,' she said. 'Thank you.'

'He doesn't understand English,' Butler grunted.

Logan looked over at Grainger and saw her cheeks blush red. He squeezed his fists together, angered at Butler's continued riling comments.

'The food was very nice,' Grainger said in what Logan knew was perfect Russian. 'Thank you.'

Fleming raised an eyebrow, impressed. Butler murmured under his breath and drank some of his wine.

Grainger then carried on, speaking in what Logan assumed was Kazakh – he didn't understand a word of it. Vassiliy tried his best to hide his laugh at what she'd said, as did the other Kazakh guards. He quickly composed himself, smiled and thanked Grainger, then stood up and began to clear away the empty bowls.

'What was that?' Butler said to Grainger. The anger in his voice was clear.

'You don't speak Kazakh?' Grainger queried. 'But you live here, don't you?'

'What did you say to him?' Butler quizzed through gritted teeth.

Grainger said nothing but held Butler's cold gaze. Everyone in the room fell silent. Logan too was staring at Butler. He had no idea what Grainger had said, but inside he was glowing that she'd managed to piss off Butler. Whatever pressure she was under, and he knew she wasn't anywhere near full strength, she still had a hard, resolute edge to her that he couldn't help but be drawn to.

'Perhaps it's time we got back to the issue at hand,' Fleming said, breaking the bitter silence.

'You're probably right,' Logan said, turning to his host.

Butler huffed and went back to his food.

Logan shot Grainger a quick look and winked at her. She didn't respond.

'So what kind of trouble are you in, exactly?' Fleming asked.

Logan thought about the question for a moment. The food he'd wolfed down was sitting nicely in his stomach but he could already feel the effects of the wine he'd drunk, making him calm and warm but also starting to cloud his thoughts.

'I'm sure Butler filled you in on Grainger.'

'He did. But what about you? How do you fit in?'

'I was traded over to the Russians,' Logan said with no emotion in his voice. 'In exchange for information. After nearly twenty years of loyal service, that was my reward. My own people left me for dead.'

'Then how does Grainger fit into that?'

'Because she was part of that dirty deal too. The CIA were trying to locate her. You can guess what they wanted to do to her. I couldn't allow that. Especially not after what they did to me. It was the CIA who set me up to allow the Russians to capture me. I'm sure of it.'

Butler looked down at his wine but Fleming's stare was fixed on Logan. The look on Fleming's face had changed. Logan saw something in Fleming's eyes that he'd not seen directed at him before. Not respect, but an understanding at least. Fleming had never given Logan a chance back in the day, but when you took away the facade, the two men had a lot of similarities, Logan knew.

'What exactly are you planning to do?' Fleming asked.

'I'm going to get my own back. I'm not going to lie down and be used as a pawn. Anyone who was involved in that deal is going to pay for it.'

Fleming smiled at that. 'I was like you once,' he said, the first time he had ever come anywhere close to comparing himself to Logan. 'Nobody likes to be wronged. But you have to choose your battles carefully. I tried to fight the system plenty of times. Most of the time I won. But the one time I lost, that was it. I was out.'

Logan assumed Fleming was talking about his discharge.

'You blame the CIA for what happened to you?' Logan asked.

Fleming gave him a blank look. 'Water under the bridge,' he

said eventually, though Logan could tell Fleming didn't believe his own words.

'And yet look at you now,' Logan said. 'I'd say it's worked out pretty well for you.'

Fleming shrugged. 'Maybe. It didn't seem like it at the time. I spent the majority of my life answering every call that came to me in the army and then, just like that, I was out. And not just out but discarded like an HIV-infected condom. You can only imagine how it felt to be put through that after everything I'd given.

'But my point is: if you're taking on the big boys, you have to know what you're doing. I tried it. I thought I had truth and justice on my side, but that's not always enough. If you're going after them, you have to be sure you know who you're going for and why.'

'I do. But it's not quite as simple as you make out. This isn't some moral crusade against the big machine of the world's intelligence community. Plain and simple, it's my life I'm fighting for. Grainger's too.'

'The stakes may be higher but the playing field's the same.'

'If you say so.'

'And don't think that you're the only one at this table who's had to fight for his life.'

Fleming held Logan's stare a few seconds longer.

'Okay. Back to work now,' Fleming said in Russian to the guards. 'Bulat, you can clean up later.'

Bulat and Maksat stood up. Vassiliy stopped the tidying that he was doing and all three men headed for the door.

Fleming took a large swig of his wine. 'I'm going to help you,' he said to Logan after he'd swallowed a mouthful.

Butler's gaze shot from his glass to Fleming, a startled look on his face.

'I'm going to help you because I understand what you're fighting against.'

Logan wasn't sure he really did, but as long as Fleming felt it, that might just be enough.

Chapter 24

Logan would be the first to admit that his turning to Fleming for help hadn't come easily. Fleming was a man he'd long despised. At one point in his life, he'd wanted nothing more than to inflict serious pain on him. But a lot had changed. As he sat at the dining table, hearing Fleming commit to providing his help, Logan was reminded of a conversation he'd had with Lena during his captivity in Russia. She'd said Logan was a survivor. That he did whatever was necessary to survive. She was right. His being there, in Fleming's house, was all about survival. There was nothing more to it than that.

'Are you sure you don't want some?' Fleming said to Grainger, swirling his wine glass.

'No. Thank you,' Grainger said. 'I want to keep a clear head.'

'I can only imagine how hard the last few months must have been for you.'

Grainger said nothing in response. Logan knew the subject of her running to the Russians for safety was an uncomfortable one, not just for her but for him too. He'd certainly not felt like broaching it with her yet. But Fleming, now that he had laid his cards on the table, was enjoying seeing Grainger squirm.

'So is it true?' Fleming said.

'Is what true?' Grainger responded, a hint of exasperation in her tone.

'Were you responsible for Frank Modena's kidnapping?'

Grainger said nothing.

'And for the lives of all those innocent agents who died in

the ambush,' Fleming added. 'It's a cold person who can pull off something like that.'

'Yes, well, sometimes people aren't what they seem,' Grainger said, her tone full of disdain and her manner making it clear that she wasn't afraid to take on Fleming. 'Are they, Captain?'

Fleming held his gaze on her. Butler looked back and forth between Grainger and his boss, clearly enjoying the awkward moment and waiting to see whether it would escalate. That was the last thing Logan wanted. He didn't trust Fleming, but he at least wanted to believe that Fleming was going to help them as he'd said he would. Challenging him was hardly going to play to their advantage.

'Let's just drop it,' Logan said.

Fleming held up his hands in defence. 'Hey, I'm just trying to understand the predicament you two have found yourselves in.'

'Move on,' Logan said.

Inside he was seething. Fleming had agreed to help, but that didn't mean Logan had to like him. Still, he knew he had to try to play nice. For whatever reason, Fleming was giving them his hospitality, and as long as that was the case, Logan and Grainger had to keep Fleming on side. Plus, Logan really didn't want to have to think about the events Grainger had set in motion that had led to Modena's kidnapping and a number of innocent people getting killed. That wasn't the Grainger he knew. The one he was helping.

'The wine's good,' Logan said, hoping a change of subject would do the trick.

'Any guess where it's from?' Fleming quizzed.

'I wouldn't have a clue.'

'No, me neither. Bulat sources it for me. I enjoy drinking wine but it's not my passion. Whisky, on the other hand, I know a lot about.'

'You can get decent whisky in Kazakhstan?'

'You can get decent whisky anywhere if you pay enough.'

'That figures.'

'Come on, why don't we finish this wine off in the lounge? Then I'll show you a thing or two about Scotch that I bet you didn't know.'

'Sounds good.'

'You like cigars?'

'No.'

'Shame. They're one of my other passions.'

'I've never smoked anything in my life.'

'You're missing out.'

'Never really saw the point.'

'Your loss.'

Fleming got to his feet and picked up the carafe.

'I'm just going to grab some water,' Grainger said. 'If I could?'

'Help yourself. The stuff in the fridge is better than in the taps.'

Butler lifted his glass and followed Fleming out of the kitchen. Logan stayed and watched Grainger pour water into her wine glass from one of the many bottles crammed into the fridge.

'You okay?' Logan asked.

'Not really,' Grainger said. 'I hate it here.'

'But what choice do we have?'

'Logan, I know that. You don't have to keep reminding me. It doesn't make being here any easier, though.'

Her forthright tone knocked Logan back. He was finding it so hard to break through to her. The affectionate moments they'd shared in the bedroom hours before already seemed so distant. It was as though she was constantly battling to keep up her defensive walls. Logan wasn't sure whether it was just the dire situation they found themselves in or whether this was just the way she was now. Maybe it was the way she had always been and the person he had met and been attracted to so strongly in Paris had just been a facade.

He really hoped that wasn't the case.

'I think I'm going to go back to bed,' she said, after drinking her glass of water and then refilling.

'Okay,' Logan said.

'You coming?'

'No, I'm just going to have a couple more drinks. I'll be up soon.'

Grainger huffed. 'Fine. I'll see you in the morning.'

She headed off. Logan immediately felt bad. It was early in the evening, though, and he thought it was important to keep up appearances with Fleming. Plus, he figured the more alcohol the three of them ploughed through, the more likely it was that any remaining falsities that Fleming and Butler were hiding behind would be exposed.

Logan headed to the lounge. When he walked in, Fleming and Butler quickly stopped talking and looked up. It reminded Logan of the Scottish Highlands, when he'd come back from fetching firewood to find the two of them deep in discussion. On that occasion, the two soldiers had been plotting how to take Logan down and leave him alone in the wilderness.

What were they plotting this time?

'Ah, you're alone?' Fleming remarked.

'She's gone to bed. She's not really with it. I'm sure you can imagine she's having a pretty hard time at the moment. She's been on her own for a year, always looking over her shoulder. She's not used to company. To socialising.'

Fleming shrugged. 'It is what it is. So what's your tipple?'

'I'm fine with the wine for now,' Logan said, sitting down on one of the threadbare sofas.

Fleming was sitting on the other. Butler was hunched on an armchair.

'Fair enough. Help yourself,' Fleming said, nodding over to the carafe. 'How about you, Butler?'

'Whatever you're having.'

'Good answer.'

Fleming got up and headed over to the tall beech cabinet next to Butler's armchair. He opened it up and Logan saw the vast array of spirit bottles neatly arranged inside. Fleming perused his collection before taking down one of the bottles from the top shelf. The labelling wasn't familiar to Logan, but he guessed it was a whisky from its caramel colouring and the style of the bottle.

Fleming poured large measures into two tumblers, gave one to Butler and then sat down with his own.

'Looks like the wine is all for you then,' Fleming said to Logan.

The three of them sat there in the lounge with their drinks, each becoming more relaxed, each becoming more inebriated. To begin with, the discussion was banal and without much focus. Just three men with a bit of time and a little bit too much alcohol inside them.

Logan was enjoying the respite, the feeling of doing something that felt like normality, even if he was in the company of two men he had long despised. But as they eased through several more rounds of drinks, Logan became more and more irked by the stuffy tone and snide comments still coming from Butler.

Retirement from the army, if you could call it that, seemed to have mellowed Fleming. Logan actually found him to be engaging and interesting, even if he wasn't exactly likeable. He had engrossing stories to tell of heroism and camaraderie, and Logan could well imagine that he had been a great leader of the men under his watch. In some ways, Fleming reminded Logan of Mackie, particularly in the way Fleming had mentored and looked after his men. Fathered them. It was exactly how Logan had always felt under Mackie: wanted, needed.

Butler couldn't have been more different to his boss. He was now bitter and morose, and much of his ire seemed to be directed at Logan.

'I bet twenty years ago you never saw yourself sitting in Kazakhstan drinking Scotch and shooting the shit with me,' Logan slurred to Fleming.

Logan knew that out of the three men, he was handling his drink the worst. It was a long time since he'd had any alcohol at all. Tonight he'd had a skinful.

'You're right,' Fleming said. 'But I'm not sure either of our lives have panned out quite the way we expected.'

'Why did you do it?' Logan asked.

Fleming raised an eyebrow. Butler stopped mid-sip.

'Why did you leave me out there to die?'

Fleming held Logan's stare for a good while without saying a word. Logan felt some clarity return to his hazy mind as he waited for the response. He wasn't quite sure why he had asked the question or what he was expecting to gain from the answer. But he wanted to know.

'I did what I was told to do,' Fleming said.

Logan frowned and shifted in his seat. 'Who told you to do what?'

'Your agency. The guy in charge there. He told me to haze you. To make you suffer. Said he needed to know you were tough. It was all part of your training.'

Through the alcohol-fuelled blur, Logan could feel anger building in his head.

'Mackie?' Logan asked.

'Yeah, that name rings a bell. He was your boss, right?'

'Yeah. He was,' Logan said. 'He's dead.'

Fleming didn't say anything to that. Logan sat contemplating what Fleming had said.

'To be honest, it was an odd request,' Fleming said and then he shrugged. 'But hey, an order is an order, right?'

'What? He told you to break my leg and leave me for dead?' Logan fumed.

'No, you brought that on yourself, you piece of shit,' Butler said.

Logan glared at Butler whose face was etched with anger, as though it was he who had been somehow wronged.

'He's right,' Fleming said. 'The hazing was one thing. And we were told to leave you out in the Highlands for you to find your own way back. They wanted to know you could handle that. On your own. That's what you are. That's what they wanted you to be. A lone wolf. But you attacked us. You broke Butler's arm. What did you expect us to do?'

'Oh, I don't know. Call for help, maybe?'

'Who said we didn't?'

'None came.'

'Well, how do you explain the trackers finding you? You think they just happened to pass the exact spot you'd crawled to? Come on, do you believe that? Just because your boss chose not to fill you in on what really happened doesn't mean it isn't true.'

Logan was raging now. Much of his emotion was directed at Fleming and Butler. They were talking about the event like it was nothing more than a mild inconvenience when Logan had very nearly lost his life.

But Logan was also angered at the role Mackie might have played in the situation. Mackie, whom Logan had long clung to as the one person in his life he could fully trust, who really believed in him. Too many times recently Logan had been made to question whether his faith in his late boss had been misplaced. Not so long ago, he would have refuted Fleming's claim outright, would have hammered him for even suggesting it. But not anymore. Why would Fleming lie? And his recounting had seemed genuine. With the amount of whisky he'd drunk, Logan didn't think the man would have the capacity or the urge to concoct such a lie.

It was just another example of how Logan had been manipulated by the JIA, been coaxed by them into performing for their ulterior benefit. And Mackie had been behind nearly every move Logan had made for the agency. It left a sour taste in his mouth that only in the aftermath of Mackie's death was Logan finding out about the other side of a man he had looked upon like a father. There weren't many happy memories in Logan's head, but he'd always thought of Mackie with genuine fondness. Now those memories were becoming somewhat tainted.

Butler began to snigger.

'What the fuck are you laughing about?' Logan spat.

'I'm glad we did what we did to you,' Butler responded, a wicked grin on his face. 'You deserved it. You thought you were the dog's bollocks, coming into our world like you did. We'd trained and fought for years to get to where we were. Why should we have even given you the time of day?'

'You know nothing about who I am or what I am,' Logan said. 'You never did.'

'We knew enough. You didn't deserve to be with us. And that was as much as we needed to know. I'm glad about what we did to you. We all were. We enjoyed watching you squirm, watching you slowly realise that you weren't the top dog you thought you were.'

Logan clenched his fists tightly, trying to keep a lid on his anger. He had been right about one thing: the alcohol had certainly brought down Fleming's and Butler's walls. The problem was Logan wasn't sure he could control himself with all of the wine sloshing about inside of him.

He went to stand up, but his vision blurred for a couple of seconds and he had to put his hand on the sofa arm to keep himself from toppling over. As he stood, Butler too got out of his chair. Logan quickly realised the ex-soldier must have seen Logan getting to his feet as a challenge.

'Now, now, boys,' Fleming slurred.

Logan had only been standing up to head to the toilet, but now that he was upright and face to face with Butler, he wasn't so sure he wanted to pass up the opportunity. Both men stepped forward. Suddenly they were within touching distance, each sizing the other up. Both men snarled. Logan's fuzzy mind was busy trying to prepare for an attack from Butler. Or should he just make the first move and be done with it?

'You might have got the better of me when I was a naive kid, but don't fool yourself, Butler. I'm not that kid anymore.'

'Just try me,' Butler said.

'You're not even worth it,' Logan said, peeling away – and glowing inside for having had the strength of mind to do so when what he really wanted to do was floor Butler.

But as he stepped away, toward the door, he sensed movement at his back. It wasn't the first time Butler had tried to take Logan out from behind. That time, Butler had been successful, crashing a rock against Logan's skull. But Logan hadn't just been bragging. He really wasn't the same person he had been back then. And when it came to moments like this, it was one of the few things he had to thank the JIA for.

Logan spun around, ducking down as he did so and lifting up his forearm to block Butler's wide, sweeping right hook. He balled his left fist and sent a crashing straight-arm strike onto Butler's nose.

Butler stepped back, wobbled and then fell to the floor, smacking his head off the armchair on the way. He wasn't unconscious but after a few seconds it was clear he wouldn't be getting up in a hurry.

Logan looked over and saw Fleming's face was entirely expressionless. He studied Logan and shrugged.

'Well, I'm sure that's not going to ease relations between you two much,' Fleming said. 'Let me speak to him in the morning. When we're all a bit more with it.'

Logan didn't respond. He just turned and headed for the door.

Chapter 25

London, England

Jay Lindegaard strode up to the door to Winter's office and gave three loud knocks. After a few seconds, he heard the bolt being unlocked and the door opened.

'Good morning,' Winter said bluntly, before spinning around and heading back to his desk.

Lindegaard gave a similarly unconvincing pleasantry and entered the room, then closed the door behind him.

'So what's the latest?' Lindegaard growled. He walked over to the desk and sat down without waiting for an invitation.

'We haven't heard from Evans since last night,' Winter said, his arms folded, his gaze stuck on Lindegaard. 'There isn't even any noise as to where he could have gone. And Nikolai Medvedev is dead, which I'm sure you've heard.'

Lindegaard huffed. 'So what are you doing about it?'

'We're trying to get information from some of our other sources, but so far no one's talking. I've never seen anything like this – it's like everyone's just stopped doing business.'

'Well, you've not really been around that long, have you?' Lindegaard said. 'It's not the first time I've seen the Russians close up shop like this.'

'Well, if you've seen it before, what does it mean then?'

'It means you need to find another way. And anyway, getting the FSB to talk isn't the main priority. What you should be doing is figuring out a way to find Carl Logan.'

'I know that. The Russians are saying he killed Medvedev. I don't believe it.'

'What? Because Logan's such a nice guy?'

'No, because I don't see any reason for Logan to have stuck around Moscow. He's on the run. The Russians are simply trying to put more heat on him. Which means two things: it's unlikely Logan is working for the Russians – which is what we'd feared – and the Russians have no idea where he is.'

'So what are you doing about it?' Lindegaard said again.

Winter shrugged and gave a nonplussed look. 'I've got other feet on the ground in Russia, but at the moment, until we hear something reliable and tangible, or unless Logan contacts us directly, we're stuck.'

'I always thought you'd be a weak link,' Lindegaard said, shaking his head. 'I just couldn't understand what Mackie saw in you.'

Winter smacked a fist down on the table and sat forward in his seat. 'I'm not entirely sure why you feel the need to constantly insult me,' he shouted. 'I don't see you offering up any solutions.'

'My job isn't to offer you solutions, Winter,' Lindegaard responded, only too happy to rise to the bait. 'It's to make sure you're doing your job properly. And right now I'm not so sure you are.'

The heated conversation paused for a few seconds and Lindegaard held the stare of the young commander. What he had said was true. He really didn't care for Winter, didn't rate him at all. But his dislike for him wasn't just on a professional level but on a personal level too. That was one of the few faults that Lindegaard saw in himself: his inability to separate work from everything else. He should have been able to look beyond the personality differences between himself and Winter and find a way to work together. But he just couldn't.

Maybe it was because of the stunt that Winter and Mackie had pulled when Logan had been investigating the Modena kidnapping. Winter and Mackie had connived to have Lindegaard's phone hacked. And the two of them had held high the dirt they had found against Lindegaard – that he'd sent a couple of gangbangers to teach Logan a lesson – ever since.

But the power in the relationship had shifted considerably

since then. Mackie was gone. For good. And Winter just wasn't up to the game.

'We're under attack,' Winter said. 'It's the only explanation. Whether by someone on the inside or outside, I think the JIA is under attack.'

'That's a bit dramatic, isn't it?'

'How many agents have we lost in just a few days? I know everyone is pinning this on Logan, but there's more at play here.'

'Wild theories will get you nowhere, Winter. We're on the hunt for a madman. Whether or not Logan is working for the Russians, that's what he is. It's as simple as that.'

'And we're on the hunt for yet another agent who's been taken hostage by the Russians,' Winter retorted. 'First they snatched Logan, and now I can only assume it's the Russians who are responsible for Evans's disappearance. I got a chance to speak to Evans a few hours before his meet with Medvedev.'

'And?' Lindegaard said, his interest in the conversation genuinely piqued for the first time.

'And nothing. He was in good spirits. There were no problems. That's the thing. It was a rushed meet, sure, but both before and after, and even with all the digging we're now doing, there's no suspicion that the Russians were onto Medvedev, or that they were planning to snatch Evans.'

Lindegaard guffawed. 'Were you expecting them to send you a letter first? How the hell did you think it would go down?'

'That's not what I meant. I meant, I had a lot of ears to the ground leading up to that meet and there was nothing untoward. No threat. Which means that either Medvedev was in on it and brought the FSB to take Evans, or the whole meet was a set-up designed to get both men.'

'Well, I think the former is unlikely, given that Medvedev was shot dead. And the latter is pretty fucking obvious. Of course it was a set-up.'

'If it's so fucking obvious, then how about you tell me who set them up and why?'

'It's your job to find that out, not mine.'

'What about the CIA?' Winter said. 'Is there anything they know that can help us? To locate Evans? To try to get him back? To find Logan and Grainger?'

'I'm not here to discuss my role with the CIA,' Lindegaard snapped. 'What I do or don't know about the CIA's operations doesn't come into this.'

'It did when it involved bargaining for Logan's release.'

'Yes. Because at that point there was a shared interest. You knew what you needed to know.'

'And there's no shared interest now?'

'I'm not saying there is or isn't. What I'm saying is that either way you don't need to know.'

'Then I really don't have anything more to add,' Winter said. 'If you're going to have me work with my hands tied behind my back, then you'd better prepare to be disappointed.'

'Don't worry,' Lindegaard said. 'I'm already well prepared for whatever disappointment you can bring me.'

Lindegaard got up off his seat and made for the door. He left the room without saying goodbye and strode down the corridor to the central bank of lifts.

Despite his abruptness with Winter, he was actually pleasantly surprised by the meeting. Because it really did seem like Winter had no clue about what he should be doing – unless he was simply pleading ignorance, but Lindegaard didn't believe that was the case.

The fact was, Winter was well and truly in the dark, which was probably the best answer for everyone. When Logan had first gone on the run, Lindegaard had been hopeful that Winter may have been useful in helping to track him down. Lindegaard couldn't afford for Logan to be out there running amok. As it was, it appeared Winter didn't know his arse from his elbow – he didn't even have a starting point.

That was fine for Lindegaard. At least with Winter dithering aimlessly in the background, he wouldn't be getting in the way. And he wasn't a threat. For now.

As Lindegaard descended in the lift to ground level, his phone began to buzz in his pocket. He took it out and looked at the caller ID. It said 'unknown' but Lindegaard had a good idea who it might be. He answered the call.

'It's done,' said the voice on the other end.

Lindegaard knew exactly what that meant.

He was happy to hear of the progress, but a very small part of him, hidden somewhere in the recesses of his mind, was also saddened. He'd made a commitment to his dying sister to look after Lena Belenov. He had done so for many years to great effect, steadily steering her through life and guiding her into a job in which she had flourished and from which he had also reaped great rewards over the years.

It was unfortunate that her being alive had no longer been viable and that his secret arrangement with her had so suddenly ended. But after the events in Moscow, which had seen Carl Logan escape from the grasp of both the FSB and the CIA, and the way in which Logan continued to evade all of his pursuers, her demise really was unavoidable. The risk was simply too great. She knew too much. And he had to expect that Logan might too.

'Good,' Lindegaard said. 'Any complications?'

'None at all.'

'I've just been speaking to our good friend at the JIA,' Lindegaard said, looking around as he exited the office building onto the street. It was quiet out but Lindegaard knew he still had to speak carefully.

'And?'

'And if he knows anything at all, he's not giving it away,' Lindegaard said.

'I don't see how he could know anything.'

'Well, let's not completely underestimate him just yet. One thing that did strike me is that he's not too happy about how the Moscow rendezvous meeting went down.'

'In what way?'

'He's been prying. Trying to find out from the other side what happened.'

'What else would you expect him to do? One of his informants was killed and one of his agents captured. Of course he's going to follow that up.'

'I'm not a fucking idiot – I know that. Just try to keep close to who he's speaking to and what they're telling him. You said yourself it was a surprise that the Russians had outed Medvedev. Or maybe even that he'd given himself up. Someone in the FSB knows more than they're telling. I want to find out who it is and what they know before Winter does.'

'Understood. Let me see what I can do. Are you coming back here?'

'Yes, I will do. I'll let you know when.'

The two said their goodbyes and Lindegaard put the phone back into his pocket. He hailed a cab and jumped in, telling the driver to head back to the Westside Hotel where he was staying, a mile or so from the office.

The taxi had only just pulled away from the kerb when Lindegaard again felt buzzing in his pocket. A different pocket. Because the call was coming through not to the pay-as-you-go phone for which only one person had the number but to a different phone, his CIA phone.

'Yes?' he said as he answered the call, which from the ID he could tell was coming from the CIA's headquarters in Langley.

The voice on the other end was his assistant's.

'There's a call for you. I was told it was urgent.'

'Who is it?' Lindegaard said.

'I don't know. He wouldn't give his name.'

'Then tell him to go away,' he blasted.

The last thing he needed was a distraction.

'Usually, sir, I would. But I thought you might want to take this one.'

'What the hell for?' he snapped.

'Because the caller said he knows where Angela Grainger is.'

Chapter 26

Aktobe Province, Kazakhstan

'Carl, wake up.'

Logan slowly lifted his heavy eyelids. His weary brain took a few seconds to process the image in front of him and remember where he was.

'Carl, come on, wake up.'

Grainger was crouched down beside him, gently shaking him. Logan turned, his head spinning wildly, and realised that he was lying on the floor, fully clothed. He held a hand up to his forehead and pressed down hard, hoping the contact would ease the sharp throbbing. He groaned and tried to lift his lead-like body up off the floor. It only seemed to make his head worse. He managed to get into a sitting position before he had to stop and wait for the pulsing in his skull to ease.

'Sore head, I take it?' Grainger said.

'Yeah.'

'How much did you drink last night?'

'Too much.'

'Can you even remember last night?'

'Most of it, yeah.'

'So you remember falling down on the floor and not getting up?'

'No.'

Grainger laughed, but Logan sensed it was an unimpressed laugh.

'You just staggered in and collapsed right there. I tried to wake you up to get you into bed but you were out of it. Completely wasted.'

'It certainly looks that way.'

'You should've just come to bed when I said.'

'Maybe. What time is it?'

'Nearly eight. I've only just woken up. I think I really needed that sleep. I'm feeling much more alive for it. You, on the other hand …'

She smirked. Logan groaned again as he tried to get to his feet. The hangover wasn't really that bad, he'd certainly had a lot worse, but it had been a long time since he'd had a drink at all and he'd forgotten just how horrendous it could make him feel.

He took hesitant steps toward the bathroom, trying not to cause his head any more discomfort. He badly needed some water – he was parched, his mouth furry and dry, his lips cracked and sore.

'Carl, I woke you up because there's something you need to see.'

'Just give me a minute,' he said, entering the bathroom.

He didn't want to focus on anything until he had some water in his mouth. He turned on the cold tap and hung his head over the sink.

'I'm not sure you can drink that, can you?'

Logan ignored her and started to lap at the ice-cold liquid. He let it wash over his face, feeling a bit of clarity and energy return to him as he did so. After a few more seconds, he turned off the tap and lifted his head, then dabbed at his face with a hand towel.

'Carl, come here. You really need to see this.'

Logan turned around to face Grainger. She was standing in the bathroom doorway. Her hair was wet, she was dressed and she looked fresh and bright. The long sleep and lack of alcohol had clearly helped her. She looked the polar opposite to how he felt. But he didn't regret having a skinful the night before. If nothing else, it had allowed him to get one over on Butler.

'What is it?' Logan said, moving over to the bedroom window.

'Out there. Take a look.'

He looked outside. The sun was shining and the bright glare

from its rays on the snowy white ground caused Logan to squint and sent another shock through his already throbbing head, the pain stabbing somewhere between his eyes. He lifted his hand to cover his face and after a few seconds, when he felt acclimatised to the piercing light, he took it away and started to slowly scan the area outside the window.

The sky was clear and blue now but the snow looked fresh. In the grounds around Fleming's home, the guards had been hard at work clearing the snow into large piles up against the outer wall, meaning the courtyard where the cars were parked was more or less clear.

Logan's gaze followed the track outside the gates that led back to the main road. After a short distance, the clearing work stopped and the track became less visible. Large grooves cut by the few vehicles passing along were the only sign that a road was there at all.

As Logan followed the track further, he soon spotted what Grainger had wanted him to see. About a hundred yards from the building's gates was a black four-by-four, its paint gleaming in the bright sunlight. It wasn't moving. It was parked with its bonnet facing the road, the driver's side of the car facing Logan. The tinted glass meant Logan had no view of the occupants.

'Who is it, Carl?'

'I could take a guess,' he said.

The list of likely candidates wasn't long.

'But how did they find us so quickly?'

'I don't know.'

'And why are they just sitting there?'

'I wouldn't want to attack a building like this. Would you? These guys would put up a hell of a fight, I'm sure.'

'Or maybe they'd just roll over and let whoever it is at us.'

'Maybe.'

'Do you think it's the Russians?'

'It could be. But it could equally be the Kazakhs, the NSC.'

Logan moved away from the window and sat down on the bed. There was only so much his fuzzy head could take.

Grainger came and stood over him. 'What are we going to do?' she said, both her voice and her look doing little to conceal her angst.

'We're going to have breakfast,' Logan said.

He looked up at Grainger. Her face was lined with worry. But what more could he say? He didn't have any more answers than she did.

'Come on, let's go,' he said, getting up off the bed.

They headed downstairs and to the kitchen. As Logan had expected, it was a hive of activity. Fleming was sitting on his seat from the previous evening. The guards too were stationed in the same positions. But there was no sign of Butler yet.

'Good morning,' Fleming beamed. 'How's the head?'

'Could be better. Could be worse.'

'Well, I'm glad it's not any worse than it is,' Fleming said. 'Because that would mean you'd drunk even more than you did and I'm not sure what mess you and Butler would've caused if that were the case.'

Grainger looked over at Logan questioningly.

'It was nothing,' he said to her, answering her unspoken question. She huffed and sat down.

'So where's Butler?' Logan asked, taking a seat.

'Sleeping it off still. To be honest, I thought you would be too.'

'I had a rude awakening,' Logan said, smiling at Grainger.

'Help yourselves. There's plenty of food.'

Fleming wasn't wrong. The table was covered with an array of offerings: bread, cheeses, meats, preserves. Nothing fancy, but lots of choice and lots of volume.

Logan and Grainger began to delve into the food. Logan piled a plate with bread and meat and filled a glass with some juice.

'So who're the visitors?' Logan asked.

Fleming glanced up at him with a serious look on his face but he didn't respond.

'The black four-by-four outside your gates,' Logan added. 'Who are they?'

'I'm guessing they're here because of you,' Fleming said. 'They're certainly not visiting me. If they were, they'd have knocked.'

Logan took a bite of bread that he'd loaded with butter and a soft cheese, then took a large swig of his juice. He eyeballed Fleming, who was sitting back from the table, casually drinking a coffee.

'You seem rather calm,' Logan said.

'You too.'

'Do you usually get visits from the intelligence services?'

'It wouldn't be the first time,' Fleming said. 'But who said that's who they are?'

'Who else would it be?'

'Fair point. But what exactly did you expect would happen? That the Russians would just wave you off at the border and you'd be home free?'

'No. That's not what I thought at all.'

'Then why are you so surprised that there's someone here for you?'

Logan thought about the question for a few moments.

'Because they had no means to follow us here,' he said. 'There's no reason at all for them to trail hundreds of miles from where we crossed the border to this place.'

'Just spit it out,' Fleming said, suddenly riled. 'What exactly are you suggesting?'

'He's suggesting that you called the Russians here,' Butler said, coming into the room.

Grainger and Logan both turned, their eyes following him as he walked over to a chair and stood over it. He glared down at Logan. His face was puffy and blotchy and his nose was a big, red, swollen mess. Dried blood caked the inside of his nostrils. There was a lump just below his left eye too, where Logan's fist had caught the cheekbone. Grainger looked at Butler, then over at Logan, and shook her head.

'Butler, you look even worse than Logan,' Fleming said, giving a wry smile.

'Yeah, well, he didn't get sucker-punched last night,' Butler snapped.

Logan huffed. It had hardly been a sucker-punch. It was Butler who had come after him when his back was turned.

'Okay, boys,' Fleming said. 'The fun's over now.'

'So is it true?' Logan asked. 'Are they here because of you?'

'No, they're not,' Fleming said, his voice raised now. 'Why the hell would I call the Russians? Or anyone else for that matter. I wouldn't even know who to call! I'm not one of you, remember.'

'Then how do you explain them being here?'

'Why should I have to? You don't even know who it is out there. Maybe you're just not as good as you think you are at evading whoever's chasing you.'

Logan didn't respond to that. It wasn't the first time Fleming and Butler had questioned his aptitude. But as much as the comment angered Logan, Fleming did have a point. Logan had been followed plenty of times recently without his knowledge. Never over such a great distance, though, or for such a period of time.

'Don't forget where you are,' Fleming said. 'This isn't England. The police and NSC and the other agencies here are anal, always on high alert, looking for anything, anyone, out of place. Particularly foreigners. This is a free state, but in some respects it might as well be communist Russia. In all likelihood, you were tailed by the NSC from the moment you crossed the border.'

'We would have seen them.'

'They're not amateurs. They don't sit on your rear end. Their whole network is connected. Your movements could have been passed from one team to the next all the way here without you ever spotting anyone on your back.'

It was certainly plausible. And Logan knew it was the best way to track across large distances.

'Then why make their presence known now?' Logan said. 'They could have stayed out of sight and continued to follow our moves.'

'How the bleeding hell should I know! This is really fucked up, Logan. Is this how you repay my hospitality? You know, it should be me questioning you for bringing unwanted heat to my door!'

'I don't get it either,' Grainger said. 'Why are they just sitting there?'

'If it's the NSC, it's because I have certain arrangements with them,' Fleming said. 'They wouldn't dare come in here without my say-so. That's all you need to know.'

'So it really is the NSC?' Grainger said, looking over at Logan, appearing almost relieved. 'It's the only explanation that makes sense.'

'I don't know,' Logan said, getting to his feet. 'But I'm not sitting here speculating any longer.'

'What the hell are you doing?' Fleming shouted, standing up.

'Well, there's only one way to find who they are and why they're here,' Logan said. 'I'm going to ask them.'

Chapter 27

Logan walked out of the house and headed to the gates. He'd thrown on one of the guard's overcoats, but as he left the house, he was still hit by the bitter cold, which seemed worse than ever. Maybe it was just because he'd become too used to the warmth of the house.

He traipsed across the cleared courtyard. The snowy remnants under his feet were slippery and hard and he had to plant his feet heavily to stop himself sliding. As he reached the outer gates, a guard jumped out of the hut on the opposite side and started shouting at Logan in Kazakh.

'Open the gates,' Logan said back in Russian as he came to a stop.

The guard didn't move, just carried on shouting. Logan heard footsteps behind him and turned to see Grainger following him. Fleming stood further behind her, by the open doorway. He shouted loudly and the guard on the other side of the gates went quiet and skulked back into his hut. A few seconds later, Bulat scurried out of the house, past Fleming, and over to a control box on the outer wall. He pressed a button and the metal gates began to whir and slide open.

'Carl, are you sure this is the best idea?' Grainger said when she reached him.

'I want to know why they're here,' he said.

'Please. Just think about this.'

She reached out and put a hand on his shoulder.

'I've thought about it,' he said, shrugging her off.

His decision to confront the vehicle's occupants might have seemed rash to Grainger but it wasn't one he was undertaking lightly. He'd already identified the occupants of the car: the Kazakh NSC. It was the only plausible conclusion.

For starters, the number plate of the four-by-four was Kazakh, so it didn't belong to another FSB surveillance team that had followed him and Grainger over the border. Sure, the FSB or CIA could have hired a Kazakh car, but Logan didn't believe either of those agencies could have tracked them to Fleming's so quickly.

And even if they somehow had, the fact the vehicle was just sitting there like it was spoke volumes. It was possible the NSC could have been there at the behest of someone else, but if that was the case, they either would have stayed in the shadows or already launched an attack.

So while he didn't fully understand *why* the NSC were there, or even how they'd found him, so far he didn't see them as a threat. And he saw no point in sitting around to wait and see what would happen. They were either friend or foe and he may as well figure out which one it was sooner rather than later.

If anything, it was intriguing to Logan that the NSC were on his tail in the first place. He and Grainger could have tried to escape and go on the run once more, but Logan saw no benefit in trying to evade them before he even knew what their intentions were.

He turned and marched through the open gates, then headed up the track toward the parked four-by-four. He didn't look behind him, but guessed from the silence that neither Grainger nor Fleming and his men had followed him out of the compound. That was fine. He didn't need them tagging along to complicate matters. He wanted to appear as unthreatening as he could.

Logan was just ten yards from the car when two of its doors swung open in unison, the front passenger door and the rear door on the driver's side. Two men emerged, dressed identically in long black coats that came past their knees, smart trousers underneath and shiny black boots. It was an unusual combination. The boots, which were more like what you would expect on a soldier, looked out of place against their formal clothing, but Logan guessed in the snowy winter they were a necessity.

The man who emerged from the rear hung casually from his open door. The other came around the car and moved toward Logan. He and Logan were only a few yards apart when the man took a hand out of his pocket to reveal a gun. He didn't point it but Logan stopped moving, as did the man.

The man said something to Logan. He spoke calmly, no hint of anger or tension, but Logan didn't understand what he had said. It did at least confirm to Logan what he'd thought – that the car's occupants were from the Kazakh NSC. Even with the man brandishing his gun, Logan still felt calm and in control.

'I don't speak Kazakh,' Logan said in Russian.

The man glared at Logan, his face giving nothing away. Then, without saying another word, he lifted his gun and pointed the barrel at Logan. He had two hands around the butt, his arms outstretched.

For a few moments, everything went silent. But then, all of a sudden, the man shouted something at Logan. He was still speaking Kazakh but his whole demeanour had now changed. Logan held his hands up in the air. He could only guess that was what the man had asked him to do. But it didn't seem to calm him down at all. He continued to shout, inching forward.

Logan remained calm. The man wasn't going to shoot him. Not if Logan didn't give him a reason to. Logan was convinced of that. If the man had wanted to kill him, he would have already. Logan glanced over and saw that the second man was also now brandishing a weapon, though he was still cowering behind the open car door.

The first man continued to move closer, until the barrel of his gun was only a few inches from Logan's face.

'What do you want from me?' Logan said, trying his best to stay calm.

From the position the man was now in, Logan could quite easily attack and disarm him before a shot was fired. Logan was of half a mind to do just that, but then he heard shouting from behind and he instinctively spun around. It was Grainger. She was running toward him.

'Angela, what the hell are you doing?' he blasted.

It was the last thing he needed. She came to an abrupt halt, her vision fixed somewhere behind Logan's right shoulder. He immediately guessed why. The man had become spooked. He was making a move.

Logan ducked down and began to spin around, but the man was one step ahead. The butt of the gun caught Logan on the jaw, splitting the skin on the inside of his mouth and sending him reeling. He fought hard to recover before another blow came, readying himself for the attack. But Logan was too slow. Maybe it was the hangover.

The thick sole of the man's boot thrust down onto Logan's neck, pinning him to the floor. From nowhere, another man appeared and quickly cuffed Logan's wrists behind his back.

Logan heard Grainger scream behind him as the two men hauled him to his feet. Logan fumed and raged, trying his best to shrug the men off him, but he soon went still when he felt the barrel of the gun pushed against the side of his head. And when he looked up, he saw a third man walking to Grainger, gun trained on her, and all of his fight suddenly waned.

The man strode up to Grainger, then reached down with one hand and pulled a set of handcuffs from his pocket. He tossed them over to her and they landed at her feet. She looked up at Logan, as though asking him what she should do. Her face was hard and defiant. Logan knew there was plenty of fight in her. It wouldn't be the first time the two of them had fought against the odds. But despite the perilous situation, Logan still firmly believed this wasn't a fight they needed. Not until the NSC had declared their hand.

In the end, he simply nodded to Grainger and she hung her head.

The two men pulled on Logan's arms, ushering him backward, toward the car. Logan didn't resist, but he also wasn't going to make it easy for them. He let his body flop down so the men had to take his weight, his boots scraping the ground as they carried him along.

One of the men pushed Logan's head down while the other shoved him in through the open rear door. Logan looked over and saw Grainger, the cuffs around her wrists, the third man marching her toward him.

Then Logan caught a glimpse of something behind her. By the gates to the compound. Two figures. Fleming and Butler. Standing, unmoving, their arms folded. They were close to a hundred yards away but Logan was sure he could see a toothy smile plastered on Butler's face.

Grainger reached the car door and was bundled in, next to Logan. The three men got back into the car and, without another word, the engine started. The tyres spun and the car lurched forward onto the track and slowly started to move along the grooves in the snow, away from Fleming and the grinning Butler.

Chapter 28

Shortly after the four-by-four started off down the track, away from Fleming's house, one of the men in the car placed a sack over Logan's head. It meant he had no idea exactly where they were heading.

Logan's mind was filled with thoughts of what was happening. The last time he'd been captured on foreign soil, he'd been held in an isolated gulag in the wilderness of Siberia. He'd spent three torturous months there at the hands of Lena and her FSB cronies, before finally orchestrating his escape.

The place they took him to in Kazakhstan was nothing like the gulag, though. When the vehicle came to a stop, Logan was escorted out of the car and the sack removed only once he was inside a building. Logan was surprised by the room he found himself in. Not a dark, dank cell, but a plain, functional interview room. The man who removed the sack released Logan from the handcuffs and then left, leaving Logan alone to roam around the small space.

The door to the room was metal and looked thick and heavy, almost like a vault door. The security was clearly tight and there was no way he could escape through the door, but it was an interview room all the same, not a prison cell.

On one wall there was an expansive mirror, which Logan knew would be two-way glass. He also knew that in a standard police station, the two-way glass was usually only a few millimetres thick – easily breakable if you used a bit of force. Given the spec of the door, though, this didn't seem to be a standard police station and he could only assume the glass here would be toughened.

He pushed his shoulder into the mirror. It didn't give at all. He tapped it gently with his knuckles. It sounded as solid as anything he'd ever seen. He wasn't going to be breaking through that.

Logan paced casually, aware he was probably being watched, wanting to give the perception that he was in control, but really his mind was in overdrive and filled with worry. Where the hell was Grainger? Had she wound up in a similar room to this? She had certainly remained in the car with him for the whole journey, but once he'd been taken out of the car, he'd lost contact with her. He'd shouted after her and heard her call back to him all the way until he'd entered the building and heard a heavy door slam behind him. It was possible they'd brought her into this place too, but it was equally possible that she'd been moved to a different facility altogether.

After mooching around the room, Logan finally sat down on one of the two chairs placed up against the simple wooden table. Other than the table and chairs, the room was bare, lit by a single fluorescent strip light that buzzed and flickered.

There was no clock, but Logan guessed he had been left for a number of hours before the door to the room finally creaked open. It was then that he got his second surprise. The person who walked in was a woman.

She was young, with dark hair and soft features, and was wearing a black suit with a plain white blouse. She wasn't stunning but was certainly nice to look at. It was clear from the way the suit clung to her slender body that she was in great shape. Her appearance reminded Logan again of his time in the Russian gulag. Of Lena, the FSB agent who had abused him, tricked him and ultimately bargained his life away. The woman who'd had Mackie killed and had passed Grainger's whereabouts to the CIA so they could hunt her down and kill her too.

Lena had been truly beautiful on the outside, but under her glossy skin and perfect face, she had been pure wickedness. This woman didn't seem to have that edge to her. The whole experience, being in this room, with this woman, was entirely less threatening than when the Russians had held him. And yet Logan wasn't going to feel at ease yet. Because he was yet to figure out how he was going to get himself out of this mess. And he had no idea where Grainger was or what was happening to her.

The woman put a notepad down on the table and then sat on the chair opposite Logan. She looked over to the mirror and then began to talk to Logan assuredly. As with the men who had brought Logan here, she spoke in Kazakh and Logan didn't understand any of her words. He was sure these people understood Russian. But for whatever reason, it appeared they didn't really want to communicate with Logan. Which only made him more concerned. Because, together with the length of time it had taken for her to make an appearance at all, it felt like they were trying to buy time.

But for what?

Logan guessed the lady was asking him questions. She would speak a few words, pause and then, when he gave no response, jot something on her notepad. She repeated the same routine over and over. Until, after what Logan thought was about half an hour, she got up and walked to the door. It buzzed open and she stepped out, then closed the door behind her.

After that, Logan was alone again for what he thought was a number of hours more. By the time the door finally reopened, he was tired and thirsty and hungry. He must have been in the room for the best part of the day and had been given no sustenance; he hadn't even been offered a toilet break.

His next visitor wasn't the lady; it was the man who had first pointed a gun at him. Gone now was his overcoat. He was wearing smart trousers with a grey pullover. He looked to be a similar age to Logan, but was shorter and thinner. His hair was light and neatly parted. His face was pointy with a jagged nose and deep-set eyes. He didn't look menacing, but there was something eerie about him.

He sat down on the chair, no pen or notepad, and began talking. In English.

'I'm Agent Jabayev,' he said. 'I work for the National Security Committee in Kazakhstan. You know who we are, right? The Kazakh KGB.'

Logan didn't respond. The man waited a few seconds before he spoke again.

'You're Carl Logan,' he said.

Logan wasn't sure whether it was a statement or a question. But it was certainly disconcerting that the NSC already knew who he was. Regardless, he said nothing.

'Why are you in Kazakhstan?' the man said after another short pause.

Again Logan didn't respond. There was absolutely no reason for him to talk to this man. Not unless he saw some benefit in it for himself.

'I understand,' Jabayev said in his thick accent. 'You think you'll be better staying silent. But it's not true. We can help you only if you talk.'

Yeah, right, Logan thought. Like they were really going to help him.

'But I'm not going to help you if you don't tell me what's happening. We don't take too kindly to people bringing their problems to our country.'

Logan sighed and held Jabayev's gaze. He was surprised at how good the man's English was. But it also irked him that they hadn't tried to engage him in conversation earlier. They hadn't given him a chance to explain himself at Fleming's place. And Logan didn't like being played with – which, for whatever reason, was exactly what they were doing.

'We tracked you from the border, in case you're wondering,' Jabayev said. 'Our border guards are there for a reason. And it wasn't hard to spot that you two shouldn't have been there.'

There was another pause. Jabayev sat back in his chair, beginning to look impatient.

'We've been speaking to the FSB,' he said. 'About both you and Angela Grainger.'

Jabayev's words finally piqued Logan's interest. But then it was hardly an earth-shattering statement. The fact the NSC knew his and Grainger's names meant it was more than likely they had been in touch with the FSB, the CIA or even the JIA, so that much had been clear from the start. But Jabayev's revelation did increase the worry that Logan was feeling. If Jabayev was being truthful, the FSB or whoever else could be waiting right outside the door, ready to take Logan out, or ready to take him back to some hell-hole like the one he'd escaped from in Siberia.

And yet, if that was the case, why all this pretence?

Buying time, Logan thought again. They were still buying time. Waiting for whoever they'd been speaking with to catch up.

Or maybe they were just waiting for the right deal to come along. The NSC were an intelligence agency, after all. Chances were, they wouldn't give up Logan and Grainger unless there was something in it for them.

But despite the intrigue that was now growing inside Logan, he kept his mouth shut, refusing to engage with Jabayev.

'The Russians, clearly, want to take you and Grainger back over to their side.'

Logan again said nothing, but Jabayev's words did at least suggest Grainger was still in the hands of the NSC. That was a welcome relief.

'Given what you two have done,' Jabayev continued, 'I'm not so sure why we should refuse their request. They're still our closest allies.'

Logan looked away from Jabayev, over toward the mirror. He wondered who was on the other side.

'You remember Lena Belenov, don't you?' Jabayev said.

This time Logan couldn't help but react to the agent's words. His head snapped back around and he caught Jabayev's stare. Logan had fully intended to ride out Jabayev's questions and statements, but his last words had taken Logan completely by surprise. He forced himself to keep quiet, biting his lip, but it was clear from the pleased look on Jabayev's face that the NSC agent knew his fishing trip was now getting closer to paying off.

Why would Jabayev bring up her name? The last time Logan had seen Lena was in an abandoned warehouse in Moscow. He'd followed Schuster, the CIA agent who'd brokered the deal that had seen Mackie killed, to a meet with Lena, where Schuster had been given his part of the deal: the whereabouts of Grainger, whom the Russians had been hiding. After spoiling the party, Logan had shot Lena in the gut and left her to bleed out as he raced to confront Schuster and save Grainger from the CIA.

He had guessed ... no, he had *hoped* Lena would die in that very spot. The wound would certainly have been fatal unless she'd quickly received medical attention, and even then it was a long shot.

Maybe she hadn't died, though. Could she even have been the one the NSC had spoken to? Logan shuddered at the thought. All of a sudden, he felt his demeanour change, felt himself deflate just a little. Perhaps Lena was already there. Standing behind that mirror. But Jabayev's next words destroyed that theory.

'Lena Belenov was murdered last night,' Jabayev said.

Logan felt his heart begin to pound in his chest. He realised that his mouth was wide open and he quickly shut it.

He knew that Jabayev had him now. Had his full attention.

'She was murdered in her hospital bed in Moscow,' Jabayev said. 'It's been all over the news there. She's been labelled a local hero. The Russian government are calling her death an act of war. And the Russians have named you as their one and only suspect.'

Chapter 29

London, England

Winter had been deliberately vague with Lindegaard when the two men had met the previous evening. Events were beginning to spiral out of control. While Winter was sure Lindegaard was either involved or at the very least knew more than he was letting on, it was too early for Winter to play his hand. He'd toyed with the idea of dropping Belenov's name into the conversation to gauge Lindegaard's reaction, but ultimately had decided against it.

No, in all honesty, he'd plain bottled it. As much as he despised Lindegaard and relished the thought of being able to get one over on him, Winter was still somehow in awe of the man, forever feeling like a naughty schoolboy in his presence. He hated himself for it, but that was Lindegaard's power.

Since that meeting, though, events had taken yet another twist. News had come through that Lena Belenov had been murdered in Moscow. Belenov had been central to the deal that the JIA and CIA had been trying to broker for Logan's release. In that regard, her involvement in the ongoing mess was clear. But given that Winter now knew of her relationship to Lindegaard, her death was a startling development. Could the Russians have found out about her? And yet if that was the case, why were the Russians blaming Logan for her death? And Medvedev's too?

The more Winter thought about it, the less sense it made. Whatever the explanation, it looked increasingly likely that

Logan wasn't in bed with the Russians, which had always been the main fear for Winter – and for Mackie, before his death.

It had been more than twenty-four hours since Winter had last spoken to Paul Evans. Winter was certain his agent had been captured by the Russians following the botched meet with Nikolai Medvedev. Someone had blown either Evans's or Medvedev's cover. Both of the Russian agents who'd been killed had links back to the JIA, for different reasons, but links nonetheless.

The only conclusion Winter could come to was that a mole on at least one side of the playing field had led to those two Russian agents losing their lives and to Evans's disappearance. Winter was increasingly coming to the conclusion that there was no one left he could trust.

Well, almost no one. There was Carl Logan. So far, the one man who everyone seemingly wanted dead was the only man whose role Winter still could not figure out. In fact, the only thing that seemed to fit was that Logan was being made a scapegoat. First for Mackie's death and now Medvedev's and Belenov's too. The Russians were gunning for Logan for sure. But was there more to it than that even?

Since Evans's disappearance, Winter had been riffling through as much information on the missing agent as he could find, looking for some hint as to who could have set him up. But Evans's work had always been so clean. Medvedev had been a key source for Evans, but the two of them had never generated any heat from their relationship. Evans's other work for the JIA was similarly seamless. Winter just couldn't grasp any answers at all.

But as he sat in his office, staring out of the window at the thick grey clouds hanging over London, he suddenly thought of something. Lindegaard and his relationship with Belenov.

From what Winter had learned, Belenov was the daughter of Lindegaard's half-sister, one of four siblings who shared the same American mother. The half-sister had been conceived in an extramarital affair, fathered by a Russian expat living in America – a communist escapee. The bastard child had held dual nationality and had long ago moved to Russia, where she'd married a wealthy Russian businessman. He'd been killed under suspicious circumstances when he'd supposedly driven his car over a bridge into a river, high on drugs and alcohol. His wife had died some five years later in much less suspicious circumstances: she'd developed bowel cancer in her early thirties and passed away a mere three months after diagnosis. Their only child was Lena Belenov. Lindegaard's niece.

The biological link was clear-cut. What was less clear was how Lindegaard had exploited that relationship. What role had he taken in bringing up Lena, who had been eight years old when her mother died? What part had he played in her landing a job with the FSB? And what destruction had the two of them wrought in the years since?

Winter didn't know. Yet. But could Evans similarly have skeletons in his past? From before his days at the JIA?

Winter began typing away at his computer, his fingers moving in a steady rhythm. He pulled up Evans's personnel file and methodically scrutinised the details of his life and career. The file gave intimate details about his upbringing, his schooling, his qualifications, his JIA missions, his psych reports, his performance assessments. But it didn't include everything. It didn't have what Winter needed.

Winter opened up a new page and began to dig further. Not on the JIA's intranet, but on the World Wide Web. Winter knew that even secret agents left traces of their lives on the internet. It was impossible not to leave footprints. Even if the world was in the dark as to the JIA's existence and methods, that didn't stop the fallout from its operations on occasion making news or being debated in chat forums. And personal information, even if out of date and spurious, was everywhere. Registers of births, deaths and marriages and electoral, land and educational records were just the tip of the information iceberg that was available quickly and entirely legitimately – not to mention the often ludicrous amounts of personal data that people willingly posted to the world through social media and other channels.

Sure, the clandestine nature of a JIA agent's existence and the fact they carried multiple IDs made the matter of matching together all of those facets of information all the more difficult, but it was there and it could be done, if you knew what to look for and how.

And it was a task at which Winter had become an ace.

After a painstaking search, he finally found something. When he did, he could hardly believe what he was looking at.

'It can't be,' he said to himself, not sure whether to laugh or fume.

He quickly went back to Evans's personnel record, double-checking the information that he had cross-matched, sure that he must have taken a leap somewhere and that he was wrong about what he had found.

But he wasn't. It was right there, no mistake. The skeleton from Evans's past.

His brain began to whir, his hands felt clammy and he fidgeted on his seat. This was a revelation that blew wide open his thoughts on what was happening in Russia. And suddenly recent events made a whole lot more sense.

There was a knock on the door and Pam stuck her head around.

Winter jumped at the unexpected intrusion and quickly closed down the pages he had been viewing. As much as Pam had helped him in the last few days, this was something he had to keep to himself.

'What is it?' Winter asked, trying his best to sound calm.

'You said you wanted to see me? Earlier?'

'I did?'

'Yeah, before I went out to lunch, you said you were having trouble accessing some of Mackie's files.'

'Oh, of course,' Winter said, remembering. He'd got completely side-tracked digging into Evans. 'Come and take a look.'

Pam came across and stood over Winter's shoulder as he clicked through restricted folders and screens until he reached the area in question. Having taken over Mackie's role, Winter essentially had free access to information on every live agent, informant and case that Mackie had worked on. In reality, as Mackie's second in command, Winter had been privy to much of that information in any case, but there were some areas that Winter either had been blocked from or just hadn't needed to know about during his time working for Mackie.

So far, Pam seemed to be the gatekeeper to it all.

'Any idea?' Winter said, turning around and looking up at Pam.

He was surprised to see concern on her face.

'Do you know what these files are?' Winter said.

'Yes,' Pam said.

'Can you get me into them?'

'I … I'm not sure, to be honest. Maybe this is one that should be checked with the committee first?'

Winter frowned. 'Are you serious?'

Pam began to rub at her neck nervously. 'I just don't know.'

'Pam, believe me, if you know what this is and how to get in, you have to tell me. Better involve me than that trumped-up prick Lindegaard, surely?'

Pam laughed anxiously. 'Yeah, I guess.'

'So what is it?'

'I really can't say much. It's probably better you look for yourself.'

Pam leaned over and scribbled something on a sticky note. Winter looked at the words – 'Operation Romana' – then back up at Pam, who smiled meekly. Without saying another word, she turned and headed to the office door.

Winter looked again at the note, then clicked onto the restricted folder. A password prompt popped up. He typed in the words on the note. Nothing happened. The page simply closed down.

He picked up his office phone and called Pam. She answered within a second.

'Think outside the box,' she said, then hung up.

'What the hell?' Winter said to the phone.

He looked down at the note again, his face creasing as he thought about what she meant.

Finally he got it.

He'd thought the words on the note referred to a past operation that Mackie had run. It pre-dated Winter's time at the JIA, but Mackie had briefed him on the details and of its importance. In the late 1990s, post-Soviet Russia was plunged into a deep economic recession. Operation Romana was a clandestine operation with the aim of hitting at the very heart of growing discontent rising among many within Russia's intelligence community and political elite who were eager for a return to the good old days of the Cold War. As part of the operation, the JIA, CIA and MI6 together had managed to turn many high-ranking officials or their family members.

The operation had to be cut short when a mole exposed the list of informants, with many suffering untimely and unusual deaths soon after – or, if they were lucky, running for their lives to the UK and US to see out their days in hiding. Nonetheless, the operation quelled a rising storm and was seen as a success and an embarrassing blow to the newly formed FSB and SVR, which had both been deeply infiltrated.

It was that angle Winter decided to explore further. The reference to Operation Romana. Could Mackie have had someone deep on the inside once more that only he had known about?

Winter loaded up an internet page and used a search engine to start digging. The first four searches revealed nothing and Winter began to question just what he was actually looking for. But then another thought came. Romana. Rome. Italy.

Going back to the other page, he clicked on the restricted folder again and typed in a name. A Russian name. A name that he knew connected Italy to Russia. To the FSB.

The password box vanished and the folder opened to reveal a list of files. Winter resisted hard the urge to do a fist pump.

His brain was racing, adrenaline pumping. Winter quickly opened the first file and read it, then the next. He scanned the documents, taking in as much as he could, reluctant to spend more than a few seconds on each, as though having the documents open too long would lead to someone finding out what he was reading.

It only took a couple of minutes to confirm what he had hoped.

With his heart pounding in his chest, he picked up the phone to Pam again.

'You got in?' she said.

'I did.'

'Just be careful. I may only be a secretary but I know what kind of damage that could cause.'

'I know. I will be.'

'And don't even think about copying those files.'

'I don't need to.'

'Okay … good. Is that all?'

'Not quite. Can you do something for me?'

'What is it?'

'I need you to get me on the next plane to Moscow.'

Chapter 30

Aktobe Province, Kazakhstan

Logan's head was spinning with what Jabayev had just told him. He just couldn't figure out the chain of events that had led to Lena being killed – although he could understand why the Russians would pin the death on him. They must have known he was nowhere near Moscow the previous night. Publicly naming Logan as the suspect was designed purely to put extra pressure on him, make his life that much harder than it already was. And they were banking on other foreign police forces and security services, the NSC included, being sympathetic to their position and therefore likely to help hunt down and turn over Logan.

He got all that.

But if Lena had survived after being shot by Logan, then who on earth had killed her and why? Surely the Russians wouldn't have? She was a major asset for them. If not the Russians, then who?

'The Russians are on lockdown,' Jabayev said. 'Another of their top agents, Nikolai Medvedev, was killed yesterday morning. Again, you've been named their one and only suspect.'

Logan's brain was now working overtime, trying to put the pieces together.

'Why are you telling me this?' he said, convinced now that he could do no harm by talking. He'd been interrogated before, he'd been tortured before, but this situation was different. He wasn't going to give anything away. But he had to know what information Jabayev had.

Jabayev looked pleased that Logan had found his voice.

'For one thing, because I know you can't have killed Belenov. You were already in Kazakhstan. The same for Medvedev.'

'The Russians must surely know that too,' Logan said. 'You must have told them that?'

'I'm not telling you a thing about what I told them. But I'm sure the Russians know it wasn't you. Which only makes this all the more interesting for us. I'm in two minds here.'

'How so?'

'On the one hand, we always like to please our neighbours. But, clearly, you're being set up here. And on the other hand, we know you're a British agent. So we're wondering how not turning you over to Russia could benefit us.'

Jabayev had an almost devilish smile on his face as he spoke. Logan had been right, it seemed. The NSC had been buying time. They were trying to figure out exactly how they could maximise their return for having captured Logan and Grainger.

But given Jabayev's words, Logan was now doubting that the NSC had been in touch with the FSB at all. That was a relief to Logan, even though it didn't really help him that much.

'So those are our options,' Jabayev said. 'But most of all, we're still trying to figure out why you came to our country and what damage your being here might cause us.'

'Where's Grainger?' Logan asked.

'I can't tell you that.'

'Is she here? Is she okay?'

'You really care for her, don't you?'

'You'd better care for her too,' Logan said. 'Anybody who harms her has me to answer to.'

Jabayev stared at Logan, his look entirely placid.

'We're not animals here,' Jabayev said.

There was a knock on the door and Jabayev looked perturbed at having been interrupted. He got up off his chair and headed to the exit.

As he reached the door, there was a buzz and it opened just a few inches. Logan couldn't see who was on the other side. Jabayev began talking, again in Kazakh. Although he was speaking quietly, it was clear to Logan that he was irate. His head was bobbing and shaking, his hands gesticulating, his words coming out in a hiss.

After a few moments, he turned back to Logan.

'Okay, we can finish this later. We're going to move you to a cell. Someone will bring you some food and water before you go.'

And with that, Jabayev walked abruptly out of the room and the door shut behind him.

Logan's mind was still racing with the information he'd been told. Lena Belenov being killed was one thing, but what about Medvedev? Logan had never heard of him, but the Russians were claiming Logan had killed him. He could only guess that the FSB, the CIA, the JIA and maybe others were all at war with each other now. Which didn't bode well for any side. It especially didn't bode well for him, given that each of those agencies had something to gain from his capture.

A few minutes after Jabayev left the room, another man came in with the promised food and water. He didn't engage in conversation with Logan at all, just put what he had down on the table and left.

Logan ate the food – some stodgy bread and what Logan took to be a type of cheese – and drank the water, and after that he sat and waited until, eventually, he nodded off from boredom as much as tiredness. He awoke when the now-familiar buzz of the door's locking mechanism sounded out again. Logan wasn't sure how long he'd slept for, but he felt groggy and confused, like you only do when you've been roused from a deep sleep.

Jabayev walked back into the room and right up to Logan, who was confusedly opening and shutting his eyes, trying his best to fight off his sleepiness.

'Come on,' Jabayev said. 'It's time to go.'

Jabayev grabbed Logan's arm and pulled. Logan wearily stood up from the chair and Jabayev clasped a set of handcuffs over Logan's wrists. Logan didn't resist at all. It was hardly a surprise that they wanted to restrict his movement while they transferred him to a different location – Logan could only guess they were now heading to a cell for the night, as Jabayev had indicated earlier.

Jabayev tugged him forward as he walked toward the door. After exiting the interview room, the NSC agent ushered Logan down a short corridor. On either side of the corridor were plain wooden doors – no clues as to what lay behind them, but the building looked like some sort of office. Probably a simple out-post for the NSC that had a solitary interview room and one or two cells.

The corridor opened out into a small foyer. There was a desk in the corner and two sets of glass doors that led outside. It was dark out and Logan saw by the clock above the desk that it was ten p.m.

Jabayev walked Logan up to the desk and spoke to the man sitting behind it. Then, after a few moments, Jabayev began moving again and tugged on Logan's arm once more. They walked toward the double doors.

'Where are we going?' Logan asked, still confused but more alert and beginning to feel the first stirring of unease.

It was clear they weren't going to a cell. Jabayev was taking him out of the building. But to whom?

Jabayev didn't answer and Logan immediately began to plan a move. He wasn't going to be held prisoner by the NSC. And he equally wouldn't let them hand him over to another agency.

When they reached the first set of doors, Jabayev and Logan stopped. The doors wheezed open and they walked through. The doors then closed behind them.

'Jabayev, where are we going?'

Jabayev said nothing.

After a short pause, the outer doors slid open and Jabayev yanked on Logan's arm, pulling him out into the bitter night. Jabayev hadn't bothered returning Logan's overcoat to him and without it, the temperature was hellishly cold.

Logan spotted a four-by-four parked directly in front of the building, its engine idling.

It was clear to Logan why it was there.

He knew he had to act. He'd already figured out how he would take down Jabayev. The only question was how the occupants of the car would react and how many of them there were. But he couldn't really plan for that – he would just have to be ready.

He was about to commence his attack when Jabayev spoke.

'You're a lucky man, Carl Logan,' he said.

He let go of Logan's arm and reached into his pocket. Logan tensed, expecting Jabayev to be reaching for a weapon, but then relaxed again when he saw Jabayev's hand emerge holding a small, silvery object. Jabayev reached down and stuck the key into the lock on the cuff on Logan's left wrist and the clasp sprang open. He then did the same with the other.

Logan's mind was now a confused mess. Why was Jabayev un-cuffing him?

'It would seem you've got some friends in high places,' Jabayev said, sticking the handcuffs into his pocket.

The front passenger door of the four-by-four swung open and Logan stood wide-eyed when he saw who was inside.

'Come on, get in,' Fleming said. 'I'm letting all the heat out here.'

Fleming reached around and opened the rear passenger door. Logan saw Grainger sitting inside the car, on the opposite side. She was looking at him, her face deadpan.

'I hope I never have to see you again,' Jabayev said. 'I think that would be best for all concerned.' He turned around and headed back to the building.

You're a lucky man.

They were Jabayev's words to Logan, but Logan felt they were equally apt directed at the NSC agent. Another second and Logan would have taken him down for good. He had been sure the NSC were about to turn him in.

Logan didn't wait for a second invitation. He stepped forward and got into Fleming's car.

Chapter 31

'What the hell is going on, Fleming?' Logan said, after the car had pulled away. He wasn't sure whether his tone was one of irritation or relief. He was feeling both.

'What does it look like?' Fleming said. 'I just saved your skin.'

Fleming was in the front passenger seat. Butler was driving. Grainger was next to Logan.

He looked over at her.

'Are you okay?' he said.

'Yeah,' she said, sounding almost offended that he had asked. 'Though next time you have the bright idea to confront an unknown target, perhaps you could discuss it with me first.'

Logan couldn't help but smile at Grainger's angry response, which only made the scowl on her face deepen. If he'd wanted, he could have reminded her that it was her running toward the already tense stand-off outside Fleming's house that had led to the situation escalating, but he didn't feel it necessary to start a fight. The key thing was they were both safe.

'I'm glad you're all right,' Logan said.

'Well, I would have been even better if I'd not been locked in a cell for the last however many hours.'

'You were in a cell the whole time?' Logan asked.

'No. They spoke to me too. Interviewed me. They asked a lot of questions. None of it made any sense.'

'Yeah, I agree with you on that.'

'What do you mean? What did they say to you?'

'I'll tell you later,' Logan said, unsure quite where to start with the story of Belenov's and Medvedev's deaths and aware that Butler was eyeing him up in the rear-view mirror. Logan wasn't about to delve into his troubles with Butler and Fleming in earshot.

Grainger humphed and looked out of her passenger window.

'What happened?' Logan asked Fleming. 'How did you get us out?'

'I told you before – I have certain arrangements with the NSC. The arrangements I have work out very well for all parties. Neither side really want that to be jeopardised, especially by the likes of you. You're a problem, Logan, but you're not my problem and you're not the NSC's problem.'

Logan grunted, not sure whether he should be offended or not.

'Those agents outside my house very nearly compromised what we have going,' Fleming continued. 'They were acting way above their station, coming to my home. Just as well I only deal with the people at the top.'

'Thanks,' Logan said, and he genuinely meant it.

Butler caught Logan's gaze in the rear-view mirror and shook his head. Logan simply looked away, caring little about what Butler was thinking.

Logan knew Fleming and Butler were likely greasing the palms of the top brass at the NSC – anyone who really mattered, in fact – in return for their turning a blind eye to his dodgy business deals. But as wrong as Logan knew that was, he was glad Fleming had the leverage to get him out of the mess he'd been in. It was a far better situation than the NSC holding on to him while they awaited the highest bidder out of the FSB, the CIA and the JIA.

'Well, you certainly owe me one now,' Fleming said.

After pulling away from the building – which, it turned out, was on the outskirts of Aktobe – Butler drove straight for the nearest main carriageway. Logan didn't know where they were heading but he could tell from the city names on the road signs that they were travelling eastwards. Fleming's house lay to the north of Aktobe so they certainly weren't going back there.

'Where are we going?' Logan asked.

'Your release wasn't entirely unconditional,' Fleming said.

'So what's the condition?'

'You have to leave Kazakhstan. Immediately. They don't want you here. They don't want to admit you were *ever* here. They want you gone so they can wash their hands of you and get on with doing their jobs.'

By 'doing their jobs', Logan assumed Fleming meant taking back-handers off wealthy businessmen like himself in order to continue having momentary relapses about how they were supposed to be doing their jobs.

But just this once, Logan could live with that.

'That sounds good to me,' Logan said.

'To be honest, you're very fortunate I'm doing this for you. Other than maintaining the status quo, there's really not much benefit in my helping you. It's not like I'm going to see an upside.'

'I'm grateful, I really am,' Logan said. 'We both are.'

He turned to Grainger, but she was facing the other way, looking out of the window at the dark expanse beyond. If she was listening at all, she didn't show it.

'We're driving you to Astana,' Fleming said. 'It's a long way. I've got four of my men following us in the Jeep, just in case. I'm not expecting any resistance from the NSC now, but you can never be too careful in these parts.

'When we get to Astana, we'll get you onto a freight train to China. The arrangements with the border guards on this side are already taken care of. You'll just have to hope for the best on the other side. I've found they rarely do a thorough check on the cargo as long as the paperwork's in place, so I'm sure you'll be fine. It'll take you a few days to reach Beijing, but that's the final destination. I'm sure you can figure out what you want to do from there.'

'It's perfect,' Logan said.

As far as he was concerned, China was neutral territory. The CIA, the SVR, the JIA, none of them had any real power there. It would be about as safe as he and Grainger could get while he formulated a plan.

They carried on driving for a number of hours with little conversation. Both Fleming and Grainger fell asleep intermittently but Logan was now buzzing. Finally a plan was kicking into place.

He knew the route that Fleming had chosen was ideal. Much easier to hide on a mile-long freight train than try to cross the border in a car or by plane. The main train route between China and Kazakhstan formed part of the famous Silk Road. The trade route had first been established more than two thousand years ago in response to the emerging and lucrative trade of silk from China to countries in Central Asia, the Middle East and Europe. It had been used ever since for all manner of trade and as a travel route for linking merchants, pilgrims, monks, soldiers, nomads and urban dwellers alike.

It was close to two a.m. when Butler pulled the vehicle off the carriageway and into the car park of a roadside lodge, the first rest spot Logan had seen for a number of miles. Fleming and Grainger both stirred as Butler put on the brakes and the car slowed to a stop.

'We'll stay here for the night,' Butler said, turning around to Logan.

'Ah, we're here,' Fleming said, rubbing his eyes and looking out of his window. 'One of my usual stopovers. It's not the Ritz but it's better than a yurt, which is about the only other type of habitation you see out here. The rooms have bathrooms and running water – sheer luxury compared to other nearby offerings.'

Logan and the others got out of the car. As Logan closed his door, he turned to see the bright twin beams of the Jeep coming up behind. It pulled to a stop next to the four-by-four and the same four uniformed guards Logan had met the night before emerged. Fleming's own mini army.

'I'll go and sort the rooms,' Fleming said, then wandered off to the office.

Logan looked over at the building. It was a basic motel, a single storey with a row of about ten rooms. The structure looked to be timber. In the amber glow from the sporadic lighting in the car park, which cracked and blinked as if it were about to give out any second, the motel itself did at least appear to be in good condition. Logan noticed, though, that there were no other vehicles in the car park save for a battered old pickup truck parked near to the office.

Fleming trudged back across the empty tarmac a few minutes

later, by which point Logan was really beginning to feel the chill and was cupping his hands to his mouth to try to blow some warmth onto them.

'Three rooms,' he said, handing one key to Bulat and another to Logan. 'Maksat, Vassiliy, you're on guard to start with. Switch over at five. Logan and Grainger, you can share. Just remember, I'm armed, and so are all of my men.'

Logan raised an eyebrow at Fleming's words. He got the message loud and clear. Though he wasn't sure why Fleming had needed to bother with the warning. It was clear that Maksat and Vassiliy were guarding not only against any potential threats to Fleming but also to make sure that Logan and Grainger didn't try anything stupid – anything that would threaten Fleming's understanding with the NSC.

'We'll give you a knock in the morning when it's time to go,' Fleming added. 'If you need me before then, just tell one of the guys.'

And with that, everyone dispersed. Butler and Fleming headed off to the second of the lodge's rooms, near the office. Grainger and Logan were two doors down; Bulat and Ilya were in the next room.

Logan pushed the door open for Grainger, who walked past him into the room and turned the light on. As Logan followed behind, Grainger halted, looking at the double bed that took up the majority of the small space. Logan felt awkwardness emanating from her as he closed the door.

'I'll sleep on the floor if you want,' he said.

'That's not what I was thinking at all,' she said, spinning around and shooting him a glare.

'Then what's up?'

'Nothing,' she said.

She went over and sat down on the bed.

Logan scanned the room. It was clearly a new-build motel and everything was in good order, but the furniture, fittings and fixtures were neutral and basic and lacking in any kind of creative design. It was just bland. Logan could see why it suited Fleming.

'What did the NSC say to you?' Grainger said.

'That I'm a wanted man in Russia,' Logan answered, closing the thin curtains.

'I guess you knew that already.'

'Except now I'm being set up for things I didn't even do.'

Logan turned around, away from the window. Grainger put her head in her hands.

'Are you sure you're okay?' Logan said.

'Yes. I'm fine,' Grainger responded, looking up again. But the resolve on her face quickly evaporated. 'I mean, it wasn't bad – they didn't hurt me or anything like that. But I was scared, Carl.'

'What did you tell them?'

'Nothing. I didn't say a word. Even if I'd known what they were talking about, I wouldn't have done. I get the impression that you're used to dealing with this, with running from your enemies, with being locked up, with being questioned and inter-rogated. But I'm just not. I've had training, sure, but this?'

'It'll soon be over,' Logan reassured her.

'How do you figure that? They're not going to stop coming after us.'

'We'll stop them.'

Grainger shook her head. 'The woman who was murdered–'

'Lena Belenov,' Logan said.

'Who was she? They showed me a picture of her. She was beautiful.'

Logan felt his cheeks blush; he wasn't entirely sure why. Did Grainger think that he and Lena had been an item? That couldn't have been further from the truth.

'She was a snake. She deserved to die,' Logan said. 'My only regret is that I wasn't the one to end her days.' He saw just a sliver of colour return to Grainger's face at his words.

'I thought that … maybe–'

'No. Nothing like that.'

'I thought that's why they were trying to pin her death on you. To rub salt into open wounds.'

'No. I'll not mourn her death for a second. She used me to have Mackie killed.'

'Oh,' was Grainger's simple response. Logan could tell she was wondering whether or not to carry on down that line of question-ing. In the end, she didn't. 'And what about the other agent?' she said.

'Nikolai Medvedev. I've never heard of him.'

'Just what is happening, Carl?'

'I don't know. It doesn't smell right, though. Agents on all sides lost their lives in me tracking you down. But there's been no public announcement about any of that. Then all of a sudden this?'

'The Russians are setting you up.'

'I know. And not for the first time.'

'But the biggest question is: why were Belenov and Medvedev killed at all?'

'And by whom?'

'Exactly.'

Logan took off his boots and went over and sat down on the bed next to Grainger. He looked over at her tired face and felt a pang in his heart.

'What did the Russians do to you?' she asked him. 'You haven't told me.'

'I'd rather not,' Logan said. 'I was a prisoner for three months.'

'But you got out?'

'I escaped. To find that my own people, Mackie included, didn't trust me anymore. Then the Russians had him killed, making it look like I did it.'

'I'm so sorry, Carl.'

'Yeah. Me too. It's done with now. Whatever chaos there is to wade through, it's better than being held prisoner in that place. I'm never going back to that.'

'And yet I bet that's exactly what you thought was happening when the NSC took us.'

She was right. It was. Logan had told himself he would never be taken prisoner again – he couldn't go back to the torture and abuse he'd suffered at the hands of the Russians, at the hands of Lena. And yet he'd barely put up a fight when the NSC had taken him in. He knew the answer to that one, though. Grainger. He'd been trying to protect Grainger. If he'd fought back against the NSC outside Fleming's home, there was a very real chance they would have shot her.

'Angela, when I came for you, it was because I had to know.'

'Not this again,' Grainger said.

Logan ignored her.

'When you left me, back in America, I was in turmoil. I wasn't sure whether I wanted to kill you or love you. I was bitter and I wanted to get my own back on you.'

'Carl, this really isn't the time.'

'Yes, it is. Because I'm only doing this because when I heard what was going to happen to you, how the CIA were planning to kill you, I knew I had to stop it. I don't want to think about whether it's right or wrong. It's just the way it is.'

'I should never have shot you,' Grainger said, turning away from him. 'I should have shot myself. Ended it there and then. Then none of this would ever have happened. The damage was already done. By shooting you and going on the run, all I've done is prolong my misery. And yours.'

Logan felt a gnawing sorrow at her heartfelt words.

'What I'm trying to say,' he added, 'is that I'm only doing this if we're in it together. This is me and you versus everyone else. But I need you to believe it too. I need to see the real you again. Because that Angela would do whatever it takes to get through this.'

She turned back to face him. Her face was teary, but in her bloodshot eyes he saw a certain resolve still there, a strength. The real Angela. The one he'd fallen for.

She moved toward him, taking him completely by surprise, and planted her soft lips onto his. It took a few seconds for his stiff body to relax, but when it did, he slowly began to kiss her back. After a few moments, they both fell back onto the bed, each gripping the other tightly.

'I'm in this with you,' Grainger said, pulling away from him for just a second.

'Then let's finish this together,' he said.

Chapter 32

London, England

From the comfort of the sumptuous white leather sofa, Lindegaard inspected John Sanderson's handsome drawing room. At least that was what Sanderson had called this room. To Lindegaard, it was simply a lounge. There were no drawing implements in there at all. Even if there were, Lindegaard would have simply called the room a studio. What the hell was a drawing room?

Sanderson, a lifelong MI6 agent and fellow member of the JIA committee, had invited Lindegaard over to his extravagant Georgian townhouse to discuss various matters before a planned committee meeting the following day. Though both men knew there was one matter that would likely dominate proceedings in the morning: Carl Logan.

It wasn't the first time Lindegaard had been to Sanderson's home, and on each visit he couldn't help but feel a puerile envy of his counterpart. Sanderson was close to fifteen years older than Lindegaard, but with his wrinkled features, wispy, balding head and out-of-shape body, he probably looked twenty-five years older. Lindegaard liked to keep himself in shape; he got extreme satisfaction from knowing that he looked and felt as strong and fit as he had at thirty. But although Lindegaard knew he was a far more impressive specimen of a man physically, he was insanely jealous of Sanderson's home.

Sanderson had fifteen years of additional wealth on Lindegaard, but even his extra years couldn't explain the money that was surely required to buy and furnish such a top-end London property. Lindegaard knew Sanderson had come from a well-to-do family and some of his wealth had been passed down to him, but he also had the sneaking suspicion that Sanderson was much better remunerated for his services to MI6 and the JIA than Lindegaard was likewise for his services to the CIA and the JIA. And that really irked him.

Sure, Lindegaard had a comfortable life. He owned two properties – one a modern apartment in Washington that was commutable to the CIA headquarters in nearby Langley, and the other the family home that was set in three acres of land in rural Georgia. But he doubted those two properties combined were worth even half of what Sanderson had paid for his London home.

Sanderson came back over from the mahogany dresser carrying two tumblers of Scotch, one neat, the other for Lindegaard with ice.

'Is the lovely Susan not here tonight?' Lindegaard said as Sanderson took a seat on the matching armchair adjacent to where Lindegaard was sitting.

'No. She's staying with my son and his wife for a few days at our place in the Cotswolds.'

Lindegaard breathed out into his whisky glass, trying to suppress his reaction. The fumes of the spirit caught in his nose and made his eyes water. Sanderson having just the townhouse had been enough to get Lindegaard's envy racing, but he had never known Sanderson had more than one home.

'I really love what you've done with the place,' Lindegaard lied, referring to the fact that Sanderson had recently redecorated the room they were in and most of the downstairs. It was gaudy and monstrously over the top as far as Lindegaard was concerned.

'Thanks. It's Susan's work, really. I just pay for it.'

'Ha, yeah, I know how that feels.'

The two men sat in silence for a few moments. Despite working together closely, they had little in common. Although Sanderson had invited Lindegaard to his home, there was as ever only brief chat between the two stalwarts. Lindegaard really had very little to say to the man.

'Shall we get down to business?' Sanderson said, breaking the increasingly awkward silence.

'We probably should.'

'So what's the latest?'

'I've been keeping on top of Winter,' Lindegaard said. 'If you ask me, he's too far out of his depth now.'

'I'm starting to come to that conclusion too. Putting him in charge of Mackie's agents was a necessary step, but it was only intended to be temporary. It's not too late to move him back down a rung to where he was.'

'Well, I definitely agree he should be removed from a commander position,' Lindegaard agreed. 'My concern, though, is whether he's even suitable for an assistant role now, given everything that's happened.'

Sanderson frowned and stared over at Lindegaard. 'He's an excellent prospect, Jay. Probably the best up-and-coming commander we have. I just think it's too soon for him. Get rid of him altogether? Are you sure?'

Lindegaard huffed. 'Maybe,' he said. 'Let's keep that one on the back-burner. We can come back to it.'

'Fair enough. So what about our two missing agents, Logan and Evans? Is there any news at all?'

'Nothing that I've been made aware of.'

'Logan I can understand. He was trained to live off the grid, after all. But Evans? Why haven't the Russians made contact? I've never known a foreign agent be captured before and a deal not be offered, or at the very least an acknowledgment from the other side as to what's happened.'

'It's a worry for Evans. That's for sure. But I don't think we should underestimate just how much damage Logan's escapade has done to relations.'

'Maybe you're right. What we need is to get access to someone on the inside, at the FSB, to see whether we can find out what's really happening.'

'Do you have any candidates?'

'On our side or at the FSB?'

'Either.'

'Yes, actually,' Sanderson said.

He leaned forward in his seat, glancing around the room as though checking for eavesdroppers.

Silly old fool, Lindegaard thought.

'I understand the JIA has a potential sleeper,' Sanderson said, his voice quieter than it had been before.

Lindegaard raised an eyebrow and almost spat out his whisky. 'We do?'

Sanderson shifted in his seat, as though uncomfortable about the information he was relaying.

'The wife of one of the FSB's deputy directors,' he said.

Lindegaard's mouth opened wide, but no sound came out. He was genuinely shocked by Sanderson's disclosure. The deputy directors of the FSB were the cream of the crop – only two pay grades removed from the overall director. Having a sleeper not just in bed with but married to such a senior official was an incredible coup.

More than anything, Lindegaard was concerned that he had known nothing about this. Immediately, he began thinking through what damage a sleeper agent in such a position could mean for himself.

'What's her name?' Lindegaard said.

'I don't know,' Sanderson responded. Lindegaard wasn't sure he believed him. 'This is about as big as it gets, Jay. If the FSB found out about her, can you imagine what damage it would do to our credibility?'

'We have to try to use her,' Lindegaard said, even though in reality it was the last thing he wanted to happen. 'Has she been activated yet?'

'As far as I'm aware, no. Never, in fact.'

'Who's her handler?'

'I understand it was Mackie,' Sanderson said. 'He was the only one to have ever dealt with her. She's been in place for years. To be honest, I don't even know if she'd be reliable anymore.'

'But she could still be a way back into what's happening at the FSB.'

'Yes, she could be. We need to discuss this with Winter tomorrow. He's the only one who has access to Mackie's files.'

'No. Let's not bring that up tomorrow,' Lindegaard said, his cunning mind in full swing. 'Let's see what Winter has to offer us first. Like you said, this is big. We don't want the wrong person to activate that sleeper. If you ask me, it'd be better for all concerned to remove Winter first and take it from there.'

'He may already know who she is, though,' Sanderson said. 'We need to find out what he knows.'

'Let me handle that,' Lindegaard said, struggling to hide a smile. 'John, if you'll excuse me, please could I use your restroom?'

'Of course. You know where it is, right?'

'Yeah,' Lindegaard said, putting his whisky down.

He got to his feet and headed out of the room, his head spinning with thoughts. The sleeper agent was a real revelation. And one that could cause untold damage to his plans if the JIA were in contact with her without his knowing. He couldn't let that happen. The radio silence between the FSB and the outside world was essential to keeping his dirty deeds in the dark and his plan on track.

When Lindegaard returned from the toilet, Sanderson was still in the armchair, facing away. Lindegaard stopped and studied a picture on the wall, a floral landscape where two bright bumblebees were feeding. Lindegaard hated it. It was garish and crudely drawn. It fitted the rest of the horrific furnishings perfectly. He guessed that nonetheless it had probably cost a small fortune.

'In many respects, I find the life of the bumblebee to be quite sad,' Lindegaard said after a few moments, moving away from the picture as he spoke.

Sanderson turned around in his chair, a quizzical look on his face. 'You do?'

'I just feel they got the rough end of the stick, so to speak,' Lindegaard said. 'The bumblebee is bigger, stronger than its counterpart, the honeybee. It's more visually eye-catching too – its colours more vivid. Overall, you'd say it was a superior being.'

'You could say that.'

'And yet it has so many apparent flaws compared to the noble honeybee. Particularly in the eyes of us humans.'

'How so?'

'Well, comparatively they're loners, their colonies significantly smaller. They don't reproduce quickly, which is one reason they struggle to maintain a nest for more than one season. They do make honey of course, but their workers are just lazy. I mean, have you ever heard of anyone selling bumblebee honey? No, because they can't make it as quickly or in as sufficient volume as those damned honeybees that congregate in their thousands and work all the hours God sends.'

'Very interesting stuff, Jay,' Sanderson said, getting to his feet and walking back over to the dresser to pour himself some more whisky.

'No, John, it really is,' Lindegaard said, more enthused now. 'Because for all its apparent flaws, you shouldn't underestimate the bumblebee. You know, the honeybee might characterise China or India or some such place. Endless drones, monotonous workers producing all the products you could ever need. Cheap labour. But what kind of life is that?'

'Do you want another one or not?' Sanderson said, shaking his empty glass.

'Yes, please,' Lindegaard said, grabbing his glass and moving over toward Sanderson.

He downed the remainder of the whisky in his tumbler and handed it to Sanderson, who poured them both another large measure before placing the bottle back into the dresser next to the vast array of other expensive-looking drinks.

'It's a novel way of looking at the life of the bee,' Sanderson said, sounding just a little condescending.

'It is, John. You're right. But to get to the point, the bumble-bee, you see, is still the king. Because it is bigger, it is stronger. It is the superior being.'

'That was your point?'

'No, John. The point is, I'm more like the bumblebee. And you're not.'

Lindegaard lunged forward toward Sanderson, who still had his back turned, and coiled his thick right arm around his colleague's neck. Sanderson squirmed and dropped the whisky glasses, which crashed to the floor. The amber liquid splashed onto the bottom of Lindegaard's trousers, angering him and making him pull harder on his arm; he used his left hand to pull the vice-like grip tighter.

Sanderson squirmed pathetically and Lindegaard pulled and squeezed as hard as he could, gritting his teeth almost in a smile as he did so. Sanderson bucked and wheezed but he had no chance.

In the end, it wasn't even a contest. Sanderson was old and soft and tired. Lindegaard still felt as strong and fit as he'd been at thirty.

Yes, he really was the superior specimen, he thought, as he happily choked the life out of the older man.

Just a few moments later, Sanderson's body finally went limp. Lindegaard released his grip and the lifeless body of the MI6 agent slumped to the floor.

Chapter 33

Akmola Province, Kazakhstan

Logan was already awake when he heard loud chattering outside the motel room door. He'd woken a few minutes earlier, a result of the light rays seeping in through the thin curtains and the noise of cars, vans and articulated lorries blasting past on the nearby road. He and Grainger were in bed together, her warm, naked body still gently wrapped around his.

When the knock on the door came, Grainger stirred, shifted off Logan and turned over to face the other way.

Logan got off the bed and walked to the door.

'Yeah?'

'Twenty minutes,' he heard Butler say from the other side.

'Got it.'

He went around the bed and kneeled down next to Grainger, pushing the hair that was covering her face away and tucking it behind her ear.

'Come on,' he said. 'Let's get a shower before we head out.'

Grainger groaned and opened her eyes, then smiled at him and Logan felt a burst of light inside him.

The two of them showered together, the mood between them infinitely more relaxed and natural than it had been over the previous few days. It seemed that resolve he'd seen in her eyes was finally breaking through.

After they'd dried and dressed themselves, they headed outside where Fleming and his men were already hanging around the two cars, chatting and smoking.

Logan shivered as the cold air hit him. He still didn't have a replacement coat and he could feel the temperature was some way below freezing. There had been a fresh smattering of snow overnight, just a half inch or so, but no attempt by anyone to move the snow from the car park area. The soft powder underfoot crunched under Logan's weight, his boots leaving perfect imprints.

The smell of fried meat in the air was rich above the cloud of diesel fumes from the carriageway. There was no restaurant or cafe on the site, but Logan wondered whether Fleming and his men had nonetheless been treated to breakfast by the motel owner. He and Grainger certainly hadn't received the invite if that were the case.

Butler said something to Fleming as Logan and Grainger approached and the two men started snickering childishly.

'Did you have a nice evening?' Fleming said.

'Those curtains are pretty thin, you know,' Butler taunted as Logan reached them.

Logan launched himself toward Butler, ready to wipe the grin off his ugly face, but Grainger grabbed his arm and pulled him back.

'It's okay, Carl. Leave it.'

Logan huffed and shook himself down.

Fleming raised an eyebrow. 'You're a touchy fellow, Logan.' He shook his head and turned to get into the car.

Butler cackled. 'Yeah. Very touchy.' He winked over at Grainger.

Logan did his best not to rise to the bait, though it took everything he had not to hurl himself at Butler.

'Come on, we've got a long day ahead of us,' Fleming said. 'Grab some food and drink of the boot before you get in.'

Butler was still grinning and he kept eye contact as he walked past Logan around to the driver's side of the car. The four Kazakhs made their way to the Jeep, talking among themselves, their own little clique, seemingly oblivious to all around them except when Fleming barked an order.

Grainger and Logan went to the boot of the car to see what supplies were there. Fleming certainly hadn't packed lightly. In the boot were three large cool boxes filled with all manner of fresh food, snacks and soft drinks. But what caught Logan's attention most was something else: weapons. Two assault rifles. Two sub-machine guns. Utility belts. Helmets, visors, night-vision goggles.

Grainger and Logan looked at each other, alarmed at the mini armoury, but said nothing. Logan wasn't sure whether the array of arms that Fleming was carrying made him feel more secure or just more suspicious.

And if all that was for just Fleming and Butler, what was in the Jeep?

After helping themselves to food, Logan got into the back of the car, behind Fleming. Grainger got in behind Butler. Then they were on the move again.

The journey, like the previous day, was long and boring. The scenery outside – vast wild steppes covered in snow and bathed in sumptuous sunlight – was initially breathtaking due to its vastness but was eventually entirely monotonous. Given Logan's own experiences with Fleming in the Scottish Highlands, and more recently in the frozen wastelands of Siberia, it was hard for him not to look upon the view as sinister and foreboding. And yet, at least this time he was safe and warm. Well, he was warm. He wasn't entirely convinced of the former.

There was little conversation between the four along the way. Fleming and Butler swapped positions twice during the long drive, giving the other a chance to sleep. Logan and Grainger also both took the opportunity to nod off.

'It certainly is a big country,' Grainger said to no one in particular as she stared at the desolate view a few moments after waking from a nap.

'There're some pretty spectacular sights actually,' Fleming said. 'Waterfalls, canyons, lakes, mountains. It's a beautiful country.'

'Just not in this part,' Butler added.

'And it's definitely not the best time of year to see it,' Fleming conceded.

He spoke as though he had a true fondness for the place, which Logan struggled to comprehend.

They drove on until the early evening. The clouds had pulled in during the afternoon, making the landscape outside appear to be an endless grey and causing the atmosphere in the car to seem all the chillier.

Logan had seen from the last road sign that Astana was now only a hundred miles away.

'We need to take a quick detour,' Fleming said. He was back in the passenger seat. 'One of the base stations we're running is out here. I've not been in a few weeks, so I want to make sure my guys are doing what they should be. We've got a few hours spare anyway and it'll only take a few minutes.'

Logan grunted in agreement.

Not long after that, they pulled off the main road and headed down a less-well-used track. They continued for close to twenty minutes before there was any sign of life at all. Then, in the distance, the base station came into view.

Small brick buildings, each only a single storey, were spread in an uneven cluster. Overground metal pipes of various sizes – some only a few inches thick, others more than a foot in diameter – snaked around the buildings and in and out of the ground. All around the complex was a wire fence, about ten feet tall, with balls of barbed wire at the top.

'What is this place?' Logan asked.

'It's a compressor station for Kazakhstan's main gas pipeline,' Fleming said. 'I supply security for all of the stations on the line, right across the country. It really is a feat of engineering. The pipeline stretches over a thousand miles across Kazakhstan and into China.'

'Sounds like a good deal for the Chinese,' Logan said. 'Easy access to one of the world's largest gas sources. But what do the locals get from it?'

'Don't be so cynical. The Chinese bring a lot of investment here. Granted, there's some ill feeling toward them having their fingers in every pie, but the Kazakhs could never have got these projects off the ground without outside help.'

Logan was sure Fleming was at least partly right. The outside investment into the country was certainly generating a lot of wealth. Just look at Fleming. The problem, as was the case in nearly all resource-rich nations, was that it brought real wealth only to the few.

'This should only take a couple of minutes,' Fleming said as they neared the outer gates to the complex.

Logan peered out of the front window. They were now only a hundred or so yards away.

'This place doesn't look like it's been used in years,' he said, feeling a hint of suspicion.

Logan could see two armed men at the gates to the complex, dressed in uniforms very much like Fleming's other guards. But he could also see now that the buildings were in some disrepair. Parts of the pipes around them had cracked and fallen from the struts holding them above the ground. Doors and windows were intermittently boarded up or just worn and old.

Fleming shrugged. 'I don't argue the toss about what goes on here or any other place. I just provide the security.'

The gates to the complex were open and Butler drove the car through, past the two armed guards, then parked on the opposite side of the open central area to where two other cars were already parked – a silver saloon whose make Logan didn't recognise and a white Toyota Land Cruiser.

'Come on, let's get this over and done with,' Fleming said, opening his door. 'Grainger, Logan, this'll be the last stop we make before Astana, so feel free to stretch your legs.'

Logan looked over at Grainger, who shrugged. Then they both went for their door handles. It had been four hours since their last stop, so this was a good chance to get out and get their legs moving.

Butler stepped from the car and made his way around to the boot. As Logan got out, his eyes followed Fleming as he made his way toward the two parked cars. When he was about midway, the driver's door of the Land Cruiser opened and a man stepped out. He was wearing a uniform much like Fleming's Kazakh house guards were. He casually walked up to Fleming and the two began a quiet conversation.

Logan looked over the car to Grainger. She was standing by her open door, stretching her arms in the air. Logan heard the sound of crunching gravel and snow as the Jeep carrying Fleming's other men arrived. It pulled to a stop right next to Grainger.

In front of him, Logan continued to spy on Fleming and the man. He couldn't hear their conversation but his mind was now racing. He looked over at the parked cars, then at Fleming and the man. Then at the two armed men by the gates. Then over to the Jeep, which the other guards were just getting out of.

Something wasn't right. The whole set-up here wasn't right. Logan was staring over toward Fleming, trying to figure out what it was he didn't like, when the front passenger door of the Land Cruiser opened and another man stepped out, this one dressed in casual clothes: boots, jeans, a thick puffer jacket. He was tall and thin and young.

Logan glanced at him, then back at Fleming.

His heart was already thumping in his chest when the face of the man who'd just emerged from the Land Cruiser clicked into place. Logan shot his gaze back to the man. Logan had seen him before. More than that, Logan knew him.

Fleming had set him up.

He was turning Logan in.

Because the man who'd just got out of the car was nothing to do with Fleming's business. He was a JIA agent. Paul Evans.

Chapter 34

Logan heard the boot to the car slam shut and was about to turn around to Butler when he felt a cold pressure against his neck. The barrel of a gun. Like a switch had been flicked, Logan was filled with unabashed fury.

'Don't even think about it,' Butler said when Logan flinched.

Logan cursed himself for having been so easily foxed. Fleming turned around to meet his gaze. Evans too was looking at him.

'Logan, no funny business now,' Fleming shouted over. 'Let's just get this done quickly and quietly.'

Logan said nothing but he was fuming, his nostrils flaring with each angry breath. He looked over the car to Grainger. She was staring at him, two of Fleming's guards crowding around her. She gave Logan a questioning look, as though asking what she should do next. He gave her the slightest of nods.

Evans walked forward.

'Winter sent me, Logan. There's no need to be alarmed. We know what's happening. We're going to help you.'

But Logan wasn't really listening. For days, he'd struggled to keep hold of his anger. He'd done his best to ignore Butler's many gibes and knowing looks. This time Logan knew it was a struggle he could no longer win. Fleming and Butler's latest betrayal was a step too far.

Logan ducked down, away from the gun barrel, acting on pure impulse, no longer caring about potential consequences. He spun around, throwing his balled right fist up into Butler's jaw. Logan's whole body leaped up at the same time, the momentum of more than two hundred pounds of weight smacking into Butler's chin. The shot was sweet, perfect contact, enough to knock out most men. But Butler was tough. His head snapped back but he didn't fall, didn't buckle.

Logan kicked out against Butler's hand, which was gripping one of the MP5 sub-machine guns that had been in the back of the car. The kick was good. Enough to see the gun fly from Butler's grip. The ex-soldier lunged at Logan, ready to counter any further attack.

As Butler came forward, Logan sent a right hook into his foe's head. Then a quick left jab into the already injured nose, then another hit with his right hand, this one full force. And then, with Butler stumbling backward, trying his best to shake himself off and regain his composure, it took just one more left fist to the nose to knock Butler to the ground.

But Logan wasn't quite finished yet. Butler groaned and rolled his head. His face was bloodied. His nose shattered. His eyes were defeated. He caught Logan's stare for just a second before Logan sent a crashing boot onto Butler's already pummelled face.

'Enough!' Fleming bellowed. 'That's enough!'

Logan, snarling, panting, spun around, his fists still balled, looking for his next target. His body was hunched over, knees bent, like a wrestler about to grapple with his opponent.

But when he saw Grainger in front of him, he suddenly straightened up and unclenched his fists. Grainger, her nose bloodied, was standing over by Fleming. Maksat, the giant, had one arm tightly around her neck. He was leaning back, pulling her up, her feet barely touching the ground. In his other hand was a gun, pointed at her head. Bulat stood a yard away, an assault rifle held high, its barrel also pointed at Grainger.

In those few moments of madness, Logan had been so consumed with inflicting pain on Butler that he'd not once thought of Grainger. He'd hoped she would have put up a fight, but had he really expected her to take on Fleming's guards on her own, unarmed? He'd done exactly what he'd been trained not to do all those years ago: he'd fought with anger, resentment. He'd lost control. And despite the predicament that he and Grainger were in, he knew he wasn't far from losing it again.

'Just who the hell do you think you are?' Fleming said, striding up to Logan.

As Logan readied himself to take on Fleming, he was taken by surprise when arms grasped him from behind. They wrapped around him, squeezing, gripping like a vice. Ilya or Vassiliy, Logan assumed.

'If you've killed him, I'm going to end your days,' Fleming said, lining up to take a shot at Logan.

Logan wasn't finished, though. He wasn't going to take any more shit from Fleming. As the ex-soldier came within striking distance, Logan lifted his legs in the air and, using the weight of the guard behind him like a springboard, he kicked out. His feet collided with Fleming's stomach, causing him to double over.

Logan slipped out of the grip, spun around and took two steps away to give him space from Fleming and whoever had grabbed him. As he looked up, he saw it was Ilya.

Fleming straightened up and the three men faced off. But after a second, Fleming's body relaxed.

'Just go,' he said. 'I'm not losing any men over this.'

'You set me up, you piece of shit.'

'What did you expect me to do?'

'Help me.'

'And why would I do that?'

'Why did you even bother to get us away from the NSC?'

'I'm a businessman, Logan. This was simply business. I wasn't lying when I said I didn't want my relationship with the NSC to suffer. So I went with the best deal. As nice as it would have been to get one over on the CIA by helping you – and I really do despise those snakes – what you were offering just didn't cut it.'

Fleming turned around and walked over to Butler, who hadn't moved an inch since Logan felled him. Logan was both surprised and disappointed that Fleming had found the strength to walk away from the fight. Business. That's what Fleming had said. It was just business to him. To Logan, it was so much more.

'Come on, Logan,' Evans said, putting a hand on Logan's shoulder. 'Let's get out of here. I'm here to help you.'

'Like hell you are,' Logan said, brushing him off.

'Believe what you want. But do I look like a threat?' he said, holding his hands in the air. 'It's not my men who are pointing guns at you and Grainger.'

'Let her go,' Logan said, glaring over at Maksat.

The guard flicked his eyes this way and that, waiting for someone else to give him an instruction.

'Just do it,' Evans shouted. 'The deal's been done now. You can all go home.'

Maksat waited just a couple more seconds but then released his grip on Grainger. She dropped down to the ground, nursing her neck. Bulat too lowered his gun, then the two guards began to slowly, cautiously, back away.

Logan walked to Grainger and pulled her back up to her feet. She wrapped her arms around him.

'Come on then,' Logan said to Evans.

Evans and his companion turned and began to walk back over to their vehicles. As Logan and Grainger followed, Logan looked over his shoulder at Fleming. He was still kneeling by Butler, who was now sitting up but looked completely out of it. A part of Logan was disappointed that Butler had been able to get up at all. And he wished he'd had one real shot at Fleming. Just one chance to fell that treacherous shit.

'You two can ride in the Land Cruiser,' Evans said. 'With me and Mason.' Evans nodded to the man they were walking with. 'The other two will follow us.'

'Where are we going?' Logan said.

'Let's just get out of here first. Before Captain Fleming has a change of heart. If he wanted to, he could kill us all and bury us out here. And you're not exactly winning him over by trying to kill his friends.'

Evans had a point. With Fleming's arsenal, it wouldn't be too difficult for him to finish everyone else off. And Logan had certainly provoked him into a fight. Evans had three men with him, only two of whom appeared to be armed. Fleming had himself and five other armed men, all skilled fighters.

Logan certainly didn't want to hang around any longer.

But he also had no intention of going anywhere with Evans, regardless of whether he was there to help or not.

As they drew nearer to the driver's side of the Land Cruiser, the man Evans had called Mason took a set of keys from his pocket.

'You get in this side,' Logan said to Grainger.

He looked over at her as he spoke and gave her a look that he hoped she'd understand. The slight nod she gave him told him she had.

Mason went to open the driver's door. Grainger stopped in her tracks.

Logan looked over at Evans, who stopped just as he reached the car and turned to the two men standing at the gate, who still had their guns at the ready.

'Wait for us to pass, then follow us out,' Evans shouted over to them.

As Evans turned back around, he was completely unprepared for Logan's attack.

Logan lunged at him, grabbed Evans's jacket at chest height and pulled him in. He sent a bone-splitting head-butt into the crown of Evans's nose. The loud crack from the ferocious blow seemed to echo off into the distance. Evans crumpled toward the ground. Before his body had even hit the deck, Grainger grabbed Mason from behind and twisted his left arm behind his back into a hammerlock. The man initially squirmed and cried out, but soon became placid when Grainger pushed the shoulder to bursting point.

'The keys,' Grainger said.

Mason groaned and held out the keys in his other hand. Logan grabbed them off him. Grainger delivered a flat-palmed smack to the base of Mason's neck that sent him to the ground. Logan raced over to the driver's door of the Land Cruiser. He dived into the seat, sank the keys into the ignition and fired up the engine as Grainger jumped in the back. He was reversing out of the spot before either Evans or his companion had even stirred.

Logan shoved the automatic gear box into drive, then slammed shut his door and pressed down as hard as he could on the accelerator. The car shot forward. The tyres initially skidded on the icy surface, but the four-wheel-drive mechanism did its job and ultimately kept traction.

The two guards at the gate barely had enough time to get themselves into firing position as the Land Cruiser swept past them. Fleming and his men seemed almost oblivious to the proceedings. Perhaps they felt it was no longer their fight.

Evans's two men let out a volley of fire, but it was clear they were aiming for the tyres rather than Logan or Grainger; the barrels of their guns were pointed low. It was only through sheer luck, or perhaps the fact the guards had been taken by surprise, that all four tyres remained intact as Logan steered the Land Cruiser away and sped down the track back toward the motorway.

PART 4

Chinks in the armour

Chapter 35

The rocky precipice that Logan was hunched behind rose eight hundred feet above the area below. The base of the rock was twelve hundred yards from the small village that lay to the north. Logan eyeballed the largest of the residential units in the village, at the far northern tip of the small enclave, through the scope of his rifle.

It was four in the afternoon and the dazzling sun in the azure sky was behind Logan and off to the west, casting a clear glow onto the buildings below without causing any glare. The light and the conditions were perfect.

Logan pulled the rifle left and right as he moved his sight around the grounds of the sprawling building complex, noting and memorising everything about the layout. There was nobody home. The building was derelict. It had been for months. Since the demise of the local businessman who had owned it, much of the village had become empty, the closest and easiest line of work gone. But while nobody lived there anymore, Logan knew the once-grand home wouldn't be empty for much longer.

Logan took his gaze away from the scope and looked up at the sky, the fierce sun making his face sting. He held the rifle up to his chest, caressing the warm metal, preparing himself. To anyone watching, it would seem as if he were in prayer. But Logan wasn't religious, never had been.

When Logan was a child, moving from foster home to foster

home, he'd always been fascinated by the sky. His upbringing had been rough – no real family, no siblings, no one who'd sincerely cared for him or for whom he'd cared. Whenever he had felt small or lonely or lost, he would look up at the sky, gazing at the vast nothingness in the day, counting and mapping the bright stars at night, all the time wondering what life was up there.

When he was twelve years old, he'd used his meagre savings to buy a battered old telescope, trying to bring himself closer to the galaxy that lay around him and the distant stars, planets and galaxies beyond. His foster brothers and sisters had taunted him over it. In fact, he'd been outright bullied. In the end, a grotesque boy by the name of Darren, who was three years older than Logan and at least twice his size, had smashed the telescope to pieces with the heel of his boot, for no reason other than that he took great satisfaction from hurting others.

Through his teen years, Logan had kept his fondness for the sky and for dreaming about what was out there. But as he'd grown up, Logan had never found any answers to what life lay beyond the misery of his existence on earth. He no longer wondered what kind of life was out there, up in the sky. Yet the ritual he'd developed remained – a homage to the person he used to be. Now it had become easy to find the life that lay at the end of his lens.

And it was just as easy to take that life away.

He looked at his watch again and then got himself back into position. Just a few moments later, an open-topped Jeep came careening around a corner – a small dust cloud billowing out behind it – and entered the building complex through the broken and open main gates. Its movement was entirely silent to Logan from his distant perch.

A few seconds later, it came to a halt and he spotted the target exiting the vehicle, his small, slight frame and his flowing black hair unmistakable. He had on a pair of aviator sunglasses that covered most of his face but Logan was certain it was his man.

The target walked a few yards from the vehicle to a rickety old bench. A few moments later, as Logan scanned the area, he caught sight of a trail bike weaving its way through the quiet, dusty streets of the village. It pulled into the gates of the large property and the driver parked, stepped off and strode over to the target, who was now on his feet.

Logan glanced down at his watch again. Bang on time. But as he looked back into his scope, he saw the driver remove the helmet and his feeling of quiet satisfaction was quickly shattered when he saw long, wavy, glistening hair – it was a woman. She walked right up to the target and the two exchanged a warm embrace – not lovers, but the contact between the two suggested they were more than business acquaintances, Logan thought.

He quickly lowered the rifle and picked up the telephoto lens that he'd laid at his side. He zoomed in as far as the lens would allow and began to snap away as the target and woman began a slow saunter around the grounds.

Logan's instruction had been simple, but the unexpected turn had flummoxed him. He had known the time and location of the target's meeting, but the intel had suggested the rendezvous was with a representative from Colombia's largest drug cartel.

The cartels in Venezuela manufactured little cocaine of their own but transported vast quantities of Colombian drugs across their country en route to the US and Europe. Disrupting the Venezuelan cartels, which was the JIA's aim and Logan's job, would not only damage the Colombian cartels' supply chain but also provide a great deal of useful intelligence about the operations of the drug barons and their extensive armies.

But this woman wasn't part of that, surely? She certainly didn't look like any cartel rep Logan had ever seen. He'd been neck deep in intelligence on the key movers and shakers for weeks and had never come across her face before.

Satisfied with the clarity of the pictures, Logan dropped the camera and picked up the rifle again, then peered down the scope and followed the man and woman as they meandered for a while, deep in conversation. They sat on the bench and after a few moments, the target reached into his jacket and pulled out a large envelope, which he handed to the woman. She took it and placed it on her lap without opening it.

'Shit,' Logan said.

He reached down and pulled the mobile phone from his pocket and dialled the number for his boss, Mackie.

'Is it done?' Mackie said without any pleasantries.

'We may have a problem,' Logan said.

'You're kidding me.'

'The meeting. It's with a woman.'

'So? What are you waiting for, Logan? Do it.'

'But I'm not sure she's from the college,' Logan said, using the basic code to refer to the Colombian cartel they had thought the meeting was with.

'There isn't time. Finish the job, then leave.'

'She's not from the college, Mackie. I need to find out what's happening here first. I'm not sure what we're dealing with.'

'Logan, have you gone deaf?'

'No, I just think–'

'I'm not asking you to think!' Mackie bellowed.

'There's been an exchange. I think she might be–'

'Do it, Logan. Do it now. That's an order.'

Mackie ended the call and Logan lay there, listening to the beeps on his phone, thinking through what to do next.

He wasn't really sure why he was so hesitant. It wasn't the morality of the order that troubled him. His inquisitive mind told him there was more to this meeting than the intel had suggested. In fact, it looked like the intel had been plain wrong.

Mackie had made himself clear, though.

Logan laid the phone down by his side and looked through the scope of his rifle once again. The woman got to her feet and the target followed suit. It looked like the meeting was over.

Logan took a deep inhale of warm, dusty air and held it in. He could feel his heart slowly pumping in his chest. Could almost feel the blood winding through his still body. The air around him was calm. Everything seemed to fall deathly silent as Logan entered a state of heightened concentration.

As he let out a long, slow and silent exhale, he squeezed the trigger, only barely aware of the thunderous crack that came from the rifle and the huge recoil of the powerful weapon that made his whole body shudder. With his eyes still on the scope, working on autopilot, he quickly locked and loaded another cartridge into the chamber. In the few seconds it had taken him to reload, the woman had turned and was running back toward her bike, her mouth wide open in what Logan guessed was a scream.

He followed her movement for just a second, pulling the line of the rifle's sight to the left of her body to account for the moving target.

He pulled the trigger again.

Chapter 36

Moscow, Russia

Winter casually strolled along the upper level of the GUM shopping centre in Moscow. He'd been there for almost twenty minutes, tracking his target, waiting for the right opportunity to approach. Above him, light was seeping in through the extravagant glass roof that reminded him of the classic British Victorian train stations. The warm glow from the sunlight gave the whole opulent expanse a balmy feel.

The GUM was deep in central Moscow, stretching some two hundred yards along Red Square, only a hair's breadth away from the Kremlin. Being within such close proximity to Moscow's historic political centre had sent goosebumps all the way down Winter's back when he arrived and, given the clandestine nature of his visit, the anxiety still sweeping through him was hard to shake.

He hadn't yet come within twenty yards of the target, Irina Tarasenko, but he knew he couldn't hang around all day. Irina was in her late twenties, tall and slender with long, wavy brown hair that shone and glowed. She was wearing a fancy beige coat that, together with her expensive accessories and nonchalant swagger, made her look every bit the designer wife the world thought she was. But Winter knew there was much more to Irina Tarasenko than that.

When she stopped outside the window of a top-end fashion store, Winter kept on going, moving toward her, determined to make the moment count. He walked right up to her, then stopped and stooped his head down to get her attention.

'Irina!' he said in Russian, beaming. 'Is that really you?'

She took her attention away from the window, her look frosty and stern.

'It's time, Irina,' Winter said, quietly now. 'I'm here because of Charles McCabe. Mackie. Just pretend you know me.'

Her expression changed at Mackie's name, her stoic glare dissolving in an instant, replaced by a look somewhere close to dread. It didn't last long, though. A split second later, her face changed again and she returned Winter's broad smile as he straightened up. Her face, smile and all, was a true picture. She wouldn't have looked out of place on the cover of a haute couture fashion magazine. And yet there was a certain coldness behind her dazzling eyes.

Winter leaned in to Irina and they gave each other a triple kiss on the cheeks. Winter looked over her shoulder and saw two broad-chested, suited men quickly closing in. They began to shout out, the larger of the two reaching his hand toward Irina to pull her away from Winter. She spun around to face them.

'What are you doing!' she blasted at them. 'Come on, this is just an old friend.'

The men stopped in their tracks but their scowls remained.

'Please, just let me have a minute,' Irina said. 'He's hardly a threat, is he?'

Winter wasn't sure whether to be offended by her words or not, but they seemed to do the trick.

'Okay. But no more touching,' the larger of the two men said.

'Shall we walk?' Winter said.

'Yes. In fact, let's go and get a drink,' she said, then turned back to the two men. 'We're going for a drink. Is that allowed?'

Her tone was terse and full of vitriol. The two men looked at each other, then nodded.

'Come on, this way,' she said and began to walk.

'How many men are there?' Winter said, looking back at the two goons, who were eyeballing him suspiciously.

'Four,' she said. 'One in the car, those two, plus the man in the brown jacket. He's at your two o'clock.'

Winter stole a cautious glance and spotted the other guard. He hadn't noticed him before. He was being way more discreet than the other two, who were clearly the muscle, the visual deterrent.

Winter wondered for a fleeting second whether the man in the brown jacket had spotted him mooching before. But the fact he had let Winter approach Irina probably meant he hadn't.

'We can't get away from them here,' she said. 'It's impossible. If I'd known you were trying to reach me, then maybe we could have worked something out.'

'I know. But there wasn't time. We can make do for now.'

His answer was only half truthful. His plan to travel to Moscow and meet with her had certainly been hastily arranged, but in reality he'd wanted that element of surprise. It would give him the chance to really gauge her – to find out whether she could be as useful as he hoped. An organised meeting with her, on the other hand, could have turned into nothing more than an ambush.

They carried on walking to an escalator and descended to the ground level. The three guards followed.

'So, is this really it?' Irina asked. 'I've been wondering whether this day would ever happen.'

'Yes, this is it,' Winter replied. 'You could say your whole life has been building up to this. But I'll be quick, I promise. No one will know we met today.'

She laughed nervously. 'I wouldn't be so sure about that,' she said. 'Alex will find out. The guards will have to write this in their logs. He reads their reports every night, then questions me about what I've been doing during the day.'

'Then you'd better start thinking about what you're going to tell him. About who I am.'

She looked at him, the same stern look now on her face that she had given the guards moments earlier.

'You're not even going to help me?' she said. 'With the story?'

'I'm sure you can think of something.'

She tutted. 'Thanks a lot.'

They headed into a coffee shop that was decked out in dark wood and had a sprawling glass-fronted cabinet that housed what seemed like hundreds of different types of pastries and cakes, all different shapes, sizes and colours. The pungent smell of fresh coffee and warm, sweet pastry filled the air and made Winter's insides grumble. They sat at a table in the window. The two suited guards found a table on the other side of the cafe and the third man stayed on the prowl outside.

A smartly uniformed waitress came over and Irina ordered a sparkling water, Winter a coffee. The lady asked whether either of them wanted some food – one of the cakes perhaps – and seemed offended when they both politely declined. Really, Winter was seriously tempted by the food, but he wanted the meeting to be quick – he was playing a dangerous game meeting her out in the open.

'How do I know Mackie sent you?' Irina said, playing with the sparkling rings on her fingers – a nervous habit, Winter assumed. 'How do I know you aren't really just setting me up?'

'If you were being set up, you'd already be dead.'

She smiled meekly. 'I guess you're right.'

'Mackie was killed,' Winter said, searching Irina's eyes for any hint of reaction. 'Just a few days ago. In Russia.'

'I know,' she said. She shifted in her seat, looking this way and that, struggling to keep eye contact.

'How did you know?' Winter asked.

'How do you think? I do what I'm supposed to do. I pry. I look for things I'm not supposed to know. I look through Alex's office, his files. I've been doing that for five years. Do you know that's how long it is since I last saw Mackie?'

'Yes, I know.'

'I couldn't believe it when I found out he'd been killed. And in Russia too. The games spies play, huh? It hit me, but I really thought that when he died – or hoped, at least – that would be the end of it. That I'd finally be free from this. That I could move on and live my life with Alex.'

'Maybe one day you can.'

'But not today?'

'No, I'm sorry, not today.'

'So this is just the start?'

'Yes. Do you have anything here with you?'

She huffed, an incredulous look on her face. Winter averted his eyes to the two goons, who were still staring, still looking less than impressed with the situation.

'Try to keep up the pretence,' Winter said.

Irina's face softened again in an instant. 'I'm sorry. No, I don't have anything here with me. What, did you think I'd been lugging around top-secret information with me every day for the last five years on the off-chance someone like you might show up?'

'I guess not,' Winter said.

'What do you need?' Irina said.

'What do you have?'

'Nothing. I've never been told to keep anything, to copy anything or pass anything to anyone. I have what's in my head. But I know how to get you information if you need it.'

The waitress came over with the drinks and Winter took a sachet of brown sugar, ripped the top off and poured it into the thick, treacly liquid.

'What happened to Nikolai Medvedev?' Winter said.

Irina's gaze caught Winter's stare. This time she held the eye contact.

'Come on,' Winter said. 'You said yourself you're in the know. I only have a few questions, then I'm gone.'

'Gone for good?'

'No. I'll be needing the files you said you have access to. You'll need to copy them somehow. But we can make arrangements for how to pass them over. It doesn't have to be face to face.'

She sank down in her seat, an almost defeated look on her face. 'Do you have any idea what it's like to live this life?' she said.

'No,' Winter said, though he thought that really he did. His own life was a constant lie to those he loved. His girlfriend, his parents. Irina's life had the extra layer of betrayal that she must constantly feel, but Winter knew his own secretive life wasn't too far removed.

'It tears me apart, do you know that? Living like this, every day a lie. It's heartbreaking.'

'I'm not here for your sob story,' Winter said, sounding as disinterested as he felt.

'I love him. I love Alex. I really do. Maybe at first I didn't, but now I do. He's a good man. A good husband.'

'And I'm sure he loves you too. But what do you think he would do if he found out about you?'

She said nothing but Winter could see her eyes begin to well up with tears. For the first time, he felt bad for her. At least he had a choice. This was the career he'd chosen. She hadn't come into her situation so easily.

Mackie had first tapped her up when she had been in her early twenties studying French in Paris. Her father had been a prominent local politician in the Crimea, but the family had fallen on hard times when he'd been ousted and jailed on bogus corruption charges put forth by his opponents. Mackie, seeing potential in her in a way only he could, had pulled enough strings to see her awarded a scholarship to complete her education.

After that, she was in his hands. He'd steadily guided her toward the powerful crowd of elite politicians and government officials in Moscow, many of whom were sympathetic to her father's position. Alex Tarasenko, a rising star in Moscow who'd previously led the KGB's and subsequently the SVR's activities in Italy, had taken an immediate liking to her. The rest was history.

She was a pawn. Mackie had played with her life for the benefit of the JIA. In that sense, Winter felt bad for her, yes. And he felt bad for having to be so blunt and emotionless with her. But only a little. It wasn't the time for sentiment.

'Come on, you need to stay smiling, if only to keep the guards at bay.'

She wiped her eyes, then returned her broad smile. The same one she had dazzled Winter with when they'd first met just a few minutes ago. He wondered how often she had to put that mask on. It certainly seemed to do the trick, though the more he saw it, the more cracks he saw.

'What do you know about Nikolai Medvedev?' Winter asked again.

'Someone found out he was a double agent.'

'Who?'

'I don't know. But they were following him that day.'

'The FSB killed him?'

'No. That's the thing. The FSB trailed him, but another surveillance team turned up. They killed Medvedev and took the British agent.'

Winter's mind began to race. What Irina had said didn't match what he thought had happened at all.

'You're sure?' he said. 'The FSB didn't kill Medvedev?'

'That's what I just told you. There were two surveillance teams. One was FSB – they were following Medvedev. They knew he was meeting with a foreign agent. The other surveillance team no one knows, but they must have been following the British agent. It was the other team that killed Medvedev and took the British man with them.'

'His name was Paul Evans,' Winter said. 'He worked for Mackie.'

'I didn't know that.'

Winter stared at her, looking for any hint of a lie in those sparkling eyes. He saw nothing.

'Do the FSB have Paul Evans?' Winter said.

'No. That's what I just told you.'

'You're sure?'

'As sure as I can be.'

Winter picked up his espresso cup and downed his shot of coffee.

'What about Lena Belenov?' he said. 'Do you know who killed her?'

'It was on the news. Your agent Carl Logan killed her.'

'Except he didn't.'

'How do you know that?'

'I just do. So tell me what you know.'

'I don't know anything about that, honestly. It was on the news. I thought it must be true. I haven't seen or heard anything otherwise.'

Winter sat staring at her for a few seconds longer, waiting to see whether she had anything else to add.

'I'm sorry,' she said. 'I really don't know anything else about that. It wasn't something I thought to follow up on.'

'And what do you know about Carl Logan? You can't tell me that he hasn't been on your radar.'

'I knew the FSB had him. Where, I never knew. And I knew later that he had escaped. The FSB are still looking for him. He attacked a team of agents not far from Volgograd, but that was two or three days ago.'

'And since then?'

'Nothing.'

'You're sure about that?'

'Why would I lie?'

Winter sighed. It was a fair point. And she had done a good job to find out anything at all. No one had been in touch with her for five years and yet she had still been quietly getting on with her job, digging and prying.

'Perhaps you'll find what you're looking for in the files,' Irina said.

'Perhaps. You need to get them to me.'

'How?'

'First you need to copy them. It'll be safer if you can write them to an external drive. A thumb drive would be easiest for you to buy and dispose of.'

'I can do that, no problem. But what then?'

Winter told her the web address for a popular chat forum and a username.

'Can you remember that?' he said.

'Yes.'

'Set yourself up a new account on that website. Send me an instant message; it's harder to trace than email. I'll reply to let you know I'm there. All you need to do is plug in the drive and I'll take the data remotely. It shouldn't take long. There won't be any trace of it happening.'

'You're sure that will work?'

'It'll work.'

'Okay, give me three hours. I'll be home by then. Alex will still be at work.'

'Well, I think we're done then,' Winter said.

'That's it?' Irina asked, surprised, but with visible relief on her face.

'For now, yes.'

Winter got to his feet and Irina followed suit. Winter threw some roubles onto the table, then leaned in to kiss Irina.

She leaned in too.

'I hope … I never … have to see you again,' she said as she kissed his cheeks.

Winter stepped back and looked at her face, looked as she fought hard to keep hold of the false smile that covered it. For just a second, he wondered what would happen that evening when Alex Tarasenko – deputy director of the FSB – confronted her about the man she'd had coffee with that day. If Alex ever found out about her, she would certainly be dead.

But there was nothing Winter could or would do about that.

Without another word, he turned away from Irina and walked out of the cafe.

Chapter 37

Barinas, Venezuela

Logan waited in the rusty car, eyeballing the tin shed on the other side of the street that passed as a bar. The temperature was baking. The car had no air con. Logan had wound down both front windows but there was little wind, and with the sun beating down on the car, heating up the metal heap, he was a sweaty, sodden mess.

It had been a whirlwind twenty-four hours since he'd carried out his orders and taken out the two targets at the abandoned village. Logan had immediately rushed down to the scene and retrieved the brown envelope from the grasp of the dead woman's hands. That in itself was a risky move to make. His orders had been to eliminate the targets and get out of there. And with the envelope in his possession, what he should have done was pass the information it contained straight to Mackie. Instead, he'd been doing anything and everything he could to identify the woman he'd killed.

Mackie had been calling him non-stop through the day. Logan had answered the calls just twice. He'd told Mackie enough information to keep him at bay but given away nothing about what he was up to. Mackie had ordered him to stay at the safe house and wait for him to arrive from England. Not this time. Logan wanted to know what trouble he'd just caused.

After printing the pictures of the woman he'd killed from the portable printer in the safe house, he'd been trailing around the local villages, speaking to every informant he could – trying to find her identity. The easiest route to identifying her would be to pass the pictures directly on to the lab at the JIA. They had some of the most sophisticated face-recognition software available, together with access to more profiling databases than any other single intelligence organisation. But this was Logan's problem. He wanted to get to the bottom of it before involving anyone else.

He didn't have to wait in the car for long – just under half an hour – before he saw the man he was waiting for. The time was a little after five p.m. and, as he did every day, the man was heading straight to the ramshackle bar following the conclusion of his shift at a local courier company.

Innocuous to look at, the man was in his early forties with wispy brown hair, stubble a few days old and nondescript clothes. He was an unassuming man who held a lowly position at the courier company. And yet his under-utilised mind contained a wealth of information far beyond his humble position. As legitimate as the majority of its business was, the company he worked for couriered goods, parcels and correspondence for the cartels. And that put him in a very privileged position indeed.

Logan opened the door of his car and stepped out into the blazing sun. He lifted his hand up to his face as his eyes adjusted to the brightness, then casually walked across the quiet street.

The man saw Logan coming after just a few strides. He stopped walking, panic etched on his weary face. Logan continued up to him.

'Hector,' Logan said.

Hector held out his hands, as though warding Logan off. 'No, please. Not here. They can't see me with you here.'

Logan took no notice. 'Turn around, Hector,' he said.

'What?'

'Turn around. Walk.'

Logan grabbed Hector's arm and tugged on him. He took him away from the bar and down the street with little resistance.

'This'll be quick,' Logan reassured him. 'Then you can go and drink as much shit beer as you like.'

Logan pulled Hector into an alleyway and they walked far enough down it so that they were out of sight from the main road.

'What do you want?' Hector said, his voice quivering.

It wasn't Logan he was scared of – it was the situation. Logan had only spoken to Hector twice before, but both times the meeting had been carefully arranged. But Logan wanted answers fast this time. He took the postcard-sized photo out of his pocket.

'Who is she?' he said, holding the picture up for Hector to look at.

Hector's pupils seemed to burst with recognition. 'I … I don't know,' he stammered.

He was lying, Logan knew. And he would have pressed Hector harder if he could. In the end, he never got the chance. It was the change in Hector's demeanour that tipped Logan off: Hector's eyes, fixed behind Logan, shot wide open in shock.

Logan reached out, grabbed Hector by the scruff of his neck, bent his knees and spun around, tossing Hector like a hammer thrower. Hector bundled into the man who had crept up on Logan. The two men fell into a heap on the ground, Hector on top.

As they scrambled to get back to their feet, Logan quickly assessed his options. He could quite easily fell both Hector and the would-be attacker. But that wasn't what he had come for. And, looking down at the man who had surely been about to attack Logan, he realised the situation had already provided him with a lot of the answers he needed.

So Logan opted for the only other choice he could see: he turned on his heel and ran.

As he exited the alley, he did a quick recce left and right down the street. He spotted two men lurking. They saw Logan and immediately began to close in on him, walking with purpose. Luckily Logan's car was in the opposite direction to where they were. He sprinted back to it, dived in and fired up the engine. He crunched the gear stick into first and thumped his foot onto the accelerator. The tyres skidded, kicking up a cloud of dust, before the car lurched forward, down the road, away from Hector and the three men.

Although it looked like he was in the clear, Logan kept on high alert as he drove on. He took an unnecessarily circuitous route back toward the safe house, then dumped the car some half a mile away in the small car park of what passed as a supermarket. He cautiously trekked back to the safe house, a roasting hot studio apartment where he had been staying for the best part of three months.

Logan came up to the door. The wood was splintered and chipped. The whole building, in fact, was rundown and in need of serious repair; the white-rendered outside walls were yellowed and had great chunks of paint and plaster missing, exposing the breeze blocks underneath.

Safe house was perhaps in some ways a misnomer. There was certainly very little secure about it in a physical sense. It was, however, entirely congruous with the surrounding area, and Logan knew that as long as he was careful about his own movements, it was entirely safe. He just had to hope he had managed to evade the heat that had clearly been on Hector.

He took the deadlock key out of his pocket, turned the lock and pushed open the door. Then froze.

'Surprise,' Mackie said.

Logan's tense body suddenly relaxed and he let out a sigh as he walked in, then closed the door behind him. Mackie was sitting casually in a worn-out brown leather armchair. He was smartly dressed, his pot belly pushing out over the waist of his pressed trousers and tugging on the buttons of his sky-blue short-sleeved shirt.

'You've got a habit of doing that,' Logan said, remaining on his feet.

'Of what?'

'Of turning up unannounced.'

'Well, if you answered your bloody phone more often, it wouldn't come as such a shock to you, would it?'

'I've been busy.'

'I'm sure you have. Busy evading me, by the looks of it.'

'That's not it at all.'

Logan moved over to the large sash window and pulled it open, letting in a blast of warm, moist air.

'Tell me what's going on, Logan. You're not a one-man show. You're my agent. You do what I tell you.'

'She was with the CIA,' Logan said, staring over at Mackie, whose face remained deadpan.

'How do you know?'

Mackie must surely have come to the same conclusion by now. Why else would he have turned up in Venezuela at such short notice?

'Because of the heat that's on me. Or at least on our assets.'

Mackie remained silent.

'When did you find out?' Logan asked him.

'A few hours after you shot her.'

'And you didn't think to tell me?'

'I couldn't get hold of you. You were running amok, hassling every asset we've worked on out here for the past two years.'

'So what do we do now? Do the CIA know about me? Know about what we're doing here?'

'No,' was Mackie's simple response. 'And they won't find out so long as you keep your head.'

'Easy for you to say.'

'Yes, it bloody is. Because I'm the one who gives the orders around here. And you're the one who's supposed to follow them.'

'I always do,' Logan said.

'And yet this time you didn't. And that worries me. You should know better than that. That's who you are, Logan. You shouldn't piss unless I tell you to.'

'Some life, eh?'

'It's the life you signed up for. The only one I'm offering you. I'm not sure you're quite understanding the seriousness of this situation. You do what I tell you. Nothing more, nothing less. That's what you were trained for. You're not Sherlock Holmes.'

'I'm not trying to be.'

'Then take this as your first and final warning. You stray from protocol one more time and that's it, you're finished.'

It wasn't Mackie's words that surprised Logan, it was his calm tone. Plenty of times Logan had seen Mackie blow up in anger. To be chastised by Mackie without his once raising his voice added a sinister edge to his words.

'I'm not straying from protocol,' Logan said, surprising himself with his own continued defiance.

'What?' Mackie said, his forehead creasing, just the first sign that maybe his bubbling anger wasn't too far away.

'This is what you trained me for.'

'I trained you to follow orders. To not ask questions of me.'

'You trained me to survive. That's what I'm doing. I'm surviving. I killed a CIA agent because of your orders – which, you'll find, I carried out to the letter. I don't know who she was or why she was there, but I know my actions will have put me in danger one way or another. You can train me all you like, but you'll never take the instinct for self-protection from me.'

Mackie stayed silent for a few moments after that. Both men stared at each other. Logan wondered what was going through Mackie's mind. He knew he was pushing his relationship to the limit. But he wasn't asking much, really. He had carried out his orders. He'd shot and killed two people on the say-so of his boss. It turned out this time that the say-so was wrong. He'd killed a fellow agent. Logan was sure that hadn't been Mackie's plan. Logan didn't regret it. He felt no sorrow or anger for having pulled the trigger. The training that Mackie had put him through had made sure of that. But what he could still feel was his own desire to live. And to seek out and eliminate any threat against that.

In the end, Mackie seemed to come to that same realisation.

'Her name was Janet Ford,' he said. 'It was a painstaking task to even get that much – after you shot her, the internal network went into meltdown. We had bad intel, it's as simple as that. We're still trying to assess why. Someone somewhere along the line isn't playing ball like we thought they were.'

'That's the same conclusion I came to,' Logan said.

He moved over to the pine dresser in the corner of the room and opened the doors at the bottom to reveal a simple electronic safe built into the wall behind the dresser. Logan input a six-digit code and took out the brown envelope that he'd prised from Janet Ford's dead grasp. He tossed the envelope over to Mackie, who took it and pulled out the contents.

'However the CIA got Ford in, she was certainly a step ahead of us,' Logan said. 'There's information there on the college's methods of operation, key personnel, locations. The man she met yesterday wasn't the college's honcho as we thought he was. He wasn't a threat. He was an informant.'

Mackie perused the documents, sighing here and there as he took in not so much the information that was in front of him, Logan guessed, but the predicament that they were now in.

'How the hell are we going to explain this?' Logan said.

'We're not,' Mackie said with no emotion or further embellishment.

'I said it didn't feel right,' Logan said, no longer able to resist pointing out the fact.

'But I don't pay you to feel,' Mackie said.

'Then maybe you should.'

Logan knew that Mackie was never going to apologise, even though it was clear to both men that the hit had been a significant error of judgement. What Logan didn't know or understand was how the JIA had been fed intel that was so far off the mark.

'We could have aborted,' Logan said. 'ID'd her before taking any action. That way we would have saved her life and still had a useful informant on our hands.'

'It's always easier to see the alternatives with hindsight.'

Logan shook his head. 'What do we do now?' he asked.

'You tell me. You're the one who seemingly wants the freedom to think all of a sudden, to tell me how we should be doing things. So tell me, please, what do you think we should do next?'

'With the information we now have, we could take the whole college down.'

Mackie smiled. 'A moment ago, you were concerned about the threat to your own life. Now you want to go all Rambo out in the jungle?'

'I never said I was concerned about the threat. Just that I wanted to find out what the threat is. Who the threat is.'

'Fair point. But we're not going to do that. Not while the CIA are out here stepping on our toes. And I'm not about to up and tell them what happened.'

'Even though there's a potential mole out there?'

'Let me think about that. I think we need to close this one down. Start afresh with the new information when we really know what's happened.'

'So we just pack up and go home? That's it?'

'Not exactly.'

'Then what?'

'I need you to do one more thing first.'

'Spit it out.'

'We've got another man in there. Deep cover.'

Logan turned to face Mackie, not bothering to hide the surprise on his face. His boss's declaration was a revelation, and yet Mackie's demeanour and tone were flat and placid, like it was nothing.

'And you didn't think that was something I should have known about?' Logan said, the irritation in his voice clear.

'No. I didn't. Like I said, I don't pay you to think. You only know what I need you to know.'

'Perhaps if you want to keep on paying me, that needs to change.'

'Is that a threat?'

'No. But don't you think this would work better if you let me in? I'm good at this. I've shown you that. I'm not asking for much. I'm just asking for you to trust me. To trust my judgement. I'll carry out your orders, I always have. But let me in. Use me properly.'

'It might not seem like a lot to you, but it's a lot to me. There's more for me to lose in this than you.'

'I don't see how. The only thing either of us has to lose is our life.'

Mackie stared at Logan but didn't say a word. Logan wished he could tell what his boss was thinking. He understood why Mackie had to be so vague and secretive, even with agents like Logan. But there came a point when the model just didn't operate effectively when Mackie withheld so much.

Logan knew Mackie's relationship was different with each agent, for the very reason that each agent he ran had different skills and uses. Logan had become, in effect, a trained killer. An assassin. The problem was Logan wasn't sure he was happy with the hand he'd been dealt anymore. Despite all the training, physical as well as psychological, he knew he had more to offer than that. And he wanted the freedom that he knew some of Mackie's other agents had. Mackie wasn't in the field day in, day out. He couldn't expect to always call every shot.

'My agent's position is compromised,' Mackie said. 'We need to extract him.'

'How do you know he's compromised?'

'Because I haven't been able to reach him for two days.'

'You think he's still alive?'

'I can't be sure. But even if his cover hasn't been blown, I think it's too dangerous to leave him in now.'

'You want me to get him out?' Logan said.

'Exactly. You want something different. This is something different.'

'Is that it?' Logan responded, surprised at the simplicity of the proposition, but also somewhat disappointed. 'I get him out, then we all go home?'

'Yes. That's it. You want to prove yourself? This is it. First, you need to find him.'

Chapter 38

Akmola Province, Kazakhstan

Butler was on the ground, half out of it, when Logan attacked Paul Evans and jumped into the Land Cruiser. His body was heavy and distant, his vision somewhat blurred. The blows Logan inflicted had taken their toll. But his mind, although not sharp, was still fully aware. He felt a cynical satisfaction as he watched Logan and Grainger speed away in the four-by-four.

The deal that he and Fleming had agreed to hand over Logan and Grainger was the best they could achieve in such a short time, though Butler had felt from the start that they could have held out for more money. Fleming hadn't been so keen. He saw Logan as a threat and simply wanted rid of him.

Butler had been somewhat disappointed at the prospect of losing such valuable assets so quickly. Giving up Logan meant Butler would never get the chance to personally make him suffer. That bastard had ruined his life. Butler had lived for the army. Lived for the SAS. When he'd been turfed out at the age of just thirty-two because of his gammy arm, his life had headed in a downward spiral. He'd contemplated suicide more than once but had always bottled it. One of the few things that had kept him going was his relationship with Fleming, who'd never lost faith in him.

When Logan had turned up out of the blue, Butler had outwardly been hostile, but inwardly pleased that he might finally get a chance for some payback. The deal that Fleming had struck had seemed to have brought to an end that possibility. But as Butler watched Logan heading off on the run once more, he felt his chance was still there after all.

That short moment of satisfaction didn't last long, though. The scene in front of Butler quite quickly changed into one of chaos and destruction.

Fleming was kneeling over him, saying something to Butler whose groggy mind was struggling to decipher the words. Fleming had seemed oblivious to what was going on behind him until the revved engine and screeching tyres caught his attention as Logan and Grainger made their getaway.

Evans and Mason lay sprawled on the floor. Evans's two armed guards were haphazardly firing their weapons into the distance at Logan's vehicle. Out of Fleming and the crew, it was Ilya who reacted first. He walked right up to Fleming and Butler. He took a handgun – a Sig – from the holster on his hip and, as nonchalantly as you could imagine, raised the gun and pointed it at Fleming's head.

Butler tried to move. Tried to shout out. He wasn't sure whether it was the state he was in or the speed of events unfolding that meant he never got the chance.

Fleming was looking over to the compound gates. He began to get to his feet. He reached for his own sidearm. With Butler frozen, it was Vassiliy who called out, who tried to alert Fleming to the fact that one of his own men was pointing a gun at his head.

Fleming half-turned before Ilya pulled the trigger. The bullet tore into the side of Fleming's face. He stumbled and fell, landing in a heap on top of Butler, whose weak body was pinned down.

All hell broke loose. There was shouting and a cascade of gunfire from all directions. Vassiliy, off to Butler's side, opened fire with his AK-47. Ilya, completely out-positioned, took at least half a dozen bullets. He collapsed to the ground just inches away from Butler who was still struggling to lift Fleming's heavy body off him.

Maksat and Bulat were both readying themselves too. Bulat, assault rifle in his hands, opened fire on the two guards at the gates. They had turned their weapons away from Logan's vehicle and were on the attack. Bulat never suspected the threat from

Maksat, standing just two yards from him. As Bulat's rifle rattled away, Maksat lifted his handgun and pulled the trigger. The bullet sank into Bulat's head and exited the other side in a cascade of blood and bone and brain matter. A random spray of fire erupted from Bulat's rifle as he plummeted to the ground.

Maksat, a top marksman from his time in the Republican Guard – probably one of the best marksmen Butler had ever seen – ducked, turned, took a split second to aim and then fired another three shots. The cry of pain followed by a thud off to Butler's right told him that Vassiliy had been hit and was out for the count now too.

Stunned, Butler looked on as Maksat lowered his weapon and Evans's two guards moved toward him. The three of them exchanged words in Kazakh. Butler didn't understand. He didn't need to. It was clear what had happened. Maksat and Ilya had sold him and Fleming out. Butler was confounded, but then he thought: money talks. There were very few relationships in life that people wouldn't turn their backs on if enough money was on offer.

Anger was now rattling around inside Butler. He tried to find the strength to move. To fight back. He heaved Fleming's deadweight body off him and grimaced as he reached out and grabbed the handgun that lay on the ground by his side. He wasn't sure whose it was – his own, Fleming's, Ilya's? Everything was such a blur. He pulled the gun up and pointed the barrel at the treacherous Maksat.

A loud crack rang out. The giant fell to the ground. Butler looked on, stunned. He hadn't pulled the trigger. He'd still been trying to find the strength. The bullet that had killed Maksat had come from the rifle of one of Evans's guards.

In the end, Maksat had got exactly what he deserved.

Just a few seconds had elapsed since the first shot had been fired. Fleming and four highly trained men had been felled. The only two men in the complex who were still on their feet had fired just one of the many shots required in the process. Butler had to admit, he was quietly impressed with the deviousness and efficiency of the set-up. So much so that in his weary state he very nearly forgot his own predicament. Only when the guards turned their attention to him, their gaze meeting his, did he snap back to reality.

By that point it was too late. As he clumsily tried to adjust his aim with the handgun, one of the guards let loose with a rifle. Bullets whizzed and ricocheted around Butler. One sank into his leg. Butler screamed. Another grazed his forearm and Butler reflexively let go of his weapon.

He was done, he knew it. He simply didn't have the strength in his body or the wits in his mind to fight back anymore.

One of the men strode up to him. The other headed over to where Evans was still flat on the ground, his companion, Mason, now hovering over him. Neither had played an active part in the slaughter that had just taken place, but Butler knew full well it was down to them.

The man came right up to Butler and held out his rifle, the barrel coming inches from Butler's chest. On the ground but with his elbows propping up his torso, Butler stared down the barrel, then up at the man behind it. The man said something to Butler. He recognised the words as Russian. His dazed brain was unable to translate them. He said nothing. Just stared at the man who had nothing but death in his eyes.

In one last desperate act, Butler propelled himself forward, aiming to tackle the man around his legs. But it was too little, too late. The man opened fire. A succession of bullets caught Butler. They tore into his chest. He collapsed back down on top of the fallen Fleming.

Butler was face down. His mouth and nostrils were pressed up against Fleming's midriff. He tried to move but couldn't. There was simply nothing left in him. As his life faded away from him, what filled his head were not flashes of his past or his family or thoughts of his many regrets – it was the smell. The smell of blood. The smell of death.

Moments later, he was gone.

Chapter 39

His eyes were closed. He was dazed and confused. The sound of rattling gunfire was only barely recognisable to his brain. After a short spell, the gunfire ceased, replaced by an uneasy silence. He tried to open his eyes but quickly shut them again when a pulsing pain stabbed at the front of his head.

As he lay there on the cold, hard ground, eyes squeezed shut, slowly becoming more aware of where he was and why, he started to feel the pain ease and the fog in his brain clearing. He finally opened his eyes again when he heard a voice and felt tugging on his arm.

'Evans?' the voice said. 'Are you okay? Evans? Come on, man, get up.'

Paul Evans looked up and saw Mason kneeling over him. He pushed himself upright, bringing his knees up toward his chest, grabbing his legs to keep his heavy torso from falling back down. A rush of dizziness washed over him. He put his head between his knees and looked down at the ground, hoping it would pass. He saw drops of blood falling from his face onto the white surface below.

'Shit,' he said, lifting his head back up to stop his nose dripping.

He felt at his nose, pulling it left and right, up and down. It was sore as hell from Logan's head-butt, but it didn't seem to be broken. It was oozing blood, though, and he could feel a laceration further up, between his eyes.

'I'll get you cleaned up in a minute,' Mason said.

'What's happened?' Evans said.

He lowered his head just a little, peering over his cheek bones toward where his two other guards were standing, near to the Jeep belonging to Fleming's men.

'They're all dead,' Mason said.

Evans began to scan the bullet-ridden and bloodied bodies that lay on the ground. There were two by the Jeep: Maksat, whom Evans had managed to pay off beforehand, plus one of Fleming's other men. Ilya, who'd similarly turned against his former boss at the offer of a measly sum of money, was the first of three bodies that Evans spotted over by Fleming's four-by-four.

That was only five.

Evans got to his feet slowly. The world seemed to sway in front of him. He took a step forward, cringing in pain.

There was the sixth body, he realised. He'd thought there were just two bodies next to the four-by-four – Butler and Fleming's remaining loyal guard. But there was actually another there, the one Evans had most wanted to see: Fleming. Butler was on top of him, his face buried in Fleming's belly. The two bosom buddies laid to rest together.

Fleming and Butler, the SAS heroes. Yet they and their four guards had been felled so easily by just two of Evans's men. Granted, two of Fleming's men had betrayed their boss only to be betrayed themselves, but it was still a damned impressive feat. Evans wondered whether Fleming and his crew had even managed to fire off any shots before they were taken out. They simply wouldn't have been ready for the ambush, too caught up in their own greedy moment. Too focused on Logan and Grainger and the money they thought was on offer for handing the runaways over.

'Tell them to come over here,' Evans said, crouching back down on the ground.

Mason shouted over to the two men, who were casually chatting among themselves. They turned and began to walk toward Evans and Mason.

'I told you they would be good,' Mason said.

'You did,' Evans replied.

The two men were Russian. Mercenaries, much like Fleming and his crew. In reality, there was nothing special about them.

They had been soldiers once, but so what? In an even fight, Fleming and Butler may well have had the upper hand. But it hadn't been an even fight. It had been a simple snare. A cheap shot.

'Good work,' Evans said to the two men. 'Pack up your weapons, then get ready to head out.'

The men nodded, then turned around to head back to the car. As they did so, Evans reached into the pocket of his puffer jacket and took out the Glock handgun that had been there throughout the whole of the planned exchange of Grainger and Logan. He lifted the gun and fired two shots.

A bullet struck each of the Russians in the back of their heads. Spatters of flesh and blood flew into the air. The bodies slumped to the ground almost in unison.

Evans lowered his gun and looked over at Mason, who simply shrugged.

'It's a shame, I guess,' Mason said. 'They were good.'

'They were replaceable,' Evans said.

'Probably. And expensive. No one likes to pay if they don't have to.'

'My thoughts exactly,' Evans said with a wry smile.

'Now let's get your face sorted out.'

Evans followed Mason over to the saloon car. Mason opened the front passenger door and Evans sank onto the seat, leaving his feet outside so that he was at ninety degrees to the seat back. Mason went over to the boot of the car and came back a few moments later with a small medical kit.

As Mason began to delve into the supplies, Evans reached into his trouser pocket for his mobile phone. He lifted it up above his tilted head so he could see the screen and dialled the number. It took a while for the connection to hold, but when it did, the call was answered on the second ring.

'Was it them?' Jay Lindegaard drawled.

Evans wondered whether he had woken Lindegaard or it was just his awful accent that made him always sound half-asleep.

'Yes,' Evans said, knowing that the question had referred to Logan and Grainger.

There had been a niggling doubt in Evans's mind as to whether Fleming and Butler were telling the truth or were playing a game with their request to do a deal over Logan and Grainger. It had been a real bolt from the blue when Butler had called Lindegaard to say that the two fugitives were staying at Fleming's house near Aktobe in Kazakhstan. Prior to that, there hadn't been a snip of the whereabouts of the two. Clearly, based on his question, Lindegaard must have had the same doubts.

In the end, Fleming had been telling the truth. But his greed had got the better of him. Following the call, Evans had done his own digging into the ex-soldiers. He found it immensely amusing that Logan had felt Fleming was someone he could turn to in his hour of need. As far as Evans could make out, Fleming was nothing more than a self-centred prick, driven by greed and his need to feel superior to everyone and everything.

Fleming had misplaced his trust, just like Logan had. If Fleming had known anything about Lindegaard and Evans at all, it was that they would never do a deal if they didn't have to. And this time, they really didn't have to. Killing the SAS men and their guards was by far the simplest solution really. No one was going to care about the deaths of two parasites who had been bleeding dry the local economy. Their deaths would be glossed over by the Kazakh authorities, who would be glad to see the back of them, as would the companies they had no doubt been fleecing.

'And?' Lindegaard said.

'They got away,' Evans said without any hint of regret.

Mason thrust an antiseptic-soaked cotton ball onto the cut above Evans's nose. The pain caught Evans by surprise and he let out a yelp, his body jolting.

'Evans?' Lindegaard said. 'What's going on?'

'Just getting cleaned up,' Evans responded through clenched teeth.

Mason came forward with a needle and thread. He paused, looking uneasy. He stared at Evans, waiting for the signal to continue. Evans nodded his head slightly and Mason began work. Evans winced as the needle pierced his skin, but he quickly focused his mind away from the pain.

'So they're on the run again,' Lindegaard said.

'Yes.'

'And Captain Fleming?'

'Dead. And Butler. And four Kazakh guards. And the two Russians we hired.'

There was a short pause on the other end.

'Are you still there?' Evans said.

'Yes, yes, I just … I–'

'I take it you're a bit surprised?' Evans said.

'No, no. Well, I'm just surprised it was so easy, that's all. I expected a bit more resistance, I guess.'

'Who said it was easy? You should see my face. And anyway, the devil's in the detail. All it took was a bit of planning.'

'I know. I didn't mean it like that. It's excellent work.'

'Thanks,' Evans said, smiling at the unexpected compliment.

'We may have a problem, though,' Lindegaard said.

'And what's that?'

'Our friend in London.'

'Winter?'

'It seems he might not be as useless as I'd hoped.'

'That's hardly a problem. In fact, he might play right into our hands.'

'Maybe. But it does add some complications.'

'Like what?'

'Nothing I can't handle myself.'

'Okay,' Evans said, frowning. He wasn't sure why Lindegaard had bothered bringing up Winter if he wasn't going to explain what the problem was.

'So everything's still going to plan,' Lindegaard said.

Evans assumed it was a statement rather than a question.

'Bang on,' said Evans, smiling again.

Logan might be a warrior, a fighter, but Evans was a tactician. Logan was part of this, but the mission didn't start and end with him. The more Evans could bring together the different elements, the easier it would be to finish the puzzle. Evans was already two steps ahead. He knew what Logan's next move would be. And the one after that. And with each move Logan now made, Evans would be a step closer to completing his work.

Chapter 40

'What are we going to do, Carl?' Grainger asked, her voice edgy. She was sitting in the back seat, having hastily jumped in the car, behind the driver's seat, after attacking Mason. 'They must be following us, surely? We've got no money, no weapons. Where can we go now?'

'We're no worse off than we were a couple of days ago,' Logan said, the anger in his voice clear.

'Yeah, but we're no better off either,' Grainger said. 'We've wasted two days with Fleming. I told you it was a bad idea.'

'You did,' Logan said through gritted teeth.

Grainger was almost disappointed with herself for rubbing salt into his wounds. She could tell from the sour look on his face and his tone that he was raging about Fleming's betrayal. She knew the situation was no easier for him than it was for her. In fact, it was clear that he'd been through much worse treatment at the hands of the Russians while she'd been cooped up in that awful apartment on the outskirts of Moscow. She felt sorry for him, for what had happened to him, she really did. But just where were they going now? What life-threatening situation was she going to be dragged into next?

When Logan had first come for her, one of the things she'd felt most strongly was hope. That maybe Logan really was the one person who could help her. She still wanted to believe that, but over the last two days, all that seemed to have happened was that Logan had drawn her deeper and deeper into his own problems. Doubts were growing in her mind about whether he could ever get them away from his troubles. She hated herself for feeling that way because a large part of her felt such a strong attraction to him still, and it was only a few hours since the two of them had felt so close to each other again in that dreary roadside motel.

He'd saved her life and she was grateful, but was this really a life worth saving?

Logan thumped on the steering wheel. 'I can't believe I thought he would actually help.'

'We all make mistakes.'

'I'm going to get him for this,' Logan snarled.

'You want to kill him now? Yesterday you wanted to be his friend.'

'I never wanted to be his friend.'

'Whatever. Revenge can't be your answer to everything, you know. You can't just kill every person who wrongs you.'

'Says you?' Logan retorted.

Grainger winced at his words. He was right, of course. Given the lengths she'd gone to in order to exact revenge on the man who'd killed her father, she was hardly one to call him out for wanting to get his own back on Fleming. And actually, she was feeling the same. Fleming had betrayed them both. She would happily see him and his crony Butler dead too.

'We got away. We're still alive,' Logan said, as though reassuring himself as much as anything.

'Yeah, but what next?' Grainger rebutted. 'We're screwed.'

'Maybe not. Because I think I'm starting to understand something now.'

'Are you going to let me in on that?'

'Let's just wait until I know for sure.'

Grainger sighed. She trusted Logan implicitly. At least she trusted that he was *trying* to steer them to safety, trying the best he could to get them away from trouble. But if he didn't let her in on what he knew, then how was she ever supposed to help? She wasn't a useless damsel in distress. One of the things she'd liked so much about Logan was that he had always seemed to get that. They'd worked as a team so effectively. But his guard was up with her now and it felt like he was keeping her in the dark, whether intentionally or not.

Who could blame him, though? She had, after all, betrayed and shot him.

Despite her doubts, she wanted to believe that Logan was the right man to help her. Once again, she couldn't help but compare her feelings for Logan to those for her ex-husband. Tom was such a charming and genuine person. Grainger knew he would walk to the ends of the earth for her and he certainly didn't carry the baggage that Logan did. He was just … normal. The problem, she knew, was that the situation she found herself in was anything but normal. Plus, she'd never had the powerful attraction to Tom that she had to Logan. There was simply something about Logan, a magnetic connection that meant she was inexplicably drawn to him.

And, perhaps most importantly, she knew Logan was a true warrior. Whatever his troubles, he would never stop fighting. Fighting for her.

'Who was that?' Grainger said. 'Were those men from your agency?'

'Evans was. The others, I don't know.'

'Is he a good guy? I mean, was he?'

'I don't know,' Logan said. 'I barely know him, really. We worked for the same man.'

'Mackie.'

'Yes,' Logan said, cringing.

'He said he was trying to help. Is it possible that you still have some friends? That there really could be someone else we can turn to? They must know you couldn't have done the things you've been accused of. Killing Mackie, killing all those other agents.'

'But I really did kill some of them,' Logan said, not a hint of regret in his voice.

'That's not my point,' Grainger responded. 'Don't you think it's possible that Evans was telling the truth when he said he was there to help? He didn't seem like much of a threat to me.'

'No, I don't think it's possible. I wouldn't have trusted Evans even before all this happened. That's just the way I've always been. But I especially wouldn't trust him now. I don't know how far the deal to sell me out went. He could have been a part of it from the start. And even if he wasn't, agents don't exactly question their orders. If Evans has been told I'm the bad guy now, then that's it.'

'So what do you expect us to do now?'

'We'll head to Astana, as planned,' Logan said.

'And then what? We'll never get across the border now.'

'Says who?'

'Well, even if we do, just why the hell do you want to go to China at all? There's nothing there for me. There's nothing there for you.'

'Because I know how to finish this.'

Grainger groaned. 'Pretty soon, Carl, you're going to have to start letting me in on exactly how you're planning to do that. Because right now, I'm having a hard time seeing it. And I'm not sure I can keep on following you aimlessly forever.'

Logan said nothing in response and Grainger's frustration grew. She didn't want to fight with him, but she at least wanted him to try to reason with her.

Without warning, Logan slammed on the brakes of the four-by-four. The tyres skidded and screeched and the car veered left and then right. Logan and Grainger both shot forward in their seats. Logan battled to keep control as the speed fell to a crawl. With the traction generated by the four-by-four system, he managed to keep the vehicle on the road, just.

'Carl, what the hell are you doing?' Grainger shouted when she had recovered from the rapid and unexpected deceleration.

Logan didn't respond. He pulled the car onto the verge at the side of the road and put on the parking brake. He then stared out of the rear-view mirror, watching as the cars, one by one, came to within touching distance of them before thundering past.

'Carl?' Grainger said, leaning forward and touching him on the shoulder. 'What's going on?'

He shifted his gaze to her.

'Look behind us,' Logan said. Grainger twisted to look out of the back window. 'What do you see?'

'I ... er, I see nothing. Just the road, a few cars. Carl, what are you expecting me to say?'

'Do you see them? Do you see Fleming's car? The Jeep? The other car that Evans had?'

'No.'

'Do you see any cars that have stopped in the distance at all?'

'No.'

'Nothing at all to suggest that anyone is following us?'

'No, but–'

'Get out of the car,' Logan said as he turned off the engine.

Logan stepped out of the car and Grainger followed just as another vehicle whizzed past. A blast of cold, wet air smacked into her face from the slipstream. Grainger shook herself down as Logan opened the boot with the remote clicker and went over to it. He inspected the inside, feeling around the boot lid, around the sides and the back. He lifted up the carpet on the bottom, felt around the space, in nooks and crannies that his eyes couldn't see.

'Nothing,' he said.

He closed the boot, sank to his knees and looked under the car. He felt around the chassis, then methodically moved around the car clockwise, looking and feeling the underside of the car and the wheel arches all the way.

'Nothing,' he said to her, then turned and walked back to open his door. He pulled the lever to lift the bonnet, then headed to the front of the four-by-four.

Grainger understood what he was doing, and she followed. Together they inspected the engine compartment. After a thorough search, Logan slammed the bonnet shut, then they both got back into the car and searched there too, looking in the glovebox, in and around the seats, on the carpets and the soft fabric of the roof.

When they had finished, they both got back out and stood at the side of the road. Grainger was shivering from the extreme cold. Logan's face was defiant.

'Let me guess,' she said. 'Nothing?'

'Exactly.'

He began patting her down, all over, his hands roaming through each of her pockets and up and down her body. She didn't resist but her mood was becoming more and more sullen.

'So?' she said, when he had finally finished.

'Let's get back in the car,' he said. 'You're freezing.'

Grainger got into the front passenger seat this time rather than the rear. Logan got in the driver's side, shut his door and looked over at her.

'I get it,' she said. 'We're not being followed.'

Logan nodded. 'We've been here what … ten minutes?'

'Yeah. Nothing behind us. We can see at least a mile. There's no one there.'

'I can't guarantee it but there's no hint of a tracker on this car either. And nothing was planted on us when they were holding us.'

'I mean, there *could* be one on the car,' Grainger said. 'Those things can be tiny. It could be in the stitching of the seats, in the windscreen washer fluid compartment, anywhere. It could be built into the car's computer.'

'There could be one,' Logan said. 'But I don't think there is.'

'Why not?'

'Because they're not following us,' Logan said. 'I'm certain of it. Evans let us get away.'

'I don't get it,' Grainger said, shaking her head. 'Why would he do that?'

'I don't know,' Logan said. 'But I'm sure one way or another, we're going to find out.'

Chapter 41

Barinas, Venezuela

Having dumped his car a couple of hundred yards away in a clearing in the dense jungle, Logan waited outside the property for more than three hours before finally making his move.

In the darkness, he made his way on foot to the edge of the compound. With the heat of the daytime sun gone, the temperature had dropped some, but it was still hot and viciously humid and Logan was dripping wet with sweat. The moist air in the jungle carried a sharp but sweet smell that seemed to cling to the insides of Logan's nostrils – its pungency together with the heat made him feel lightheaded.

He shook himself down to regain his focus, then looked up at the fortified wall in front of him that ran around the perimeter of the compound. The wall, covered in sloppy yellow render, looked basic and easily scalable. The main gates, off to Logan's right, were wooden and would probably only take a few kicks to knock down.

There was an elevated guard post just inside the compound at the main gate, but it was hardly Fort Knox. Logan knew the main security would come in the form of the many armed men he had to expect would be inside the compound. From the spot where he had been hiding, he had made out two guards in the elevated lookout, both armed with scoped rifles. There were two more guards on the ground outside the gates, each carrying automatic weapons slung over their shoulders. Four men to take down just to get in through the main entrance.

And no one in their right mind, not even the local police or army, really wanted to take these men on. Nobody wanted a war on their hands. Logan, similarly, had no intention of heading in all guns blazing.

Which was why he wasn't going in through the main gates.

Logan used a simple grappling hook to help him scale the wall in one swift movement. He jumped down and landed softly, immediately moving into a crouch. The area he'd entered was about as dark as he could hope for, out of the direct line of each of the four spotlights that lit up much of the inside of the compound almost as well as bright sunshine. If someone were looking in his direction, though, they'd surely still be able to see him.

As he quickly scanned the area, Logan was surprised at just how quiet it was. Other than the guards at the gates and in the watchtower, there wasn't a person in sight. The inside of the compound was made up of a large central building that looked like it had once been a pleasant mansion with its decorative red roof tiles, ornate windows and white-painted walls. But it was in poor condition and the grounds around it, with ramshackle outbuildings, barns and a series of vehicles including Jeeps, cars and a flatbed truck, made it look more like a military barracks.

Logan planned a route that would take him to the main house with as little time in the open as possible, then quickly moved away from his position against the wall. Moving cautiously but with purpose, it took him a couple of minutes to reach the main building.

He came to a stop at a side door that he had spotted was ajar, crouched down and pushed it fully open. It creaked as it swung on its rusted hinges and Logan grimaced, hoping the noise hadn't alerted anyone. He froze in position for just a second until he was satisfied there had been no reaction to the noise from either inside or outside the house. Then he made his way into the dark interior.

There were no lights on inside and Logan contemplated putting on the night-vision goggles he had brought with him. He soon realised, though, as he moved along the corridor, that there was enough illumination coming from the spotlights outside for him to make out the layout. Plus, he hated wearing those damned things. No matter how many times he used them, they just didn't feel natural, diminishing his full range of view quite drastically.

Logan reached the bottom of a twisting staircase. There had been no signs of life at all in the downstairs of the house. Logan was almost surprised at just how little resistance he had so far encountered. He had a fleeting thought that maybe it meant Leo Pinilla, the deep-cover JIA agent, wasn't there after all. If that were the case, all of Logan's efforts over the last three days would have been a waste.

This was his chance to prove himself. Mackie had finally given Logan an opportunity to show his full worth. Logan couldn't be sure what ructions he'd caused by shooting Janet Ford. He'd certainly had no hint of a threat against him, no heat on him at all, since that last encounter with Hector. Maybe Mackie had pulled some strings after all.

Logan had met with two other assets as he tried to pinpoint Pinilla's whereabouts. For three days, he'd been buried deep in intelligence, matching the information he'd been provided with the vast array of information – much of it uncatalogued and uncorroborated – that was available to him through the JIA.

It was the first time he had truly been let loose under Mackie's authority. Albeit Mackie was keeping a watchful eye over his every move and Logan had briefed his boss on every detail of what he had found and what he had planned. Everything had brought Logan to this place: a building far off the grid that the JIA had previously known nothing about. But doubts were now beginning to creep in.

Maybe Pinilla wasn't there.

Maybe he was already dead.

Logan really hoped that wasn't the case.

He dropped the L85 rifle, which fell to his side, the strap tight on his shoulder, and took the dart gun out of the holster on his waist.

He knew the property was used by some of the cartel's most senior soldiers. But the intel he had also suggested their wives and families stayed there. Although Logan had no qualms about getting into a firefight with the cartel's guards and foot soldiers, he had no intention of killing innocent people. That was what the dart gun was for. He certainly didn't want to kill a child or an innocent family member, but he had no problem at all in shooting a tranquilliser dart at them. Better to shoot first with the dart gun and ask questions later than run the risk of killing an innocent with the rifle.

As Logan ascended the stairs, he could feel the adrenaline beginning to surge through his body. He was alert, focused, ready. But he also felt edgy. Not nervous exactly, but he knew that he was without doubt well and truly in the lion's den. One false move now and it would be game over for him.

When Logan reached the top of the staircase, he paused and took a deep breath as he scanned the area. He counted five doors along the main corridor on the first floor. Four of the doors were shut. Taking slow cautious steps, Logan moved forward to the first door. The one that was ajar. He pushed the door fully open with the barrel of the gun. The curtains were open. Light seeped into the room from the outside. Logan quickly realised it was a child's bedroom, with playful patterns on the walls and toys stuffed on shelves and lying all around the floor. But the bunk bed in the middle of the far wall was empty.

Logan breathed a sigh of relief. He moved on to the next room. He reached out and turned the doorknob. When he felt the catch release, he froze for just a second. Then he slowly pushed the door open.

This room was also a bedroom. The curtains were closed. But they weren't blackout drapes. The meagre light coming into the room from outside immediately told Logan one thing: this room wasn't empty.

Logan's heart began to thud in his chest. His hand clenched as hard as it could around the grip of the dart gun.

Because lying in the large bed in front of him were two figures. A man, Leo Pinilla, was fast asleep on the right-hand side. But the other, a woman, wasn't asleep. She was sitting up in the bed.

Her eyes were wide open, staring at Logan.

Chapter 42

There really was only one option: the path of least resistance. Logan was there to rescue Pinilla, not kill him, but the woman in bed with the undercover agent had no way of knowing that.

Before she even had a chance to scream, Logan took aim and fired. The dart gun had a silencer but the noise was still stark in the otherwise quiet house. Logan could only hope it wouldn't alert anyone else. He rushed forward and grabbed the woman, placing his hand firmly over her mouth to muffle the scream he knew was coming. Her smothered cries were quiet, probably not enough to be heard outside the room they were in.

Within seconds, the tranquilliser started to take effect and her resistance and cries died down. Logan let her go and she flopped onto the bed as she battled through her last seconds of consciousness.

But her wails had been enough to rouse Pinilla from his sleep.

He murmured and groggily opened his eyes. Logan quickly loaded another dart into the gun and pointed it at Pinilla, who was slowly coming to. After a few seconds, he must have finally got it because he suddenly sprang up in the bed.

Logan put a finger to his lips.

'Pinilla, Mackie sent me. Don't be alarmed.'

'What the–'

Pinilla looked down at the woman next to him. His expression turned to one of horror.

'It's okay,' Logan whispered. 'She's just unconscious. She'll wake up with nothing more than a headache.'

'Why are you here?' Pinilla hissed. His anger was unmistakable.

'I'm here to get you out. It's over. Time to go home.'

'You're fucking kidding me, right?'

'No.'

'Do you know what this place is?'

'Yes,' Logan said.

'Three of the cartel's most senior soldiers are in the rooms next to us. They'll kill us all. They'll skin us alive, for fuck's sake. I'm really not kidding about that. I've seen it done!'

'Not today they won't.'

'Are you serious? Do you know what they do to their enemies around here? They'll cut our fucking heads off and piss down our necks!'

'Then I suggest we go.'

Logan reached out and grabbed hold of Pinilla's arm. Pinilla quickly snapped his arm away.

'I'm not going anywhere. I'm not throwing away three years of my life at the drop of a hat.'

Logan sighed. But then, he could understand Pinilla's point. He certainly wouldn't be happy if someone turned up out of the blue to tell him a half-run mission was getting canned.

'I'm sorry. But it's over,' Logan said. 'Those are Mackie's orders. It's too dangerous.'

'Damn fucking right it's dangerous.'

'You're coming with me one way or another,' Logan said, pointing the gun at Pinilla.

Pinilla stared at the dart gun. Logan could see the man mulling over his position.

'I'm not going anywhere without her,' Pinilla said, looking over at his woman.

'That's not the deal.'

'I don't give a fuck what your deal is. She comes with me. I'm not leaving her to the wolves. Just what do you think they'd do to her when they find out I've scarpered?'

'It's not my problem,' Logan said.

'It is now.'

Logan let out another long sigh. The fact was, he really didn't want to have to use a tranquilliser dart on Pinilla. If he did that, he'd have to drag the man out of there. He wanted to escape with Pinilla back over the wall, under cover. The cartel wouldn't know Pinilla was missing until morning, by which point they would be long gone.

But it looked like Pinilla wasn't going to give Logan that option.

'If you hadn't shot her, it would have been easier,' Pinilla snapped, as if catching on to Logan's thoughts.

'Who else is in the house?' Logan said. 'How many men?'

Pinilla rattled off three names. Logan tried to hide his reaction. He recognised them all. They were notorious, kingpins of the cartel. And Pinilla was right there, living among them. The intelligence Logan had seen had suggested that senior soldiers and their families came to this place, but to have so many of them there at the same time was a huge surprise.

And, potentially, a huge opportunity.

'I've been doing this for three years,' Pinilla said. 'I'm not just some errand boy. I'm part of the inner circle. Now do you realise why it would be foolish to run?'

'You're right. It would be foolish to run,' Logan said.

Pinilla raised an eyebrow. 'What does that mean?'

'What's her name?' Logan asked.

'Erika.'

'Okay, you take Erika. Get her to one of the vehicles. I'm presuming you know where the keys are?'

'Of course. What are you going to do?'

'I'm going to make sure the coast is clear.'

'You can't kill them all!' Pinilla protested. 'Do you know what that would do? You'll start a goddamn war.'

But Logan was barely listening. Mackie had sent him to prove himself. This was his chance.

Suddenly there was a knock on the door. Both men jumped and spun around.

'Is everything okay in there?' said a man in Spanish.

Pinilla began to respond but the man wasn't waiting. He stuck his head around the door.

It was the last thing he ever did.

Logan grabbed hold of the rifle at his side, brought the barrel up and fired a quick double-tap. Even with the suppressor, the noise of the rifle was piercing in the quiet house.

'I guess there's only one choice now,' Logan said. 'You need to get Erika out of here. Use your cover for as long as you can.'

'Fuck!' Pinilla hissed in frustration.

Logan was already moving quickly toward the bedroom door. He stared down at the man he had just killed as he walked over the threshold. It wasn't one of the three men Pinilla had named.

'How many guards are there?' Logan said.

'Seven. Well, no, six now.'

The four on the gate plus two others, Logan thought. Together with the three senior soldiers Pinilla had named, there were still nine men to get past.

Logan looked out of the room, scanning the corridor left and right. There was still no noise, no alarms or shouting coming from outside. But he had to assume that anyone else in the house would by now be on the alert.

He crept along the corridor to the next bedroom. As he reached the door, he stopped and listened for just a second before swinging the door open quickly and rushing into the room, his speed making him a more difficult target.

The room had much the same layout as Pinilla's. Logan spotted two figures in the bed at the far side. He quickly lifted his gun and fired. The two bullets hit the man in the chest. He never even got the chance to open his eyes. The woman he had been sleeping with jumped up, screaming. Logan reached for the dart gun and fired at her. Then he turned and left, her wailing cries filling the room.

Any hope of a silent escape was now well and truly void.

As Logan edged back into the corridor, he heard quick footsteps approaching from his right, where the staircase was. He pointed the rifle and waited. At the first sight of the bobbing heads coming up the stairs, he fired again. Three shots in total, two more kills.

Logan was about to turn when he was grabbed suddenly from behind by thick, strong arms. Logan winced as the man squeezed on his neck. He reached down for the hunting knife on his belt and slashed it across the man's arm. The man screamed in pain and let go.

Logan spun around, taking only a second to adjust himself. He plunged the knife into the man's chest and pushed the blade as far as it would go. The man grimaced and spluttered as the knife tore into flesh and pierced his lung. Logan twisted the knife before pulling it out. A spatter of blood hit him in the face. The man slumped to the floor gasping and wheezing. Logan looked down at him.

Only one target left. Plus four more guards.

Logan was about to move toward the next bedroom when the door suddenly sprang open. A man jumped out, firing a handgun. Logan threw himself to the floor. Bullets ricocheted off the walls nearby. White paint and plaster dust filled the air. Logan fired a shot. The bullet caught the man in the ankle and he tumbled to the ground, screaming. The next bullet hit him in the face and he went silent.

For a few moments, there wasn't a sound to be heard. Three of the cartel's most senior soldiers had been eliminated in about sixty seconds.

Logan knew the fight wasn't over yet, though. He jumped up, turned around and headed back toward the staircase. As he reached Pinilla's room, he saw the undercover agent was still in there. He was dressed, trying his best to rouse his naked girlfriend.

'What the hell are you doing?' Logan said.

'I'm not taking her out there like this,' Pinilla said.

'There's no time. Grab her and go.'

Logan headed off to the stairs, his rifle held out. He retraced his steps down to the ground floor, then back to the side door. When he reached it, he peered out into the courtyard. There was still an eerie silence outside. Logan had thought the guards would have gone into red alert – sirens blazing, spotlights searching, men shouting as they rampaged through the property. But there was nothing of the kind.

Logan took a step out. Just as he moved his head to get a look at the gates, there was a snapping noise as a bullet smacked into the wall an inch from Logan's ear. He quickly retreated, realising the shot must have come from one of the two snipers in the watchtower. There was no way he was getting out of the house that way.

Crouching low, he headed back and moved into the first room he came to – a lounge. He crept up to the window, across which thin drapes were drawn. He pulled himself up against the wall. Using the tip of the rifle's barrel, he lifted the corner of a curtain just an inch. He had to assume the two guards would be busily scoping the entire building, but he seemed to get away with the twitching curtain. Without further disturbing the drape, Logan moved into position behind the rifle and peered out through his scope. He only needed a slight adjustment to spot the guard tower some thirty yards away.

With his target fixed, he pulled on the trigger twice, then quickly moved the barrel half an inch to the right. Two more shots. Only two men left.

Just then, Logan heard a car engine starting.

Pinilla.

Logan jumped to his feet and rushed back toward the side exit. He only quickly glanced about this time as he ran outside. He had no idea where the remaining guards were. He just hoped they weren't in sniper positions. The watchtower was clear. He was certain of that. Most likely if he contended with them at all, it would be a melee attack, so moving with speed was as good an option as any. And Pinilla was ready to go, so moving fast was definitely Logan's preferred option.

When Logan reached the courtyard, he turned and sprinted toward the waiting Jeep. Pinilla was in the driver's seat. He turned just as Logan approached and leaned over and pushed open the passenger door. Logan jumped in and Pinilla pressed on the accelerator. The car jerked forward, Logan's legs dangling out of the still-open door.

Logan adjusted himself, sitting properly on the seat, and reached out to shut the door. He looked up at Pinilla. The undercover agent had a sour scowl covering his face. He was fuming.

'What happened?' Logan said.

Pinilla didn't say anything. He just indicated behind him. Logan looked. He saw Erika sprawled on the back seat. She was still unconscious. Pinilla had managed to cover her naked body with a thin nightgown but it was covered in thick, wet blood.

She'd been shot.

'Shit,' Logan said.

Pinilla snarled as he pressed his foot further onto the accelerator, pushing Logan right back in his seat. The two men braced themselves as they crashed through the wooden gates. The impact sent a painful jolt through Logan's body but the Jeep was barely damaged.

Logan looked behind as they sped away, but then winced when the back window of the Jeep suddenly shattered and glass shards filled the air. The car swerved this way and that. Logan rocked in his seat. They were being fired upon. The two remaining guards. At first Logan thought a tyre had blown, the way the car had violently swerved. But as he looked over at Pinilla, he realised the situation was much worse than that. Pinilla had a gushing wound in his neck.

'Just keep going!' Logan screamed at him. 'You're going to be fine. Just keep going!'

Pinilla had one hand up against his neck, trying to stem the tidal flow of blood. Logan looked at the man's groggy eyes. Pinilla was already losing consciousness. The hand he had on the wheel was clumsily steering this way and that. His eyes were glazed and closing.

Logan sat back in his seat and braced himself for the inevitable. And in the few seconds that remained before the car ploughed into the jungle, Logan couldn't help but think one thing: he'd failed.

Mackie had given him the chance. It had been there for the taking. For the first time, the opportunity had been there to really prove his worth. But he'd got greedy. He'd seen a means to take more from the mission than Mackie had asked for; he'd killed three of the cartel's high-ranking soldiers just like that!

In the end, it was all for nothing.

Because Logan knew, even before the oncoming collision with a thick tree, that Leo Pinilla was dead.

Chapter 43

Moscow, Russia

Peter Winter fished the vibrating phone out of his pocket and stared at the caller ID, not quite knowing what to say if he answered. It wasn't that the call was completely unexpected – he had certainly hoped it would come – but given the events of the last few days, the call had taken on a whole new importance.

'Logan? Is that really you?' Winter said as he tentatively answered.

'Yes,' was the simple response on the other end.

Even from the single-word answer, Winter knew it was Carl Logan.

His voice brought back a rush of memories. The two men had never been particularly close, but all of a sudden Logan's familiar voice brought a degree of comfort. How different to the last time he had spoken to Logan, just a few days ago, when Winter had still believed Logan was responsible for Mackie's death.

'I wasn't sure if you'd have left my number open,' Logan said after a few moments of silence.

Each of the JIA's field agents had a unique phone number that acted almost like an ID. It didn't matter whether they used a mobile or a landline or a pay phone, they could call their assigned number from any phone in the world and they would be routed to their commander. Now that Winter had stepped into Mackie's shoes, calls to Logan's ID were directed to him. He'd debated in his own mind whether or not to cancel Logan's account – he had already deleted much of the other evidence of Logan's existence when Logan had been on the run in Omsk – but in the end he'd left it operational. Given the events of the last two days, he was now very glad about that.

'I was hoping you'd call,' Winter said as he stood up from the chair and gazed out of the window of his Moscow hotel room.

'Of course you were,' Logan said, his tone terse. 'So has Evans filled you in?'

'I haven't spoken to Evans in more than two days,' Winter said, frowning as thoughts raced through his mind.

There was another silence on the other end for a few seconds.

'Logan, have you seen Evans?' Winter asked.

'He came after me. He didn't succeed.'

'Is he dead?' Winter said, not sure what answer he was hoping for.

'He was alive when I left him.'

'Evans was sent to Moscow to trail you,' Winter declared. He immediately wondered whether or not he should reveal his full hand to Logan. In the end, he carried on. He had to at least test the waters. 'He went to meet with a JIA asset. That asset, Nikolai Medvedev, was killed in a street in Moscow. I understand the FSB are blaming that on you.'

'I understand that too,' Logan said. 'But it's not true.'

'I know. That meeting was the last anyone saw or heard of Evans. It seemed the FSB captured him.'

Logan didn't respond immediately and Winter realised he'd given Logan new information that he was mulling over. Winter just hoped his gut instinct in doing that was right.

'Evans hasn't been kidnapped,' Logan said. 'I can assure you of that.'

'Then where is he?'

'Kazakhstan.'

That figured, Winter thought. He knew Logan wouldn't have stayed in Russia for long and would have headed to one of the neighbouring countries. Irina had said the last place the FSB had sighted Logan was near to Volgograd in southern Russia, not far from the western border of Kazakhstan.

But why would he go there? And what the hell had Evans been doing there?

Winter stared out of the window, looking across the sprawling Moscow cityscape but not really seeing anything. His mind was too filled with thoughts as to why it appeared his agents were running amok. For the last few hours, he had been sifting through the data he had received from Irina Tarasenko, which had downloaded to his computer seamlessly. It had given him many of the answers he needed while creating many more unanswered questions. And it had confirmed some of his worst fears.

With what Winter had come to know, his life was very much at risk.

'I'm taking from your more amiable tone toward me that you know I'm not behind whatever's going on here?' Logan said.

'I'm starting to come around to the idea,' said Winter.

'You know I didn't kill Mackie.'

'I know you didn't. And I know you didn't kill those other agents, Medvedev and Belenov, in Moscow.'

'The CIA killed Mackie.'

Winter was silent for a moment. He knew that now too, yet the words sounded surreal.

'I know,' Winter said. 'Jay Lindegaard okayed Mackie's death. In exchange for the Russians handing over Angela Grainger.'

'Yeah, sorry about that. Looks liked I've buggered up that deal then, doesn't it.'

'It wasn't my deal.'

'No, but you knew about Grainger. You were only too happy to sell me out. You and Mackie both.'

'You can't seriously believe that, Logan? Mackie would have fought for you to the bitter end.'

'If you say so.'

'It's the truth, Logan. I know how important Mackie was to you, but I worked closely with him too. So is Grainger still with you?'

Logan went silent. Winter took the lack of response as affirmation.

'I can help you,' he said. 'Both of you.'

'Evans said he was there to help me,' Logan said. 'You really didn't send him?'

'Sure, I sent Evans to find you. But last I heard he'd been snatched in Moscow. I would say we can both agree that Evans is no longer acting on my authority. And I had no idea you were in Kazakhstan.'

'Who said I still am?'

'Then where are you?'

There was silence on the other end of the phone once again. Winter turned away from the window and went and sat down on the bed, hanging down his head, which was throbbing with confusion.

'Why me, Winter?' Logan said. 'What's happening?'

'That's what I'm trying to find out,' Winter responded. There was still so much he needed to figure out. But he knew one thing for certain: Carl Logan was relentless; he would never give up. Exactly what Winter needed right now. He decided to dangle a carrot for Logan to chase.

'Maybe you should take a look at yourself, Logan. Maybe your past is finally catching up with you.'

'What the hell is that supposed to mean?'

'I always knew you were different,' Winter said. 'I saw the way Mackie treated you. He had a fondness for you that he didn't have for anyone else.'

'I'm touched that you noticed.'

'The thing is, I couldn't understand why. I admit, for a time you were a brilliant agent. You had all the talent in the world. But it wasn't enough for you. You wanted more.'

'I carried out every assignment I was given. I gave my life for the JIA.'

'But you started to question your orders, or at least question your role in carrying out those orders, even though it's the biggest taboo. You showed signs of life when the JIA expected none.'

'Is there a point to this?'

'Do you remember South America? Venezuela?'

'Of course. I did everything that was asked of me there. I always have.'

'You're right, you did,' Winter said. He didn't add that in addition, Logan had made big mistakes out in the Venezuelan jungle. 'But you also asked a lot of Mackie. That was the turning point, you see. That was when the chinks in your armour first appeared.'

'What are you talking about?' Logan said.

'The questioning, the bargaining for more power. What Mackie should have done was throw you out – you were finished. But instead he gave you the leeway you craved. He was willing to let go of the leash and let you make decisions for yourself, as long as they fitted his need, obviously. Yet that was never the path Mackie had intended for you.'

'You're saying this has something to do with what happened in Venezuela? Leo Pinilla?'

'No, I'm saying this has everything to do with you. The enemies that you've collected along the way.'

'Okay, Winter. Enough of this bullshit. You need to tell me what's going on.'

'I don't have all the answers. Not yet. We need to meet. It's about time we both took our sides.'

'The only side I'm on is my own.'

'Me too. Help me figure this out, Logan. No one else is going to listen to you now. If they get to me, and I have to assume they're going to try, then you really will be on your own.'

'And who is they?'

'Not over the phone,' Winter said.

'Then where?'

'How about London?'

'No chance. How would I even get there?'

'Don't you worry about that. I'll get you wherever you want to go.'

'I'm sure. You'll send someone else out to help me, right?'

'I told you, Evans being in Kazakhstan looking for you is nothing to do with me. I thought he'd been kidnapped by the Russians just like you were.'

'So Evans was the agent who met with Nikolai Medvedev?'

'Yes. But clearly the whole thing was a sham.'

'To kill off Medvedev.'

'I think so.'

'And Lena Belenov?'

'From what I gather, it certainly wasn't the FSB who did that.'

'So who's Evans really working for? Lindegaard?'

'It's a long story.'

'One you can only tell me face to face.'

'Exactly.'

There was silence again for a few moments. Winter wanted to say more but was reluctant. As much as he needed an ally, he wasn't sure how much he could trust Logan – even though he trusted Logan more now than he trusted just about anyone else.

'I'll be in Beijing in four days' time,' Logan said.

'Okay. Call me when you're there,' Winter said, but he was talking to an empty line.

PART 5

The art of deception

Chapter 44

Moscow, Russia

Jay Lindegaard moved slowly through the dense pine forest. There was sparse illumination coming from the near-clear sky above, the light of the full moon largely obscured by the dense foliage overhead. He'd parked his car some distance away from the house, hiding it from sight in a narrow passage that led into the forest. To get onto the sprawling housing complex where he now was, he'd had to scale an eight-foot-high perimeter fence. For a man like Lindegaard, that had been a cinch. He was now edging through the southern end of the grounds toward the agreed meeting point: next to the boathouse, which looked out onto a large man-made lake.

After a few more steps, the gaps between the trees seemed to widen. Not long after, Lindegaard found himself at the edge of the treeline, staring at the boathouse twenty yards ahead. Though to describe it as a boathouse didn't really do the building justice. It was the size of most deluxe mansions. But that was corrupt, super-rich Russians for you. Rarely discreet or tasteful in showing off their ill-gotten wealth.

The house he had come to was in the Rublyovka district of Moscow. A rich man's playground. Over just a small number of years, the suburb on the outskirts of the city had been overtaken by the newfound wealth of the few. Opulent and overly extravagant residences were springing up almost as fast as the land could be spuriously grabbed.

Beyond the high walls of the residences lay extremes of fantasy brought to life, ranging from mock castles and palaces with balustrades, towers and flying buttresses, to space-age white mansions with endless sleek curves and contours. The owners of these monstrosities playfully, or perhaps arrogantly, referred to their homes as cottages, but they really were anything but. It made Lindegaard sick to see such brazen and tasteless displays of wealth.

Lindegaard looked around and, happy that the coast was clear, began to trudge across the frozen grass toward the boathouse, the design of which reminded him of the wood-framed lake houses that he and his family often vacationed at in the Rocky Mountains. When he reached the building, he pressed himself up against the wooden slats of the near wall and began to creep around the outside, checking that he was alone.

For now, it appeared he was.

Just a few moments later, though, he heard rustling off in the opposite direction to where he had come from. He saw the outline of a figure coming through the trees. His body tensed but soon relaxed when the figure came into view and he saw who it was: Irina Tarasenko. The sleeper agent whom Sanderson had told him about. And who, Lindegaard had come to learn, had been visited very recently by Peter Winter.

Irina was moving slowly and with unease, looking around her all the time. She had on heavy black boots but Lindegaard could see that her legs were otherwise bare, covered from the knees up by the thick coat that she had wrapped around her. Lindegaard guessed she had come out into the gardens from her bed and he wondered what she had on underneath the coat – a skimpy lace negligee perhaps or maybe nothing at all. He felt the faintest twinge of arousal in his groin at the thought.

'You're alone?' Lindegaard said when Irina was just a couple of yards away. He spoke to Irina in English.

'Yes. I think so,' Irina said in a thick accent. 'It's two a.m. Everyone thinks I'm in bed.'

'Your husband? Will he notice you're gone?'

'He's not home tonight.'

'Okay. Great. I'm really glad you could meet me.'

'I wish I could say the same. Sorry, I don't mean to be rude.

It's just that I thought after the meeting with your colleague that I wouldn't be seeing anyone else from the agency for a while.'

'Yeah, sorry about that. But that's actually one of the things I need to talk to you about. The meeting you had, that is.'

'Okay,' she said, the look on her face changing from one of anxiousness to one more of suspicion.

'Can we go inside?' Lindegaard said, nodding to the boathouse. 'You look freezing.'

'Yes, come on. I have the key.'

Lindegaard followed Irina to the door, which she unlocked with a key from her coat pocket, then they both went inside. Neither of them bothered to turn on the lights – there was no need to draw attention. In the dark, it was hard to make out the layout of the room properly. It appeared to Lindegaard to be some sort of large, open-plan lounge-cum-dining room.

'We should do this quickly,' Irina said. 'The longer I'm gone, the bigger the chance of getting caught out.'

'I understand. This will be quick, I promise. Tell me about the meeting you had.'

'It was out of the blue. Not planned, like this. I always expected it to be more like this. He just came up to me when I was shopping.'

'His name is Peter Winter. He works for me.'

'He didn't tell me his name.'

'But you believed he was from the agency?'

'He said he worked for Mackie. Until Mackie was killed, that is. I had no reason to doubt him.'

'No, no, that's fine. He was telling the truth.'

'Then I don't really understand why you're here.'

'What did he talk to you about?'

Irina sighed, her shoulders slumping, as though resigned to the fact that she would have to just grin and bear the questions.

'All sorts,' she said. 'He wanted to know about the two FSB agents who were killed: Nikolai Medvedev and Lena Belenov.'

'And what did you tell him?'

'I told him what I know, which isn't much. I don't actually work for the FSB, remember. Everything I know is either from Alex or from digging into his files.'

'I appreciate that. But what did you tell Winter? What do you know?'

'That Medvedev wasn't killed by the FSB. They were tracking him, but it was another surveillance unit that killed him and took the British agent. The Russians don't have the British agent. Evans, I think your man said he was called.'

Lindegaard nodded, his face expressionless even though inside he was seething. Winter was certainly getting closer than Lindegaard had expected. He needed to find that weasel fast.

'And Lena Belenov?'

'I'll tell you the same thing I told him. I have no idea who killed her, but I'm sure it wasn't the FSB. And according to your colleague, it wasn't Carl Logan either.'

There was silence for a few moments. It didn't seem like Irina was going to willingly offer any more.

'What else?' Lindegaard said.

'There's nothing else to say. I sent all of the electronic files I gathered to your colleague, Winter, just like he asked me. That's everything I have access to right now. Honestly. I'm not sure what else you people are expecting me to say. If there's something specific you need me to do, then just tell me.'

Lindegaard tried his best to suppress his surprise at Irina's words. Electronic files? Just what the hell had she given Winter access to? It looked like the young commander was becoming a big problem.

He stared at Irina's face for a good while, but she didn't offer anything else. The dim light meant he was struggling to fully read her expression, but it seemed to have changed to exasperation. She was certainly a cool character, given the circumstances. But then Lindegaard guessed that her whole life was based on a lie, so keeping her real feelings under wraps probably wasn't too difficult.

'You're tired of this,' Lindegaard said.

'This?'

'This life. The uncertainty. I can sense it.'

'I'm tired of living a lie, yes. It's hard to get by not sure whether today might be the day that you have to betray the people you love most.'

'But it is what you signed up for.'

'It's what I was signed up *to*. I wasn't really given much of a choice.'

Lindegaard chuckled. He was fully aware of how she had been drawn into the clandestine world. She'd been barely out of her teens when Mackie had begun the process of setting her up as a sleeper agent. In essence, she'd been blackmailed into that position. She had no ties or any real allegiance to the UK or the US. Yet Mackie had delivered perfectly, first ensuring she was indebted to him and then skilfully steering her toward a relationship that made her potentially one of the most powerful informants Lindegaard had ever known.

'Yes, Mackie did have a rather unique manner of persuasion. Gentle was rarely his thing.'

'He was nice,' Irina said, her positive affirmation surprising Lindegaard and angering him a little. 'I always trusted him.'

'He was an honourable man,' Lindegaard said through clenched teeth.

The truth was, he'd hated Mackie. Hated who he was, how he operated, how he always seemed to get the upper hand in any situation. Well, not anymore. Lindegaard had always seen Mackie as a threat, largely because Lindegaard knew just how good he was at his job. It was one of the reasons that Mackie's carefully calculated demise had been such a blessing for Lindegaard. And that would have been the end of it, if it hadn't been for Carl Logan. If only Lena had done her job and taken care of Logan when she had the chance, it would have prevented all of the current chaos.

'So are we done?' Irina said. 'I've told you what happened. You said that was what you came here for.'

'You're doing a good job here.'

'I'm not so sure it's done any good so far.'

'Believe me, it's been very useful.'

'If there was a way to get out of this, I would. I do love Alex. I told your friend the same.'

'There might be a way.'

'Really?'

'Yes, really. I need to show you something.'

Lindegaard took a step toward Irina and moved his hand up to his chest to reach inside his coat. As he took another step, Irina shuffled back, away from him. His fingertips were just on the inside, heading toward his pocket, when she shouted out.

'Don't you fucking think about it!'

Lindegaard froze in position, his hand still up to his chest. In the darkness, he'd barely seen the move, but there was no doubting that the object that she had thrust toward him was a gun. Its dark metal seemed to glisten even in the dull light. Lindegaard was taken aback by her tactile move, but not in the least worried about the position he found himself in.

'Move your hand slowly away,' Irina said, her pitch raised but her tone defiant.

'Irina, I think you've mistaken my intentions,' Lindegaard said, taking his hand away from his coat.

'Really? This is bullshit. The whole thing is bullshit.'

'It's not. It's really not. Please, just put that away, then we can carry on talking about how to get you out.'

'Not a chance.'

'You won't shoot me,' Lindegaard said. 'How the hell would you explain that to your guards? You'd be better off putting that gun to your own head and blowing your brains out. It would surely be a nicer death than what will happen if they find out I was here. If they find out what you really are.'

Irina said nothing in response but Lindegaard could see the confidence in her stance melting away. She seemed to shrink down and her outstretched arm began to quiver.

'Just lower the gun and then we can carry on talking.'

Hoping to calm the tension further, Lindegaard raised both his hands into the air.

'Come on, Irina. You have to trust me. Like you trusted Mackie. I'm the only one who can get you out of this mess now. If that's what you really want.'

'No. There is no way out,' Irina said, lowering the gun and bowing her head. 'I realise that now. There is no way out for me. I can't leave Alex. I love him too much. And it means that I'll always have to live with this. With what I am.'

'Irina, believe me. There is a way out. If that's what you want.'

She looked up at him. 'Yes. I do. But how?'

Lindegaard lunged forward and grabbed her. He spun her around into a choke hold, an arm wrapped around her neck. With his free arm, he seized her wrist and smashed her hand off the wall behind. She writhed and cried out.

Lindegaard squeezed harder on her neck, stifling her screams. After another smack, she dropped the gun and he released her hand. He then swiftly brought his free hand up to her neck, a large hunting blade extending from his closed fist.

'Shhh, Irina. Come on. You don't want to wake the guards.'

She continued to writhe and coil but it was no use. Lindegaard's thick, muscular arm had her trapped.

'I told you there was a way out,' he snarled, pressing the tip of the knife into her skin, eliciting a desperate, strangled murmur. 'I'm a man of my word, Irina. Just like Mackie. You can trust me. You can trust me when I say that I can get you out of this.'

Slowly, meticulously, Lindegaard pushed the knife into the side of Irina's neck as she fought with all her strength to free herself. The razor-sharp blade sliced through her flesh with ease, piercing her windpipe as Lindegaard pushed the knife as far as it would go. Irina rasped and her body spasmed.

Lindegaard paused for just a second, savouring the moment, then thrust the knife outwards, cutting right through and out to the front of her neck. A spray of blood hissed out of the wound. Lindegaard lowered the weapon and threw her body down onto the floor, discarding her like the piece of rubbish she was.

Irina lay on the floor, eyes wide in panic, her body twitching as the life drained from her. Lindegaard listened intently as she gargled for breath, choking on the blood that was flowing fiercely, filling her mouth and lungs. Not long after, when her heart ceased beating, the gargling stopped and the noise of the blood fizzing from the open wound began to die down.

After a few moments more, there was only silence.

'And now,' Lindegaard said, smiling broadly, 'you're free.'

Chapter 45

Beijing, China

From the safety of the car, Logan had a near-unobstructed view of the hotel's expansive glass-fronted lobby. He was parked on the opposite side of the street to the hotel, in the Dongcheng district of Beijing, where the meeting with Peter Winter was due to take place.

Logan and Grainger had arrived some two hours before the planned meet. Largely because Logan was caught in two minds about Winter still. Either Winter was playing Logan, in which case he wouldn't be coming to this meeting alone. Or Winter really was trying to help Logan. That was clearly the lesser of two evils. But even if that were the case, Logan reckoned Winter was probably now being tracked by the enemy, just like he was, and caution was undoubtedly still required.

The near-four-day train ride from Astana had been long and dull but had given Logan and Grainger a chance to rest and talk. In the end, boarding the freight train had been simple. When they had arrived at Astana, they had sold the virtually new Land Cruiser to a car salesman who ran a second-hand garage on a main road in the city. He had given them five thousand US dollars in cash for the car, no questions asked. Logan reckoned the dealer would probably sell the four-by-four for close to ten times that amount, but that wasn't a problem. The man thought he'd got a good deal – which he had – but was clearly aware of the risk to himself in purchasing a vehicle of dubious origins. In any case, as far as Logan was concerned, five thousand dollars was enough to get them everything they needed.

After that, all it had taken was some gentle persuasion from Grainger, who'd used all her skills and feminine charm – and the obligatory palm-greasing, of course – and they had been able to stow away in an empty wooden container for the duration of the train journey into China and on to Beijing. Along the way, there had been no hint of disturbance, neither at the border crossing into China nor at the two rest and refill stops en route.

From there, the money had allowed them to hire a clapped-out micro car from a dodgy rental company in Beijing and buy cheap mobile phone handsets and provisions. It had also put them up in a rundown but discreet hotel the previous night. And they still had more than half the money left.

The journey had given Logan and Grainger plenty of time to talk. To grow closer to each other once more. Coming away from the failed exchange with Fleming and Evans, the mood between Logan and Grainger had been tense, but they'd both mellowed over the following days. Despite their predicament, the intense attraction that Logan had first felt for Grainger in Paris was back. And it was a good feeling. One he had long wondered whether he would ever have again. Although they were still far from in the clear, Grainger seemed to be filling up with life bit by bit too. It changed her expression, her mannerisms and her outlook. This was the old Grainger. The one he'd hoped he would find again.

'I'll go and wait inside,' Grainger said when it was two thirty – half an hour before the rendezvous.

They had both already scoped out the interior separately, noting the layout of exits, corridors, stairwells, toilets and all other potential hiding places and escape routes. Winter had asked to meet Logan in the lobby bar – the area Logan was spying on – but Logan had no intention of sticking to that arrangement. It was a no-brainer that both men wanted to meet in a public place, but Logan wasn't going to let Winter have the advantage of determining where.

'Okay,' Logan said. 'Take a seat in the bar, on the lounge chairs in the far corner. And keep your head down.'

Grainger tutted. 'Carl, I think I know how to surveil.'

'I know you do.'

'Keep the phone line open, so we can talk.'

'Of course,' he said.

Grainger dialled the number for Logan's phone and he pressed the button to accept the call. She then opened her car door, got out and crossed the busy street over to the hotel.

Logan watched as she strolled through the bar and then took a seat in the corner, as they had discussed. He was to wait in the car. Separated, they were in a better position to surveil a wider area, and the car gave Logan good cover on the outside of the hotel.

With Grainger sitting down, he could only see the top of her head; the rest of her body was obscured by the headrest of the seat opposite her. But that wasn't a problem for Logan. He knew where she was and between the two of them, they now had eyes on the whole bar and lobby area, together with the street outside the hotel.

After a few moments, a waiter came over to Grainger and Logan heard her order a soda water. Neither he nor Grainger spoke more than a few passing words of Mandarin, but the hotel was a typical business establishment where English was widely accepted, albeit spoken clumsily by the majority of the local staff.

Logan had visited China on numerous occasions but never for any great deal of time and he'd never had the opportunity or need to properly learn the language. Compared to many other countries, he'd always found it more difficult to move around due to the fact that the majority of locals, even in the big cities, had about as much English as he had their native tongue.

'Nothing happening in here so far,' Grainger said when the waiter left her.

Logan glanced at the clock in the car. Twenty minutes to go. But as he looked up, his eyes were immediately drawn to a figure moving cautiously along the pavement toward the revolving doors of the hotel.

It was Winter.

His body was stiff as he walked and he was doing a bad job of being discreet, his head darting this way and that as he scanned the area. Logan felt a pang of satisfaction at seeing a man who had on more than one occasion criticised Logan's skills appear so amateurish.

Or maybe it was all a show, Logan thought.

'Okay, this is him now,' he said to Grainger.

'Early, just like we thought.'

'Of course. He wants to get the lay of the land first. Just as we did.'

Winter walked in through the revolving doors and then glanced quickly left and right as he made his way through the lobby area. He wasn't stopping. He kept on going and soon was out of Logan's field of sight.

'I've lost him,' Logan said.

'It's okay. I can still see him. He's gone around the reception. Toward the restrooms ... and now he's gone in.'

'Looks like he's just being careful. Let me know when he comes back out.'

'Sure. And likewise, let me know if you spot anything out there.'

'All I see at the moment is an attractive brunette drinking on her own.'

Grainger laughed. 'I would ask you to join me, but I'm working.'

Logan smiled. 'Maybe later.'

'Maybe. I hope so.'

There was silence on the line for a good five minutes after that. Logan couldn't help but clock-watch the whole time, feeling the nerves inside him growing by the second as the hands on the car's clock edged painfully slowly toward three p.m.

'He's out,' Grainger said. 'And he's heading to the seats on the other side of the bar to me. You should see him any second.'

'I've got him,' Logan said as Winter came into view.

Winter sat down on a lounge chair. From the position he had chosen, his face was pretty much in clear sight of Logan, who sank down in the car just a little, aware that Winter would still be scoping the area outside the hotel. Logan couldn't help but think that Winter looked even younger than he had the last time Logan had seen him, almost a year ago. The weight of the world on his shoulders had somehow brought out the youth in the man.

But Winter didn't look nervous. Not at all. He looked confident and full of life. Logan didn't like that. He knew Winter was a tough cookie, mentally at least – he'd worked for Mackie for a number of years, after all, being groomed for a commander position. But Logan was still surprised by his relaxed demeanour. Either he was a brilliant actor, or he was up to something. Either way, Logan was planning to take the upper hand.

'Still nothing at your end?' Grainger asked.

'Nothing. Right, it's almost time.'

'Yeah. I see our guy. He's heading over to him now.'

As Logan glanced to the right, back toward the main doors, he saw a young Chinese man in a bellboy uniform heading over to the bar area. He moved with purpose, waltzing around the tables and chairs toward where Winter was sitting. Winter looked up at the young man with a sudden suspicious expression on his face. There was a brief exchange and the man handed Winter a piece of paper, then spun on his heel and walked off in the same direction he had come from.

Winter looked around him, confusion now washing across his face, then unfolded the paper. A second later, he jumped up out of his seat, turning this way and that. And then he fixed his eyes directly across the street at where Logan was parked. Logan slunk even lower in his seat, hoping Winter hadn't spotted him.

After a few moments, Logan risked a peek and was surprised to see Winter had gone.

'Where is he?' Logan said.

'Doors,' was the simple response from Grainger.

Logan's eyes darted toward the main doors and he saw Winter coming out of the hotel. By now, Logan's heart was thudding in his chest, and he breathed a sigh of relief as Winter walked off to the left, away from the hotel and away from where Logan was parked.

It wouldn't have been a disaster if Winter had spotted him, but it would certainly have taken away the element of control that Logan and Grainger knew they'd have if they could direct Winter to the rendezvous spot they'd chosen, which Winter wouldn't have had time to scope out beforehand.

'Okay, he's on the move,' Logan said.

'I'm following.'

Logan watched as Grainger came out the hotel and began sauntering down the street. He stayed in the car and waited, wanting to make sure that Grainger and Winter were far enough out of sight to make his own presence inconspicuous before he headed for the rendezvous location.

Within a few moments, Logan could no longer see either of them. 'Keep on him,' he said.

'I am.'

'And keep on the–'

'Shit, Carl,' Grainger said.

'What is it? You haven't lost him already, have you?'

'No. Worse than that. I don't think we're alone. He's got a tail.'

Chapter 46

'Who is it?' Logan asked, opening his door and stepping from the car.

'I don't know,' Grainger said. 'Not Evans. Or any of the other guys he was with before.'

'Is he following you or Winter?'

'Winter, I think. He's in front of me. I didn't see where he came from. I have to hang back. I might lose sight of Winter, but I don't want to spook whoever this other guy is.'

'That's fine. You know where Winter is heading so just keep going that way.'

'Yeah, will do.'

The place they had chosen for the Winter meet was in Beihai Park, a former imperial garden deep in the centre of Beijing. Now a public park, it was popular with tourists and locals alike, and at this time of day, Logan knew the main parts of it would be bustling. The piece of paper the boy had handed to Winter in the bar gave directions to the Nine-Dragon Wall – a six-hundred-year-old screen at the northern end of the park within easy reach of the nearby streets. It was out in the open, giving Logan and Grainger the lay of the land, but also somewhere they could easily run from, losing themselves in the crowds in the park or in the streets if they needed.

But that was all assuming Winter was actually heading there. Right now, Logan's simple focus was on catching up with Grainger.

'What does the tracker look like?' Logan asked. 'I'm heading up behind you.'

'He's tall, about your height. Cropped jet-black hair. Blue jeans, dark-grey coat. I think he's a local. Chinese, I mean.'

Logan wondered whether he was with a surveillance unit from the Chinese Ministry of State Security. But then, why would the MSS have had Winter or Grainger on their radar? It was possible that he and Grainger had been followed since coming off the freight train at Beijing West station the previous day. But it was more likely that the man was affiliated to Evans or Winter.

Was he with Winter or surveilling him?

Either way, Grainger was very possibly heading straight into an ambush.

'I'll be with you in a minute,' Logan said, his quick speech matching his breathing.

Logan could feel his tension slowly starting to rise. He hated being blind to what was going on, unable to control the situation.

'Can you still see Winter?' he said.

'Only just. The streets are getting really busy here.'

'Yeah, I can see that,' Logan said as he bumped shoulders with another pedestrian who cut across him. The crowded streets would make his own presence less visible but it also meant progress was slow.

'Winter's quite far ahead now,' Grainger said. 'I'm not going to be able to keep sight of him for much longer. Wait … no, that's not him. Shit, I think I've lost him.'

'Damn it.'

'But I can still see the tracker easily enough.'

'Okay, keep on him. I can't be far off you now.'

Lost in the conversation and busily scanning the crammed street for any sight of Grainger or the mystery man, Logan was almost caught out when the pedestrian crossing lights ahead changed to red. He took a step into the busy road and a car slammed on the brakes and skidded to a halt, only narrowly avoiding him. Logan cursed to himself, then gave a meek wave to the angry driver before carrying on across the road, darting between the moving cars.

'Are you still on the main road?'

'No,' Grainger said, causing Logan to shake his head. 'We turned onto a side street. Take a right when you pass the electrical shop on the corner – red sign. It's quieter now. Easier to follow.'

'Easier to be seen too,' Logan said. 'But still no sign of Winter?'

'No.'

'What's the street name?'

'I didn't catch it. Wait a second. He's turned right again. Second right.'

'The tracker?'

'Yeah, I still can't see Winter.'

'That's not the way.'

'I'm going to follow him. Winter must have turned too.'

'No, Angela, leave him. Keep on top of Winter.'

'But I can't see him.'

'I don't like this. Just go to where we planned. Winter will be there.'

'Unless he's done a bunk on us. You head to the rendezvous. I'm following this guy. We need to know who he is.'

'Angela, don't do it. It's not safe.'

But she wasn't listening. This really was the old Grainger. Dogged, determined. It was the woman he had fallen for. Yet he wished just this once she would stop and listen. Logan didn't like this. She must too have realised the situation wasn't right?

'I've turned up the street behind him. It's just an alley. Pretty much deserted. I see the tracker up ahead, about thirty yards from me.'

Logan swore again. He wasn't getting a good feeling about the situation at all. He tried to pick up his pace. Tried his best to dodge between the many pedestrians. But it was near-impossible to force a clear path.

'What's happening, Angela?' Logan said, his impatience clear. 'Where are you?'

'Damn it. I think he might have spotted me.' Her breaths were heavy and fast, her voice filled with tension. 'I'm hiding behind some bins.'

'Get out of there, Angela!' Logan shouted. 'Turn around and just get the hell out of there. I'll find you back on the main street.'

'And now he's gone. I've just looked up and he's not there anymore.'

'Angela, get the hell out of there!'

Logan knew what was happening but was entirely powerless to stop it. And already it was too late. Because the next thing he heard was Grainger's shrill scream.

'Angela!'

The phone line went dead.

Chapter 47

Fighting against the tide of people, Logan did his best to burst into a sprint. After one too many collisions with startled pedestrians, he began to dart in and out of the road. As he moved, Logan scanned each side street he passed.

He followed the few directions she'd relayed to him. He took the turns she had and he found the alley, the set of bins she must have been hiding behind. But there was no sign of Grainger. No sign of life there at all.

In the end, frustration and anger gripping him in equal measure, Logan turned and rushed back toward Beihai Park. It was more than a mile away. By the time he reached the ornate gates at the northern tip of the park, he was a sweaty mess. His legs felt like they were on fire. He was panting almost uncontrollably. He stopped to regain his composure for just a few seconds before entering the park and heading toward the meeting point.

Logan had been to Beijing before, both for work and for pleasure. It was a fascinating city, a strange mix of ancient history and modern exuberance, with the impact of the communist era still evident all around in the buildings and the way people acted. But the impressive ancient sights within Beihai Park – the temples, pavilions and halls with their spires and pointed, upswept eaves and intricate decorations – were completely lost on Logan today.

The park, as expected, was busy with tourists enjoying the sunshine and the sights, happily clicking away on their cameras, holding aloft their ridiculous selfie sticks while they gurned like there was no tomorrow. Logan brushed past them, focused only on one thing. Winter.

The young JIA commander was casually meandering alongside the metal railing that surrounded the Nine-Dragon Wall, looking every bit the worry-free tourist. Just like at the hotel, there was no hint of anxiety, of tension, on his face. Logan strode up to him, feeling the absolute opposite to how Winter looked – his body rigid, his head ready to explode.

When Logan was just a couple of yards away, Winter turned to face him. There was just the slightest hint of a smile on his face when he saw Logan. It was soon wiped away when Logan thrust an arm forward, grabbed hold of Winter by his scrawny neck and almost lifted his whole body off the ground.

'Where is she?' Logan boomed.

'Logan, get the hell off me.'

'Where is she? Where's Grainger?'

'What are you talking about?' Winter rasped and wheezed. 'I've no idea where she is.'

Logan caught sight of the people around who had stopped to stare. He cursed under his breath. The last thing he needed was to draw unwanted attention from the local police, who still kept order with an iron fist. Being banged up in a Chinese jail really wasn't going to help matters.

And Winter's surprised reaction to Grainger's disappearance seemed genuine.

He released his grip on Winter, who crumpled down, grabbed his knees with his hands and began coughing and spluttering.

'Walk,' Logan said, hauling Winter back upright and dragging him along by his arm.

'What's going on?' Winter gasped.

'We were followed. Either you or us.'

'What? I'm sure no one followed me.'

'Then where's Grainger?'

'How should I know? I made my way here. Just like your message said.'

Logan stopped and tugged Winter to a halt.

'If you're lying to me, I *will* kill you, Winter.'

'Your macho bullshit doesn't work on me, Logan.'

Logan pulled Winter into him again and grabbed him by the

scruff of his neck. He pressed his face up to Winter's, snarling like an angry dog.

Logan felt pressure on his side.

'Let the fuck go of me before I stick this in you,' Winter said, his voice absolutely calm.

Logan looked down and saw the pocket knife, its silvery blade pushed up against his side, right by his kidney. A spot Winter had surely chosen with purpose. Logan had on a thick jumper and overcoat. Probably an inch or so of protection. But the four-inch blade could still do plenty of damage if Winter wanted it to. If it pierced the kidney or the artery nearby, Logan could be dead within minutes. He let go of Winter's neck and the JIA commander slumped down and withdrew the knife.

'You might think of yourself as an unstoppable force,' Winter said, 'but don't kid yourself that I'm just some plank off the streets.'

'Winter, even with that knife pressed up against me, you don't worry me in the least. I just don't want to make a scene out here.'

Though really, Logan was a little surprised that Winter had made a move on him, and he did respect the young man for it, even if he wouldn't admit to it.

'Come on, let's keep walking,' Logan said, anger still dominating his mind but feeling a sense of clarity returning.

'Tell me what happened,' Winter said.

'Grainger was on foot, following you here.'

'I figured one of you would be.'

'But someone else was too. A man. Grainger said he was Chinese. Tall, black hair, grey coat.'

'Logan, that could describe about five million people in this city.'

'Yeah, well, she was sure he was following you.'

'There was no one following me.'

'And you haven't made any new friends here?'

'I haven't made contact with anyone here other than you, if that's what you're asking. The Chinese authorities have no idea I'm here.'

'Well, whoever it was, he got the slip on Grainger. He's got her now.'

Winter stopped and turned to face Logan. 'Are you sure about that?' he said.

'Sure about what?'

'That someone's snatched Grainger. Are you sure you can trust her?'

'I trust her more than I trust anyone else. You included.'

'But it wouldn't be the first time she's betrayed that trust, would it?'

'She's been snatched,' Logan said through gritted teeth. 'I know it.'

'Well, if she has, it was nothing to do with me.'

'Maybe. Maybe not.'

'You see what's happening here, don't you?' Winter said.

'You tell me,' Logan responded. 'Not so long ago, you were blaming me for killing Mackie. I was the bad guy. You wanted to hunt me down and end my days.'

'A lot's changed.'

'You don't say. Now, all of a sudden, you want to play nice. And yet no sooner have we planned to meet than Grainger gets kidnapped.'

'If that's even what's happened to her, I assure you it wasn't me,' Winter said. 'And I know now that you didn't kill Mackie.'

'You really thought I could kill Mackie, after everything we went through?'

'Yes,' Winter said without thinking. 'I think people are capable of anything in the right circumstances. Given what happened to you, being locked up like that, do you really blame me for thinking you did it?'

'No. But I do blame you for leaving me in a torture chamber for three months.'

Winter tutted, as though fed up with going over old business. But Logan felt fully justified in bringing that up. He was yet to have any sort of apology from Mackie or from Winter or anyone else for his having to spend three months in the hands of the FSB in that godforsaken gulag.

'You know that's not how it was,' Winter said.

'If you say so.'

'You were set up, Logan. And it wasn't me or Mackie.'

'Lindegaard,' Logan said, venom in his voice.

'You knew?' Winter said, clearly surprised by the fact.

'I've been putting the pieces together. It was always Lindegaard.

But I'm not sure why. He's always had a beef with me, but this?'

'It's not just Lindegaard. It's Evans too. And they've both got a beef with you.'

Logan raised an eyebrow. 'I've barely ever spoken to Evans. How could that be?'

'I told you your past was coming back to haunt you.'

'Yeah, but I'm finding it hard to believe this is all about me. Too many people have died for that to be the case.'

'You're right, it's not. And you don't know the half of it. John Sanderson was killed in his home in London two days ago. Did you know that?'

'No, I didn't,' Logan said.

He hadn't known Sanderson well, but his death was still shocking, given his senior position at the JIA. Together with Mackie's death, it was like the heart of the JIA was being torn out.

'And in Moscow, you already know about Medvedev and Belenov?' Winter asked.

'Of course. Apparently it's me who's copping the flack.'

'Well, something you might not know is that three days ago another JIA agent was killed there.'

'Who?'

'Irina Tarasenko.'

Logan racked his brain but the name didn't fit anything he knew.

'She was a sleeper agent.'

'Mackie's?'

'Yes. I met with her in Moscow. The information she gave me helped me to piece together the final pieces of the jigsaw. I thought I had a real asset on my hands. But the following day she was found dead with her throat slit.'

'And you're telling me you're not being followed?'

Ever since escaping from Evans outside Astana, Logan had wondered why there was no sign of anyone following him. And now it was making sense. It was Winter they were tracking. Not just his movements but probably his phone calls with Logan too. Evans and Lindegaard had been banking on Logan and Winter meeting, because they knew Winter was getting too close to the truth.

'Look, Logan, don't you see what's happening here? These deaths aren't unconnected. You might be central to what's happening now, but only because you're one of the few men who could ever stop it. You've rubbed the wrong people up the wrong way and you're on their hit list.'

'But why? You said something about Venezuela before.'

'Logan, there was so much fucked up about Venezuela you wouldn't believe it.'

'The CIA agent I killed – Janet Ford. She was Lindegaard's agent.'

Winter stared at Logan, an impressed look on his face. But Logan had known about that for years. It was the first time that Lindegaard and Logan had crossed paths. It had taken a lot of work by Mackie to keep the CIA off Logan's back.

'What I bet you don't know is that Erika Sandstrom was his agent as well,' Winter said. 'But she was deep, deep cover. Only three people ever knew about her. Pinilla wasn't one of them.'

Logan tried to hide his surprise at the revelation. Leo Pinilla's girlfriend. The woman Logan had shot with a tranquilliser dart. The woman Pinilla had insisted on bringing with him as they tried to escape from the cartel.

How could Logan not have known she was another agent, even after all this time?

'So what, this is just some kind of revenge against me?'

'No, not at all,' Winter said. 'Certainly that's been a catalyst for a lot of things that have happened since, the bad blood that there's been between Lindegaard and the JIA for years. His dislike of you, me, Mackie. All of us.'

'Then what else is there?'

'Take a guess.'

'Lindegaard. He's playing us. The JIA, the CIA. It's the only thing that makes sense.'

'You've hit the nail on the head. Lindegaard has been dirty for years. I've got all the evidence now. He sold out you and Mackie both. But when you escaped in Russia, his whole world was turned upside down. You got away. You messed up everything for him. He knew with you on the run it was only a matter of time before you got to the bottom of what he's been doing all these years. He's been trying to take out anyone who's had a whiff of his dirty deeds ever since.'

'You included.'

'Absolutely. Oh, I'm sure he thought I wouldn't be a problem, but clearly he underestimated me like he did you. You know, the JIA only exists because we operate in the shadows, away from prying eyes. There's only so long the sponsors will put up with all of these inexplicable events. Logan, Lindegaard is trying to take down the JIA. And once we're out of the way, I'm not sure who's left to stop him.'

Logan's mobile phone began to chirp in his pocket. Winter and Logan looked at each other, both knowing what this meant. Logan reached down and took out the phone and looked at the caller ID, which confirmed what he already knew. It was Grainger's number.

He pressed the button to accept the call and put the phone to his ear without saying a word.

'Logan, I know you're there.'

It was Evans.

'I'm going to keep this really simple for you. Look down.'

Logan looked down and saw a small red dot hovering on his chest. He held his hand up, intersecting the laser a few feet in front of his body. He found the line of sight where the beam was coming from. He couldn't tell exactly how far away the sniper was, but the laser was coming from the buildings to the north, the nearest of which were at least a couple of hundred yards away.

'Very clever, Logan, you've figured out where the shooter is. But it's not going to help. As soon as the call is finished, we're moving.'

'What do you want?'

'I want you to do exactly as I say. If you don't, Angela Grainger is dead.'

Chapter 48

Evans stood over Angela Grainger, who was slumped on the chair in front of him. They'd transported her to the empty industrial unit in the nearby Xicheng district in a battered old minivan. The vehicle had been supplied by a thirty-year-old Chinese man who called himself Jeremy and had previously worked for the Beijing police, but had long been a useful informant for the JIA. These days, he was effectively a mercenary. Much like Evans's other helper, Mason.

But then, Evans figured, wasn't that what all JIA agents really were? Largely they were paid not to think, not to question orders, but to just bloody well carry them out. It was the way of the world. Secret agents were looked up to as heroes when really they were just gutless, self-centred arseholes who cared for no one but themselves. How else could they get through life doing the things they were told to do without ever questioning their morality?

Really, though, Evans didn't mind that. If anything, it made his job all the easier because the likes of Jeremy and Mason and the countless other men Evans used didn't care to ask why. They just took their money and did as they were told.

Evans kneeled down by Grainger's side and reached forward, extending his forefinger and lifting Grainger's eyelid. Her pupil was big and black, taking up almost all of her eye. There was only the slightest movement as the pupil shrank a little, reacting to the dim light. She was clearly still out of it, but Evans guessed it would only be minutes before she started to come around.

Everything had happened so quickly after Winter had left

the hotel where he'd arranged to meet Logan. The move hadn't taken Evans by surprise. He had guessed Logan would try to lure Winter elsewhere. What he hadn't known was where. So he'd had Jeremy follow Logan and Grainger to the hotel some two hours before the planned meeting. Then, when Grainger had gone inside, leaving Logan in the car, Mason and Jeremy had taken up positions, ready to tail. When it became clear that Grainger was following Winter, and with Logan nowhere in sight, Evans had decided to snag Grainger.

Once Jeremy had lured her into a quiet alley, Mason delivered the blow – a tranquilliser-filled syringe. Not a big dose, just enough to knock her out. Much like what had been delivered to Evans himself during his faked kidnapping back in Russia.

Now, an hour later, Evans knew it wouldn't be long before Grainger started to stir.

He lifted her head up. She held it in position for a few seconds and then it lolled left and right as she struggled to maintain control. Finally it flopped down again. He lifted her head up again and smacked her lightly on the cheek. This time, she seemed to take notice and her head snapped back stiffly and her eyes opened and closed a few times.

Grainger moaned and groaned and fought to keep her eyelids open. When she finally managed it, her gaze fixed on Evans's smiling face. All of a sudden, she seemed to find the strength to fight. She began to jump up and down in her seat, her arms and legs bucking and flailing. Evans just grinned. There was nothing she could do. Her ankles were taped to the chair legs, her wrists to the chair arms. The chair itself, a simple metal structure, had been bolted to the floor.

'Hello again,' Evans said, still smiling, when Grainger stopped her fruitless resistance.

Grainger didn't respond. She took her glare away from Evans, an angry look on her pained face.

'I bet you're feeling pretty drowsy. It'll wear off soon, though. Do you want some water? It might help.'

'Why are you doing this?' Grainger slurred.

'Doing what?'

'I don't understand what you want from me. I don't even know you.'

'You're right. It's who you know, I'm afraid. Wrong place and the wrong time. Or something like that.'

'If it's Logan you want, then why am I here?'

'Do you really need to ask that? That man is crazy about you. Or maybe he's just crazy. I can see why, though. You're a looker. Clearly a bit mental, what with you organising the kidnapping of the Attorney General, but definitely a good-looking lady.'

'Fuck you.'

'I really don't care about you, Angela Grainger. The Americans might want you to face justice, whatever that might mean, and the Russians probably want you dead, given the trouble you've caused them. But I don't care what you did. I don't care about the people who lost their lives in Paris because of you, or the trail of bodies Logan left behind in hunting you down. This isn't about you.'

'I never asked to be saved,' Grainger said. 'I don't even know why Logan did it. Don't forget I shot him so I could get away from him.'

'Ouch,' Evans said, then laughed.

Her response surprised him, but he assumed she was just trying to bluff. He had to admit, he was impressed by her resolve, given the circumstances. But then, he guessed, she must be a cool character to have organised the plot to kidnap Frank Modena.

'It's just as well Logan isn't around to hear you say that,' Evans added. 'It'd break his feeble little heart. But it does play nicely into what we have planned for you.'

'Which is what? You use me to lure Logan here, then kill us both?'

'Not far off, I have to admit. But there's a bit more to it than that. We thought you might be so good as to help us.'

'Who is us? And why the hell would I help you?'

'Us is me and my associates. You've met Mason before.'

Evans turned around and pointed at Mason, who was sitting on a chair at the far side of the expansive but bare room.

'And there're others as well. You'll meet us all in due course. You help us, we'll help you.'

'I can't see that happening. You could say we've got off on the wrong foot.'

Evans sighed. 'Why don't we just stop this now? I can see you think you can get through this situation with your tough girl bravado, so well done for that. But you'll see why you'll help us. We've got a very good reason.'

'And what's that?'

'Ah, in time. First of all, I need to tell you what you're going to do for me. For us.'

'Which is?'

Evans leaned over to Grainger and whispered in her ear. She snorted. Evans carried on, telling her the plan. But just as he began to move away, her head shot forward and she sank her teeth into his cheek.

Evans screamed in pain and laid a fist into Grainger's stomach, then another into her head. The blows made her release her grip and Evans stood straight, feeling at the wound on his cheek. Blood poured down onto his clothes and filled his mouth. He moved his tongue up and realised she had bitten right through the flesh of his cheek.

Grainger looked up at him, defiant, red liquid dripping from her mouth and covering her teeth, making her look manic and crazed. She spat out a mouthful of blood and smiled.

Acting on instinct, Evans lunged forward and sent a crushing blow into Grainger's nose. Her eyes rolled and her head bowed again. Evans kneeled back down next to her and tugged on her hair sharply, lifting her heavy head back up.

'You will help us,' Evans said, blood dribbling down his chin.

Evans nodded over to Mason, who stood up from his chair, completely relaxed and unmoved by what had just happened – which only made Evans all the angrier. Mason moved over to the large steel door that led to the storage room, pulled the lever and slid the door open.

Grainger was managing to hold her head up but she was clearly dazed from the punch; her eyes were closed, her nose streaming thick red blood.

'Look!' Evans shouted at Grainger. 'Look, you stupid bitch!'

Grainger slowly opened her eyes and Evans waited. It took a few seconds for her to fully focus, but when he saw the terror in her eyes, Evans knew he had her full attention.

Standing in front of Grainger was Jeremy. Not a big surprise really – Grainger had been following him earlier, after all, so she surely could have guessed that he'd be there too. But it wasn't Jeremy she was looking at, Evans knew. She was staring at the second man. The one who was on his knees at Jeremy's feet. The one who had the barrel of a silenced revolver stuffed into his ear. His hands were tied behind his back and glossy tape was wrapped around his head, covering his mouth.

Finally, Grainger's resolve broke and she began to sob.

Even with the pain that was coursing through his cheek, Evans couldn't help but smile.

'Now that I've got your attention,' he said, 'why don't we start again.'

Chapter 49

Logan parked the car on the road outside a looming red-brick industrial unit. The location Evans had directed Logan and Winter to was just past Beijing's 3rd Ring Road, about four miles from where they had started, though with the traffic the journey had taken the best part of an hour.

'You know they're setting us up,' Winter said as he got out of the car.

'Of course,' Logan replied as he opened his door and got out. 'But what choice do we have?'

'I could call some other people here. Get this done properly. I know you like to take on the world, but it doesn't always have to be that way. We could have a Chinese ops team here in no time to sweep through the place.'

'Evans gave us two hours. More than half of that has gone already.'

'Evans wouldn't know what to do if we didn't show. Trust me. We'd have the time. He wants you, Logan. He's not going to just disappear if we don't show.'

'It's not just about me. He'll kill her. I don't think he's bluffing. I'm not risking Grainger's life. I've come too far for that.'

Logan looked up at the structure in front of him. Although the brickwork was in good condition, it was clear the property was no longer in use. Its windows were either boarded up or broken, weeds were growing uncontrollably out of the ground surrounding the building and the rickety chain fence along the perimeter was in a state of serious disrepair.

The building itself looked like an old factory or textile mill that wouldn't have been out of place in the industrial heartlands of Victorian Britain. It was surreal to see such a structure close to the heart of Beijing.

'So what's the plan?' Winter asked as the two men made their way along the deserted street, looking for an entrance.

'There isn't one,' Logan said.

'You're kidding, right?'

'No.'

He knew it wasn't what Winter wanted to hear, but they weren't in control of this situation. Evans was. Logan still fully believed he'd get a chance to turn that around, but for now he had to just go along with what Evans had said and wait for the opportunity that he was certain would come.

'Neither of us is armed even,' Winter said.

'It's what Evans asked for. No point in taking a chance.'

'But how the hell are you expecting us to get out of this alive if we don't even have a plan?'

Logan stopped and Winter followed suit.

'If you want to run, then run,' Logan said. 'Nobody would think any less of you.'

Winter scoffed and looked offended. 'I'm not going to run. I just thought it would be better to have some sort of plan.'

'Okay. The plan is we kill them all and rescue Grainger.'

Despite the sarcastic nature of the comment, that was exactly what Logan intended to do.

'To think we gave you all that tactical training,' Winter said with a wry smile.

Logan shrugged. 'You didn't. Mackie did.' He set off again with Winter scurrying behind.

'I admire your confidence, Logan,' Winter said. 'But do you think that maybe you've bitten off more than you can chew this time?'

'No.'

They came up to what looked like the original gated entrance to the factory, a simple wire mesh that was closed but not locked, beyond which lay a short pathway that led to a set of large, wooden double doors. The paint was peeling and the doors were covered in grime and mildew, but they looked structurally intact.

Without saying a word, Logan opened the gate and walked up to the doors. He reached out for the handle of the normal-sized door in the middle of the left-hand loading door and pushed the handle down. The latch released. He looked over at Winter, standing by his side. Winter nodded, and Logan swung the door open and then walked in.

It took Logan's eyes a couple of seconds to adjust to the darkness that ate up the majority of the inside of the building, due to the many boarded-up windows. Bright rays of light pierced the black here and there from the few panes that remained unobstructed. When his eyes focused, Logan immediately knew they were in the right place. Because in the darkness, he could quite clearly see the narrow beam of a red laser reaching out from the distance to his chest. A second beam intersected the first, trailing to Logan's right, onto Winter's chest.

'Close the door behind you,' Evans said, coming into view from behind a large metal girder about ten yards in front of where Logan and Winter were standing.

Logan saw that, as well as a gash on his eye from where Logan had butted him back in Kazakhstan, Evans had a fresh wound on his cheek and dried blood was caked on his face and clothes. He felt a sliver of satisfaction. Grainger was a fighter. That was for sure.

And so was he.

Winter back-stepped, the trail of red light following him as he did so, and he pushed the door shut.

Logan stared at Evans who, despite the injury, had a smug look on his face, his hands behind his back, striking an altogether nonchalant pose.

'I like what you've done to your face,' Logan said. 'It suits you.'

Evans didn't respond to the taunt.

'Where is she?' Logan said, his voice calm.

'She's right here,' Evans said, indicating over to his right. 'Come on, let's go.'

Evans turned and walked away, across the barren expanse toward a set of sliding doors at the end of the room.

Logan began to edge forward, in pursuit of Evans, scanning the area as he moved, taking in the surroundings. The room they had walked into was large, probably a thirty-by-thirty-yard square. The poured concrete floor was in good condition but the room was entirely empty, with the exception of the load-bearing metal struts that lay at regular intervals and the thick layer of dust that covered the floor and filled the air. Whatever previous use the building had seen as a factory or an office, it had been entirely cleared of anything of use and value now.

As Logan kept stride with Evans, his gaze followed the path of the red laser hovering over his chest. At the end of the beam, out of the darkness, a figure appeared. It was the man who had been at the exchange in Kazakhstan. Mason. Logan looked off to his right, following the beam targeted at Winter's chest. Another man came into view. Logan hadn't seen him before. He was tall and wore blue jeans and a dark-grey jacket. He looked Chinese. The man Grainger had followed.

The two armed men closed the distance to their targets. When they were just a few yards away, Logan could see that the guns they were holding were M4 carbines. Not playthings: these were heavy-duty guns. Serious weapons.

'So how much did you have to pay Fleming to give me up?' Logan asked Evans, who was still walking away.

'We didn't pay him a thing,' Evans said without turning around.

Logan guessed what the response meant and his heart sank. He wouldn't mourn Fleming's or Butler's passing for a second, but he was disappointed. After what those two had done, Logan would have happily killed them both. Still, at least it was one less problem to consider. More than anything, Logan was surprised Evans had managed to fell the SAS men at all. Fleming, in particular, was someone Logan had never once managed to get the better of. And there weren't many people like that.

Logan walked past Mason, who hadn't yet moved, eyeballing him the whole time. As Logan approached the doorway which Evans had stopped at, he felt pressure on his back. The muzzle of Mason's M4, he guessed.

Evans slid open the large inner door to reveal a near-identical room on the other side. Except this room wasn't entirely bare, like the first had been.

In the middle of the room was Grainger.

'And here she is,' Evans said, a smile on his face. 'Another reunion for the lovebirds.'

'Are you okay?' Logan said as he entered the room.

Grainger nodded, tears rolling down her face.

Logan stopped and looked around. Winter came up two yards to his right, a rifle barrel pushed up against his back, the mirror image of Logan. Evans walked between them and up to Grainger.

'You let her go now,' Logan said. 'That was the deal.'

'I'm a man of my word,' Evans said to Logan. 'You've done everything I asked you to do.'

'Let her go.'

'Don't worry, man. I won't kill her. What the Americans or the Russians do with her is up to them. But you can't hold me responsible for that.'

'Just let her go!' Logan shouted.

Evans laughed but then scowled. 'I will. But first, I want her to see you die.'

Logan had been trying his best to control himself, breathing deeply, repeating a mantra in his head that had seldom helped his rage but he was hoping would this one time. He knew he had to control himself if he was to get out alive. Once the red mist descended, all bets were off. But seeing Grainger so helpless and Evans so mocking was making Logan's task all the more difficult.

'Kneel down,' Evans said. 'It's time to say your last words.'

Out of the corner of his eye, Logan saw Winter get to his knees. But Logan stayed on his feet.

'I said kneel down!' Evans shouted.

'It's time,' Logan said, turning his head toward Winter.

He just hoped Winter would put up a fight.

Logan had known Winter for a number of years. The young man was a pencil-pusher, but Logan knew he must have had at least basic combat training. Commanders didn't work the field like agents did, but they had to be prepared for situations like the one they were in. Plus, Winter had managed to pull a knife on Logan earlier with ease. He wasn't a complete no-hope. Either way, Logan didn't have enough time to save himself, Grainger and Winter. And when it came down to it, the hard truth was that Grainger's life was worth more to Logan than Winter's. He had to save Grainger first. For now, Winter would just have to take care of himself.

Logan spun around, bending his knees and then springing upwards like a jack-in-a-box. He clenched his right fist, thrust it up and crashed it into Mason's jaw, snapping his head back. It was perfect contact. The noise suggested to Logan that Mason's jaw had probably been shattered to pieces. And the way that Mason's body tumbled to the ground told Logan the single blow had been enough to put him out of the fight for good.

As Logan threw himself to the floor, he glanced to his left to see whether the other gunman was a threat. He was pleased to see Winter scrabbling on the ground with his foe. Logan hit the deck right next to Mason's crumpled body. He lifted up the M4 that had come from Mason's grip, though its strap was still around the fallen man's shoulder.

Logan yanked on the gun. He pointed it toward Evans.

The move had taken barely a couple of seconds. Evans had gone for defence first and taken cover behind Grainger. He was crouching down behind her. His head and torso were entirely hidden as he brought a handgun around and placed the barrel against Grainger's temple.

From their relative positions, there was no way Logan could deliver a fatal shot. But he didn't need to see all of his target to make a difference.

He took aim and fired.

Logan hadn't checked the settings on the weapon before pulling the trigger, but he knew the M4 had selective fire options. The quick treble blast of fire told Logan the weapon had been set to three-round bursts. Evans let out an animalistic yelp as each of the .223 calibre bullets tore into his ankle. He rolled to the ground, screaming.

Logan heard a volley of fire from his right and his body tensed for a second. But the fact he could still hear Winter and the Chinese man grappling suggested the shots had all been wayward, whoever the intended target had been.

Before Evans could even contemplate his next move, Logan aimed again and let off another burst of fire. This time the three bullets caught Evans in his arm and shoulder. He instinctively dropped his weapon as he continued to scream in agony.

Logan yanked harder on the M4, pulling the strap from the fallen Mason. As he got to his feet, Logan turned his weapon.

He pointed it toward Winter and the Chinese man, who were tussling on the floor. He tried for a second to take proper aim, but the bodies were writhing too much. As with Evans, though, Logan didn't have to shoot to kill. He fired off three more shots and heard two more screams.

He'd hit both men. But his shots had been aimed at their legs.

The two men rolled off each other, giving Logan the target he needed. He fired again. All three bullets hit the Chinese man in a small cluster in his chest. Then Logan spun and sent another volley of fire into Mason's chest – he couldn't take any chances.

Winter was clutching his leg, screaming, but Logan barely heard. He was only focused on one thing. He strode up to Grainger and kicked the handgun out of the reach of Evans, who was still writhing in agony on the floor. And Logan could see why. The multiple bullets he'd fired, landing in such close proximity, had very nearly severed both Evans's ankle and his arm. Another round of fire would probably have seen his foot and arm taken clean off. Logan was tempted to put him out of his misery, but he knew the fight wasn't over yet. He still needed Evans.

He leaned down next to Grainger and undid the tape wrapped around her wrists and ankles. She virtually fell off the chair into Logan's arms, burying her head deep in his chest. After holding the pose for a few seconds, Logan stood her up.

'Are you okay?' he said, holding on to her shoulders, craning his neck to look into her eyes.

'Yes,' she said.

Logan took his hands off her, studying her for a couple of seconds to make sure she had the strength and wherewithal to keep herself upright.

'Come on. We need to finish this,' he said.

Her expression suggested she was reluctant, but she nodded.

Logan moved over and used his foot to turn Evans over onto his back. Evans's face was creased with pain, but as their eyes met, Logan thought he could see the faintest of smiles still on Evans's face. It made Logan want to pound the life out of him. But he knew he had to restrain himself. Evans was the only man in the room who had the answers Logan needed. He had to at least try to get something useful out of him.

Logan was just about to speak when he heard an entirely unexpected noise. He knew what it was as soon as he heard the click. A handgun being cocked. What surprised him was that he could see the glint from the shining metal out of the corner of his eye and he knew the barrel was pointing at him. He could still hear Winter's cries from over the other side of the room. And Evans's other two men were down for good. Logan was sure of that.

Which didn't leave many other candidates who could be holding the weapon.

Logan turned to face the gun. His eyes moved from the barrel to the person standing behind it.

Grainger.

'I'm sorry, Carl,' she said, her face streaked with tears. 'I really am. But it's the only way.'

Chapter 50

'Angela, what are you doing?'

Logan's mind took him back to the log cabin in the Appalachian Mountains over a year ago. The place where Grainger had fulfilled her desire to exact revenge on the man who had killed her father. The place where she had shot Logan and then gone on the run, into the hands of the Russians.

That day, she had left Logan in turmoil. She had betrayed him in a most grievous way. Since that day, he had fought hard with himself to come to an acceptance of what she had done. In the end, he had wanted her back. He had fought to have her back, to rescue her from the grips of the CIA who were hunting her. He'd seen some good in her. And some hope for himself.

But had it all been in vain?

Because here she was again. Pointing a gun at him. After everything he had done to help her.

He should have been feeling enraged. The red mist should have been clouding his mind. But it wasn't. Not this time. Instead, he felt entirely empty.

'I'm so sorry, Carl.'

'You've said that to me before.'

'I know. But I have to do it. It's the only way to stop this.'

'To stop what?'

'You'll never be free, Carl. Don't you see that? They'll come after you. They'll keep on coming after you. They'll come after me. As long as you're still alive.'

'They won't stop just because I'm dead.'

'But it's not just about you.'

'Then who is it about?'

'Carl, they've got Tom. Lindegaard has Tom. They've taken him away. I don't know where to. But if I don't do this, they're going to kill him.'

And where before he had been empty, Logan now felt a wave of unexpected emotion. Something akin to dismay but infinitely more powerful rushed through his body. The wave was so sudden and severe it made him feel faint.

Tom Grainger. Angela's ex-husband. A man Logan had never met but felt he knew so much about.

'Angela, put the gun down,' Winter said through laboured breaths. 'You're safe now.'

'Keep out of this,' Logan blasted without turning his focus from Grainger. 'You were given a choice,' he said to her.

Grainger didn't respond but her hand was now shaking, her bottom lip quivering.

'You chose him over me,' Logan said.

'It's not like that! I chose for this to be over. No more killing. No more fighting or dirty deals. I love you, Carl, but just look at the destruction that follows you.'

'I did it all for you.'

'But I can't do it anymore.'

'Once this is over, you won't have to.'

'That's right. And there's only one way to end it.'

'You're wrong about that,' Logan said, but he could tell from the look in her eyes that his confidence was doing little to sway her.

Grainger bowed her head for a second and Logan took a step forward.

'I can't let someone I love be pulled into this mess,' she said. 'I couldn't live with that.'

'Tom pulled himself into this mess, remember? He came to you in Moscow.'

'But I pushed him away again. I didn't want him involved.'

'You still love him.'

'Of course I do! Not like I did, but you can't just stop caring for someone. They will kill him. I have to save Tom.'

'Let me help.'

'You can't help me anymore,' Grainger said, but there was a little less conviction in her voice now.

She was a shaking mess. Even if she pulled the trigger, and despite the short distance, Logan wasn't sure she would hit him.

'Just do it!' Evans said.

The show of strength from the fallen man surprised Logan. But it also took away some of the turmoil inside his head. And the gap that was left filled with something familiar: anger. At Evans. At Lindegaard. At everyone who had betrayed Logan and caused him to be in this place.

'Kill him, Grainger!' Evans shouted. 'Or it's over for you.'

Logan took another step toward her. Then another.

'If you really think it'll make a difference,' Logan said to Grainger, 'then do it. You won't get a better chance than this.'

'Kill him!' Evans screamed.

Logan stopped. He was now only inches from the barrel of the gun.

'Well?' he said.

He stared into Grainger's bloodshot eyes. But he saw nothing. He didn't see the woman he cared about so much. He only saw a target. A problem.

Grainger let out a cry. Her finger twitched on the trigger.

Logan wasn't sure whether she would actually do it. In the end, it made no difference. Logan was already moving. His balled fist caught Grainger in the gut as he lunged forward and she exhaled painfully, doubling over. Logan sent a blow to the back of her neck and Grainger collapsed.

'I'm sorry, Angela,' Logan said, looking down at her.

He reached down and grabbed the gun from her limp hand and strode back to Evans. He kicked him hard in the groin, then stood on Evans's injured ankle, grinding his boot into the bloody mess. Evans's mouth gaped open, his head shook, his eyes bulged, looking like they would pop right out of his head. He let out a long, silent scream.

When it looked like Evans was on the brink, Logan took his foot off. He wanted to punish Evans, but he couldn't let his need for revenge get in the way of what was still left to do: he had to find Lindegaard. Tom Grainger too. He had to finish this. And Evans might be the only man who could help him do that.

Logan kneeled down on top of Evans and pushed the barrel of the handgun into Evans's shoulder.

'Talk,' Logan said.

Evans panted and gasped but didn't say anything.

Logan pushed the gun down harder and Evans's face creased up.

'I can do this all day,' Logan said.

'You can't stop it now,' Evans shrieked. 'It's too late. Grainger was right. You have to die, Logan. It's the only way.'

'Where is Lindegaard?'

Evans pursed his lips, a show of defiance.

'Tell me where he is!'

'Don't you get it, Logan?' Evans said, managing to laugh in between his pained breaths. 'I'm just like you. I was trained just like you.'

And Logan did get it. Evans wouldn't talk. Not like this. And Logan didn't have the luxury of time.

'You're nothing like me,' Logan said.

'It doesn't matter whether you believe it or not. I won't help you. I'm dead already. I know that.'

'Fine by me,' Logan said.

Yes, he wanted to hurt Evans. He wanted to hurt him badly. But Logan knew that once the anger had subsided, he would get no real satisfaction from having made Evans suffer. He wasn't a sadist.

Logan stood off Evans and cocked the handgun, then pointed it at Evans's head.

'Wait!' Evans begged. 'Wait.'

Logan hesitated but didn't say a word.

'Don't you want to know why?' Evans said. 'Don't you want to know why I did this?'

'No,' Logan said.

'You killed my father!' Evans screamed.

Logan wasn't listening. His finger was already pulling the trigger. Evans's words hadn't even registered before the bullet tore through his skull, leaving a small, dark hole in his forehead.

And just like that, he was dead.

Chapter 51

'Angela, come on, get up.'

She opened her eyes groggily and closed them.

'Wake up, Angela,' he said.

She opened her eyes again and fought hard to keep them from shutting. Logan was standing over her. Winter was at his side.

'Come on,' Logan said, putting his hand under her shoulder and hauling her to her feet. 'It's time to go.'

It took a few seconds for her to take her own weight. When she had properly come around, she shrugged Logan off.

'I'm sorry,' she said, looking down.

'Yeah, I know,' Logan said, sounding less than convinced.

There was an awkward silence. Grainger didn't know what to say. A small part of her was surprised she'd woken up at all. It wasn't beyond comprehension that Logan might have pulled a gun out and shot her for what she'd just done.

Really, did she deserve anything more?

'We know where Lindegaard is,' Winter said to her.

Grainger said nothing but looked down at Winter's leg. A torn piece of cloth was tied around his thigh.

'I've got Logan to thank for that,' Winter said. 'The bullet took a good chunk of flesh out of my leg, but I guess I fared better than that lot.'

He pointed over toward the bodies lying on the ground. Grainger glanced at them. At Evans. He'd been alive, screaming at her to kill Logan, just minutes earlier. Now he had a hole in his forehead that was dribbling blood. She quickly looked away again.

'Come on, let's go,' Logan said.

She hesitated. This wasn't the reaction she had expected from Logan at all. She'd just been pointing a gun at his head. He was acting almost as though nothing had happened.

Had she really intended to pull the trigger? She didn't know. She just knew she had to do *something* to save Tom.

'I didn't know what else to do,' Grainger said to Logan. 'I was scared. Confused.'

'I know. No need to explain. I'll help you save him. Lindegaard is finished. I'm going to make sure of that.'

'Why are you still helping me?'

'If you'd really wanted to shoot me, you would have done. I know you, Angela. You're an ace with those things. Your stance, the grip on the gun, the finger on the trigger. You're a professional. What I saw when you pointed that gun at me was something else. That wasn't you. I knew you wouldn't do it.'

He certainly sounded a lot more confident about that than she'd felt.

'What now?' Grainger asked, her tone wary.

'We think we know where Tom is,' Winter said.

'How?' Grainger said, surprised.

'While you were out of it, we found a phone on Evans's body,' Winter said. 'There weren't too many numbers on there. One of them was Lindegaard's.'

'You called him? You spoke to him?'

'No. We debated it. In the end, we decided against it. But we did find a number of recent calls on the phone to a hotel in central Beijing.'

'Lindegaard may still be there,' Logan said.

'We need to get out of here, head back to the city,' Winter added.

'Come on, we need you for this,' Logan said, holding his hand out to her.

Grainger hesitated.

Her head was filled with confusion. She had been desperate. There was no other explanation for her actions. Of course she hadn't wanted to shoot Logan, but it had seemed like the only option.

Twice she'd held a gun up at Carl Logan. Somehow or other,

twice he'd forgiven her. If she was in any doubt about whether he was the right man for her, whether he was the right person for her to partner with on what was undoubtedly a troubled road ahead, that surely gave her the answer she needed.

She took his hand and he pulled her in, then wrapped his arm around her shoulders. The three of them headed back through the derelict building to the parked car outside.

Chapter 52

It was dusk as they made their way back into central Beijing. The traffic was still heavy and it was fully dark by the time they passed back into Dongcheng district. There had been little talk on the way. Logan's mind was filled with thoughts as to what had happened and why. With both Grainger and Evans.

Despite his words of reassurance, Logan was left with a bitter taste in his mouth. He wasn't sure whether it was from Grainger having pointed a gun at him or from his lack of remorse at knocking her out. Regardless, he felt he could understand the turmoil she had been in. She hadn't wanted to kill him. She'd just wanted a way out. A way to make all of the torment stop. Killing him wasn't the answer to that, though. He figured that deep down she knew that too. Despite what had happened, he still trusted her. He had to. It was the only way he could make sense of how he felt for her.

As for Evans's dying words, they were still resonating in Logan's head. He had barely heard them at the time, but he was now replaying them over and over again.

'How did you find out?' Logan said to Winter, who was sitting in the back seat of the car. 'About Evans.'

Logan realised his question had been vague, but Winter seemed to understand what he meant.

'It just took a bit of digging,' Winter said. 'It's not the only family connection in this.'

'No?'

'Lena Belenov was Lindegaard's niece. It was what tipped me off about Evans.'

Logan froze, almost losing control of the car as the words rattled in his head.

'It was Lindegaard's big secret,' Winter said. 'He's been playing the agencies against each other for years. Lena was his way into the FSB. The two of them have been concocting dirty deals and tit-for-tat missions to exploit their power ever since she joined.'

Finally, everything that had happened started to make sense to Logan. The deal to hand him over to the FSB had been Lindegaard's work all along. Logan had suspected it, but hadn't been able to pinpoint why. Lena, who had become Logan's nemesis during his time in the Siberian gulag, had been working with Lindegaard from the start.

And it had been Lindegaard who had sold out Mackie too. He might not have pulled the trigger, but Mackie's blood was on Lindegaard's hands.

'Lindegaard is trying to bring down the JIA,' Winter said. 'There's a long trail of dead bodies following his moves. And right now, he's not far off completing his mission.'

'But why?' asked Grainger.

'Because we were too close,' Logan said. 'Too many cooks in the kitchen. With the work we were doing, it was only a matter of time before his link to Belenov was uncovered.'

'Exactly. You crossed paths with him one too many times,' Winter said. 'We all did. And with you running amok in Russia, I think he panicked. He was quite content while you were in the hands of the FSB – which was his doing in the first place – but when you escaped, everything changed. That's what kicked this all into action. He had to move fast before you tore apart everything he'd worked to build.'

'What about all the other people who've helped him, though?' Grainger said. 'It's not like he was working alone. They can't all have been in on it with him.'

'Maybe, maybe not,' Winter said. 'Evans certainly was. The others may have been dirty or just doing what they were told.'

'So what did you find on Evans?' Logan asked. 'He said I killed his father.'

'Well, I had the family connection with Lindegaard. So I wondered what Evans could have in his past. And if anyone had cause to want you dead, Logan, then Evans certainly did.'

In a way, Logan could relate to Evans's cause. And he was sure Grainger could too. It was her scheme to exact revenge on the man who had killed her father that had first brought Logan and Grainger together.

He wondered what she was thinking now. Whether she had sympathy for Evans. Whether that very reason had convinced her to turn the gun on Logan.

'Who was it?' Logan asked.

'John Webb,' Winter said.

The name, one that Logan hadn't heard for years, sent a rush of memories through his head of a baking rooftop in Marrakech.

A strange thought then occurred to Logan. In all the years that had passed since, all the water that had gone under the bridge, all of the troubles he'd been through and all of the changes in his outlook on life, he had never once asked Mackie why. Why Webb, a fellow JIA agent, had been a target.

But Logan had been a different man back then. At that time, as a young man in his twenties, he had revelled in the newfound responsibility he held.

The questions, the doubts, the chinks had come much later.

'Who was John Webb?' Grainger asked.

'He was a JIA field agent,' Winter said. 'Like Logan.'

Logan winced. It was true. Webb really had been like Logan – the younger agent had even looked on his ultimate foe as someone to emulate.

'You killed him?' Grainger said to Logan.

'Yes.'

'Why?'

What could he say? The truth was, he didn't know why he'd had to kill Webb. Logan had no way of justifying his actions that day other than he had done what he was told to do. He knew today he could never operate like that. He couldn't pull the trigger now unless he knew he was justified in doing so. But his morality hadn't always been so established.

'Webb was a rogue agent,' Winter said, coming to Logan's rescue. 'If Logan hadn't killed him, chances were he would have had Logan killed soon enough.'

Winter's qualification seemed to do the trick in pacifying Grainger's interest. And the commander's words were also more than welcome to Logan's mind too, giving him a very belated justification for what he'd done all those years ago.

'And then there was Venezuela,' Logan said. 'I killed two of Lindegaard's agents there. One directly. That was my first run-in with him. In his eyes, I've been a marked man ever since.'

'But what you didn't know was that even then Lindegaard was working against us.'

'What?' Logan said.

'Janet Ford, the CIA agent you killed. She wasn't just extracting information from the cartel – she was passing it back too. That meeting you came across, the CIA were selling out Leo Pinilla. You know, what you did gave him a fighting chance of survival at least. And his death was certainly quicker and less painful than it would have been otherwise.'

Logan didn't respond. Not for the first time in the conversation, he was shocked. Pinilla's death had long been a dark cloud over Logan's career, at least in his eyes.

'Like I said,' Winter carried on, 'Lindegaard has been dirty for a long time. Way before he came to work for the JIA.'

'Yeah, well, that's about to come to an end,' Logan said, gripping the steering wheel as tightly as he could, trying to channel the fury that was building inside him.

Not long after, they arrived at the deluxe, high-rise hotel. Logan pulled the car over and killed the engine.

'Please tell me you have a plan this time?' Winter said. 'I'm not sure I can take being shot again today.'

'Yes,' Logan said. 'This time I have a plan.'

Chapter 53

Logan explained the ploy to Winter and Grainger. Needless to say, Grainger was fraught with worry. Tom Grainger was nothing more than a pawn in a grand scheme of deception and betrayal. As far as Grainger was concerned, saving his life was now the goal. But Logan knew that whatever action they took from here was a gamble. They had to at least try, though. And one way or another, he would get Lindegaard. Of that Logan was certain.

He took out Evans's phone and made the call. Lindegaard picked up on the third ring.

'Evans, where are you? I was wondering what the hell had happened to you.'

'Think again,' Logan said.

There was a brief pause. Logan could almost hear the cogs turning in Lindegaard's mind.

'Logan. So Evans is dead.'

'What do you think?'

'I think you don't know when to quit.'

'I could say the same of you. But no, Evans isn't dead. What use would he be to me dead?'

'We had a deal with Angela. It looks like poor Tom isn't going to come out of this too well.'

'You certainly know how to make a deal,' Logan said, glad that Grainger couldn't hear Lindegaard's words about Tom. 'How about a new one?'

'What could you possibly offer me?'

'Your life. And Evans's life. In exchange for Tom Grainger.'

'How do I even know Evans is still alive?'

'You don't.'

'Put him on.'

'No.'

'Then I may as well just kill Tom Grainger now.'

'No, you won't.'

'Logan, you're annoying me now. Goodbye.'

Logan's heart skipped a beat as he wondered for a split second whether he'd just signed Tom Grainger's death warrant. 'You put that phone down and I'll never stop, Lindegaard,' he blurted out, thinking on his feet, hoping his forthright tone would keep Lindegaard's interest. 'You should have figured that out by now.'

No one spoke for a few moments, but Logan could hear Lindegaard's heavy breaths so he knew his adversary hadn't hung up. Tom Grainger was still alive – Lindegaard's words had all but confirmed that. But unless Logan could keep Lindegaard on the phone and get him to agree to the plan, Tom was a dead man.

'What's the deal?' Lindegaard said.

'You give us Tom Grainger. You get Evans back. Everyone walks away.'

'That's it?'

'What have you got to lose?'

'Quite a lot, actually. But seeing as you're still alive, it does seem like my options are running thin.'

'I'm glad you're finally seeing sense.'

'Where and when?'

Logan gave Lindegaard the address for the bogus exchange. Logan had no intention of going to the place. It was simply a ruse to get Lindegaard into the open.

'You and Tom come alone,' Logan said. 'You've already mixed enough people up in this. No point in adding any more bodies to the list.'

'I'll be there in an hour,' Lindegaard said before ending the call.

Logan put the phone down on his lap, relief washing over him. He looked up at Grainger, whose expression told Logan that she wasn't feeling quite as confident as him.

'So what do you think?' Winter said.

'He'll show,' Logan said. 'He thinks he's smarter than you and me.'

'But do you think he'll be alone?'

'Not a chance. But he won't have time to call in additional people. So it'll be him and whoever else he's got up there in his hotel room.'

'And what if he's not actually here?' Grainger said. 'We've taken a leap there.'

'It's all we've got,' Logan said.

Grainger huffed. 'If Lindegaard's not here, you may have just got Tom killed.'

'We're playing the odds,' Logan said, sounding calmer than he really felt. 'That's all we can do now.'

It probably wasn't the response she wanted, but it was the plain and simple truth. If they did nothing, Lindegaard would surely kill Tom anyway. This way, at least he had a fighting chance of survival.

Logan opened his door and got out. Grainger followed. Logan leaned down and stuck his head back into the car.

'Wait here until I call,' Logan said to Winter. 'If you haven't heard from us in thirty minutes just go, get out of here. You've got the evidence. Tell everyone what Lindegaard is. You'll find some friends, I'm sure.'

'I will. And good luck.'

'Luck doesn't come into it,' Logan said as he shut the door.

He looked over the car to Grainger on the other side. Logan couldn't read her expression at all. He had no idea what was going through her mind. In Kazakhstan and on the train to Beijing, he'd finally thought that their stuttering relationship may be making progress. Then she'd pulled a gun on him. Again. He knew he could trust her for this final assault; if nothing else, she wanted to save Tom's life. That meant they shared a common enemy. After that – who knew?

He moved to the boot of the car and opened it. Logan looked around, waiting for the solitary pedestrian in sight to move away, then took out the M4 and, as discreetly as he could, stuffed it inside his coat. It was bulky and heavy but they didn't have far to move in the open, and with Grainger taking the handgun, it was the only option if he wanted to be armed.

'Come on then,' Logan said as he shut the boot.

Grainger nodded and they looked left and right, then dashed

across the road toward the hotel. They cut left and walked around the side of the hotel, away from the main entrance. Winter, in the car, would keep guard at the front of the hotel, the other M4 on his lap in case he needed to take Lindegaard out. But Logan didn't think Winter would need it. Because Lindegaard wouldn't be leaving the hotel on foot.

As they made their way around the side of the hotel, they came to the exit ramp that led down into the basement car park. There was a barrier on either side. CCTV cameras were placed above both the entrance and exit sides to record movements, but there was no manned booth. Logan stooped under the barrier on the exit side and Grainger followed just two steps behind.

They headed down the ramp and into the car park below.

'Looks like a single level,' Grainger said when they reached the bottom. 'Makes it easier.'

'Yeah. But two stairwells into here. He could come from either.'

'So what do we do?'

'We sit either side. But stay at this end, nearer to the ramp. Wait and see which stairwell he comes from.'

'Okay. I'll go left, you right. When we know where he's coming from, the other can move across.'

'Exactly.'

They headed in their respective directions. Logan crept from car to car, edging closer to the stairwell door. He came to a stop up against a minivan, the vehicle's height providing him with good cover from the door, which was only ten yards away.

He looked around him, trying to see whether he was in view of any CCTV cameras. He spotted three more cameras dotted about, but it seemed that from where he was hiding, he was invisible to them all. In any case, he assumed there wasn't a guard viewing live footage of all feeds. Most likely the cameras were in place to record incidents. A hotel that size would have hundreds of cameras, far too many to make it feasible for security staff to be watching each feed twenty-four hours a day.

Logan looked over to the other side of the car park, trying to spot Grainger. There was no sign of her. He scooted down and looked underneath the cars and saw one of her feet behind a tyre.

He felt a wave of relief. For just a fleeting moment, Logan had wondered whether Grainger had duped him. But she was there, on the far side of the car park, almost in line with him.

Logan was just about to stand back up when he heard a clunk and then a bang as the stairwell door on his side of the car park opened and then slammed shut on itself. Logan waited, his body relaxed and calm, as he heard footsteps coming toward him.

He risked a peek and saw a woman, smartly dressed. Her arm was interlinked with the casually dressed man walking by her side. It wasn't Lindegaard. Logan pulled his head back in quickly, hoping they hadn't spotted him. The lack of change in the rhythmic pattern of their footsteps suggested they hadn't.

Logan held his breath and waited. He hoped the twosome would simply get into a car before they reached him and drive off none the wiser. But the nearer they got, the less likely that prospect seemed. Logan was about to start to move around the minivan, to keep himself out of sight, when he heard a double beep and the indicator lights of the van flashed.

He cursed his bad luck. He had to move before the two strangers got to the van. The last thing he wanted was for these two to become spooked and run off to tell the police before Lindegaard had even made an appearance.

But just as Logan was about to move, he heard the door on the opposite side of the car park open and then close.

And then he heard Grainger's voice.

'Stop, now!' she screamed. 'Hands in the air. Both of you.'

Logan tensed, bracing himself for action.

A second later, a gunshot rang out.

Chapter 54

There was a chorus of shouts.

'Get in the van, now!' shouted a woman.

It wasn't Grainger. The voice hadn't come from the other side of the car park, where Grainger had been waiting, but from much closer by.

It was at that moment Logan realised what was happening.

He had only glimpsed the smartly dressed woman and the man she was with for a brief second. He had taken the whole picture in but not really thought about what it was telling him.

The woman, he had assumed, was on business. Logan guessed many of the hotel's residents were. The man had been somewhat more casually dressed. The woman had been holding on to the man, her arm interlinked with his, so Logan had thought the two were a couple. He hadn't thought it unusual that the man was walking with both hands behind his back. But the reason was clear now. Logan had never seen the man before, but he realised who it was.

Tom Grainger.

There was shouting over on the other side of the car park. More gunfire. Logan heard hurried footsteps coming from nearby. He spun on his heel, pulling the M4 around with him.

When he darted out from behind the minivan, it was Tom Grainger he caught sight of first. He had a grimace on his face. An arm around his neck. The woman was behind him, pushing him along. But she was too focused on her job – trying to get her man into the waiting vehicle. She hadn't spotted Logan at all.

Logan lifted the M4. He saw Tom Grainger's eyes open wide in panic. Logan pulled the trigger, releasing a single bullet – he'd changed the firing selection in order to save ammunition.

The bullet sailed from the muzzle. It whizzed past Tom Grainger's right ear, striking the woman who had hold of him just above her eye. She fell down into a heap, taking her hostage with her.

Logan lowered his gun. He rushed over to the two bodies. The woman was dead. No doubt about it.

'You okay?' Logan said hurriedly.

'Yeah. I think so,' said Tom.

'Just stay out of sight until this is over,' Logan said, turning and heading off before he'd finished his sentence.

He looked over to the other side of the car park as he moved toward the exit ramp.

'Is that you, Angela?' shouted a man's voice. It was Lindegaard. 'And I'm guessing Carl Logan is here too.'

Silence. Logan kept on creeping.

'Nice little trick you played there,' Lindegaard shouted. 'Ambushing us like that. Pity me for actually believing you wanted to do a deal. But you've just fucked any chance of you and your hubby getting out of this alive.'

There was another gunshot. Logan instinctively ducked, though he soon realised the shot hadn't been aimed at him. He reached the end of the car park and cut back across, over to the side where Grainger was. He pulled up against a concrete pillar and peered around.

Out in the open, near the stairwell door, was a crumpled body. It looked like a man. But it wasn't Lindegaard.

Five parking spaces in front of him, Logan saw Grainger. She was hunched behind a car bonnet, peeking out every few seconds. Other than the body in the middle of the car park, there was no sign of Lindegaard or anyone else.

Logan edged forward, crouching down, moving from one car to the next. He whispered to Grainger. She didn't react at all. She mustn't have heard him.

Logan was three cars away when Grainger took a step out around the front of the car that she had been hunkered behind.

'No, Angela,' Logan said in a hushed voice.

This time she did hear him. She turned and glanced at him. But never saw the threat coming from the side. Logan hadn't seen it either, even though he'd guessed what Lindegaard had been doing. Seemingly from nowhere, Lindegaard rushed toward Grainger. He came into view too late for Logan to make a difference. Lindegaard had outflanked her, moving around to take her out from behind.

Logan hastily raised his gun. He let off two rounds. But Lindegaard had the element of surprise. Neither of the shots hit him. Lindegaard flung himself into Grainger, tackling her like a rugby player and sending her crashing to the ground. She lost her gun in the process. Logan rushed forward. He raised his gun, looking for a shot.

But in the end he didn't take it. There was too much at stake. Logan froze.

Lindegaard hauled Grainger up. There was a large red graze on her cheek where she had hit the deck. A line of blood trickled from her nose. As she looked up, her pleading eyes bored into Logan. Lindegaard stood behind her, twisting Grainger's arm behind her body in a hammerlock. His other hand pushed the barrel of a gun into her back.

'Now what?' Logan said.

'We had a deal,' Lindegaard spat.

'Sorry about that.'

'Well, no more deals now.'

'You hurt her and I'm not just going to kill you. I'll make you suffer.'

Lindegaard laughed. 'Look where you are,' he said. 'Police will be storming this place any minute. Remember who you are. You two are both wanted in several countries.'

'I guess it's just as well that Winter is so good at digging then,' Logan said. 'Pretty soon, you'll find the tables have turned.'

Logan couldn't see all of Lindegaard's face as he hid behind Grainger, but even from the narrow glimpse that he had, Logan could tell his last words had washed some of Lindegaard's arrogant confidence away.

'You're finished, Lindegaard,' Logan said. 'Whatever happens here, your life is over.'

'I should have killed you years ago,' Lindegaard said.

'You're right, you should have.'

'All you've ever done is cause me problems.'

'I'm sorry for doing my job so well. And for having some real loyalty.'

'Loyalty? To what? To the JIA? To your country? To Mackie?'

The mentioning of Logan's long-term mentor sent a shiver down his spine. This was going to end here. Lindegaard wasn't getting out of the car park alive.

'You're not loyal, Logan. You're dumb. You were a toy for Mackie. Nothing more, nothing less.'

'Like Lena was to you? I know you're a cool man, Lindegaard, but having your own niece killed?'

'You've no idea what you're talking about!' Lindegaard shouted, clearly riled by Logan's words.

However much Lindegaard wanted to be, he simply wasn't in control of this situation, Logan realised.

Logan raised his gun. He knew he didn't have a kill shot. But he had to do something. He just hoped Grainger would forgive him.

A split second later, a gunshot rang out.

But Logan hadn't fired it.

Logan looked off to his right. It was Tom Grainger. He held a revolver in his hand, pointed at Lindegaard. He fired again. The sound made Logan jump.

Logan looked back at Lindegaard, who took a half-step sideways before his body slowly crumpled to the ground. Tom had hit him twice. Once in the side. Once in the neck. Lindegaard would be dead in seconds.

But as he fell, another gunshot blasted. Lindegaard's last act of defiance. Grainger stumbled, her mouth open, a look of shock plastered on her face. Both Logan and Tom shouted out almost in unison. Grainger flopped to her knees, then keeled over onto her side.

Logan dropped his gun and rushed over to her. Tom did the same. Logan reached her first. He spotted the hole in the back of her jacket. The material around it was wet with blood. Tom came up beside Logan. Without thinking, Logan lunged forward and threw his fist toward Tom's face.

'You did this!' Logan screamed, getting to his feet as Tom reeled backward.

Tom wiped at his lip with the back of his hand and looked at the bloody mark that it left. Then, without saying a word – averting his gaze from Logan – he stood up and went back over to Grainger. She was sprawled on the floor, gargling and gagging for breath.

Logan tried his hardest to fight against the rage building inside him. His head was on fire, his heart bursting in his chest. He thought he could feel his veins throbbing with fury. But he fought it off as best he could. Tom's rash move had led to Grainger getting shot. But it had also felled Lindegaard. Logan himself had been seconds away from taking a similar gamble.

Fighting to keep his emotions in check, he crouched back down next to Grainger.

He took her hand. He looked into her bloodshot eyes.

'I'm so sorry,' Logan said.

Grainger stared deep into his eyes. Her breaths were fast and shallow. She didn't say a word.

'Angela, be strong,' Tom sobbed. 'Please, you'll get through this.'

Grainger shut her eyes. Her face contorted in pain. When she opened them again, she was staring straight up at the ceiling. Her eyes glazed over. Logan wondered for a second whether she had gone.

But then she opened and closed her mouth and pained sounds came from her lips. As though she was trying to say something but couldn't.

After a few moments, she finally found the strength.

'I love you,' she spluttered as bubbles of blood burst from her mouth.

Logan and Tom looked at each other. Logan knew what Tom was thinking. Neither was sure which man she had been speaking to. Perhaps it had been to both of them. Logan looked back at Grainger, completely still, ghostly.

And then she closed her eyes again.

Chapter 55

Two months later

Logan stood on the balcony and looked down at the crashing, frothing waves below. The dull grey sky seemed to blend into the water, making it impossible to pinpoint the distant horizon.

There was a cool breeze and Logan folded his arms and hunched his head down into the neck of his woollen jumper to escape the cold. Although the scene in front of him looked bleak today, it was a whole lot better than what he had become used to in the frozen wastelands of Europe and Asia over the last few months. And he knew that come summer, this place would be the paradise he craved.

Hell, compared to where he had come from, it already was.

After the paramedics had arrived in the car park in Beijing, Logan had called straight in to Winter. The JIA commander had still been parked in the car opposite the hotel. He rushed as fast as he could on his shot leg down to Logan and helped to straighten out the situation with the local police who, understandably, had wanted to lock Logan up.

From there, Winter had somehow been able to extract Logan from China with little opposition from the Chinese authorities. Logan didn't know how Winter had managed it, but he was certainly grateful for it. And Winter, naturally, was thankful to Logan for his help in bringing to an end Lindegaard's life of lies and deceit, and in doing so very possibly saving the JIA's existence.

The news story that played in the press explained how the fugitive lovers – Carl Logan and Angela Grainger – had both been killed in a shoot-out in Beijing. Lindegaard and Evans were hailed as the heroes who'd helped bring them down. That was fine by Logan. A fresh start was all he wanted.

Although Winter could never entirely wipe Logan's slate clean, Logan knew the JIA commander would have done everything he could to get Logan back into business at the agency. It was the last thing Logan wanted, though. For years, he'd carried out Mackie's orders without a second thought. Then the chinks in his armour had appeared – in Venezuela first, there was no doubt about that. But it was his time at the hands of Youssef Selim that had brought the walls crashing down.

Angela Grainger had been the one who had helped him to rebuild those walls, to rebuild a life. But those walls weren't as high or as strong as they used to be.

Logan knew he could never go back to the way he had been. He would never carry out orders religiously, unquestioningly, like he had before. He would never kill a man or a woman on nothing more than another person's say-so. And that was fine. Logan didn't want his old life back. He just wanted a life.

Winter had been happy to give him that. A new identity, a new location. A fresh start.

Logan knew he would still be on the Russians' blacklist. The CIA's too, possibly. He had to believe those agencies knew he was still alive. His enemies weren't gone for good and they wouldn't forget. There wasn't much he could do about that. He knew he would never be able to truly free himself of his past. It was a dark cloud that would forever hang over him.

He was sure one day someone would come knocking, whether Winter, in need of his help, or the many enemies he'd picked up through his troubled and complicated life, come to seek their vengeance.

That was fine. Whoever came for him, Logan would be ready. He was sure of that.

As for Grainger, well, Logan hadn't been quite sure what to think in the end. There had been so many ups and downs, so many lies in their fraught relationship, that it was difficult to identify what was real and what wasn't. But some of it had been real, he believed. His feelings for her, for sure. And there had been more to his feelings than just lust. From the moment they had first met, Logan had been drawn to her, had felt a powerful connection that just didn't seem to diminish no matter what problems were thrown their way.

He had always hoped she had felt the same. She had betrayed his trust more than once and yet each time he could understand her intentions. She had loved Tom Grainger, that much was clear. While he might have been naive in love, Logan wasn't so naive that he hadn't seen that Grainger still had feelings for her ex-husband, even though their marriage had long since finished.

Had Grainger still loved Tom like a partner all along? Logan didn't know.

Had she ever loved Logan? He didn't know the answer to that either, and yet he hoped it was the case.

Logan closed his eyes and listened to the crash of the ocean, the waves rolling and sweeping ashore, the noise of the wind whistling over the coastline.

With his eyes shut, he took himself away to another place. A place where he could still feel Grainger's electric touch. The way it had been the first time they had kissed in a motel in the French countryside. He could feel the warmth of her body, the way they had fitted together so naturally the first time they had made love and each time after that. He could hear her soft voice whispering in his ear and smell her rich femininity.

Would he ever feel like that again?

He held himself in the moment, eyes shut, not moving, just thinking about her. As he drifted off into a world of his own, the sound of the ocean and the wind faded. All he could hear was the gentle rhythm of his heart beating calmly in his chest.

Lost in his thoughts, he heard the patio door slide open behind him. Imagined the soft footsteps approaching. He still didn't move. Didn't open his eyes. He felt the touch of the hand on his shoulder. The feeling of electricity jumping up through the ground, into his feet and through his entire body. The powerful sensation reminded him just how explosive her touch was. How alive it made him feel.

He smiled, then opened his eyes.

Epilogue

War-torn Bosnia had been the first time in his life he'd felt such mind-numbing pain. The bullet had torn through his shoulder, wreaking a path of destruction through the muscle and tendons and nerve fibres there. Two inches to the right and the bullet would very likely have left him paralysed from the neck down, if he'd survived at all. In fleeting moments, he'd contemplated whether that would have been a better outcome – it would at least have taken away the ferocious pain that swept through his body.

He'd been travelling with three other men. Their mission was to extract a high-ranking officer of the Scorpions – a Serbian para-military unit believed to have been involved in various atrocities in the Bosnian War, including the Srebrenica genocide.

The mission had run its course. It was a success. Their man was bound and gagged and lying shackled in the back of the pickup truck as they raced back toward the safe zone, where the prisoner would be transported out of the country for good.

It was only through sheer bad luck that everything turned to shit.

Deep inside territory held by the Army of Republika Srpska, one of the front tyres of their vehicle exploded when they rode over a piece of shrapnel. They frantically battled to fix on the spare wheel, but it wasn't long before Serb forces found them. Outnumbered and outgunned, they would all have been killed at best, captured and tortured at worst, if it hadn't been for a heroic helicopter rescue team that plucked them to safety.

In the process, he'd been shot. As had two others on the team. The first man died in the helicopter, the other two days later in a military hospital.

His mind was replaying those moments – the bombardment by Serb forces, the bullet tearing into him, the agonising helicopter ride that followed – over and over as though he were living it all once more.

The pain he felt was real, that was for certain. Pain that strong, that horrific, couldn't be imagined. This time, it wasn't emanating from his shoulder, though, but from his head. It was almost unbearable. It seemed to be rushing through his bloodstream, infecting every inch of his body. If someone had offered to put him out of his misery there and then, he very possibly would have agreed.

Yes, the pain was real. But he wasn't in Bosnia anymore. It was only when he finally opened his eyes that his weary brain began to recalibrate. It took him a few agonising moments to recall where he was and why.

Kazakhstan. The planned exchange.

He should have walked away from that place a rich man. Instead, he'd been betrayed.

He tried to move but couldn't. Yet he could feel his arms, his fingers, his legs, his toes. So why couldn't he move? He looked down and saw the answer.

Using all his strength, he heaved the deadweight body off him. The lifeless mass rolled away. He looked at the face of the dead man and a strange concoction of emotions washed through him: sadness, fear, hatred. It was the hatred that stuck. Not for the blood-soaked man who lay dead next to him, but for the man who'd caused this to happen.

Carl Logan. This was all down to Carl Logan.

In that moment, Captain Fleming determined two things. First: he wasn't giving up. He would survive. He would battle through the pain; he would fight on. Eventually he would recover. And second: one day, he would make Carl Logan pay.

To receive updates, sneak previews and enter giveaways for future releases, head to http://www.robsinclairauthor.com now to sign-up to Rob's email mailing list.

Want to know where it all began for Carl Logan? *Dance with the Enemy* and *Rise of the Enemy* are the explosive first two books in the *Enemy Series*.

Read on for more details…

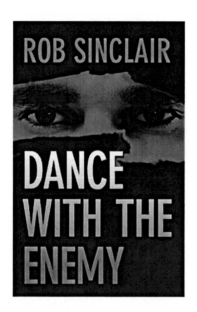

Carl Logan was the perfect agent. A loner, with no real friends or family, he was trained to deal with any situation with cold efficiency, devoid of emotion.

But Logan isn't the man he used to be, or the asset he once was. Five months ago his life changed forever when he was captured, tortured and left for dead by Youssef Selim, one of the world's most violent terrorists.

When Selim mysteriously reappears in Paris, linked to the kidnapping of America's Attorney General, Logan smells his chance for revenge.

Pursuing his man relentlessly, oblivious to the growing trail of destruction that he leaves in his wake, Logan delves increasingly deep into the web of lies and deceit surrounding the kidnapping.

Finally, he comes to learn just what it means to Dance with the Enemy.

Prologue

They say that before you die your whole life flashes before you. But nobody can know for sure what happens in those moments before death. If you do see your life flashing before your eyes, does that mean you've got no chance? And if it doesn't, does that mean you're going to be okay?

Carl Logan didn't know. Five months ago, on the day he almost died, no bright light had been calling him in, no images from his childhood flickering through his mind. There had been only pain and suffering.

Logan had been on his last breath. His brain had submitted. His body, too. He shouldn't have been alive. But after his heart had beaten its last beat, it had beaten one more time. And then it had beaten again.

And it had kept on going.

It hadn't been his time to go.

But he hadn't been saved. Not by a long stretch.

Chapter 1

Maybe the psychologist had been right. Maybe he was an addict. Who else would put themselves in these positions willingly? Knowingly?

He had the man in a hammerlock. It was a classic submission hold. Its ease of application, and the fact it could be used from an upright position, meant it was a favoured hold of bouncers and law enforcement the world over. Logan was in neither of those professions, but it was a move that he had found to suit many purposes nonetheless.

He pulled the man's wrist further up towards the shoulder, feeling the resistance as the shoulder joint was pushed to bursting point. The man let out a yelp at what was becoming an inevitable outcome. His friends, just five yards in front of Logan at the other end of the bar, continued to look on, forming a physical barrier between Logan and where he wanted to be – the exit.

'Move out of my way. Now,' Logan said. 'Don't think for a second I won't do it.'

Despite the threat, the man's three friends stood their ground. They weren't about to back down. But they weren't looking like they were about to make a move either. For now, it was a stand-off. Neither side wanted to take it to the next level.

Yet.

Logan looked them over, one by one. Rednecks would be a harsh way to describe them. They were probably just average

323

working guys letting off steam on a weekend; albeit guys who were bulked up through steroids and overuse of weights, and fuelled by alcohol and God knows what else. Each one of them was big and menacing. And judging by the non-situation that had started this, they were looking for a fight tonight.

And for no sane reason, other than he was who he was, Logan was prepared to grant them their wish. He wasn't the tallest or the strongest guy in the world, but he could handle himself just fine. Despite the odds, he still fancied his chances against this lot.

'I warned you,' Logan said.

He pulled the man's wrist further, as hard and as fast as he could, pushing against the resistance until he heard the tell-tale pop as the man's arm dislocated from the shoulder. The way it suddenly flopped in his hand told Logan it had probably dislocated at the elbow too. The man shrieked in pain and slumped to the floor as Logan let go, readying himself for the next stage of his latest battle.

The three friends, wide-eyed and staring, looked shocked at what had just happened. Maybe their macho stand-offs didn't normally go this far. And yet they continued to stand their ground. Logan was a little surprised by that.

But then he saw it. The man on the left. It was nothing more than a flinch. Maybe just a twitch, even. But it was enough for Logan. Enough to tell him that this wasn't over yet. And that man was now his next focus.

But just as Logan was about to leap forward, something unexpected happened.

He heard the noise before he felt anything. A dull thud. He was on his knees before the searing pain in the back of his leg took hold. Then came the thud again. This time pain shot across his back.

In an instant, unable to stop himself, he was face down on the floor.

He tried to stand up, but the combination of whisky and whatever had just hit him was too much. Instead, he just lay there, hearing the thuds that kept on coming. Feeling the pain with each strike, but unable to muster a response. He saw boots crowding around him. Saw them pulling back and kicking him. Pulling back and kicking. The thuds kept on coming across his back.

He took a boot to the face and felt his lip open up, blood pouring into his mouth. The blows kept on coming but Logan didn't move. He wasn't sure he could anymore. He closed his eyes, wondering how things had gone so wrong this time. Maybe he was losing it. Maybe he had never really got it back. He had been out of action for too long. Five months had gone by now since his last fateful assignment. Five months of hell.

His mind began to wander, his awareness of the blows raining down on him fading. Before consciousness left him, he felt a slither of an unlikely smile form on his face.

The psychologist was right. He was an addict.

But it wasn't the fighting that he was addicted to. It wasn't the pain either – he was no masochist. Too many years had gone by living a life that wasn't a life at all. He didn't want to be their machine anymore. He couldn't. That was his addiction – the clamour for some sort of normality. He just wanted to live and to feel like everyone else did. Nights like this, in a twisted logic that made sense only to him, allowed him that.

He just wanted to be normal.

And yet he knew that would never be the case.

***

To carry on reading head to Amazon.com where a longer sample is available.

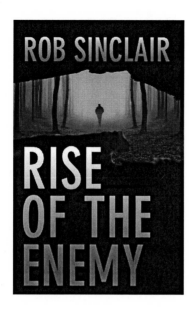

Everyone has a breaking point. Carl Logan might just have found his.

The Joint Intelligence Agency sends agent Logan on a routine mission to Russia. It should have been simple.
But when his cover is blown, Logan is transported into a world of hell he thought he would never see again.

Something is different this time though, and before long, doubts begin to surface in Logan's mind as to why the assignment went so wrong.

Logan has never been short of enemies. And sometimes the enemy is close to home than you think.

Could his own people really have set him up?

Prologue

Dance with the enemy and your feet will get burned. An old friend once said that to me, many years ago. The same old friend who was now sitting in front of me, across the table of the café. I think he'd misquoted the saying, but it always stuck with me nevertheless. And recently, his words had come back to bite me with a vengeance.

I'd made the mistake of getting too close to people I thought were friends. People I trusted. Angela Grainger was one of them. We'd had a connection like I'd never had with anyone before. I still thought about her every day. Mostly, despite myself, I still thought of her fondly. But she'd betrayed me. Betrayed my trust. I'd let her get too close and my feet had been burned.

The man sitting before me was another one. Grainger's betrayal was something I would never forget – it still dominated my mind. But in many ways the betrayal of this man hurt the most.

He was the person I had trusted more than anyone else in the world.

I never imagined that we would end up like this. Talking in this way. The accusations. The insinuations. Speaking to each other like we were natural enemies rather than two people who had worked so closely together for nearly twenty years.

They wanted me to kill him. Until a few days ago, the mere suggestion would have been laughable. Something had changed, though. I didn't know what and I didn't know why, but our lives would never be the same again. The fact we were sitting here like this told me that.

And if it came down to it, I would do it. I would kill Mackie. My boss. My mentor. My friend. Because it might be the only way for me to get out of this mess alive.

***

To carry on reading head to Amazon.com where a longer sample is available.